T0354765

THE RIVERS OF JOY AND SORROW

A NOVEL

JUSTIN ROBERTS

ARCHWAY
PUBLISHING

Archway Publishing books may be ordered through booksellers or by contacting:

Archway Publishing
1663 Liberty Drive
Bloomington, IN 47403
www.archwaypublishing.com
844-669-3957

ISBN: 978-1-6657-3022-8 (sc)
ISBN: 978-1-6657-3023-5 (e)

Library of Congress Control Number: 2022917969

Print information available on the last page.

Archway Publishing rev. date: 10/10/2022

Eventually, all things merge into one, and a river runs through it. The river was cut by the world's great flood and runs over rocks from the basement of time. On some of the rocks are timeless raindrops. Under the rocks are the words, and some of the words are theirs.

Norman Maclean, A River Runs Through it

If you are neutral in situations of injustice, you have chosen the side of the oppressor.

Desmond Tutu

Goodness is stronger than evil;
Love is stronger than hate;
Light is stronger than darkness;

Desmond Tutu, An African Prayer Book

And joy is stronger than sorrow.

Colleen Roberts

ONE

SURELY THAT ROCK MUST BE SOMEWHERE CLOSE. THERE ARE MANY rocks along the brink of the Blyde River Canyon, but the one Justin was looking for, Colleen's rock, held some special memories. It was here all those years ago—a different life time in reality—where he and Colleen had first kissed, where they had crossed the boundary between dating and becoming a couple. The landscape had changed since those happy times. The rutted track that used to run near the edge of the canyon was now an improved road. Many of the old landmarks were gone, the old foot paths obliterated. But as he continued his hike he became increasingly confident that he was closing in on his destination. And suddenly there it was. He climbed up onto its flat surface and drank in the grandeur of the canyon below. He felt in his shirt pocket for the photo of Colleen that he always carried with him, but of course, it was not there. He had had to leave it behind along with anything else that might provide a clue as to his true identity.

Thinking rationally, he knew that there was not the slightest chance that Colleen would be on this rock. And yet somewhere in the deepest and more desperate reaches of his consciousness he had hoped somehow, just somehow, that she might actually be there. But of course she was not. The feelings of utter loss and loneliness once more engulfed him, as so often they had during these past couple of years. He tried to push these feelings aside by filling his mind with memories of the day that they had met for the first time and of the many happy hours that they had spent together subsequently. So many happy memories indeed, and yet that is all that they were now—just memories. They belonged to the past, not the future or present.

It was not the happy memories of the past but the anxiety of the present that now flooded his mind. Had things gone according to plan, by now he would be back in England, safe in his secure but meaningless exile. Instead, here he was sitting on the brink of the canyon wondering whether this foolhardy escapade would end in disaster. Why was he even here in South Africa, using a false name and passport? How had he been sucked into this foolhardy venture? What were the turning points in his life when he might have taken a different road? Why was he not the successful lawyer that he had once aspired to become rather than a lonely exile with no prospects? He began to examine the turning points in his life.

What if he had never gone to that meeting on education for Africans? It was not as if he had intended to do so. He was one of the few second-year students who owned a car, albeit a beat-up Volkswagen Beetle. Some of his friends had persuaded him to attend the seminar mainly because it would afford them a ride. As a result, he became increasingly involved in the illegal endeavour of helping African students obtain an education—students who were politically active and refused to be part of Bantu Education.

What if he had avoided student politics as did many of his more career-minded compatriots? In those days student politics were inextricably bound to protests against apartheid. But his involvement in African education seemed to lead seamlessly to participation in the national student protest movement.

What if he had never met Colleen? After their first date he had been surprised that a girl as beautiful and vivacious as her had even considered going out with someone like him. He was even more surprised when their dates blossomed into a love affair, which is how it came about that she was to become his Achilles' Heel.

What if he had never agreed to assist with the Institute for Racial Reconciliation's curriculum resources project?

What if he had flown to Cape Town for that emergency meeting of the national student organisation instead of driving? Then Sipho and he would never have spent the time together on the way back from Cape Town to Johannesburg—time that inevitably dragged him deeper into the struggle.

What if his escape from South Africa had been foiled by the Special Branch?

What if he had made his way to Canada, as per his original intention rather than being seduced by the lucrative, but in the end empty, offers of scholarships by a number of British universities?

Above all, what if he had refused to be persuaded to undertake this madcap mission by that shadowy stranger who had appeared out of the blue at his university office only a few days ago?

What-ifs can drive a person to madness, and so Justin decided to focus his attention on the surroundings. The Blyde River Canyon is surely one of the great sights in the world. It is sixteen kilometres long and eight hundred metres deep. What sets it aside from other great canyons of the world is that is is known as a green canyon. Other than the vertical cliffs, it is covered in verdant vegetation. From his rock, Justin gazed out over the magnificent vista. To the north were the rock formations known as the three rondavels, their domed heads iced in green and their sides stained with fiery orange lichen. Beyond them Mariepskop, one of the portals of the canyon, where the edge of the escarpment gives way to the mouth of the canyon. And beyond the canyon mouth the flat Lowveld stretched away into the far horizon. To the south, but out of sight at the head of the canyon, lay Bourke's Luck Potholes, a series of cylindrical wells and plunge pools carved out by the swirling waters at the confluence of the Blyde and Treur Rivers. The river that mesmerized Justin as he watched the swirling water at the bottom of the canyon contained a mixture of these two rivers, the river of joy and the river of sorrow. Somehow this intermingling was apt to his mood as he contemplated both his past and present.

He wondered if tourists ever questioned how these two unusual names came about. Some time around the middle of the nineteenth century a voortrekker leader named Hendrik Potgieter made several attempts to forge a path to Delagoa Bay. On one of these excursions the expedition was on top of the escarpment looking for an easy route down to the Lowveld. To expedite his quest, Potgieter took a few men and broke away from the main party to search for a route. When the men did not return from their trip on the expected date, the trekkers who had remained behind, which included all the women and children, expected the worst—that Potgieter and his men had not survived. And so they decided to move on. They appropriately named the river at which they were camped the Treur River, the River of Sorrow. However, a few days later, Potgieter and his men caught up with the trekkers unharmed, and there was much rejoicing. It was then decided to name the river along which they were now camped the Blyde River, the River of Joy.

Gradually, the beauty and tranquillity of the natural surroundings soothed Justin's troubled mind. Natural beauty had always had this effect on him, but none more so than his beloved Eastern Transvaal. He removed his shirt and lay back on the rock, drinking in the warm, calming rays of the afternoon sun. It was Colleen who had first introduced him to this region, but since then he had returned to it as often as possible, sometimes with her and sometimes alone. At first they had visited the main tourist areas, God's Window, Berlin, Lisbon, and MacMac Falls, and of course the canyon itself. But later they explored and delighted in the hidden gems, unknown but to the privileged few. When members of the Student Council had been advised to find out how well they might be able to withstand solitary confinement, a common form of torture in those days, he had chosen to spend a week in this area in complete isolation. It was a week during which he had learned much about himself, and also about the area.

Sitting on Colleen's rock, he watched as a couple of hawks played in the wind. The easterly breeze was creating an updraught along the edge of the canyon. The hawks would gain height, then dive and flatten out their descent in the direction of the canyon wall. Just when it seemed that they would smash into the wall, the updraught would fling them back high into the sky, as if they were riding on an express lift. They repeated this manoeuvre again and again. Down below in the thickets an emerald-spotted wood dove was singing its plaintive song, ending in a series of descending notes fading away into silence.

Perhaps he dozed a bit, for now the vista before him transformed itself into the final scene of Das Rhinegold. A rainbow bridge, a glorious illusion, stretched out from his rock, over the River Rhine, ending on the Three Rondavels, now transformed into Valhalla, which shimmered in the golden light of evening. But unlike the gods, he would not be crossing that rainbow bridge. He would not join Wotan's fabled heroes, and he would not be reunited with Colleen in Valhalla.

As the sun began to sink toward the horizon, Justin woke with a start, and his thoughts returned to the extraordinary meeting that had set his current trip in motion. Only a week ago he had been sitting in his office playing solitaire. Actually to call it an office was something of a misnomer. In the past it had likely been some kind of storage room. It was devoid of windows and was no larger than six square metres. Besides the desk and one chair, the only other furniture was a dilapidated book shelf. It had no phone and certainly not one of those new personal Apple computers that were just beginning to make their appearance on the campus. He had done little to brighten up the dingy room. Other than a Pierneef print that he had picked up cheaply at a second hand junk store, no pictures adorned the walls. When he had first arrived at the university he had been something of a celebrity, and thus had been given a decent office with a view of the campus. But his star had waned fairly quickly, as had his studies. He suspected that the Dean now regretted his impulsive offer of a position in his department. Rumour had it that he would be asked to leave at the end of the current term. He suspected that his downgraded 'office' was part on an attempt to get him to resign, thus avoiding the unpleasant prospect of getting rid of him.

His ears had perked up as he heard the sound of Miss Davenport's footsteps pounding down the corridor towards his room. It was her angry walk, and so he was fairly certain that she was on her way to see him. She was an elderly spinster who had run the department as its secretary for as long as anyone could remember. She had not taken kindly to his appointment, and her attitude towards him had not improved since then. He had done nothing to offend her, as far as he could tell, but she continued to snub him at every possible occasion. He suspected that she had not been consulted regarding his initial employment, and perhaps he had taken the place of one of her protégées. Before she reached the door to his room, he hastily packed away the cards that he was playing with, grabbed a book, and pretended to read.

She entered without knocking. "I have told you this before and I will tell you again, I am not your secretary."

"I have never assumed that you are."

"Then why do you expect me to answer you phone calls."

"I am sorry. I have already told all my friends never to call me at work." It had not been a difficult task since he could count the number of friends he had on the fingers of his left hand if that.

"Well a friend of yours is on the line now."

"Perhaps it is not really for me. It might be the representative of a publishing company. Did he or she give a name?"

"It is a he and he refused to give a name. He sounded foreign and uneducated". So it was out in the open. The caller must be an African. Had the foreign accent been German she would most likely have said it sounded intelligent, or if French sophisticated. "He did say it was very urgent. I suppose you had better take it. But make sure that this never happens again."

Justin followed her back to her office, which was next to that of the Dean. She handed him the receiver and returned to her chair behind her desk. She clearly intended to listen to every word of the conversation.

"This is Justin Roberts."

"I need to meet with you urgently."

"Who are you?"

"You may call me Themba. When and where can we meet?"

"But I do not even know you. What is this all about?"

"One of your friends in South Africa is in grave danger. That is all I can say at this point. Will you meet with me?"

"I am free now. We could meet at the Black Swan. It is a pub just off the campus."

"Do many students go there?"

"Yes."

"It is best if we are not seen together. Suggest some other place."

"There is the Kings Arms, a pub near the station. I could be there in about fifteen minutes."

"Excellent. I will see you there."

"How will I recognise you?" But Themba had already hung up.

Justin returned to his office, his mind in turmoil. He was inclined to forget the whole episode. Perhaps it was a hoax, or worse some kind of trap. His student days in South Africa had taught him to be cautious of strangers and of possible set ups. On the other hand he was in England now and far removed from danger. It would not hurt to see what Themba really wanted, and any excuse to be away from his office should be welcomed. Besides, he had found his brief phone conversation with Themba most intriguing. Accordingly he wrote a memo to the effect that he would be gone for the rest of the day and then rode his bike to the Kings Arms.

As it turned out Justin need not have worried about recognising Themba. When he scanned the customers in the pub, only one was black. What did surprise him was that Themba recognised him instantly and beckoned him to come over to where he was sitting in a secluded booth with a good view of the door. Once he had settled in, Themba asked, "What will you have?"

"A pint of bitter will go down well."

Themba signalled for a waiter and ordered two pints of bitter. Without a pause he continued, "Let me explain why I asked to meet with you." This opening gambit surprised Justin. In Africa one does not come to the point immediately. The polite manner of paving the way for what is to come is to inquire about one another's health, and that of family members and friends. One might also explore people that each might have in common and places where each might have lived. The abruptness of the approach made Justin a little uncomfortable and put him on his guard. He felt the need to find out more about his new companion. "I was surprised that you were able to recognise me when I walked in. It is not if I stand out from others that are in here."

"You mean that you are not black", Themba laughed. "Actually we have a whole dossier on you, including a number of photos."

"I guess I should be flattered, but who exactly is 'we'?"

"I am surprised that you should have to ask—a clever fellow like you. Is it not obvious?"

"I could hazard a guess, but then I might be wrong. I would rather you tell me."

"Let me say then that I am a member of the Movement, the one to which Sipho has dedicated his life. The same Sipho who is now in grave danger."

"Sipho is a common name. It is possible that I knew a number of Sipho's, or perhaps none at all. It is hard to remember. It has been a long time." Part of Justin's training had come back to him. *If questioned by the police, never admit to knowing anyone or to reveal any names.*

There ensued one of those mildly uncomfortable moments when each waited for the other to continue. In the end it was Themba who broke the silence. "You are right to be cautious. It shows that you have discipline. Let me lay my cards on the table."

"Before you begin, may I assume that your name is not Themba."

"You are right, but for your sake it is better if you do not know my real name. May I continue?"

"Sure. Go ahead."

"I am sure you know the Sipho that I mean. It is Sipho Dlamini, the person whom you got to know on the drive back to Johannesburg from Cape Town. The Sipho that you kept in touch with afterwards. And although you were not a member of the Movement, it is the

Sipho for whom you occasionally did—what what shall we call them—favours from time to time."

"Okay, so I do know Sipho."

"After you left, Sipho continued his work underground. He has become one of our most successful and elusive operatives. He is known as the Black Houdini. He is regarded as the number one enemy by the Special Branch."

"Why are you telling me all this?"

"It is because Sipho is in grave danger. There is nothing the Special Branch would like more than to capture him, and I do not have to tell you what they would do to him if that happens. I am almost ninety nine percent sure that our London operation has been infiltrated by the Branch. Once they uncover the details of how we communicate with him, he is a goner."

"That is terrible, but what has it got to do with me?"

"I want you to go back to South Africa and warn him—to tell him not to act on any instructions from London."

"But that is crazy. I am a wanted person. I would be arrested on the spot at the airport."

"You would not go as yourself. We would provide you with a false name and a British passport."

"This is all very sudden. Why don't you go? In any case I would have no way in which to get in touch with him."

"I am too well known by the police. There is no way I would be able to enter the country without being apprehended. On the other hand a white British tourist could slip in without trouble. As to how to get in touch with him, you would be given some detailed instructions."

"This is a big ask. I am at a loss as to how to respond."

"I understand. If I were not desperate, I would not have come to you. I am not asking you to make a decision right now. I am sure that you are a busy man and have lots of commitments here. Think it over, and I will get in touch with you tomorrow."

Did Themba really think he was a busy man, or was that intended as a barb? "Okay, I will think it over."

"I will give you a phone call tomorrow morning."

"No. Don't phone. Are you staying over night. Can we meet at your place?"

"I will be staying in town tonight, but it is best if I do not tell you where. We could meet here again, but it is best not to use the same place twice. Let's meet at the coffee shop in the station itself at say nine tomorrow morning. You can give me your decision then one way or another."

The sun was beginning to set, bringing out the colours of the rocks and lichen on the far wall of the Blyde Canyon. Justin replaced his shirt and set off to where he had parked his rented car. From there it was a half hour's drive to Pilgrims Rest where he planned to spend the night. In his student days, he had often passed through the village without bothering to explore its features, or even contemplate its history. It had struck him as a rather uninteresting, old mining town whose time had past. Most of the cottages, and indeed the hotel itself, were made of lumber and corrugated iron sheets. This time he was going to stay in the hotel, where he had already registered.

Ironically much of the history of this area, and indeed of South Africa as a whole, had been learned during his years in England. As a young man, like many of his age, he had lived in the present, oblivious of what had gone before him. He had explored and enjoyed this area for its scenery, for what it was, not what it had been and where it had come from. As his exile in England stretched from weeks, into months, and then years, he found himself spending more and more time reading about the history of his land of birth. It was perhaps one reason why his studies suffered.

The first gold rush in the area took place in 1873 when payable gold was discovered on the farm Geelhoutboom about five kilometres from Pilgrim's Rest. President Burgers, who visited the site, officially named the area the New Caledonian Gold Fields, but he jokingly referred to it as "MacMac" and the name stuck. It became known as the MacMac Diggings, named after two Scotsmen who worked there.

The area spawned its share of characters. Alec 'Wheelbarrow' Patterson for example, arrived at the MacMac diggings pushing a wheelbarrow with all his belongings in it. He had gotten rid of his donkey after it kicked him and he had then decided that pushing a wheelbarrow was a less painful means of transporting his belongings. He pushed this wheelbarrow all the way from the Cape to the gold fields, a distance of some one thousand six hundred kilometres. Alec left the crowded MacMac diggings and went off on his own to explore new territory, where he struck it rich in a small stream later named Pilgrim's Creek. Alec was a solitary man and did not share his new find with anybody—he quietly kept on panning. But not for long. Another digger, William Trafford, also found gold in the same stream and registered his claim with the Gold Commissioner at MacMac.

The news sparked off the biggest gold rush of the time and on 22 September 1873 Pilgrim's Rest was officially proclaimed a gold field. In January 1874 the Gold Commissioner, Major MacDonald, moved his office from MacMac to Pilgrim's Rest as some one thousand five hundred diggers were working about four thousand claims in and around Pilgrim's Creek. By 1876 most of the tents were replaced with more permanent structures, usually built from timber and corrugated iron, and traders moved in supplying the diggers with necessary equipment and provisions.

By the 1880's alluvial gold started to dwindle and many diggers moved along to newly discovered gold deposits in Barberton. With more capital and larger equipment, the mining companies started to dig deeper for gold-bearing ore. Gold production declined steadily after 1914 and in 1972 the last operational mine closed.

Another of the area's characters was the celebrated robber, whose grave may be found in the town's cemetery. It is placed in a north-south orientation as opposed to all the others, which are east-west. It is emblazoned simply with a cross and the large type words 'Robbers Grave'. One legend attributes it to a robber who was shot, perhaps having first been lynched, when he was caught stealing a tent from another miner. However a mysterious grave inevitably gives rise to colourful myths. One such legend is that the robber was a highway man who robbed the stage coach of the gold that it was transporting. He then returned to town with his ill-gotten horde and proceeded to buy drinks for all and sundry. When the law arrived, he did not resist arrest and was simply carried out to the jail in a drunken stupor, where he subsequently passed away from the excessive amount of alcohol that he had consumed.

Justin drove up the main road of the town, essentially the only road, to the front of the hotel. As he passed the front desk, he heard the receptionist call out to one of the guests, "Mr. Roscoe." When the guest did not respond, she called out again, more loudly this time, "Mr. Roscoe." Finally she came out from behind the desk and ran after Justin calling out, "Mr. Roscoe, sir. Just one minute." Justin berated himself. During the afternoon he had delved at such length into his past that he had neglected to respond to his false name. It is the kind of mistake that amateurs are prone to make, the kind of slip up that can be costly. "Mr. Roscoe, sir, the manager has asked me to give you this voucher for a free drink at the bar. Also will you be eating with us tonight? If so I have a copy of the menu, which I can give to you now." She spoke with a sing-song accent marking her of Afrikaner descent. "Also here is a brochure which will give you some information about the hotel itself. Sies tog, you look quite tired. A good drink will pick you up."

Justin thanked her and then retired to is room, grateful that his slip up had gone unnoticed. He took off his shoes and lay back on the brass bedstead. For want of something better to do he scanned the brochure. The hotel had been started in 1894 to cater to the needs of visitors to the gold fields. It went by the name Royal Hotel for reasons not explained in the brochure. It boasted of eleven bedrooms in the original structure, but the hotel management was in the process of buying up some of the old miners' cottages and refurnishing them as an annex to the hotel itself. The hotel's claim to fame was the Church Bar, which had originally been a school chapel somewhere near Delagoa Bay, and had been brought to this spot piece by piece on ox wagons. It was in this bar that he had been invited to enjoy a free, pre-dinner drink.

As he rested on his bed he tried to decide whether or not to go out again. His recent lack of vigilance had shaken him more than he cared to admit. There was always the possibility, however remote, that he might run into someone who knew him as Justin Roberts. He was not from this part of the country, and during the time that he had spent exploring the countryside while a student, he had avoided contact with others. On the other hand, he and Colleen had attended a number of parties in neighbouring towns. What if he ran into one of Colleen's former friends? In the end his need for something to eat and drink was stronger than these misgivings, and he headed for the Church Bar. He was pleased to note that most patrons had left the bar, presumably for dinner, and that the only two occupants, most likely locals there for the duration, were sitting at the bar counter chatting to the barman. He ordered a cabernet sauvignon, and retired to one of the few small tables. The room itself was smaller than he had anticipated. It must have been the chapel of a rather small school. There was not much to show that it had once been a chapel. The counter stretched from where the pulpit might have been to the windows that looked out over the main road. Behind the counter the whole wall was taken up with an impressive selection of every possible type of drink, neatly arraigned in row upon row. He sipped his cabernet sauvignon with pleasure in the knowledge that a wine this good in the UK would likely cost thrice as much. Despite their value for money, good South African wines were hard to come by in the UK due to the boycott of that country's produce. As a student he had not appreciated the wines that were available to him. Almost everyone he knew drank Lieberstein, fondly known as Liebies, if they drank wine at all. All that seemed to matter to him and his colleagues was that it was cheap and effective.

His wine finished, he made his way to the Digger's Den restaurant for dinner. He was relieved to see that most of the guests had already left. He was shown to one of the smaller tables nestled against the far wall, where he placed his order. Only two other tables were occupied. An elderly couple were just finishing up their meal, but their argument was far from over. The bone of contention seemed to revolve around what they should do with the one remaining day of their holiday. The other somewhat larger table was occupied by a family consisting of four children ranging from about five to ten years old. They were obviously tourists and spoke in some foreign language which Justin could not place. The children had obviously had enough of sight-seeing and were restless and crotchety.

Again his mind drifted back to the past. Had things turned out differently, would he and Colleen have been married by now? Would they have had children? If so, what would these children be like? Surely better mannered than those brats across the room from him. Justin was suddenly overwhelmed by a vision of Colleen surrounded by beautiful children. Clearly she would be a loving and caring mother, but they would not be his. Get a grip he admonished himself. Before leaving London he had been repeatedly warned never to step out of his assumed role of a British tourist named James Roscoe. Yet time and time again since his arrival he had reverted to being Justin Roberts, clinging to all the baggage of his past. He was not really cut out, he realised anew, for the role of a secret agent.

Sitting alone at the table, Justin had never felt so lonely in all his life. He was sure that he stuck out like a sore thumb. What were the other diners thinking about him? Did they even care? What did one do when forced to dine alone? He wished he had thought to bring a book to read with him at the table, but then he had never considered himself to be one of those lonely souls sitting in solitude at a restaurant table reading a book. With nothing else to do, his thoughts drifted back to that first meeting with Themba, less than two weeks in the past, but what now seemed to be part of a former lifetime. Themba had given him the rest of the day to make up his mind. He had returned immediately to the flat he shared with three other post-graduate students, thereby foregoing the pleasure of refusing to satisfy Miss Davenport's desire to find out more about that curious phone call. Two of his flat-mates were women and the other a male. Each had their own rooms, but shared a common kitchen cum dining room. It was an agreeable arrangement, as women were generally regarded as being more considerate when it came to sharing space. Fortunately his other flat-mates were not around, giving him the quiet he needed to sort out his thoughts. Justin rummaged through his shelf in the fridge to see what was available. Enough of last night's Chinese take-out remained to make one more meal. While this was being heating in the microwave, he poured himself a glass of cheap Spanish claret.

While partaking of this instant feast he tried to sort out the turmoil in his mind. What Themba was asking was preposterous—or was it? It would be crazy for him to go back to South Africa where he was a wanted man. Besides he had no training, or even an aptitude, for clandestine work. Could he even trust Themba when that was not even his real name? Even if he did go, what were the chances of success? On the other hand, if there was a chance of saving Sipho, should he at least not try? If nothing else a paid holiday in South Africa was a welcome prospect. And then there was the deal-breaking question, would it not revive his spirits to take a break from his current dismal life here in England? Questions upon questions, but no answers. He decided to sleep on it. Tomorrow morning he would make his decision, and then meet with Themba to let him know what he had decided.

Justin's reminiscing was interrupted by the arrival of his dinner, consisting of rump steak, baked potatoes and peas—the best the Digger's Den had to offer. By the time he had finished eating, he was the only one left in the restaurant. The only remaining option was to retire for the night, but sleep did not come easily. Tomorrow would be the final day of his quest to meet with and warn Sipho. With luck he might make it back to Johannesburg in time to catch the late night British Air flight back to London. With sleep eluding him, snatches of his life, and in particular the events leading to his current quest, passed through his mind like a sequence of tableau's. It had all begun during his second year at university.

TWO

JUSTIN'S SECOND YEAR AT THE UNIVERSITY HERALDED TWO SIGNIFICANT changes to his life, one to his living arrangement and the other to his political awareness. His educational track, however, remained essentially unchanged. His somewhat vague goal in life was to go into some aspect of the law and hence he had opted for the BA followed by an LLB route. The main decision at the beginning of his first year was to choose majors for his BA. At school his best subject had been mathematics. It was the only subject in which he had obtained a distinction in the matriculation examination. Hence it seemed only natural to choose mathematics as one of his majors. Whether it would help his proposed legal career was an open question, but at least it could not hurt. English seemed the logical choice for his other major especially if his future occupation involved reading, writing, and speaking.

During the break between his first and second years, one of those fortuitous and unforeseen events occurred. Much of the city had simply grown rather than been planned. As a result some of city's major arteries, once simply tracks through the bush, were narrow, two lane roads subject to endless congestion. The municipality had decided to widen some of these arteries and had initiated this intention by expropriating some houses, which in the course of time would be demolished to make way for a wider road. Lack of money delayed the completion of this project and the municipality found itself in possession of houses which would not be demolished for another five

years or so. One of the roads in question was within walking distance
of the university and many of these houses were subsequently rented
out to students at low rates.

Justin's first year at university had been spent in one of the
residences. While not unpleasant, it was not really his cup of tea. He
and his friends had talked from time to time about moving out and
renting a flat. However the rental was prohibitive, and for the most
part their talk of moving out on their own was merely idle chat rather
than definitive planning. So when the low rental houses opened up,
they were among the first to claim one of them. Justin and his best
friend, Ian McCall, took the initiative. The house that they settled on
had three bedrooms. They figured that the living room and garage
could be converted into make-shift bedrooms, and at a push the
servant's quarters could also be used. It did not take much effort to
sign up another four persons, and so during the first week of Justin's
second year the six of them moved in. Since Justin was the only one
of the six with a car, if a beat up Volkswagen Beetle with over two
hundred kilometres could even be called that, it was in use all day
ferrying their assorted belongings from all over the place to their
new abode.

Ian was a third-year student majoring in political science, and
besides that he was one of those natural leaders. He knew enough
about politics to know that any functional society, even one as small
as six guys, needs some form of organisation and governance. On
the day that they all moved in, Ian bought pizza and beer for all and
hosted an informal meeting. "We need to make some decisions and
also agree on some ground rules."

"Such as?" asked David Cohen. David, along with Tony Forester,
was one of the two house mates who had not been in the same
dormitory during the previous year. He and Ian had a history together,
but Justin was quite sure what it was. David was one of those students
that most universities collect—students who seem to regard studying
as a career rather than a stepping stone to something else. He was well
known on the campus, if for nothing else for his frequent disputes

with the university administration. He had also spent a number of nights in jail following protests broken up by the police.

"Well, for a start, who gets which room."

"I suggest that Ian and Justin get first pick seeing as that they acquired this house in the first place," suggested Tony Forester.

"I am not comfortable with that suggestion", countered Justin. "It sort of sets us apart."

"Well perhaps we could draw straws", suggested Neville Perkins.

"Or perhaps we could each state our preference and see if things work out on their own," added Andy Kaplan.

"Let's try Andy's suggestion first, and if that doesn't take care of things we can draw straws", decided Ian. "Andy, you go first."

"It may sound weird, but I would choose the garage. To have all that space—it is a double garage—would be like heaven. As some of you know, I am a speech and drama major. I would fix up one corner as a bedroom, and could use the rest of the space for things like set building and even rehearsals."

"Well that takes care of the one room nobody else would want", said David. "For myself I would choose the servant's quarters—small but very private."

"And with quick access to the lane behind the house if the police ever come looking for you", quipped Ian. Neville added, "Hey David! Don't worry. If the police come for you I will beat them up with a hockey stick."

"That leaves the three bedrooms and the living room. Any other requests?"

"I would choose the living room. It has its drawbacks, but I like the size", said Neville Perkins. "With that amount of space I could set up my exercise machine."

Since there was little difference between the three bedrooms, the remainder of the room allocation was swiftly concluded. The rest of the meeting was concluded fairly quickly. Those who had lived in the dormitory were used to being served three meals a day. Here they would have to provide for themselves. Restaurants would be too expensive as a permanent solution. It was decided that each member would be responsible for dinner for all one week at a time. All would chip into a kitty to fund dinners. Breakfast and lunch were individual responsibilities. Each would take care of his own room, and cleaning the common areas would also be rotated on a weekly basis. The question of female guests provoked the most heated debate. In the end it was decided that nightly visits would be permitted, but no long-term stays. It was not so much a matter of puritanical intent, but the pragmatic realisation that the morning demand on the bathroom would already be considerable. David pointed out smugly that his digs, the former servant's quarters, had its own toilet facilities, meagre but upgradable.

Justin could trace his political involvement to one of the dinners three weeks into their occupation of the shared house. Dinners for the first two weeks had been a nightmare, so much so that Justin had seriously considered returning to dormitory life. The best meal that he could remember comprised of burnt hamburgers, half raw potatoes, and uncooked frozen beans. The others were even worse. However during the third week, when Andy took on the task of providing dinner, matters improved considerably. He produced one gourmet meal after another. His only comment to the compliments that flowed was, "I hated seeing you plebs suffer so." Halfway through the week Neville announced, "I can get free tickets to Saturday's Currie Cup match. Any takers?" Neville had an amazing number of contacts in the sporting fraternity. He himself was rumoured as being consider for a provincial hockey cap.

"Who is playing?"

"Transvaal against Western Province."

"Count me out!" from Andy. "I never did see the point of twenty two Neanderthals bashing each other over an oddly shaped piece of leather."

"That just shows your ignorance, you arty-farty dweeb. There are fifteen players per side in rugby."

"Oh! So that makes it much better. Thirty rather than twenty two neckless brutes having a go at each other."

Although the banter was light-hearted, Ian thought it best to intervene. "I would love to go, but I already have a commitment."

"Where are you going?"

"Actually it is something Tony got me into. Let him tell you about it."

"I don't know that much about it myself. You know that I am taking a class from Prof. Armstrong. He has been approached by a group of students in Soweto asking for help. Ian and I volunteered to go with him to Soweto this Saturday."

"What kind of help?"

"That is what we hope to find out. Actually we need some help ourselves. Prof. Armstrong's car is already full of other students. We have to make our own way there."

"Good luck taking the train."

"Or one of the dreadful taxis."

"Actually I was hoping you, Justin, would take us in your car. Besides you might find the whole experience quite interesting."

"No way! Count me out. I have no interest or experience in education. You can take my car if you like."

"Thanks for the offer. But you know very well you are the only one who knows how to drive that heap. It wouldn't go more than one hundred metres with me at the wheel. Come on. Be a sport."

"I will think about it."

"Just say yes. If you will come with us, I will stand you to all you can drink at the Dev afterwards."

"All right. You are on. But I will hold you to the offer of drinks."

With Justin at the wheel, Ian in front and Tony in the back, they followed Prof. Armstrong's car into Soweto. It was the first time Justin had been there. The main road into the township was narrow but paved. However it lacked any kind of side walk. Both sides of the street were crowded with pedestrians who stared at the white occupants of the two car convoy. The stares were not hostile, nor were they welcoming—simply blank stares. Justin wondered if the others felt as uncomfortable as he did.

They followed the main road for a while and then turned, crossed over a railway line, and then turned again. For the most part both sides of the road were dotted with small, square houses, each a carbon copy of the one next to it. Each of the houses had a small plot, less than one tenth of a hectare, most of which was just bare ground. Now and then an occupant had tried to grow some vegetables, or in rare instances flowers, but such efforts were few and far between—and seemingly not very successful. A few of the yards had what appeared to be spindly fruit trees. In the back corner of each plot stood a pit toilet, a few of which had been painted. Besides the houses, they passed an occasional shop, school, or church—but mostly little square houses. Row upon row of them. At some point it seemed an effort had been made to grow trees along the side of the road, but most of these were no more than stumps. Reading his mind, Ian observed, "Trees are the only source of fire wood around here."

After a while they turned off the main road onto a rutted, dusty track that looked identical to countless other tracks that they had already passed. Justin had no idea how Prof. Armstrong had chosen this particular one. There were no street signs or anything else that distinguished this track from any of the others. They passed row upon row of identical houses, making a left turn here and a right turn there, until Justin was totally disoriented. He noted that the occasional house had what appeared to be a makeshift addition—a room leaning up against one of the outside walls—but no real landmarks by which to navigate. "I am surprised more people don't try to improve their houses. How big are they anyway?"

Ian replied, "It is not surprising at all. Africans here are not allowed to own homes. They rent them from the municipality. So if they do put their own money into a house, it is the municipality that benefits. And since they can be evicted at any time, there is no incentive to improve the place where they live. To answer your question, each house has four small rooms." Justin thought he detected a note of bitterness in Ian's reply—something he had never heard before.

Finally they came to rest in front of what appeared to be a church. Obviously they were expected as a figure immediately appeared and dragged the broken gate open. There was just enough room to park the two cars. Their greeter closed and locked the gate, and then went over to Prof. Armstrong's car and shook his hand in the typical African manner—shake, hold thumbs, shake again. As the others piled out of their cars, their host went around shaking the hands of each in turn. "Watch how we shake hands and do the same when it is your turn," Ian whispered to Justin. Following handshakes, they were all then led into the building.

There was not much to indicate that this was a church other than a small sign reading 'Church of Christ'. The front door led immediately to a room the size of a small hall. The far wall had two doors in it leading presumably to a vestry or perhaps a small kitchen. Windows were spaced along the two side walls, but it seemed they had not been washed for months. A number of the panes were cracked and some even missing. Chairs were arranged in rows with their backs to the entry door, occupied by some twenty youngsters. The new arrivals were shown to a row of chairs at the front of the hall facing those already present. It was a classical us-them or givers-takers type of arrangement, making all uncomfortable, but secure in their assigned roles. Prof. Armstrong immediately upset this established order. "Let us sit in a circle rather than facing one another like two opposing teams." His request was acted upon immediately and soon all present arranged themselves in a single, large circle. However no one seemed quite sure how to proceed. In the end, Prof. Armstrong suggested, "Peter, why don't you introduce yourself and tell us why you invited us here."

"My name is Peter Sisulu, and I am one of many struggling students here in Soweto. The others that you see here are all in the same boat. But before we proceed any further, perhaps Prof. you would be so kind as to introduce your students."

"That sounds like a good way to begin. Immediately to my right is Jenny Marsh, who is on the Student Council—vice president if I am not mistaken." Jenny nodded and stood up briefly to a smattering of applause. "Please hold any applause for now. Next to Jenny is Patricia Case, who is a third-year zoology student. Going on down the line, Jonty Webb is the president of the Student Council, and has one year of physics. Next is Neil Abrahams who is a second-year chemistry major. To my left are Ian McCall, Tony Forester, and Justin Roberts. I don't know much about them, but I am sure that in the course of the morning we will find out more. So tell us more about your group."

"Sir, I am not sure I want to burden you with all their names." Was Peter being polite or discreet? It was common knowledge that most whites found African names difficult to pronounce let alone remember. "But I will ask a few of them to tell you their stories and explain what it is that has brought them here. Kagiso, perhaps you could go first."

"Thank you Peter. I was a student at Fort Hare until the end of last year. It was an exciting year, but also dangerous and frustrating. There are those who have adopted the slogan, 'No education until freedom'. Of course every student there wants freedom, and an end to apartheid, but not everyone, myself included, was willing to abandon their studies. The more radical students organised boycotts and sit-ins, and generally tried to disrupt campus life. Most of us were forced to go along. As things came to a head, the university would shut down and we would all be sent home. The university authorities would then try to identify the ring-leaders and exclude them from returning to the campus. However senior administration and almost all the white faculty did not even know our names, nor could they put a name to a face. The white police who were called in to break up the boycotts were in the same boat. The administration relied on impimpis, informers, to find out who the ring-leaders were. These impimpis were expected to come up with a certain number of names. They were too frightened to give the names of the real ring-leaders, because if they were found out they would in all likelihood be killed. So they submitted the names of ordinary students. Last year the campus closed down three times, and then reopened again. The third time was just before the exams, and I then received a letter saying that I would not be readmitted since I had been identified as an agitator. I am not only excluded from Fort Hare, but all the other black universities as well. So now I am trying to find a way to continue with my studies."

Tony burst out, "Prof. could we not find a place for Kagiso at our university?" From the embarrassed silence that followed, Tony realised he had asked either a naive or a stupid question. Prof. Armstrong tried to let him down gently. "Tony, your heart is in the right place, but that is not an option. To register officially with us he would have to get permission from the Department of Bantu Education, and that would certainly be refused. Some of us at the Institute of Racial Reconciliation are exploring the possibility of helping students like Kagiso get a university education overseas. However, there is a problem with this option too. In order to study overseas, Kagiso, and others in his situation, would have to apply for a passport. Since he has already been identified as an agitator, this would almost certainly be refused. With luck he might be able to leave on an exit permit, but then he would never be allowed to return. There are no easy solutions, but we have come here to listen. Perhaps this group has some idea of ways in which we can help."

"Thank you Prof. for explaining the situation so well," continued Peter. "And thank you Tony for being so willing to help. We all have a lot to learn about how the other half lives. Let me ask another of the group to tell you her story. Lerato, it is your turn. Lerato was hoping to write her matriculation examination at the end of this year, but she no longer goes to school."

Lerato began her tale hesitantly, in a soft voice. "Some months ago one of our favourite teachers told us that he had recently been at a meeting where they were warned that we might be forced to use Afrikaans as the medium of instruction. He said if we wished to prevent this from happening it was up to us. We were not sure what to do, but in the end we decided to make some posters, which we hung on the fence near the school gate. The posters said things like 'No to Afrikaans' and 'Afrikaans is the language of the oppressor'. Soon other schools started displaying posters of their own. After about a week the police moved in and tore down all the posters. Next about ten teachers were fired, including the one who had warned us what was about to happen. Instead of putting an end to our protest, these actions really made us angry. We decided that we would boycott classes on the following Monday and march from school to school carrying posters demanding the reinstatement of our teachers and no lessons in Afrikaans. The march went as planned. At each new school more and more students joined in. We were all very excited. We were doing something we had never done before. As we marched we sang songs, danced, and waved our signs."

Lerato paused for a moment and a hush fell over the audience as if they knew what was coming next. "The police arrived in hippos, and without warning they charged at us. We scattered and ran, but they chased us. Those of us who were too slow were beaten with sjamboks. Next they started shooting us with rubber bullets as we ran. I was hit in the back, which caused me to trip and fall, hitting my head on the ground. However my friends quickly picked me up and carried me to safety even although my head was bleeding badly. They decided to take me to hospital, which, as it turned out, was a bad mistake. The police were waiting in the reception area and anyone with rubber bullet wounds was immediately arrested. About twenty of us were put in a big van and driven to John Vorster Square. One of the boys knew some catchy songs, which he taught to the rest of us. Two of the were 'Dubul'iBhunu' and 'Umshini wami', but at the time I did not know what they meant. So by the time we arrived we were all singing and in quite high spirits. Even when we herded into a cell, we kept singing until a warden came and threatened to beat us unless we shut up.

"After a few hours I was taken by myself to a small room with no windows. The only furniture was a desk and two chairs. Also there were two policemen. They made me take off my clothes and stand on a brick. They kept asking me who had organised the protest march, but I kept telling them that I had no idea. I told them that I simply saw the students going by my house singing so I decided to join in. I told them I had no idea what the march was all about. They just kept asking the same questions over and over again, telling me that I would have to stand on the brick until I gave them the answers that they needed. After a couple of hours my legs started trembling and I fell off the brick. One of them hit me with a wet towel and made me get back on the brick. Each time I fell off the same procedure would be repeated. After maybe ten hours I must have fainted. By then I had no idea of what time it was, even if it was day or night. They threw water on my face and when I came to a senior officer was in the room. He said to give me one more working over. So I they made me stand on the brick again for a couple more hours. In the end the senior officer came back in and said, 'We are wasting our time with this kaffir meid. Let her go.' So I was given back my clothes and pushed out into the street. I had no money on me and no idea how to get back home. So I went to the taxi rank and when I told people what had happened to me one kind driver said he would take my home for free. He even dropped me off at my own house.

"Since then I have never gone back to school, but I tried to keep studying on my own. Then I came across Peter and this group, and now we try to help each other with our studies. That is why I am here today."

The silence that followed Lerato's story was broken when a well built lady entered from one of the back rooms carrying a tray on which were two tea pots and a number of assorted mugs of different sizes and shapes. "I see Aunty has brought us some tea," announced Peter. "Let's take a short break and get to know one another. Prof. will you go first."

Prof. Armstrong allowed himself to be led to the table with the tea, which was being poured into the mugs by two of the female students. Justin and Tony tried to hold back and allow others to go next, but Peter urged them forward. "You are our guests." Justin found the tea different from what he had expected, but not unpleasant. The milk and sugar had already been added, making for a sweet, milky brew. Once everyone had been served, clusters began to form as the individuals from such different backgrounds tried to get to know one another. Justin found himself surrounded by four or five Soweto students. They pressed him for details about what life at university was like. Clearly it was something that they all aspired to. After a while Justin took the opportunity to ask some questions of his own. "I was shocked at what happened to Lerato. Were any of you in that protest march?" It turned out the everyone in the group had partaken in protest marches, if not the one mentioned by Lerato, then others. "Did any of you get shot?"

A student called Amos replied, "Sure. I still have the marks." With that he pulled up his shirt and pointed to scars on his back. "I also have some on my butt if you would like to see those."

"No thanks. I believe you. I am sorry you had to go through that experience."

"Not at all. These scars are now a badge of honour. If you don't have any you are not really considered a man. It is like being initiated."

"So true," added another of the group. "Hau! There was this guy in my class who showed off his 'rubber bullet wounds'. You know what he had done? He cut himself with the point of a knife. He thought we would not see the difference between bullet and knife wounds. Besides we all knew he avoided protests like the plague."

This story provoked much laughter and mirth. "What a mampara!" was voiced a number of times. Amos grabbed a teaspoon and pretended to poke holes in Justin's back. "There, now you too have been initiated." And indeed, perhaps it was a kind of initiation. Other slapped him on the back, provoking more laughter.

Another group, including Jenny and Patricia, coalesced around Lerato, who was now sobbing. There was no laughter in this group. Patricia had her arms around Lerato, who was trying to regain control of herself. "It's okay Lerato. We are all with you. We will do all we can to help you with your education."

"Yes we will," added Jenny angrily. "But more than that. We need to erase this evil from our midst. I am truly sorry that these beasts have done these things to you."

"Thank you Jenny and Patricia. I know not all white people are bad. I know that there are others like you."

"Yes, but not enough." Jenny was still furious.

Peter called everyone back to order. "I hope that you have enjoyed your tea and conversations, but let's get on with the meeting. Will you all take your seats please."

"Prof. let me try to explain the situation to you. We are but a few here. There are hundreds like us in Soweto. Most are like Lerato in that they have left school. Many were expelled, while others have suffered some kind of trauma. Then there those who have dropped out simply because they do not want to be part of Bantu Education. However almost all of them wish to continue with their studies. We are trying to find ways to help them."

"So are you trying to start some kind of alternative school?" asked Prof. Armstrong. "There may be difficulty getting it registered."

"Excuse me Prof.," Ian interrupted. "I do not think that they are trying to start a school and get it registered. From what I can gather they already have a school going. They are asking our help in supporting this school. Am I right, Peter?"

"In a sense, yes, you are right. We do all meet in a number of venues on Saturdays and Sundays to study. Most of our high school students would like to sit for the Cambridge examination. There is a school in Swaziland that seems willing to take us on as external students, but there are a number of issues to iron out, such as where to write the examination. Perhaps Prof. you could help us with these negotiations. For the most part we are coping with learning in groups, helping each other as much as possible. There are some teachers from our schools who stop by to help us when we are stuck, but many of them are afraid to be associated with us. Some subjects are difficult for us and we are struggling with them"

"What subjects, for instance?"

"It is the science subjects that are giving us the most trouble. Also mathematics."

"Perhaps we can help you there."

"That would be most appreciated, but let me first mention the other category of student that we are trying to help. We have a number of students like Kagiso who would like to continue their university education. It is unlikely that they will be accepted at any South African university, except perhaps the University of South Africa. Perhaps Prof. you could give us some insight as to whether they could study for an overseas degree."

"As I understand it, there are two main issues. The one is to find ways in which your students can obtain degrees or some form of high school certification. It is not something that we can deal with immediately. However if we work together with the Institute for Racial Reconciliation, we can perhaps come up with some solutions. The other issue is to help your students with their ongoing studies. It is something we can begin to address today. What exactly are your needs?"

"Well sir, at the moment we meet in study groups and use the curriculum materials that we have at hand. Most of the time we are able to help each other, but there are subjects that often stump us. No one in the study group understands the materials. As I said before its is physical science, biology, and mathematics that cause us the most headaches. If you could find students that would help us with these subjects we would be most grateful. Then we are also in need for more curriculum materials, especially text books that are aligned with the curriculum that we study. For example for most of our high school students, these would be books aligned to the Cambridge examinations."

"Those of us who came here today will try to recruit students to act as mentors to your study groups. We already have two science students here who I am sure will volunteer."

Ian piped up, "Justin here is a maths student."

"But I only came as a driver."

One of the Soweto students called out, "A maths teacher and a driver. We are doubly blessed."

Prof. Armstrong clarified, "No one will be coerced into volunteering. All those who decide to help will do so because it is something that they really want to do. We must go now, but thank you for your hospitality. Peter, please keep in touch so that we can get the ball rolling on both counts as soon as possible."

As Prof. Armstrong and those that had come with him were preparing to leave, they were overwhelmed by the Soweto students wishing to thank them and shake their hands. If Justin did not know about the 'African' handshake before, he was an expert in it before he finally left.

There was a sombre silence in the beat up Volkswagen as the three friends made their way back to their digs—none of the usual good-natured banter. It was Justin who eventually broke the silence, "I had no idea things were this bad."

"Same here," added Tony.

"Yes, the government makes sure to keep the truth from us whites. We need to do something about it. An article in Campus News might be an option."

"But you knew how bad the situation really is?" Justin asked Ian.

"Unfortunately, yes. I have been here before."

They rode on in silence.

Eventually Ian asked, "Are either of you going to volunteer?"

"It is really not something I want to do, but after what I heard and saw today I don't see how I can just sit back and do nothing," said Justin. Even as the words came out of his mouth he realised the inadequacy of his response. His state of emotional turmoil left him unable to properly express his feelings, or to articulate an appropriate response. He reflected on Jenny's blazing anger as opposed to the calm demeanour of most of the Soweto students. They had even joked about some of the events. But while he did not entirely embrace Jenny's anger, he nevertheless was deeply disturbed by what he had heard. Up until this point in his life, like most other whites, he was able to turn a blind eye to the injustices of the government's policies. 'Best to leave matters to the government. They know what needs to be done' was an all too familiar refrain. But when he thought back to Lerato's story in particular he knew inaction was no longer an option. He could no longer plead ignorance or stand on the sidelines.

Ian continued, "You should only volunteer if it is something that you really want to do. It is not going to be easy. You do realise that it is against the law."

"What do you mean? That it is illegal to show someone how to solve a quadratic equation?"

"More than that. A strict interpretation of the Bantu Education Act is that no unauthorised white person may teach anything to an African."

"That is crazy."

"But true. Do you realise that we broke the law by coming to Soweto?"

"How so?"

"No white person may enter Soweto without a permit."

Justin digested this new information for a while. He realised that Ian was giving him a chance to honourably withdraw. Is that what he really wanted? It would certainly be the easy way out. The alternative was fraught with unknown dangers. But could he live with himself if he turned his back on what he now knew and what justice demanded? Finally he said, "What you have told me clinches it for me. You can count me in."

"What about you Tony?" asked Ian.

"I am not sure if I can help, but I would like to. I did take physical science and maths for matric. If I brushed up on them a bit I might be able to help with the easier topics."

No one said anything for a while. Eventually Justin said, "It was not really my car that you needed was it."

"No. I guess it was you."

Somehow the promise of free drinks was forgotten. Life for Justin would never be the same again. The Rubicon had been crossed.

THREE

LIFE IN THE HOUSE SOON SETTLED INTO A COMFORTABLE ROUTINE. ONE aspect, for which everyone was grateful, was that the dinners had improved markedly. Andy had gone to the trouble of investing in a popular book of recipes, Cook and Enjoy It. Not only had he provided this book, but he had also highlighted five easy to prepare dishes which, as he put it, "Not even the least talented of you hopeless plebs could mess up, although no doubt some of you will try." The upshot was that while there was less variety, there was certainly greater quality, so much so that Ian did not hesitate to invite Jenny, Jonty, and Norman to stay for dinner after their meeting.

The meeting had been called by Ian to follow up on a thought that had been eating away at him ever since their trip to Soweto. What can be done to make more people aware of the atrocities that were being committed under the guise of state security? Besides the three guests, Justin and Tony had also attended the meeting. The six of them had crammed into Ian's room, which like much of the rest of the house was sparsely furnished. Besides the bed, the only other furniture was a desk and chair, all of which had been scavenged from departing students. Jenny, Jonty, and Norman were seated on the bed, which Ian had hastily made just before the meeting. Tony had bagged the chair and Ian was perched on the desk, leaving Justin no option to make himself as comfortable as possible on the floor. The meeting was lively with many ideas bandied around, some grandiose, expensive, and impractical, while others were more modest and doable. In the end they decided to start with something that they could initiate without any outside help or funding. The student run newspaper, Campus News, of which Norman Barker was editor, would run a series of articles featuring the stories of some Soweto students. The envisaged tutoring sessions would give them the opportunity to hear and collect the details about the difficulties experienced by some of the students in the study groups. The main point of concern was to protect the identity of those whose stories were published. It was agreed that this could be done by changing names, places, and dates, but at the same time portraying an accurate picture of what had transpired. It was a challenge that even the most experienced journalist might find difficult to accomplish. It was also agreed that nothing would appear in the paper without the overall approval of Peter Sisulu and his committee. Jenny and Norman undertook to prepare the first of the articles in the series.

The dinner that followed broke ground in a number of ways. It was the first time guests had been invited, which gave rise to some logistical problems. For one, there were not enough plates or knives and forks to go around. Neville, who was the cook for the week, offered to eat out of the pan in which the food had been prepared. A pot and its lid made up for the rest of the deficit. For some, spoons were substituted for forks. Up until then meals had been eaten sitting on the floor, since there was no dining room table with chairs, and so the custom continued with guests present. Before the guests arrived there had been a cleaning frenzy—fast, but as it turned out not very effective. Jenny gamely tried not to look horrified as she eased herself down onto the none-too-clean cushion on the floor and observed the cracked plate that was handed to her. Watching her, Justin remembered the discussion that they had had on first moving into the house—the one about whether to allow girls to stay overnight. It seemed redundant now. Surely no girl in her right mind would ever want to spend more time here than absolutely necessary. Justin grinned to himself as he envisaged some fair maiden fleeing down the driveway, shrieking in horror at what she had just seen.

However it was the discussion that made the dinner really memorable. It turned out to be more thought-provoking than many a college seminar. Those who had made the trip to Soweto described some of what they had seen and learned, and went on to describe what they hoped to achieve in terms of coaching the students in the difficult subjects. Jenny and Norman went on to explain how they planned to publish the plight of some of the students that they had met or that they hoped to meet. It was David who set the cat among the pigeons, "Why are you doing all this? What good will it do?"

"I should think it is obvious," replied Norman somewhat huffily.

"Don't get me wrong. I am full of admiration for your intentions. But what will all of it really achieve?"

After some blank looks, David continued, "Think about it. Okay so you help get these guys a certificate or a degree. Have...."

Jenny interrupted, "There are girls there too."

"Yes, of course you are right. My apologies. But have you thought beyond that. Will they be able to get a decent job? Will they be able to vote? Will they suddenly be afforded all the privileges that you enjoy? They may have a piece of paper in their hands and some new knowledge in their heads, but will they be any better off than they are now?"

"Aren't you over simplifying things?" asked Tony. "Surely they will be better off in some respects."

"Am I? Think about it."

"So what is your solution? Just do nothing?" retorted Justin.

"Not at all. Please don't get me wrong. I think that you should continue with your plans. I really do. And I am not suggesting that all of it will be futile. Only that these are merely first steps. I am just asking that you realise that the day might come when more action will be needed. Educating these students and publishing their stories is not going to give them the freedom that they deserve."

"Then what will really help them?" asked Tony, but most in the group already knew the answer that would be forthcoming.

"They will not be free until we get rid of the apartheid government."

"And just how do we do that?" asked Justin.

"You don't. Not now anyway. All I am suggesting is that if and when the time comes you be ready for it. In the meanwhile you cannot do better than what you are already planning."

"Do you really believe that the time will come?"

"I have no doubt about it. Apartheid belongs in the dustbin of history. That is what Karl Marx said about capitalism, but I am sure it is true of apartheid as well. It may not come soon. Certainly not soon enough for my liking, but it will happen. Perhaps not even in our life times, but it will happen."

"How do you think it will happen?"

"Some revolutions are violent and some are peaceful. I can only hope that ours will be peaceful. I will say this. The more we can educate people—all people, white and black—the more stake they will have in a future non-racial society and the more likely that the revolution will be peaceful."

At this point, to everyone's surprise, Andy joined the conversation. Of all the house mates, he was perhaps the least political. "No future society will ever be complete without the arts—music, painting, theatre. How many of you here even know the extent to which the arts have inspired people to revolt? I bet none of you realise the extent to which Verdi's Nabucco or Beethoven's Fidelio for instance, aroused people to action—more so I dare say than Marx's Das Kapital."

Jonty looked at Andy with a renewed interest and respect. There was more to him, it seemed, than an aspiring poet or actor. He had an arresting face, thin and angular, framed with black hair. He reminded Jonty of a character in Sesame Street, the Count. He was also dressed more stylishly that the others in the room, in that he was even wearing a tie and jacket. A handkerchief was sticking out from his left hand sleeve. Where had he seen him before? And then it came to him. Andy had played the role of Bunthorne in the Operatic Society's recent production of Patience. It seemed that in real life he was attempting to recreate this role—that of an enigmatic poet given to the promotion of the arts. Yet he was not without some political awareness.

Now that Andy had everyone's attention he continued, "Actually what I really wanted to do was to share some good news with you. I have been asked to direct this year's production of the Dramatic Society. We will be performing Macbeth."

"Congratulations," said Tony. "Isn't Macbeth a matric set book this year? If so you should have no difficulty filling the theatre."

"Yes it is, but that is not the only reason we chose it. The play portrays a real abuse of power, which should be of interest to all of you aspirant politicians."

"Very interesting," chimed in Jenny. "I look forward to seeing how you interpret the main themes of the text—the corrupting influence of power, the escalating use of violence, and so on. It could be very relevant to our situation. Have you cast Lady Macbeth yet?"

"No, I was only appointed director today. Are you interested in the role?" Andy made a square with his two hands and peered at Jenny through it. "I can just see you as the perfect Lady Macbeth—cruel and ruthless, with blood dripping from your hands."

"Thank you very much for such a flattering image of me. Actually I already have too much on my plate, but thanks for thinking of me anyway."

At this point Jonty said, "We probably need to get going, before Andy starts casting the rest of us. Thanks for the dinner, Neville. Justin and Tony, we will stay in touch about the coaching project and the articles. Thanks to all for an interesting evening."

The next day Neville buttonholed Justin as he returned to the house from the campus. "I have some good news for you. I have found you a date for tomorrow night."

"I don't remember asking you to find me a date, and in any case I don't do blind dates."

"It is not exactly a blind date. You have probably seen her around at some of my cricket games. She and her sister often come to watch. I am dating her sister at the moment."

"So what you are saying is that you want me to come on a double date with you."

In Justin's mind a double date which included Neville ranked somewhere below a colonoscopy. Neville was a star—girls swooned over him. Before university he had attended a boys' private school where he had excelled in sports. He represented his school in the first team of most of the sports offered. Once he started his university career he had decided to specialise in cricket and hockey. His face was rugged rather than hansom, and his lopsided grin was enough to melt the heart of many a fair maiden. He wore his curly, honey blond hair fairly long and unkempt, which many girls found endearing. It gave the appearance of one who did not really care about his looks. Justin, on the other hand, had never had a girl swoon over him or comment on his good looks. Truth be told he had a very ordinary face topped by straight black hair. He had never got beyond a first date with any girl, and there had been few enough of those. So in Justin's mind, a double date which included Neville would end up with two girls clinging to Neville while he sat abandoned like a wall-flower.

"Thanks for the offer but I am not interested."

"Come on. Be a sport. I don't want to have to disappoint Julie."

"What is it that you have in mind?"

"There is this hot party that Julie wants us to go to. Colleen is Julie's sister."

"So why don't you just take her and find another date for Colleen?"

"Another complication is that we need a ride to the party. It is just out of town in the mink and manure belt."

"So that is what this is all about. You are looking for a ride and I am your best option."

"No, it's not only that. Colleen really does want to meet you." The 'heavens knows why' was left unsaid but hung in the air. "Please say you will come. You will have a great time I promise you."

"I will think about it."

Justin did think about it, but in the end Neville was a hard person to refuse any favour. Besides it had been months since his last ill-fated date.

Neville pushed his way into Justin's room without knocking. It was not the custom of the house to knock when entering a room, and in any case doors were mostly left open. "Don't tell me you plan on going to the party dressed like that."

"What is wrong with my outfit?"

"You look as if you are going to a funeral. No one wears a coat and tie to a party."

"Well, I have never been to a party in Rivonia. How would I know what the mink and manure set wear to parties."

"For heaven's sake, just put on something casual. I will come back for you in a couple of minutes."

Justin changed quickly and was ready before Neville returned. "We will pick up the girls and drive straight to the party from here," Neville informed Justin as they climbed into his car. "They share a flat near the campus."

"What is the name of my date again?"

"Colleen. Colleen Jansen. You might try to remember it."

"What else can you tell me?"

"Julie and Colleen are sisters. They are from Sabie, which is a small town in the Eastern Transvaal. Colleen is a second-year student, majoring in Latin and French. Julie is a fresher and will most likely major in speech and drama."

"Anything else you can tell me?"

"They are both gorgeous."

"Yes. You did mention that before." Neville was known for his overly optimistic assessment of women, and indeed life in general.

"By the way, hockey season is just beginning. Why don't you come and try out. You did play hockey at school didn't you?" Justin wondered if Neville was deliberately changing the subject, or if it was a serious suggestion. "I was never much good at it, but I did enjoy playing."

"Other than the first team, most guys just play for fun and exercise. Come to the practice next week."

"I suppose you are looking for a ride to practice?"

"Stop being such a grouch. And no, I always jog to hockey practice. It is not that far."

"Okay. I might just do that."

"Turn left here and park around the back of this block of flats. We had better go up to their flat as most likely they will not be ready."

Justin followed Neville up a flight of stairs and along a corridor until they came to the right door. It turned out the Neville's prediction was wrong. Julie opened the door immediately and gave him a quick kiss. Both girls were ready and waiting. In some ways they might have been twins. The main difference between them was that Colleen's hair was shoulder length, whereas Julie had hers cut short. Both were wearing the now fashionable mini-skirts.

Neville made the introductions. "Colleen, this is Justin. Justin, Colleen."

"Hi Colleen." His heart leapt and sank simultaneously. She was indeed gorgeous. She had long blond hair and blue eyes, but somehow there was more to her than that. A pleasant, friendly smile touched the corners of her mouth. She did not sport that haughty look so commonly found among blonds who knew that men found them gorgeous. Her face was soft, but her nose perhaps just a little on the large side. Yet its size made her even more endearing to Justin's mind. But in the end it was not her beauty that impressed, but that special presence that only a few are blessed with. Justin knew immediately that she was way out of his league. He watched her face for that look of disappointment as she appraised him, but either she hid it well or it was not there. Perhaps the evening would not be a total disaster. At best they would keep up the appearances of a date and then each thankfully go their own ways afterwards.

"Best we hurry," said Neville. "The party will already be under way." He and Julie climbed into the back seat, leaving the front seat next to Justin for Colleen.

"Which way now?" asked Justin.

"Take Oxford Street all the way as far as it goes."

For the first ten minutes of the drive Neville kept the conversation going, talking mostly about the past cricket season, during which time he had scored a number of centuries, and the upcoming hockey season, where he hoped to score a record number of goals. After a while he stopped talking, and a glance in the rear mirror confirmed Justin's suspicions. There would be no more conversation from Neville or Julie for the duration of the trip. That meant that either the rest of the trip would be made in silence, or he and Colleen would need to start a conversation—but who would make the first move? In the end Justin asked, "So what are your majors?" He already knew the answer, but he could not come up with a more original way of breaking the silence.

She told him, and then asked, "What about you?"

"Mathematics." He had given this answer before and knew from experience that it was a conversation stopper, accompanied by sympathetic or embarrassed looks. Mathematics majors did tend to be a collection of odd-balls and social misfits.

"I understand that your other major is English." So she did know more about him than she had let on. "I am hoping to minor in English."

"If that is so, and if I fail a year, we might end up in the same class."

"I doubt if that will happen, I mean your failing. Neville says you are one of the smartest persons he has ever met." Justin reflected that Neville did not really move in intellectual circles, but kept the thought to himself. "Neville also mentioned that you have been out to Soweto recently and have plans to coach some of the out-of-school students there. Please tell me more."

Justin gave her a sanitised version of the trip that they made and some of what they hoped to achieve. He did not mention the articles that they planned to write for fear that he might then have to stray into tricky territory. He certainly did not want to venture into Lerato's story with someone he was meeting for the first time. Besides relating the details of how a young woman had been tortured was not the kind of thing one talked about on a first date. Even Justin knew that much.

Colleen turned out to be an attentive listener. At the end of Justin's narrative she remarked, "I am most impressed by what you are planning. Perhaps there is some way I might be able to help."

Before Justin could follow up on this opening, Neville called out from the back seat, "Take the next right." Had he just surfaced, or had he been more aware of the progress that they were making all along?

As Neville had predicted, the party was well under way when they arrived. Clearly he was well known in these circles. A number of friends came over to greet him and to meet his companions. Introductions were made, but Justin knew he would not remember any of the names. They were shown to the tables bearing food and drinks, and invited to help themselves. Strident music was blaring from the next room, which was full of gyrating couples. Justin surveyed the scene with a jaundiced eye. His mind strayed to the elegant waltz's of old Vienna, and the beautiful symphonies and opera's of the nineteenth century. Has civilization really deteriorated this far, he wondered to himself?

Justin could not fail to notice that the entry of Julie and Colleen had stirred considerable interest among many of the males, both on the dance floor and around the food tables. Perhaps this was the moment, he reflected, when Colleen would detach herself from him and seek out a more desirable partner. From the looks that she was receiving she obviously had any number of choices should she so wish. Instead she took him by the arm saying, "Let's dance first and work up an appetite. We can eat later when there is less of a crush at the food tables."

"I am not really good at dancing," he protested. She led him onto the floor anyway. She started to twist and turn gracefully. He did his best to follow her movements, but only succeeded in executing a number of uncoordinated, stiff jerks and stumbles. Her face lit up with laughter—not the derisive kind, but rather hinting of friendly mirth. "You really don't dance do you. Come over to the side of the room and let me try to give you some lessons."

They found a relatively unoccupied corner. "Now pretend you are wet. Imagine you have just come out of a shower."

"Without clothes?"

"If you like," she replied impishly. "Now hold a towel behind your back with both hands. Next move your hands and body so as to dry your back down by your waist. Shake and twist."

He did his best to comply, but he was still stiff and awkward. Plus the image of his doing this naked was so ridiculous, that he burst out laughing. "What is so funny?"

"Can you not think what this would look like if I had no clothes on."

It took a moment for the penny to drop and then she too burst out laughing. "You are a riot. You really are."

She continued to try teaching him but in the end gave up. "You are right. You really are hopeless at this. Did you never learn to dance?"

"At school I did have to take some dance lessons. I think I might be able to remember how to waltz if that is okay with you."

"No one here is going to put on any waltz music. I tell you what. Once they start playing some slower music I will teach you the nightclub shuffle. In the meanwhile let's get something to eat."

Back at the food table Justin surveyed what was on offer. No expense had been spared in providing a sumptuous buffet. They helped themselves and retired to the next room to eat. Colleen turned down several requests to dance, indicating that she was busy eating. After she had declined the third offer, Justin suggested, "Why not go and have some fun on the dance floor. I will be okay."

"Are you sure?" He nodded yes. As she went off on the arm of a potential partner she called over her shoulder, "Don't go away. You still have to learn the shuffle." He was grateful that she had let him down so gently. He went back to the food and drinks tables. He could, he supposed, drink himself into oblivion, but then who would drive home. Neville was known as someone who should not be behind the wheel of a car. He would nurse a beer or two and nibble at the food table until it was time to go home. However, as it turned out, there was a flaw to this plan. From time to time a girl would eye him with an 'ask me to dance for heaven's sake' kind of look. He would try not to meet her eyes by carefully studying his drink to make sure no insect had made the suicide plunge. In the end to escape, he tried to take a stroll around the garden, but it was that time in the course of a party that couples were drifting into nooks and crannies behind shrubs, tool sheds, or any other suitable cover. Maybe he would run into Neville and Julie, or even worse Colleen and whoever might have latched onto her. With that in mind he returned to the drinks table.

Before he could pour himself another drink, Colleen put her arm around his. "I have been looking for you everywhere. Time for you to learn the nightclub shuffle." With that she led him back to the dance floor, where the music was now much softer and slower. "Just do as I tell you. Put your arms around me." He held her right hand in his left, and his right hand lightly on her waist. "No. That is the ballroom style. Put both your arms around me." He complied. "Now for the most part we just shuffle and sway a little. Put your weight on your right foot, now back to the left. Shuffle your right foot to the left, your left foot to the left and then a quick, left, right, left." He tried it as she was speaking and found it quite simple. "Very good! That is all there is to it. We can keep going to the left, or reverse direction and go back to the right." Within minutes he had perfected the manoeuvre and together they drifted slowly around the floor. He was intensely aware of her arms around him and the closeness of her body. As one song gave way to the next she showed no signs of wanting to stop, and Justin for the first time that the evening, hoped that the music would never end.

His bliss was interrupted by a thump on his shoulder. It was Neville, "Time to go home."

"But it is still early."

"No it's not. Look around. There is hardly anyone left." Justin opened his eyes and found that they indeed were one of the few couples left on the dance floor. Reluctantly he released Colleen from his arms. Earlier in the evening he could not wait to leave. Now all he wanted was for the night never to end.

They had no sooner pulled out of the driveway when Justin realised that he would not be getting any help with directions from Neville. He and Julie were already fully engrossed with one another. In order to avoid having to listen to the noises from the back seat he decided to engage Colleen in conversation. The same thought seemed to have struck her as well.

"Neville tells me that you are from Sabie. What is it like there?" Grateful for the opening, she launched into a detailed description of of the area surrounding her home town. She spoke of waterfalls with names such as MacMac, Berlin, Lisbon, Forest, and Bridal Vail. She described scenic spots such as God's Window and the Pinnacle, the precipitous escarpment and the Blyde River Canyon. "Have you ever been there?" she finally asked.

"No but you have certainly whet my appetite."

"I do hope that you will get the opportunity to see at least some of it. I would be happy to take you around if you are ever in the area."

"I would like that."

She hesitated for a while and then said, "You know what I like about you Justin, you are real."

"What do you mean?"

"You seem content to be just who you are. You do not pretend to be anyone but yourself. And you have not trotted out any of those god-awful pick-up lines."

"I guess I have never thought about needing a pick-up line."

"That is exactly what I mean. You should hear some of the dreadful ones that have been tried out on me. For example, just tonight this guy comes up, and in a syrupy voice says, 'Let's go and look at the moon together.' So I humoured him and said, 'Why?' And then he says, 'I want to see it turn green with envy when it beholds your beauty.' I nearly puked all over him."

"He sounds really pathetic. But funny in a way. Do you have any others?"

"Lots. Another favourite is, 'I must have died and gone to heaven and met a beautiful angel.'"

"Corny."

"And another is, 'If Helen's face launched one thousand ships, yours would launch one million.'"

"Don't they see how they are making fools of themselves?"

"No. And that is because they are not real. They are pretending to be someone else—a modern-day Casanova or something. You, on the other hand, do not try to be anything but yourself."

"If that is a compliment, thanks. Some might see it as an insult."

"I will think of you as my Velveteen Rabbit. Do you know that children's story?"

"I think I might have heard it. Remind me."

"The Velveteen Rabbit is a child's toy. It is old, scruffy, and missing parts, but it is loved and that is what makes it real. It does not try to be like the other fancy toys."

"I guess the old and scruffy might be a good description of me."

"No you are not old and scruffy—or at least not old. But you are real. That is the point I was trying to make. My favourite line in the book is, 'When you are real you don't mind getting hurt.'"

Justin tried to digest all that had just transpired. Did he really seem old and scruffy, not to mention missing parts, to some people? He did not think that that was what Colleen really meant. She was trying to tell him that she appreciated that he was real. But then there was that rider about the rabbit being real because he was loved. What did that mean? Who did she think loved him? Was he reading too much into what Colleen had said? After all, she had said that she did not mean to imply that he was old. They arrived at their destination before he sorted out that one in his mind.

"Come up for a quick cup of coffee," invited Julie as they disembarked from the car. While the two sisters made the coffee, Neville and Justin made themselves comfortable in the lounge. "I hope you enjoyed your evening."

"It was fine. How about you."

"A okay." Polite chatter did not really become the two of them. In the end Neville said, "Be sure to come to hockey practice on Wednesday afternoon."

The girls returned with coffee and they chatted mostly about who and what they had seen at the party. Justin kept waiting for Neville to signal that it was time for them to leave, but he showed no signs of wanting to go. Instead he and Julie kept looking at him expectantly. And then it dawned on Justin. Neville was planning to stay the night and they were willing him to leave. He quickly got up got up saying, "I guess it is time we left. Coming Neville?" He had the satisfaction of making Neville reply, "No. You go on without me."

Colleen followed him to the front door, and gave him a quick peck on the cheek as he was leaving. "Don't be a stranger."

Driving home alone, Justin reflected on the evening. All things considered it had not been an unpleasant experience. Colleen had treated him kindly. He had survived his blind date and could now forget all about it and get on with his life. On the other hand her parting words had been ' Don't be a stranger', but surely that was simply a manifestation of her good manners.

Colleen, on the other hand, was less dismissive. She felt sure that when they were doing the nightclub shuffle, that there had been a definite physical attraction, an energy exchange, a spark. She loved the fact that he was a little mysterious and deep. She knew that she wanted to see him again, to get closer, and to ask questions that would invite him to show himself more. But as she thought about the evening she realised that what she now felt went beyond Justin himself. She had never had the experience of hearing about the suffering of others first hand. Just the opposite. Her first year at varsity had been a series of parties and romances. Not once on all these dates had there been any talk about topics such as the struggle of African students for a meaningful education. She had surprised herself when she responded to Justin's explanation of his visit to Soweto, asking if she could help. Was Justin helping her find her true self? Was that perhaps one of the reasons that she found herself attracted to him?

As arranged, Justin attended the hockey practice on Wednesday. Most of the time was spent on drills and then sorting players into groups. There were those who were trying out of the first team that would play in the premier league. At the other end of the scale were those who merely wanted to have some fun together with friends. They would be assigned to teams in the lower leagues. Justin was, both by choice and inclination, in this latter group. The words of his high school coach still rang in his ears. "Justin's lack of talent is matched only by his enthusiasm and effort."

A more important meeting took place that same week. Prof. Armstrong arranged for all who were interested in coaching in Soweto to meet with him and the student committee from Soweto headed by Peter Sisulu. Altogether about twenty students had volunteered, including the six who had originally made the visit to Soweto. Prof. Armstrong kicked off proceedings by introducing Peter and explaining the purpose of the meeting. "Peter will be far better than I at telling you what his committee has come up with, so I will hand the floor over to him."

"Thank you Prof. We have had much discussion and consultation leading up to the project that I will explain to you shortly. I do not want to bore you with all the details, but you do need to understand something of the tensions that surround this project. In Soweto, and indeed across the country, there are basically three groups of students. There are those who are saying that there should be no education until we have achieved freedom. Then there are those who contend that Bantu Education is better than nothing at all. In the middle are members of my group who are attempting to get an education outside of the structures of Bantu Education. It is the first group that initially opposed our project. By the way, teachers are also divided into the same three groups. In the end, ironically, it was the striking teachers who helped us convince the 'no education' group that we had the right to study. Some of these teachers have even agreed to help us.

"So let me now explain how we are organised, and how you can help us if that is what you want to do. We plan to meet as a group every Saturday. We have already secured a venue. There will be four sessions of about one and a half hours each. At each session, four subjects will be covered; mathematics, physics, chemistry, and biology. This arrangement means that those who so wish can attend all four subjects during the course of the day. However some may wish to attend only one subject, say mathematics. We will pick a topic for each day ahead of time. For example this coming Saturday the mathematics topic will be quadratic equations. Students will prepare on their own during the week. The Saturday session will be used to answer difficulties that the students have experienced and to help them to solve these equations. The same lesson on quadratic equations will be repeated four times during the day."

The rest of the meeting was taken up with logistical matters such as who would volunteer for the coming Saturday, who would cover each of the four subjects, and what transport would be needed for the volunteers. As the meeting was breaking up, Jenny and Norman buttonholed Peter. "What did your committee have to say about our idea of writing up some of the stories of your students?"

"They are all for it. Even if we are identified and punished for it, we decided that it would be worth it in the long run. So go ahead. I will introduce you to others who have interesting stories to tell on Saturday."

At this point no one had any idea of the far reaching consequences that these articles would have.

FOUR

IT WAS DECIDED BY THOSE INVOLVED THAT A SMALL TEAM WOULD BE dispatched to Soweto on Saturday, two persons for each of the four subjects; mathematics, physics, chemistry, and biology. Justin was assigned to the mathematics group, along with Tony Forester. It had proved difficult to find a second maths person, and so Tony volunteered despite his not being a mathematics major. Besides the eight tutors, Norman and Jenny would join the group in the hopes of unearthing more stories, and also to show the draft that they had written about Lerato for her approval. And so it was that Prof. Armstrong and ten excited, if nervous, students set out for Soweto in a kombi.

The venue was a different one this time—a much larger church hall. Justin estimated that at least one hundred students had shown up. Each of the four subjects had been allocated a corner of the hall including rather rickety looking blackboards perched on wobbly easels. The Soweto students were quickly divided into four groups, and the tutoring sessions got under way. The two morning sessions flew by rapidly, and after a quick boxed lunch, so did the two afternoon ones.

A few years previously, Prof. Armstrong had been a visiting professor for six months at Hiroshima University. While there he was exposed to, and had learned to appreciate, the Japanese custom of reflecting on lessons. He decided to apply this technique to the Soweto tutoring project. At the end of the afternoon, once the Soweto students had left, he asked those who remained to take a seat. He surveyed the group wondering how best to begin. He scanned the expectant faces, all wondering what would come next. Besides the ten tutors who had come with him, were Peter Sisulu and three of his committee, as well as two striking teachers who had come to help.

"When I was in Japan I learned how valuable it is to reflect on what we do. Consider, for example, what went well and how we might improve in the future. So please feel free to share your impressions and thoughts. This will take no more than half an hour."

It was an unfamiliar request, and no one volunteered to speak. "Did anything impress any of you in particular?"

In the end it was Tony who broke the uneasy silence, "I am not sure if this is what you are looking for, but I have one impression I could share. When I was at school we tried to avoid maths as much as possible. We would try to side-track the teacher, to waste as much time as we could, and get out of as much homework as possible. These students actually asked us for more homework! They wanted to learn everything that they could about quadratic equations. They kept pressing us for more. I was amazed."

"Thank you Tony. Why do you think that they are so keen?"

It was Peter who eventually answered. "When you are denied something it becomes valuable in your eyes."

"Good point. Thank you, Peter. By the way I am not looking for any particular answer. It is up to you to share what seems best to you. Anyone else?"

Justin started out hesitantly. "My first session did not go very well. I guess I overestimated what the students knew about quadratic equations. I had been given the impression that all we were expected to do was maybe fill in a few gaps and to answer a few questions. In the following three sessions I started off with a quick lesson, which seemed to help. With a few basics covered, the rest of the session kind of fell into place."

"Thank you Justin. Did anyone else experience difficulties, or come up with improvements?"

Jonty Webb raised his hand. "We were dealing with Ohm's Law, and the ratio between potential difference and current in general. I found that most students had memorised as much as they could, including the diagrams. But when I probed, it seemed they had very little understanding of what they had memorised. For example when I asked them what the voltmeter in the diagram was they would reply something like, 'a circle with an arrow in it.' In other words, the diagram conveyed no meaning. It was simply a series of lines and shapes to be memorised."

"Well what do you expect from someone who has never seen a voltmeter," retorted one of Peter's committee members.

"You are right, and I am not trying to blame or belittle them. I am trying to figure out how to make these physics concepts meaningful and understandable. It is not like we have a laboratory here that we could use."

One member of the Soweto student committee spoke up. "Actually there is an NGO that makes portable laboratories. We had some in the school that I used to go to. They had everything we needed including electricity stuff."

"I am not sure we could fit a laboratory into our kombi."

"Perhaps I used the wrong word. They are more like kits. The box that everything comes in is only about this big." He held up his arms with his hands about thirty five centimetres apart.

"I know some people involved with this NGO," said Prof. Armstrong. "It is called the Science Education Project by the way. Perhaps they would donate a kit or two for our use."

Another Soweto student spoke up. "I have heard that these kits were developed at Fort Hare. And now they are used in government schools here. That means they must be part of Bantu Education. If so we should have nothing to do with them."

"Actually it is not that cut and dried," broke in one of the striking Soweto teachers. "One of the mining houses wanted to supply schools here in Soweto with these kits. However the director of the project was reluctant to be seen to be undermining our strike. He came to us to ask our advice. We debated the issue among ourselves and then gave him our verdict. In a nutshell we decided that despite our strike, we acknowledge the need for our youngsters to receive an education, especially in the sciences. We will need their knowledge when we obtain our freedom. So we told the director of the project to go ahead. We felt it would do no harm, and perhaps even some good. So if you use the kits here it will be with our blessing."

"Very interesting," said the prof. "I will contact the director of the project. Any other comments or suggestions?"

"Yes, one," said Jenny. "And please don't the rest of you shoot me. I for one felt very uncomfortable eating lunch when the students had nothing. I think that we should either bring lunch for all, or else eat nothing ourselves."

"That would mean finding at least another one hundred lunches," observed Jonty. "We don't even have a budget for this project. I don't even know how the prof found money for our transport and lunch, and no, I am not going to ask. Some things are best left unknown."

Peter came to the rescue. "There are some business men here in Soweto. I will approach some to see if any of them will sponsor a lunch for all, including you guys. That way we will either all eat, or none of us."

"Thanks Peter. Well, I see our time is up. Best we get going before dark."

On the way to the kombi, Justin asked Jenny about Lerato's reaction to the proposed article. "She is all for it. We have set the action in Durban rather than here, and of course changed her name. Other than that the details of what were done to her are accurate. Despite the name changes it is still fairly clear that it is about Lerato. However, she is one hundred percent okay with the article. She says that even if they do trace it back to her, all that they can do is torture her again. She maintains she has experienced the worst and could take it again."

"Brave girl. But I suspect that they could do much worse. I hope she knows that. So will you be publishing the article?"

"Yes it will be in this coming week's edition of Campus News."

The following day, Sunday, Justin experienced one of those minor milestones that make up the tapestry of life. It occurred during his first time wearing university colours on a hockey field, albeit a friendly match. The main season was yet to start. He had been assigned to the fourth team—there were only four. His position was right half back where it was deemed he could do the least damage. The two full backs were a team's last defence against an opposition attack, and hence had to be reasonably good players. It was up to the forwards to score the team's goals, so they too had to be able to hit the ball true and hard. As long as the half backs ran around enough and passed on the occasional ball, no one paid them too much attention.

Sometime during the second half of the match, Justin's team forced a short corner. It was Justin's task as a half back to push the ball from the opposing goal line to his forwards waiting on the edge of the circle. If all went to plan, one of the forwards would then take a shot at goal. As it turned out everything was going exactly to plan, and the forward who had stopped Justin's push was lining up to take a mighty shot at goal. Too late Justin suddenly realised that he had jogged away from the goal line and was now exactly between the goal and the forward lining up his shot. To avoid being hit on the shin, Justin leapt as high as he could into the air, saving considerable damage to his being. However he had neglected to lift his hockey stick as he leapt, and the shot at goal deflected off his stick to beat the baffled goal keeper. Justin had scored his first, and as it turned out, the only goal of his career.

If scoring a goal was not enough, the day held one more surprise for him. After the match, Neville tracked him down and asked, "How would you like to go flying this afternoon?"

"What do you mean, flying?"

"I am taking lessons. Do you want to go up with me."

"You mean in one of those small planes?"

"Of course. You do not learn to fly in a Boeing 707."

"How safe is it?" Justin had never been in any kind of plane.

"Safe as houses. An instructor will be flying with us. I am not allowed to fly by myself with passengers until I have my licence."

"Where are you taking these lessons?"

"Out at Grand Central. It is just off the Pretoria road."

"I get it. You need a ride and I am available."

"You are such a cynical bastard. I don't know why I even bother with you. If you look around almost everyone you can see has offered me a ride to the airport just for the chance to fly with me. I am trying to do you a favour you stupid cretin."

Chastised Justin replied, "Sorry. Thanks for the offer. Yes, I would like to give it a try."

Neville and Justin sat in the flying club lounge waiting for the instructor to finish debriefing his previous student. "We will be flying in a Cessna 172 today. It is a four seater. Most of my training to date has been in a two seater. However I want to include both the Cessna 172 and 182 on my licence when I get it. So I am doing some of my training in these models. Today will be my first cross-country flight and my instructor will be treating it as a comprehensive check flight. In other words he will be grading me on everything I do from start to finish."

Out on the apron, Justin looked on as Neville inspected the plane from the outside under the watchful eyes of his instructor. No detail seemed too trivial. Nuts, bolts, and hinges were all inspected, not to mention the more obvious details such as fuel and oil. It was most reassuring. That completed, Justin was shown how to climb into the rear seat, after which the instructor and Neville claimed the two front ones.

"I though you were going to fly this thing," Justin whispered in Neville's ear.

"I am. The pilot sits in the left hand seat. It is not like a car."

Justin watched as Neville checked every switch and gauge, of which there were a bewildering number. Finally Neville opened the window, stuck his head out and yelled, "Prop clear!" With that he started the engine, and then went through another series of checks, all carefully watched and noted by the instructor. Finally he picked up the microphone and said something Justin could not catch. The reply came, "Cleared to holding point runway 35." And they were on their way.

At the end of the runway, Neville went through another series of checks, including making sure that Justin's seat belt was fastened. Clearance for take off was granted from the tower. Neville lined the plane up with the runway, gunned the engine, and they began their take off roll. Justin gripped the seat, but then relaxed as the plane lifted and the ground gently dropped away beneath them. He was airborne for the first time in his life. He watched entranced as the houses below him drifted by getting smaller and smaller as the earth seemed to recede beneath the plane's landing gear. It seemed that he was floating as the terrain below him shrank to Lilliputian dimensions. He suddenly realised that he was holding his breath, not from anxiety, but from exhilaration. He had never felt so free.

It occurred to Justin that he had no idea where they were going. He wanted to ask but realised that Neville had his hands full. Not only was he flying the plane, still in climbing mode, but was also responding to a series of commands concerning altitude and direction coming over the radio. Grand Central, it occurred to Justin was surrounded by other airports, including Jan Smuts, the country's main international terminal. There were also two air force bases and a couple of other general aviation fields in the area. He sat with his eyes glued to the window and continued to enjoy the unfolding vista. Finally a landmark that he could recognise, the Hartbeespoort Dam, came into view. The plane banked slightly to the left and now the majestic Magaliesberg range stretched out below them. As a first-year student, Justin had joined the university's hiking club, and had spent many a happy weekend exploring the numerous kloofs and pools that define this mountain range. He now looked down eagerly to try to identify places that he had hiked to during the previous year. The crystal clear pools made for ideal spots to swim and generally laze the day away. It is strange, he mused, how much smaller that area looked from the air than when hoofing it on foot. Silently the easily recognisable Rustenburg Kloof slipped into view, and then the mountain scenery gave way to farm lands.

It occurred to Justin that he still did not know where they were headed. Neville appeared to be more relaxed now, and was even chatting with the instructor. Tapping him on the shoulder he asked, "Where are we going?"

"Zeerust will be our first point of call. We will be landing there and spend a few minutes on the ground. Make it your bathroom break."

Sure enough, it was not long before Neville started to busy himself with preparations for landing. As he cut back on the power, the plane began to descend. The airport, Justin noted, was some distance from the town itself. Having checked the windsock, Neville chose to land in a northerly direction, joining a left hand downwind for runway 04. After what appeared to Justin to be a near perfect landing, Neville taxied the plane to the only building on the premises. It was good to be on firm ground again and stretch one's legs. The airport appeared to be deserted, and so the three visitors settled themselves around a table on the verandah of the building. Neville spread out a map on the table, and began to do some calculations. Justin looked on intrigued. "Are the lines you have drawn on the map our route?"

"Yes, exactly. We have just flown from Grand Central, here on the map, to Zeerust." He traced out the route with his finger. "From here we will fly to Nylstroom and then back to Grand Central. No more stops."

"I see we will be flying over the Pilanesberg. Any chance of flying close enough to the ground to spot some animals?"

"No way. We maintain altitude along the whole route. Anyway it is forbidden to fly low over game reserves."

"What are those little circles along our route?"

"Those are the check points I have chosen to mark our progress. By timing how long it takes to get from one to the next I can get an accurate measure of our ground speed. It is also a way to make sure we are heading in the right direction."

Neville continued with his calculations. "What are you doing now?"

"I am factoring in the latest information that I have on the wind speed and direction. That way I can predict how long it will take us to reach our check points, and how much correction to add to my desired headings."

"It sounds complicated."

"Not really once you get the hang of it."

Once Neville was ready, the three of them boarded the plane to continue the trip. Pilanesberg viewed from the air was an amazing sight, the outlines of the collapsed caldera clearly visible. Justin savoured every minute of it, his face glued to the window. He could not help but recall the famous poem on flying by John Mcgee. He decided to share it with Neville later on.

Back at Grand Central, Neville was debriefed by the instructor. From what Justin could overhear, Neville had done an excellent job. As they were leaving, the instructor said to Justin, "Any time you fly with Neville you will be in safe hands. I do not say that about all my students."

On the drive back home Neville asked, "Well, how was it? At least you did not throw up as some have done."

"It was absolutely fantastic. I enjoyed every single moment. It was exhilarating. While in the air I remembered a poem that I heard back in high school. It describes my feelings about flying exactly."

"How does it go?"

"I don't remember it all, but it begins, 'Oh! I have slipped the surly bonds of earth, and danced the skies on laughter-silvered wings.' Then the end is something like, 'I've trod the high untrespassed sanctity of space, put out my hand, and touched the face of God.'"

"Yes, that is very descriptive of how I feel too. Thanks for sharing it. Who wrote it? I would like to read the whole thing."

"It was a guy called John Mcgee. I might even have it somewhere still."

As they continued on their way home, Justin had another question. "Neville, it seems you are too poor to own a car, so how can you pay for flying lessons? They must be very expensive."

"Yes, they are. Not having a car is not related to money."

Justin waited for more. "I don't like this getting around as it does not make me look good. A while back I pranged my old man's Merc—it was a write off. Had my licence taken away at the same time. Blood count was way too high. After my old man cooled down he made a deal with me. If I promised not to drive for two years, he would gift me one hundred flying hours."

"That was very generous of him."

"Yes and no. He is in the aviation industry, and hopes that I will join his business as a pilot. He gets a whopping discount on the flying time at that school at Grand Central. I also overheard him telling the old lady that he hoped that the discipline of learning to fly will rub off on other aspects of my life."

"Sounds like a good deal to me."

"Yes it is. Say, if you would like to take flying lessons, I will spot you some hours."

"That is more than generous, but I don't see how I could accept."

"Well think about it. I only need about forty hours to get my pilot's licence."

"Okay, I will." Justin reflected that the last time he had promised to think about it, he had been coerced into a double date. Neville usually got his way.

When the weekly edition of Campus News appeared on Wednesday it was snapped up very quickly. Justin could not find a copy until he got home late that afternoon. Fortunately some of the others in the house had bagged a copy. He turned quickly to the sports page, and after a short search found what he was looking for—hockey news. He quickly scanned the scores and descriptions of what the first two teams had achieved. Right at the bottom of the page was what he was looking for. 'Fourth team lost 1-2. Lone goal scored by Justin Roberts.' His moment of glory for all it see, albeit in small print.

Turning to the front page he discovered what had made the paper an instant sell out. The article about Special Branch torture based on the information supplied by Letato and a couple of other Soweto students filled most of the front page. The headline across the whole of the front page read **'POLICE TORTURE STUDENTS'**. There was also an editorial denouncing torture and the laws that permitted it. By now the house mates were assembling for dinner. Since it was Andy's week to cook, no one was absent. David Cohen was the last to arrive.

"I see you have all read the article on the front page. There is going to be a silent protest just outside the main gate on Friday evening during rush hour. I hope most, if not all, of you will come and support it."

The protest went off as planned, although David was disappointed that only a hundred or so students actually showed up to participate. Placards were handed out, which were then waved at passing motorists. Prominent among the messages displayed were 'END POLICE TORTURE' and 'NO DETENTION WITHOUT TRIAL'. Justin was interested to note the reaction of passing motorists. Some waved and gave them the thumbs up sign. But a few, more than he would have anticipated, seemed angry with the students, and even hurled abuse at them. However the largest reaction by far was simply to ignore the protest. As the rush hour traffic started winding down, the protest was declared a success and most headed for the Dev, or other watering holes in Braamfontein or Hillbrow.

Meanwhile Andy Kaplan was attempting to get Macbeth off the ground. He had already held auditions on the previous day, and was reasonably happy with his cast. Macbeth was to be played by Donald Campbell, and exchange student from England, who already had considerable experience in the theatre. Diane Linder, a veteran of Dramatic Society productions, was to play Lady Macbeth. The other major roles were to be played by actors with at least some experience on the stage. All things considered, Andy felt reasonably confident that he would be able to mount a first rate production. The fly in the ointment was that he had been pressured to accommodate a number of Speech and Drama students. There was not much he could do about it as the Department sponsored and more importantly provided some funding for the production. He had to find roles for about twenty Speech and Drama plebs. He assigned them some of minor roles, and then made up a number of non-speaking parts such as serving wenches. Julie Jansen was one of the latter, but at this point Andy had not made the connection between her and Neville. With the roles assigned, Andy had brought the whole group together for the first time to get to know one another and to set times for rehearsals.

There is always one in every group. Andy had already picked out Paul Bowser as a smart-alec trouble maker. Paul was a third-year Speech and Drama student, which was one way of saying that he was taking first-year level classes for the umpteenth time. He spoke up with a loud voice, "I think that the serving wenches should be topless."

"You may not have noticed it, but the play is set in Scotland and not ancient Rome. We are not going to have an orgy," was Andy's response.

"Why not set it in Rome."

"It is going to be set in Scotland."

"Too bad we don't have an imaginative director. Think of all the innovative things we could do with Macbeth set in Rome."

As Andy drew himself up to his full height, an expectant hush fell on the cast. "There is a label here on my chest. Read it." There was in fact no label.

"I don't see any label."

Donald, catching on, chimed in, "I can see one."

"Any actor worth his salt can see this label," continued Andy.

"Oh yes. I do believe I can see one now."

"Then read it."

Paul pretended to fumble for his glasses. "Oh dear. I seem to have misplaced my glasses. Could you read it for me." Maybe Paul did have a future in acting.

"Gladly. It says 'Andy Kaplan, Director. His word is final'. There is also a label on your chest. Read it to me."

"Oh yes. I can feel it. But it is upside down. Could you read it for me."

"Gladly. It says, 'Paul Bowser, Wannabe actor – expendable'."

"Okay. I get it. No topless wenches."

The message Andy had meant to convey went far beyond topless wenches, but he was satisfied with the outcome and let it rest. He had read about a director who had used this tactic on an obstreperous actor, but at the time had doubted whether it would yield results. One learns something new every day.

Robin Anderson, who would be playing Mcduff, tried to defuse the situation, "We expect to have lots of school kids coming to our performances. If the wenches were topless they would be stopped from coming."

"Maybe they would only find out too late. Do you remember what happened last year with the Canterbury Tales?"

Donald, sensing an interesting story, said, "Tell me more."

"There is this Afrikaans medium high school somewhere on the East Rand. The kids wanted to have a matric dance, but the principal ruled that a dance was too sinful. Their English teacher came up with an idea to compensate for their disappointment. He had read somewhere that one of the great classics of English literature was being performed in a theatre in Johannesburg. So the whole matric class was loaded onto buses and taken to the theatre."

"Was this a Dramatic Society performance?"

"No. It was a professional group. Naturally they included the Miller's and the Wife of Bath's tales. The fallout was unbelievable, and quite funny really."

"Did the teacher not know what he was taking them to see?"

"No. He had vague notion that Canterbury Cathedral was the headquarters of the Church of England, and assumed therefore that it was a religious play.

"If he knew that little, how come he was teaching English."

"Apparently they had no one else, and he had at least spent a year in Durban."

"I don't get it."

"Durban is the one city in South Africa where you never hear Afrikaans spoken. Some buildings still fly the Union Jack. When the English cricket team plays there it is not only the Africans who root for the visitors but whites as well. It is that kind of place."

"I get it. So what happened to him?"

"Well the matric class voted him the teacher of the year. But he was fired anyway."

The rehearsals for Macbeth were making progress off stage as well as on. The next day when Andy opened the wardrobe closet to find his director's jacket, he saw Macbeth entwined around one of the serving wenches. They were so startled by his appearance that some of their clothes dropped to the floor as they sprang apart. "Rehearsal starts in five minutes," he said laconically, and then closed the door on them. He was thinking what a great dinner-time story this episode would make as the actors assembled on the stage. Macbeth and the serving wench were reasonably well dressed by this time, but their make up was a mess. It was then that Andy did a double take. The wench was Julie Jansen, Neville's girl friend. Oh well, not all good stories can be told.

The weekend slipped by uneventfully. The coaching in Soweto continued as planned. Prof. Armstrong had come through with two science kits, one for use by the physics group and one for chemistry. He had also recruited a few other lecturers to work with those students taking university level courses. Peter had made good on his quest for lunches for all. The next day Justin played his first league hockey match and emerged unscathed, if not victorious.

On Monday evening, as the house mates were gathering for dinner, Neville stormed into the room. "You Roberts, are the most idiotic imbecile that I have ever come across. True as God, I don't know why I even bother with you. You are a hopeless case."

"What's he done now?" asked Tony.

"It's what he hasn't done. He has just met one of the most amazing and beautiful girls he is ever likely to come across in the whole of his pitiful life. For some unfathomable reason she seems to like him, calls him her rabbit, and wants to see more of him. But this pathetic idiot, instead of getting his lame arse into gear and..." Before he could finish, a bombshell was dropped. David came panting into the room. "Jonty and Norman have been detained. No one can find out where they have been taken."

FIVE

David's announcement was met with a stunned silence. It was Neville, unfortunately, who was first to speak, "So what are they charged with?"

David exploded in anger, "Where have you been living. Don't you know anything at all?" He took a few deep breaths to calm himself. "Sorry. It is not you with whom I am angry. Call it misplaced anger if you like. People are not charged any more. They are simply detained and locked up. That is what is happening to Jonty and Norman."

Neville, in trying to recover, only dug himself deeper into a hole. "Well of course I have heard of the ninety day law. But it only applies to communists, doesn't it?"

David did all in his power to keep his temper. "First of all the name 'ninety day law' is a misnomer. It means that the Special Branch can detain anyone they choose incommunicado for ninety days, and at the end of the ninety days for another ninety days, and so on indefinitely. Those thus detained have no right to see a lawyer or even family members. Their location does not even have to be disclosed. No reason has to be given for their detention. And no, it is not just aimed at communists, but anyone who opposes government policies."

Ian intervened, "So we have no idea why they were detained and where they are."

"Exactly."

"Have any others been detained?" asked Tony.

"It is likely, but I have only just found out about Jonty and Norman. By tomorrow we may have a fuller picture."

"Well I am glad to see you were not detained," added Justin.

"Actually, I was picked up and interrogated for a couple of hours. They wanted to know who had organised the protest, but in the end I convinced them that I knew nothing about it. Surprisingly they then let me go."

"Thank goodness for that."

"But I thought that you were one of the main organisers." Neville clearly had a bad case of foot-in-mouth. The rest of the house mates shook their heads sadly.

Despite the bombshell of the detentions, Neville's admonishment had stung Justin, and it continued to fester in his mind. Perhaps he should try to contact Colleen, but how? There was no phone in the house, but in any case he would rather not issue any invitation over the phone. It would be easier for her to refuse his request for a date if it was not done person-to-person. He would ask her out by letter. Julie, he had learned, had a role in Macbeth. He would ask Andy to give his note to Julie with the request that she give it to Colleen. Several days later, and after about ten drafts, he finally produced an invitation, and handed it to Andy to give to Julie.

Dear Colleen,

I would be most honoured if you would consider accepting my invitation to dinner and a film show next Friday. I believe Doctor Zhivago is well worth seeing. However please do not feel under any obligation to accept as you may well have other plans.

Yours hopefully,
Justin Roberts

No sooner was the invitation on its way than misgivings crowded Justin's mind. Was the note too formal, or was it perhaps too forward? How would she respond? Would the rejection be tinged with disdain, or would she let him down gently?

The answer arrived the next day.

My dear, gallant Justin,

Nothing would delight me more that to accompany you to dinner and the film. I will await your presence, shall we say, at six o'clock on Friday.

Yours in anticipation,
Colleen Jansen

Justin spent much of the next week fretting about where to have dinner with Colleen. In the end, he threw caution to the winds, and on the day before his big date made a reservation for two at Chez Andre, one of Hillbrow's most fancy restaurants. It was the kind of establishment where tables were covered with white table cloths and immaculately set with candles, wine glasses, and silver cutlery. He had seen the menu and had all but fainted at the prices. The evening would wreck his budget for at least half the year, but he deemed it worth the expense.

At four o'clock on Friday afternoon he showered and then dressed. By five o'clock he felt sweaty and impatient, so he showered for a second time. He got dressed again, but this time in his very best shirt, jacket and tie. At six o'clock promptly he knocked on the door of Colleen's flat, which was opened immediately. Colleen was dressed in a t-shirt and jeans. "My goodness, you do look fancy. Where are we going? One of us is not dressed for the occasion."

"I have reservations at Chez Andre."

"Good heavens. That is the fanciest place in town. Hold on a sec. I will need to put on something more appropriate. I won't be long."

Five minutes later, true to her word, Colleen was ready to go. She had changed into a soft, powder blue dress that showed off her shapely body to perfection. Justin hoped she had not noticed how long be had been rendered speechless. "You look stunning," he finally blurted out.

He opened the passenger door of his car for her to get in, and could not help but stare as the dress rode up her shapely legs.

At the restaurant the maître d', dressed in an evening suit and white bow tie, stiffly showed them to their table. If he was wondering whether this impecunious looking student could afford his prices, at least it did not show in his face. He was too well trained for that. If Colleen was shocked at the prices, she too did not show it. She was too well brought up for that. In the end she selected the least expensive entrée on the menu, worried that Justin might be over-extending himself, but flattered that he considered her worth the expense. Justin chose the same dish. The next decision was about what wine to choose. Sensing his bewilderment, Colleen helped him select a wine that would go with the food that they had ordered.

Sensing that his demeanour thus far might be construed as that of a star-struck schoolboy, Justin decided to strike a more adversarial attitude. "I have a bone to pick with you."

"And what is it?"

"Neville now refers to me as The Rabbit."

"Oh no! Really?"

"Yes. And he credits you with the name."

"What a jerk. Julie and I were talking about what makes people real. I did not think he was even listening. There was some cricket match on the radio. I must have mentioned how you reminded me of the Velveteen Rabbit. Sorry."

"Not at all. I was just kidding about picking a bone. Do you think Julie and Neville are serious?"

"No, I don't think so. Julie is flattered to have the attention of a popular sports hero like him, but I suspect that in time she will mature and outgrow him. I also suspect that by this time next year he will be surveying the new crop of freshettes."

"Yes he does get around, but he has a good heart and is a generous friend."

The arrival of the wine brought conversation to a temporary halt. The wine steward poured a little in Justin's glass. "Please serve the lady first."

Colleen whispered in his ear, "He wants you to taste the wine and tell him if it is satisfactory."

Justin complied as best he could.

"Is it to your satisfaction? The temperature just right?" asked the wine steward with a hint of sarcasm. "Yes, very nice thanks."

The wine duly poured, conversation continued.

"So tell me, have you lived all your life in Sabie?"

"Yes, born and bred."

"Did you go to school there?"

"I went to primary school in Sabie, but high school in Pretoria."

"Does Sabie not have a high school?"

"Yes it does, but it is Afrikaans medium."

"Is that why you did not go there?"

"It is a bit more complicated than that. My father is Afrikaans speaking and my mother English. Both languages are spoken in our home and so I am pretty well bilingual. My mother wanted me to receive my high school education in English, but my father was not that keen on the idea. But what really tipped the balance in my mind is that my father is the principal of the Sabie High School, and my mother teaches English there as well. Can you imagine the embarrassment of going to a school where your parents are teachers?"

"I can see a number of disadvantages."

"The choice of school was more than just a language issue. Almost all the teachers and students at the Sabie school are vehemently pro-Nat. My mother is one of the few who do not support the government and who are against apartheid. She wanted me to be exposed to a more liberal education."

"Discussions must get quite heated at times in your house."

"Actually for the most part we avoid political discussions. My parents seem to have agreed to disagree on some issues. But they do agree on a surprising number of things, such as kids should help around the house!"

"Mine agree on that too. Must be something in the water."

"So tell me more about your family, and where you went to school."

"I am the eldest of three kids. I have two younger siblings, a brother and a sister. We grew up on a farm in the Standerton district. We all started our education at a small, dual medium farm school that went as far as standard two. I completed primary school in Johannesburg, where I stayed with a great aunt. When I went to high school, also in Johannesburg, I became a boarder. I guess you must have been a boarder in Pretoria too."

"Yes I was. It was at a girls high school."

"What about the rest of your family?"

"You have met my sister. I have a younger brother, Gerald. He elected to go to the high school in Sabie despite the obvious drawbacks. Then we have a dog called Bambi and a cat called Chessie. My brother said she grins like a Cheshire Cat."

For a while they chatted about books that they were reading. Finally Colleen got around to something that had been bothering her. "I read last week's Campus News. I suppose you saw it as well."

"Great. So you saw about the goal that I scored."

"Sorry. I somehow missed that bit of news. It was the front page that really caught my attention. Did those things really happen to that girl?"

"Yes. Everything that was written is true."

"How do you know? Have you met the girl? According to the article she lives in Durban."

Justin found himself in a quandary. If he admitted that he knew Lerato, it would reveal that she lived in Soweto. In the end he decided to level with Colleen. "In the article, names and places were changed to protect the identity of the individual. But yes I have met the girl. I was there when she first told her story to us. It made a deep impression on us at the time. That was when we decided that her story needed to be told."

"I am glad that you did. What they did to her was monstrous. It makes me angry even now just thinking about it. I want to do something to stop that kind of abuse by the police. Any suggestions?"

"It might be best if you don't get involved right now. It could be dangerous, and I would not like to see you get hurt. Have you heard that Jonty and Norman have been detained?"

"Yes. I did hear that."

"David was also interrogated by the police, but then released."

"I had not heard that. So what?"

"So you see why it might be best if you do not get too involved."

"Justin Roberts, we need to get a few points clarified. First I appreciate your concern for me. You are a gallant soul. But never, ever think that because I am a girl I need to be prevented from doing what is right, or protected from danger, as if I were made of china. We females can be a lot tougher than you imagine. Take the girl in the article for instance. She has put herself at risk by telling her story, but she did it anyway. That is all I have to say. Please try to understand."

"You are quite right. You have put me in my place, and rightly so. I will think about your request."

They were quiet for a while, and then a grin broke out on Justin's face.

"What are you grinning about?"

"The slogan, *'You Strike the Woman, You Strike the Rock'*. It goes back to the women's march of 1956. You can call me a rabbit and I will call you a rock."

Her eyes twinkled as she laughed merrily. Close call, but I think I got out of that one, thought Justin to himself. For the rest of the meal they chatted about safe topics.

Dinner finished, they drove into the city centre to where Doctor Zhivago was playing. The Colosseum was one of the two premier cinema theatres in Johannesburg, the other being His Majesties. Justin had been to the Colosseum a couple of times in his life, but it never ceased to fascinate him. The auditorium was designed to give the impression to the audience of being inside the ancient Colosseum. The walls of the auditorium were made to look like those of its ancient namesake in Rome. The ceiling was designed to replicate the night sky. Hundreds of stars festooned the heavens, and wispy clouds drifted languidly overhead. They were shown to their seats by an usherette in a smart maroon costume and pill hat.

Soon after the film started, Colleen reached over to take Justin's hand. And thus they remained, hand in hand, as the classic film deftly steered them through the full gamut of emotions—love, fear, suffering, cruelty, and betrayal.

It seemed to Justin that those around him were in a pensive mood as they quietly filed out of the cinema at the conclusion of the film. "Let's grab something to drink before we go home. There is a place just across the road," he suggested to Colleen. "I would like that. I am not ready to leave the world of the Russian revolution quite yet. I need to work through some of my emotions."

They found an empty table and ordered a cup of coffee each. There was much about the film that Colleen wanted to explore, but she was not sure where to begin. In the end she started with a trivial remark, "I overheard Neville say that he would give his right arm to spend just one night with Lara, with Julie Christie that is."

"That sounds like Neville."

"She seems to have that effect on most of the guys I have spoken with. I wonder why?"

"She does project a kind of animal magnetism. She has that beguiling face and exudes an innocent sexuality. I can see what draws men to her."

"Does that include you?"

I am on dangerous ground now thought Justin, but Colleen would expect an honest answer. Was she fishing for a comparison between Lara and herself? She would certainly reject any trite compliments such as 'You are one hundred times more beautiful'. "If I were in that situation I might well be bewitched by Lara. She is hard to resist. But if she were to be struck, and it does happen to her, it turns out she is not a rock. In the end she is found to be lacking. So I might be seduced by her, but regret it in the end."

"An interesting answer."

"But what about Zhivago himself. How would you react to him?"

"He is very handsome in a spaniel type of way. By the way, did I tell you that Bambi is a spaniel? But from all appearances he did not even try to be faithful to Tonya, his wife? So yes I might be attracted to him, but I think I would be more cautious about getting involved. What bothered me about him is that he did not seem to give a second thought about leaving Tonya for Lara."

"Do you think it was shallow of Zhivago to let the Count—what was his name? Komarovsky—take Lara away at the end?"

"No that was a heart wrenching choice. He could either give her to Komarovsky or let her be taken and likely to be killed by the Bolsheviks. He made his choice, but I think that is what really killed him in the end. What would you have done?"

"It is really a Hobson's choice. Suppose that there is this girl that I really love with all my heart. If I stand by her terrible things will happen to her. On the other hand, if I abandon her she is remains unharmed, but we are separated for ever. That is such a hideous choice that I pray to God that I never have to make one like it."

Once they had finished their coffee and driven home, she had given him a quick kiss, not just a peck on the cheek, but not a proper kiss either. Before retiring to her flat she had whispered 'Good night rabbit' to which he had replied 'Good night rock'. It had been the best evening of his life.

But if Justin was elated after the date, Colleen was more thoughtful and disturbed. It had been an unusual date to put it mildly. At least she had been able to confirm her first impressions of him. The time that they had first met she had loved his humour and had enjoyed teaching him to dance. She loved the way he responded. He had tried everything she suggested, although this was extremely uncomfortable and difficult for him. Even back then she had sensed somehow that he was real, someone who had depth. And then this evening he had called her a 'rock'. Over the past years she had received many flattering compliments, but had never before been called a rock! Up until now she had mostly been perceived as something of a party girl. However tonight it was she who had first raised the issue of police torture, and Justin had answered her honestly. Would he accede to her request to become involved in whatever he was up to politically, or did he too see her only as a shallow, party girl? Did he really mean it when he referred to her as a rock? What would be the price of political involvement, and was she really prepared to pay it? Was she really ready to shed her image as a party girl and become politically active? She would have to wait and see if Justin did accept her request to become involved. And then there was the haunting image of the two lovers, Zhivago and Lara, being wrenched apart for ever. Could that be the price of her involvement? And then the big question, what did Justin really think of her? He had not even tried to gain entry into her flat (or bed) for 'one quick nightcap'. Did he not like her enough, or was he just too shy? It had been an enjoyable but confusing evening.

The events of the next week somewhat dampened Justin's exhilaration at his date with Colleen. The first indication of the events to follow was that his afternoon mathematics lecture was cancelled. A post-graduate student had come to the lecture room to make the announcement. When asked why, he replied that he had no idea, but had simply been told by the Head of Department to make the announcement. It was only later that he learned that Dr. Carter had been detained. The police had searched her office and found a box of explosives. She had explained that she was keeping the box as a favour for a friend, and was not aware of what it contained. However she refused to divulge the name of her friend and so was detained.

With his lecture cancelled Justin went home early. To his surprise he found Jonty, Norman, and Jenny in serious conversation with

David. They were startled by his entry, but recovered quickly when they saw that it was only him. Realising that he had interrupted something important, he offered to leave again. "Thanks but you may as well come in," replied David. "It will all come out in the end anyway."

"Why are you all here?"

"Jonty and Norman were released this morning. We have just started to find out what happened to them. There are some decisions that we may have to make."

"Don't mind me then. Carry on."

"So you still don't know where you were taken?" asked David.

"No, we were blindfolded. I am fairly sure it was not John Vorster Square. It took longer to get there. It might have been Marshall Square."

"What was the line of their questioning?"

"Since I am the editor, basically they wanted to find out who had given us the details in the article on police torture and who had written it."

Justin interrupted, "Since Jenny wrote the article why did they simply not detain her."

"Didn't you notice that I did not give Jenny her by-line," replied Norman. "They worked on me for days, but I held out. I did not give them any names. At least they never tried to deny the truth of the article."

"Did they torture you?"

"Physically no. The worst that I experienced were long interrogation sessions. They tried the good cop bad cop routine, but I was ready for it."

"How about you Jonty?" asked David.

"They did ask me a little about the article, but I explained I had nothing to do with the paper and had not even seen the article before it was published. They seemed to accept that. I was mostly questioned about the protest. Again all I would tell them was that it had not been organised or even authorised by the Student Council.

They wanted the names of the organisers but I maintained that I was totally unaware of any of the details."

"It sounds like the two of you handled the situation well. Now think very carefully both of you. Was there any indication, even the slightest hint, that they might have been after more than just the article or protest? Any suggestion that they suspected that you might be able to give them other vital information?"

Both shook their heads.

"Again think carefully. If you are detained again, could you hold out a second time?"

"I could handle the interrogations again. But we saw other things that really scared me. The cell that they put us in only had bars for a door, so we could see everything that went on in the passage outside. We saw other detainees, mostly Africans, being taken off for interrogation and then saw them again when they returned. Most of them came back badly mutilated and had to be carried."

Norman continued Jonty's account. "There was this guy next door. When they brought him back he was groaning and crying. It went on for most of the night, and then it got very quiet. I think that he might have died. David, I would like to think that I could withstand that kind of torture but I just don't know."

Jonty concurred.

Justin was horrified by all he had heard. He knew of course that these things were happening, but when friends and colleagues were involved it really hit home. He wished his lecture had not been cancelled. These were things he would rather not hear.

David continued. "Thanks for your bravery and also honesty. I suggest you go home now and take things easy for a while. Justin, perhaps you would drive them home."

Once the three had left, David addressed Jenny. "We may have to get them out. One or both of them might be broken quite easily. What do you think?"

"How much do they know?"

"Not a whole lot, but enough to cause some real damage."

"You may be right. Let's sleep on it for a day or two."

"Would you be willing to take over as the President of the Student Council?"

"I may have to, although I would have preferred to remain out of the spot light."

"We might also have to look for a new editor."

As the week drew towards an end, it was clear that there was a nation wide campaign of detentions. Particularly hard hit were labour organisations and academic institutions. Nevertheless it was decided to proceed with the Soweto tutoring project. From the outset, the atmosphere seemed different to Justin. For a start Prof. Armstrong and his fellow lectures seemed more subdued. However given that some of their colleagues had been detained, it was understandable. When they arrived at the venue a number of vehicles were visible that had not been there on previous Saturdays. It became immediately obvious that far fewer students had shown up compared with the previous sessions. Peter was one of the missing ones. Nevertheless, they carried on as before as best they could.

As they were leaving, one of the students slipped a note into Justin's hand. It read, 'On your way home, stop at Tshabalala's garage and ask for a petrol attendant called Simon.' Justin, who was driving the university vehicle, pulled into the petrol station and asked that an attendant called Simon fill up the tank. As he was performing his task, Simon whispered to Justin, "When we are through here, go around to the back of the garage where the air dispenser is located."

Justin did as asked. Before he could pump any air into the tyres a figure emerged from one of the bathrooms. It was Peter. "Can you give me a lift into town?"

"Sure. Hop in."

"Thanks. Let's get out of here as soon as possible. Forget about the air."

As they were driving away, Justin asked, "Peter, what is going on here?"

"The police are looking for me. Didn't you see their vehicles at the church hall?"

"I did see some vehicles, but I did not realise that they were the police."

"Special Branch actually. Unmarked cars."

"Okay, we can get you out of here. You might want to duck down low if we are approached by any suspicious looking cars."

Once they had left Soweto the occupants of the vehicle began to relax somewhat. "Where do you want us to take you?"

"Anywhere is fine."

"Don't be silly. We can take you to wherever you are going."

"I don't want to be of any more trouble to you. You can even drop me off here if you like."

"Peter, it is no trouble at all. Just tell us where you are going."

"Well I am meeting my contact at Park Station, but not until tomorrow."

"So where will you spend the night?"

"Anywhere that I can remain invisible and out of trouble."

"Then come and spend the night at my place."

"I cannot ask you to place yourself at risk."

"It is something that I would like to do. Please accept."

"Are you sure?"

"Yes, I am sure."

Justin first had to drop off the other tutors and then collect his own car. Finally he and Peter were on their way home.

"I will drop you off at the station tomorrow. Will you be taking the train some place?"

"No I am just meeting my contact there. It is very busy there and so a good place to meet without being noticed."

"So where are you off too?"

Peter seemed very hesitant.

"You don't need to tell me if you don't want to."

"No. I should trust you, but not a word to anyone else. Okay?"

Justin nodded.

"I have been accepted at the ANC training school near Morogoro in Tanzania."

"Wow. How will you get there?"

"Even I don't know that. All I know is that I will be smuggled out of the country tomorrow. The unfortunate thing is that now I have made you an unwitting accomplice should anything go wrong."

"Don't blame yourself. After all it was my choice. I knew the police were looking for you."

"Well, thanks again. By the way, where are you taking me? Do you live with your family?"

"No. I live in an old house with a bunch of guys. Which reminds me, what should I tell them about you?"

"The other tutors already know that I am on the run from the police, so we could tell them that. But not a word about Tanzania."

By the time Justin and Peter arrived at the house dinner was already under way. They now had what served as a dining room table. It had been scrounged from the side of a road somewhere and only had three legs. A couple of wooden crates compensated for the fourth leg. A number of assorted chairs had also been added to complete the setting.

"Hi guys. This is Peter. He will be spending the night. I hope there is still something to eat. We are starved."

"There is still plenty," said Andy grumpily. "Neville cooked tonight's glorious repast. Eat it at your peril."

"Don't pay any attention to him. It's not that bad although to be honest I did get the salt and curry amounts mixed up. Come. Take a seat."

As Justin and Peter moved towards the table a problem became apparent—there was only one vacant chair. "Here take my place," said Andy to Peter. "I have to go to a rehearsal anyway. It will be best if the cast does not see their director grovelling on the stage in pain. They might think that it is because of their acting."

"What play are you directing?" asked Peter.

"Macbeth. Have you heard of it?"

"Oh yes. It is one of my favourite Shakespeare plays."

"Where did you come across it?"

"I was majoring in English at Fort Hare. We had this wonderful lady lecturer who really made Shakespeare come alive for us. She was one of the few old-timers who stayed on after Bantu Education took over the institution."

"But now you are no longer there. Have you graduated?"

"No. I only got as far as first year and then I was kicked out. Now I am trying to complete my education at a British university."

"Peter is one of the organisers of the study groups in Soweto that we are supporting," explained Justin.

"I missed seeing you there today. How come?" asked Ian.

"The police are looking for me so I though it best to stay way."

"Been robbing some banks recently," quipped Neville.

"That is not funny, Neville," retorted Ian. "Did you know that all teaching and learning without the express blessing of the Bantu Education Department is illegal?"

"Sorry. No offence was meant. I was just trying to lighten things up a bit."

"Actually I did find it quite funny," added Peter diplomatically. "Maybe I should go into the bank robbing business. It probably pays more than studying."

"And is a less serious crime," added Justin.

"Where did you grow up?" asked Tony.

"In Soweto."

"Tell us what it was like growing up there and going to school."

As Peter started regaling them with his life in Soweto, David, who had been oddly quiet until then, with a nod of the head, indicated that Justin should follow him into the next room. "How well do you know this Peter?"

"As I already said, he is one of the organisers of the study group."

"And how do you know that the police are after him?"

"He told me."

David looked sceptical. "Plus we did see some unmarked cars near the church hall today."

"So you don't really know."

"David. Why are you of all people objecting to my helping someone evade the police?"

"I am not objecting to it at all. The reason that I am asking these questions is that it is a known fact that the Special Branch plants spies in our organisations. These are people who pretend to espouse our cause, but then give vital information to the police. I just want you to be sure that Peter is not one of those."

"Yes I see. I cannot say why, but I just don't think that Peter is a spy."

"I am inclined to agree with you. But since you seem to be getting yourself into deeper waters I felt that I needed to have this word with you. Always be careful and on your guard. Let's go back to the others."

It seemed Peter had finished talking about Soweto and was commenting on his present whereabouts. "Believe it or not, I have never been in a white house before. It is not quite what I imagined."

"What do you mean?" asked Tony.

"I somehow thought it would be fancier. To be honest there are a lot of houses in Soweto that are..". Peter struggled for the right word. "... better looking than this. Your white food is also a little strange."

Justin laughed. "This is certainly not a typical white house. In fact it has been condemned and we are just staying here until it is pulled down. And please don't think that what you were given to eat tonight is typical white food. We are no cooks, but the food is getting better. You should have seen what we ate when we first got here."

The next morning Justin drove Peter to the station, or to be accurate, near the station. "Drop me off at Joubert Park."

"I don't mind taking you all the way."

"It's not that. I cannot be seen with you. If my contact sees a white guy dropping me off he will assume the you are Special Branch and that I am a plant. It would be tickets for me. It is Sunday, so lots of the servants who work in the flats around here will be attending church services under the trees. I will be able to fit right in, and then walk to the station from there."

Once at the park they shook hands African style. "Goodbye my friend. I will not forget you."

"Me neither. Good luck. Hamba kahle. Go well."

"Sala kahle."

When Justin returned to the house he found David, Ian, and Jenny huddled around the table talking in hushed tones. Their tone and attitude alerted him that something serious had happened. "Is there a problem?"

They looked at one another, and eventually David said, "We may as well tell him. It will likely involve him at some point anyway."

"What is it?"

"Jonty and Norman have fled the country."

"Why?"

"Sit down and we will fill you in."

SIX

"JONTY AND NORMAN HAVE FLED THE COUNTRY." JUSTIN WAS astounded.

"But the good news is that they made it safely," added David.

"Where are they?"

"In Botswana for now. Eventually they will likely go on to the UK, Canada, or America."

"They left just because of the article?"

"No. There is more to it than that. While they were in detention they witnessed how some of the detainees were tortured. They think that the man in the cell next to them might even have died from his injuries."

"I did see in today's Rand Daily Mail that a detainee had died. The police claimed that he slipped on some soap while taking a shower and hit his head on the floor," contributed Justin. "I wonder if that is the same man."

"It is quite possible. Anyway the point is that the two of them, Norman in particular, felt that they would not stand up to that kind of treatment. We deemed it best that they get out while they could."

"But by now everyone has read the article. How would punishing them do any good?"

"It is not just about the article. They know things that could be very damaging to us. Fortunately they were only questioned about the article and the protest."

"What kind of things?"

"Best that you know nothing about them."

"Come off it David. When I walked in you said something to the effect that it might involve me. Now you want to keep me in the dark. So what is going on here?"

Ian tried to smooth things over. "We have been talking about how to fill the gap now that Jonty and Norman have left. Jenny is willing to take over as president of the Student Council. I have agreed to stand as a candidate for the Council now that there is a vacancy. The main problem is the paper, Campus News. We were wondering if you would be willing to help fill the gap in one way or another, perhaps by proof reading or even taking over some of the editorial functions."

"Try to find someone else if you can. My hands are already full."

"If we can't, would you at least consider it?"

"I suppose so."

At this point Tony, ashen faced, broke into the room. "They have caught Richard."

"Who is Richard?" asked Justin.

"Richard Levine."

"I don't know any Richard Levine. Who is he?"

"Do you mean to say that you have never heard of him?"

"No I haven't."

"He is president of the South African Student Association, SASA for short."

"The name is still not familiar."

"He is from Cape Town."

"Well that explains it. But what happened to him?"

"He was caught trying to cross the border. He had been alerted that his name was on the list, but he left his escape until too late. They were waiting for him."

Tony's interruption at least postponed Justin's need to decide about Campus News.

For Justin, the next couple of weeks resembled a phony normalcy, or perhaps just the calm before a deluge. There were no more arrests or detentions. Lectures continued as normal, a substitute having been found for Dr. Carter. The attendance at the Saturday tutoring project picked up again, although most of the organising committee had fled. He was enjoying playing hockey and was even improving his skill-level. He was helping out with Campus News as a part time proof reader. His main concern was what to do about Colleen. He wanted to take her out again, but was flat broke. He had also promised to find a role for her in exposing police brutality, but had run out of safe options. However he did come up with one idea that might solve both his dilemmas.

He went around to Colleen's flat and was pleased to find her at home. She was delighted to see him, invited him to come in, and offered him a glass of Liebies. After exchanging some pleasantries, Justin put his proposition to her, "Would you consider coming out to Soweto with us this coming Saturday? A number of the students are having difficulty writing up their assignments in English. I have been trying to help some of them, but most of my time is taken with maths. It would be of enormous benefit to have someone around that they could call on at any time."

"Sure I would love to come with you. Thanks."

"There is something else. As students get to know you, some of them might open up about things that have been done to them by the police. We might even come up with enough material for another article. Of course I cannot guarantee anything, and it might take some time."

"Of course. I understand that. At least I feel I will be doing something. And we will be doing it together."

Colleen felt both pleased and anxious. Justin had made good on his promise and clearly he saw her as more than just a pretty face. They would be seeing more of each other, not just as Saturday night dates but as colleagues doing something worthwhile for others. On the other hand it was clear to her that she was reaching a turning point—a point of no return. She had never been to Soweto or had even previously interacted with Africans other than her family's servants.

But this is what she had asked for and in her heart knew it was what she wanted. The die was cast. There would be no turning back.

Justin was surprised to receive a request to meet with Prof. Armstrong in his office the next day. At the appointed time he made his way from the library, where he spent much of his time between lectures, to the Main Block. It housed Prof. Armstrong's office and was indeed the venue of most of Justin's lectures and tutorials as well. He paused to gaze at the building before continuing up the main steps and entering the building via the front entrance. The Grecian pillars proclaimed the university to be a place of ancient learning.

"There is someone I would like you to meet." That someone, it turned out, was Anton du Toit, director of the Institute for Racial Reconciliation. After introductions had been made, Prof. Armstrong stated the purpose of the meeting. "The Institute is committed to helping students like those we have been meeting with in Soweto with their education. However theirs is a nation-wide effort. They are particularly interested in providing support materials. But I will let Mr. du Toit explain his request himself."

"Yes, thank you. We have become aware of how many African students are either opting out of the formal education system, or else being throw out. We have seen how many of them are struggling to continue with their education by distance learning, often in conjunction with an overseas institution. Some of the lucky ones do find some help, such as what your group is providing in Soweto, but many are on their own. What most of them are asking for are books, study guides, and lecture notes to help them on their way. Even those who have the kind of help that you are providing would benefit from such curriculum materials. Are you with me so far?"

"Yes, it makes perfect sense," replied Justin.

"So here is where you come in. Since mathematics is perhaps the most challenging subject for most of the students that I am talking about, that is where we wish to start. The first step will be to do a comprehensive analysis of the various curricula that these students are following. Your experience in Soweto will be invaluable here since you are working closely with them. However you may need to spread your net a little wider as similar groups, say in Durban, may be using different sources. Make sense?"

"Yes, I think I could be of some help."

"The next step will be to assemble and/or develop curriculum materials, starting with mathematics. It is possible that there are some existing textbooks that are suitable. In fact it is more than likely. The larger challenge will be to then find or develop lectures and study guides based on these texts. Again there may be some out there as other countries are ahead of us when it comes to distance learning. However we may need to adapt some of these or even create our own.

"I have been in touch with a foundation in New York that is interested in funding this project. In fact I will be going there later this year to firm up the details. Before I go we need to at least be on top of phase one, and perhaps even made a stab at phase two. So that in a nutshell describes some of our plans."

Prof. Armstrong added, "Since our Soweto tutoring project will be named as a pilot site, our activities there will be fully funded. And of course we will have full use of the materials as they are developed. I know you are busy, but do you think that you could spare some time to work on this project?"

"It sounds like a very exciting and worthwhile venture. Yes, I would like to be part of it."

"Excellent. We will be in touch. Thank you very much. I look forward to working with you."

As he made his way back to the library Justin chastised himself. He really must learn not to say 'yes' to everything. Were there any courses that taught a person how to say 'no'?

Two more surprises were in store for Justin, both involving Neville. After his hockey match on Sunday Neville approached Justin,

"I will be flying with my instructor again this afternoon. Would you like to fly with us again?"

"Yes, I would love to." Another yes! "Are you flying cross-country again?"

"No. This time I will be practising some of the basic procedures. I will be taking my final check flight before too long. My instructor says that I am ready for it."

"Sure, count me in. Thanks."

At Grand Central airport Justin watched Neville go through all the now familiar pre-flight checks, after which they boarded the C172 and taxied to the holding point of the runway. Once airborne Justin again experienced the exhilaration of 'dancing in the skies on laughter-silvered wings'. It felt intoxicating. He watched carefully as Neville practised turns, stall recovery, emergency landing procedures, and the like. Finally they returned to the airport where Neville executed a perfect landing.

It was as they were exiting the plane that Neville sprung his surprise. "I have put some of my flying hours into your account. Also the instructor is free to take you up right now for your first lesson if you want to."

"Right now! But I still haven't decided if I can accept your kind offer."

"Well at least take this first lesson. If you don't wish to continue after that, nothing is lost. What do you say?"

"Why not! Thank you so much."

The instructor, who had been listening to this exchange spoke up, "Normally I have my students read up on basic flying procedures before their first lesson, but I will take you up for a short flight. I will do most of the flying, but I will give you a chance to try things out." With that they took their places in the plane, Justin in the left hand seat.

"Okay. We have our clearance. Taxi the plane to the holding point."

Justin immediately realised that he had a problem. "There is no steering wheel."

The instructor laughed. "Keep your heels on the floor and use you feet. If you push on the right pedal, the plane will turn to the right. Left pedal to turn left. And, this is important, if you want to stop, step on the top of both pedals with your toes. Now open the throttle about halfway and let's be on our way." Fortunately Justin found that steering the plane was easier than it sounded.

At the holding point the instructor ran through the check list and then told Justin to turn onto the runway and line up for take off. "Next push the throttle to full and use your feet to keep heading straight down the runway. Good work. Now ease back slightly on the yoke." And suddenly they were airborne. Justin had achieved his first take off. "Keep heading in the same direction and keep the airspeed at seventy knots." They then headed for the general flying area where the instructor taught Justin how to make both left and right hand turns without losing altitude. After about half an hour of practice the instructor said, "We will now head back to the airport. I will guide you into the traffic pattern, but once we are lined up to land—it's called the final approach—I will take over."

Once the engine had been shut down, the instructor said, "For someone simply thrown in at the deep end, you did very well. Do you think you will be continuing with your lessons?"

"I don't know. I will have to think about it." But even as he spoke these words, he knew that he was deceiving himself. He knew that he was hooked.

On the way home, Neville spring the second surprise. "Do you remember that we send a hockey team down to the Lowveld every June?"

"I do remember you going last year."

"Well, I am busy selecting the team for this year's outing. I want to include you in it."

"Surely you want to have your strongest team."

"Not really. After all, it is just a social event. Most of the chaps we play against are over the hill. In any case a number of the first team players cannot make it this year. What do you say?"

"Are you sure?"

"Yes of course. It will be a ball. They are wonderful hosts and we always have a great time."

"Yes, it does sound fun. Count me in."

Still not able to say no, he thought. But perhaps there was more to the Lowveld trip than just hockey. Is that why Neville had chosen him? Had Julie prevailed on Neville to make the selection? Or had Colleen prevailed on Julie to prevail on Neville? How many layers of potential intrigue were there?

During dinner that night, Neville regaled the house mates with much exaggerated accounts of Justin's exploits as a fledgeling pilot. "He even executed a barrel roll!" was his closing remark.

"Right. Sure thing."

"I hate to move on to a more mundane topic," chimed in Ian, "but I wanted to let you know that I am standing in a by-election to fill Jonty's position."

"That is great news. Let me be your campaign manager," offered Neville.

"Thanks, but there is no need for a campaign. No one else is dumb enough to stand."

Colleen was pleased that Justin had asked her to join the Soweto tutoring group. On the first Saturday she had been introduced and her role explained. Only a couple of students had come to her for help with their English at first. But on the following Saturdays more and more came to speak to her, not just for help with English, but also simply to socialise. It began to open up a whole new world for her. The only Africans that she had ever interacted with were household servants. Now she was meeting young folk her own age, whom she began to realise had much the same hopes, dreams, and interests as she did. It was also uncomfortable to realise how different her privileged background was to the struggle of their daily lives. Books, a place to study, electricity, a room and bed of her own, were all luxuries foreign to most of the girls who came to share their lives with her. Her political awareness, or lack thereof, was thrown into sharp relief. She had had no idea about the consequences of the government's policy to force as many Africans as possible back into the homelands. Families were broken up on a routine basis by forced removals. She could not get over how causally a young girl might say something like, "My older brother was sent back to the Ciskei last week as a superfluous dependent". It was painful to realised that these things had been going on for years while she remained blissfully ignorant of the suffering of others.

Another benefit of being part of the Soweto group was the time it afforded her to spend time with Justin. Not only did they drive both ways together, but had fallen into the habit of sharing the day's experiences over a glass of wine once they got back to her flat. Just talking to Justin was a great way to sort through her feelings and impressions.

"One of the girls told me today how the police had raided her house at three in the morning. They said that they were looking for subversive material. However they used the raid as an excuse to completely trash the house just for pleasure. I am disgusted by their behaviour."

On another occasion she said, "We were always taught that separate development is the most just solution to the racial question. Different races develop along their own cultural lines and thus live in harmony. But all I see is misery and suffering."

And also, "Why are we all so ignorant about the effects of apartheid? Have we chosen to be blind?"

Justin, for the most part, let her vent her feelings. He was a sympathetic and non-judgemental listener. Some one with less empathy might well have retorted with comments from time to time such as 'where the hell have you been living that all this is new to you'.

It was on Colleen's fourth Saturday that she was approached by one of the girl students. "Do you know who it was that wrote the story about Lerato?"

"I am not sure I know what you mean."

"Your student newspaper wrote about how Lerato was tortured by the police."

The penny dropped. Colleen had never been told the real name of the victim. "Oh! Now I know what you mean. Yes I do know. Why?"

"My brother has just been released after about three months in detention. He is ready to talk."

Colleen remembered how she had told Justin that she wanted to do something to stop this kind of atrocity. Now that she had been given an opening she was not sure how to proceed. "I think I could put you in touch with someone. Would your brother be prepared to come and talk with us?"

"Yes. In fact I could go and get him right now."

"Could you tell me your names."

"Mine is Thembi. My brother is called Lucky."

Colleen looked over to where Justin was busy tutoring. "When we are finished here for the day, come and speak to me again. If you brother is willing, he could come as well." The die was cast.

As soon as Justin was finished, Colleen filled him in. Soon afterwards Thembi appeared with Lucky in tow. Justin was first to speak. "Colleen tells me that there is something that you wish to tell us."

"I wished to speak with the person who wrote the article about Lerato in your newspaper. Is it you?"

"No. He was detained and has since fled the country."

"So I am too late."

"Yes, but you could speak to me if you like. I do have something to do with the paper."

Lucky proceeded to give details of how he had been treated while in detention. When he had finished Justin replied, "Colleen and I will try to write down most of what you have told us. We will not publish anything until you have approved what we have written. And of course, as with Lerato's story, we will try to hide your identity. Come and see us next week to approve of our draft article."

The next Saturday they showed what they had written to Lucky. "You will see that we have changed your name to Jonas."

"It really doesn't matter because Lucky is not my real name anyway."

"Under what name did they detain you? Not Jonas I hope."

"No. They had my real African name. I wish that they had used Lucky. Imagine your headline, 'A guy named Lucky is beaten up by the police'." With that he doubled over in laughter. After he had recovered, he added, "You have captured most of what I told you. Please go ahead and publish it."

The main problem now lay in who would authorise publication. Since the departure of Norman, the paper was kept going by staffers and volunteers like Justin. Different people acted as a temporary editor for each week's edition, but none felt that they had the authority to handle an article as hot as this one. In the end it was Jenny, as Student Council president, who took it upon herself to make the decision to go ahead. She was not only courageous, but had a wicked sense of humour. "We will publish it under the by-line Norman Barker. He is safe in London now, but maybe we can trick the police into thinking that he has snuck back into the country."

The article was duly published in Campus News the following week. As expected, it created quite a stir. However Justin was surprised, and perhaps both a little disappointed and relieved, that it provoked no response from the police. On the up side, Thembi and Lucky became stalwarts of the Saturday turoring programme, filling a vacuum that Peter's departure had created.

The hockey trip to the Lowveld was scheduled to take place at the beginning of the winter break. At the final practice, Neville handed out the itinerary.

Itinerary for Lowveld Hockey Tour

Thursday   12:00   Bus departs from sports pavilion.

             17:00   Arrive in Nelspruit. You will be met by your host, where you will spend the night.

Friday   10:00   Practice at the White River sports club. Your host will deliver you to the field.

             12:30   Lunch hosted by the White River Hockey Club.

             15:00   Match against the White River Hockey Club.

             18:00   Reception by the Eastern Transvaal Hockey Association to thank hosts for providing accommodation. Attend with your host.

Saturday Free day for sight seeing. Our bus will take those who wish to go to the Kruger National Park. Others may wish to spend the day with their host family.

Sunday   10:00   Match against the Sabie Hockey Club. Your host will deliver you to the field.

             12:30   Lunch hosted by the Sabie Hockey Club.

             14:00   Bus departs for campus.

See attached list for your host. It is suggested that you give your host some memento of your visit to thank them for their hospitality.

Justin was not surprised to find that a Mr. and Mrs. Jansen of Sabie were to host Neville and himself. Neville had clearly given much thought to this tour.

It was Colleen and Julie who met the bus at Nelspruit. Neville and Julie quickly claimed the back seat of the car, leaving Colleen to drive and Justin in the front seat. As they left Nelspruit and started climbing through the hills towards Sabie, Colleen pointed out the various landmarks. It was all so new and different. The lush Lowveld vegetation was in stark contrast to the more austere Highveld where Justin had grown up. Here everything seemed to grow in profusion. Farms were laid out between the naturally forested areas. Colleen

pointed out the various types of fruit growing on trees on the farms—
oranges, pawpaws, mangos, bananas, and avocado pears seemed to be
the most common.

"I like this place and could willingly waste my time in it," mused
Justin, mostly to himself.

"What on earth are you trying to say?"

"It is just a quotation from Shakespeare that seems apt. It captures
how I feel at the moment. You live in an incredibly beautiful place."

"Is Shakespeare part of the second-year curriculum?"

"Yes, and I have this wonderful lecturer, Dr. Sherman. He seems
to know every play off by heart, and when he recites passages it almost
makes one's hair stand on end. He somehow imbues his students with
a love of and wonderment for the Bard. If you have a chance next
year, make sure that you sign up for one of his classes."

"Thanks for the tip."

On their arrival Mr. and Mrs. Jansen were at the front door to
welcome their guests.

"Pa, this is Justin, and this one is Neville."

"Aangename kennis, meneer Jansen," Justin greeted his host in
his home language. His mother had always impressed on him the
importance of making a good initial impression. "En u ook, mevrou."

"You are both very welcome. I am glad to meet you both. Dinner
is already on the table, but let me first show you to your rooms."
The boys followed her into the house. "Neville, we have put you up
in the guest room. Make yourself at home. Justin if you will follow
me, we have put you out by the pool. We have converted one of the
changing rooms into a make shift guest room. I hope you will be
comfortable there."

Having looked over the room, Justin replied, "More than
comfortable, thank you. It is sheer luxury after what I am used to."

"Come back to the dining room as soon as you are ready."

A few minutes later everyone was comfortably seated around
the dining room table. Mr. Jansen offered a blessing in Afrikaans,

and then the soup was served. It did not take long before Mr. Jansen broached a subject that had obviously been bothering him. Looking at Justin he said, "I hear that you are taking my daughter into Soweto with you. I cannot say that I am happy about it."

Colleen intervened, "Pa. Justin is not taking me anywhere. I am going to Soweto of my own accord because I want to. Besides I have found it very rewarding to help some of the students there with their English."

Mrs. Jansen saw her opportunity to defuse the situation. "That sounds wonderful. Maybe you will become an English teacher like me. What is it like working with these students?"

"Some of them find English rather difficult, but they are so keen to learn and they try very hard. They are so appreciative of any help I can give them."

"That's more than I can say about most of my students. Talking of my English classes, this year's matric Shakespeare play is Macbeth. How are your rehearsals going Julie?"

"The play is coming along. Since I am only in one scene, I do not have to go to most of the rehearsals."

"What part do you have?" asked Mr. Jansen.

"I am one of the serving wenches. It is a non-speaking part. You know what? Some dork wanted us wenches to appear on stage topless, but the director nixed that idea. A pity really. It might have been rather fun."

"You see what happens when you send my daughters to a bloody English, liberal university."

"Ag skattie, don't be such a stick in the mud. You might want to remember some of the things we did when we were students."

Julie's eyes lit up. "Do tell. I am all ears."

Time to change the topic again. "Talking of my English classes, Justin can you suggest any new novels that I might be able to recommend to my students?"

Justin seized the opportunity, and steered the conversation into a discussion about some likely books. As this topic exhausted itself, it was Julie who quite inadvertently steered the conversation back into troubled waters. "Before I forget pa, I have brought Dora's pass book for you to sign."

"Dora? Do I know any Dora's?"

"She is the cleaning girl."

"What Julie is trying to say is that she is the lady who comes and cleans our flat."

"Oh! So now we are expected to call them ladies and gentlemen."

"Well, why not. Have you any idea how hurtful it is for grown men and women—Dora is in her forties for heaven's sake—to be called boys and girls?"

"So this is what they are teaching you in that hot bed of liberal nonsense."

It was Mrs. Jansen who again intervened. "Skattie, don't you think that Colleen has a point. After all you have never been one to hurt people on purpose. I am sure you at your age would not like to be referred to as a garden boy."

"Of course I would not like it. For one I don't work in the garden." Then after a pause, he added, "Yes, I can see your point. 'Boy' and 'girl' are labels we just use without any thought."

Mrs. Jansen felt that the point had been made and that it was time to move on to a safer topic. "Neville, how do you rate our chances against the New Zealand rugby team when they tour next month?"

It was Colleen's brother, Gerald, who piped up first. "Of course we will moer them."

Neville gave his more measured response. "I think that we will be able to give them a good run for their money, but they do have some very strong players. It should be an exciting series."

"However it seems that they may not come after all," observed Justin.

"Why ever not?" asked Julie.

"The New Zealand selectors have included some Maori players in the squad. After all their best winger is a Maori. But our prime minister has said that unless the Maoris are dropped, he will cancel the tour. That prompted a number of New Zealand players to say that unless the team is selected on merit, and not on the threat of our prime minister, they will refuse to go on the tour. So unless someone backs down the tour may be off."

No sooner had Justin given his explanation, than all hell broke loose in a free-for-all Jansen dust up. "Why should our boys have to play against blackies?"

"You think it will give them cancer of something?"

"It is our country. They must obey our laws."

"Which are stupid."

"Why should they leave their best player behind?"

And so on and so forth. Justin listened with amazement, not to the content of the fight, but to how it was being conducted. All the participants were switching back and forth between English and Afrikaans, and were apparently totally unaware that they were doing so. Often the switch occurred in mid-sentence. He had never before witnessed such a display of bilingualism. He found himself trying to figure out what prompted a switch. Did the rise in fervour prompt a change to one's home language? But then did any of them, especially the children, really have just one home language? Perhaps one or other of the languages had more descriptive words when it came to expressing a particular thought. Afrikaans, he was sure, had better swear words than English. It was a mystery to him, but nevertheless a fascinating spectacle. Then as quickly as it had flared up, the argument subsided and normal conversation resumed. Safe topics were hard to come by in apartheid South Africa.

After dinner everyone retired to the living room for coffee. A short while later Mrs. Jansen said, "Kom skattie, let's go to bed and give the young ones some time to themselves." When Gerald did not move she added, "That includes you too."

"But I am one of the young ones."

"Yes, but not young enough." She then laughed at her gaff before Gerald could point it out. "Off to your room, now, young man."

The remaining four 'young ones' sat around expectantly until Colleen took the initiative. "Come Justin. I would like to take Bambi for a walk."

"Bambi?"

"Yes, my dog. You have not yet met him. He likes his walks in the park across the road and it is quite a pleasant evening. Here in the Lowveld it does not get as cold at night."

When they returned, Neville and Julie were still on the sofa in the living room and did not seem over pleased to have them back.

"It's been a long day, and you have another big one coming up tomorrow. Let's get some shut eye. By the way. What do you want to do on Saturday?"

"If you can manage it, I would love to see some of the places that you described to me."

"I would like that too. Let me make sure that we can use one of our cars."

Mr. Jansen was making the most of the school holidays to catch up on his golf, and consequently left the house at the crack of dawn on Friday morning. After he had left, Colleen slipped into her mother's bed. It was the place where they had their most intimate mother-daughter discussions.

"Are you awake?"

"Ja, skattie. What's on your mind?"

"So what do you make of Justin?"

"I like him very much. He is certainly better than some of the blokes that you have brought home."

"Yes, I guess I have brought some doozies home, but what do you like about him?"

"Well, he does seem to be a decent sort, well-spoken, intelligent, sensitive, sincere in his beliefs, and compassionate in his actions." She paused for a moment.

"And?"

"I think that he is seriously in love with you."

"Yes, you may be right."

"But it does not really matter what I think. It is what you think that counts."

"I do like him for all the qualities that you listed. Okay, to be honest, yes, I do love him, or I think that I do, although it is hard to explain why. He seems to value me, not just for my looks, but as a real person. Do you know what he called me on our first date. A rock!"

"A rock! Yes, he seems very perceptive. You are a strong woman and he senses that. Most of your other boy friends only saw your beauty."

"But do I want to get seriously involved with him—to start thinking of a future together?"

"So what makes you hesitant?"

"I have this sense that life with him will not be easy. He is passionate about putting an end to police brutality, and about helping others with their education. His colleagues have already had some run ins with the Special Branch and I am afraid that he might be next."

"So is it an easy life that you are after?"

"No. In fact it was I who asked him to involve me in some of his activities. I guess that I am not making much sense at the moment."

"Being in love is confusing, and I think you are in love with him, perhaps more than you realise."

"Perhaps you are right. I wish I knew what to do."

"You need to come to a decision as soon as possible. The last thing that you should do is to string him along for the next few months and then tell him that there is no future for you together. He is more vulnerable than you imagine. If you are going to hurt him, do it soon and do it as gently as possible. On the other hand, if you do see a future together, don't leave him hanging in suspense. Let him know where he stands. You owe it to the both of you to make up your mind. There is also something else that you need to consider."

"What is it?"

"You do realise that you are on a collision course with your father. You are developing values, and acting upon them, in ways that are incompatible with those of your father. I have had to pull back from acting on my beliefs in order to keep the peace. If you decide to throw in your lot with Justin, it could well end with a rift with your father. All I am trying to say is that you need to know that there are consequences for what ever you decide to do."

Mrs. Jansen looked over to her daughter and saw that there were tears in her eyes. She put her arms around her and held her tight.

"I know you will do the right thing. Love is difficult. I suspect this is the first time that you are properly in love. It is confusing. And on top of it you have to decide how important your values are to you."

For a while, neither of them spoke.

"Dankie ma. You have always been here for me. I will think about what you have said." With that Colleen slipped out of the bed and went back to her own room.

The Friday morning hockey practice session went badly for Justin. Over the prior weeks his skills had gradually improved, but now they seemed to have deserted him entirely. After the practice he ruefully commented to Neville, "With me on the team it will be like fielding ten players."

"Too true. You have hit the nail on the head."

Justin had been hoping, if not for an outright denial, at least for a less robust affirmation of his prognosis. Neville continued, "But you have given me an idea. We must reduce the opposing team to ten players as well. That is where you come in."

"Surely you don't expect me to incapacitate one of them?"

"No, but listen. Their best player is on the left wing. In the past he played for Natal. Your job as right half will be to make sure he never touches the ball. Just stick close to him, and any time the ball is passed to him, get in the way. Stop the ball with your stick if you can, but your foot if needs be. Even if you give up a free hit, that is better for us than his getting the ball."

The strategy worked well during the afternoon game. The opposing left wing only received the ball twice, and scored on one of those occasions. Neville found the opponent's goal twice leaving the visitors the winners, 2-1.

Saturday morning dawned as one of those perfect Lowveld days. After a quick breakfast, Colleen and Justin set off to explore the sights of the Eastern Transvaal escarpment. "My mom has packed us a lunch, but I could do with a cup of coffee. I will get us some at the café in town." Justin sunned himself, leaning against the car, while Colleen went inside to get some coffee. He surveyed his surroundings. Sabie was a pleasant looking town. They were parked on the main street which was lined with the kind of shops one expects to find in a small town. Justin watched as shoppers of all races went about their business. His attention was suddenly caught by an anomalous sight—a small, emancipated looking African girl wearing a colourful, though dirty and scruffy school blazer. Colleen arrived back at that moment. "Oh my. That girl is wearing the Sabie High School blazer. It must be one that someone threw away." As they watched a strapping young white boy, wearing the same blazer, stormed up to the girl. Justin and Colleen watched in horror as he tried to wrench the blazer away from the girl, and when she held on tightly to it, made ready to hit her. The young girl was trembling with fear. Justin was a stranger to the community, and every instinct advised him not to get involved. However when it appeared that no one was about to intervene, he decided that it was up to him. He walked over to where the confrontation was taking place. "What is going on here?"

"This girl is wearing the blazer of my school."

"Did she steal it from you?"

"No, but she insults my school by wearing this blazer."

"Has she broken a law?"

"No, but..."

"No she has not. If you steal that blazer from her, you are the law breaker. Now bugger off you big bully before I have you charged for attempted theft." It was of course and empty threat. No policeman would ever act against a white boy harassing an African girl. But a fifteen year old boy would probably not know that.

For a moment Justin thought that the boy was about to punch him in the face. However, he eventually unclasped his fist and slunk off quietly. Afrikaner youth are raised to defer to authority. It seemed, as Justin looked around, that the whole town had been holding it collective breath. The girl had disappeared. But with her departure, the town came back to life.

"Let's get out of here," said Colleen. Then she put her arm around his waist and whispered, "I am so proud of you." It was at that moment that she made up her mind. She now knew what she would say to Justin.

Their first stop was at the MacMac Falls and Pools. Justin found the falls a mesmerising sight—the twin streams of water drifting down into the gorge below. From where they stood a rainbow hovered above the falling water—a bridge that the gods might well use to cross the gorge. The pools looked inviting, but it was a little too cold for a swim. "We often come to swim here in the summer, although there are better, more private places. I will show you one of them some time."

Next they drove through the little town of Pilgrims Rest, not much more than a ghost town in Justin's estimate. It comprised a series of corrugated iron houses hugging either side of the road. There was also a run down hotel. All the while that they drove, Colleen filled him in on what they were seeing and what they were not seeing, but might see at some later date. She talked about the history, the geology, and the flora of the area. It was music to Justin's ears.

Their next stop was Bourkes Luck Potholes. Here the river had carved a deep, narrow canyon into the landscape. Having done so, it then appeared to have suffered a fit of madness. In a fit of frenzy, so it seemed, the river had then carved a series of large, round holes as if trying to disappear into the bowels of the earth, giving up, and then trying again in another spot. Justin stood entranced as the water gurgled and swirled from one pothole to the next. In the end Colleen had to entice him away. "Next comes the grandest sight of all. Let's keep moving."

"What is it?"

"The Blyde River Canyon."

As they drove towards the canyon Colleen explained, "There are no designated view points or even a road that parallels the rim.

I know of a few vantage points, but we will have to walk to most of them. However the view will make it all worthwhile."

They left the main road and followed a track which eventually petered out. "We will walk from here," Colleen announced. There was no path—only the unscarred veld. As they walked, the far wall of the canyon came into sight and grew progressively larger. And suddenly they came to the edge of the canyon, and a magnificent vista spread out before them—the Blyde River Canyon. She led them to a flat rock that stretched out over the rim, where they made themselves comfortable. They ate lunch in silence, drinking in the grandeur of the scenery.

Finally Colleen said, "This is my special rock." Justin said nothing.

"I come here on special occasions." Justin remained silent, knowing that there was more to come.

"Sometimes I come here to grieve, like when an acquaintance, or even my previous dog, died."

"Sometimes I come here to celebrate, when something wonderful has happened. When I just feel so full of joy that I could burst."

"Sometimes I come here to think, like when I have an important decision to make."

There was a long silence, and then Justin asked, "And today?"

"Today I come here to tell you that I love you. That I love you with all my heart. And, you know, I don't even know why. Perhaps it is because you are so different from any one else that I have gone out with. You are such a special person—a real person." With that she placed her arms around him and kissed him fully on the mouth. "I love you too." They then lay down on the rock in one another's arms, kissing and hugging. How long they held tightly onto each other Justin could never say. Finally Colleen said, "I wish we could stay here for ever, but I guess we need to be getting back."

"It is so appropriate that we have found one another in sight of the Blyde River," said Justin. "The name says it all."

"Yes but remember that the waters of the river below are the combination of the Blyde and Treur Rivers."

Colleen took a different road back. They stopped off to see God's Window, Lisbon Falls, and the Pinnacle on the way back. Each were spectacular, breathtaking, but Justin's mind was in turmoil and nothing really registered. Nothing like this had ever happened to him before. That night when he went to bed, he was still in shock. It took some time for him to eventually drop off to sleep. He felt that he must be dreaming when he saw his bedroom door quietly open, Colleen slipping out of her night gown, and sliding into bed with him. When he woke up the next morning, Justin was alone in his bed. Had it really happened or had it simply been a dream? At times dreams can be very realistic. Surely this had been one such dream. On the other hand could a dream be that realistic?

The university team won their Sunday match 3-0. Justin played like he had never played before, and actually won Neville's praise for his performance. After lunch Neville assembled the team for a group photo, just before setting out for home. He handed his camera to Colleen and asked her to take the shot, remarking that the photo might well be accepted by Campus News. Then, as an after thought, he asked her to take a photo of Julie and himself. Not to be outdone, Colleen got Julie to take a photo of herself with Justin. Later Neville gave both Justin and Colleen copies of this photo. Little did Justin know at the time that it was destined to become his most precious possession.

Justin was in a pensive mood during the bus trip home. The victorious team was celebrating its triumphs, but Justin remained closeted in a world of his own.

When Justin and Neville entered their house, Ian and David had solemn looks on their faces.

"Anything wrong?" It was Ian who answered. "Prof. Armstrong and Mr. du Toit have both been arrested."

SEVEN

"WHAT!" EXCLAIMED JUSTIN. "PROF. ARMSTRONG AND MR. DU TOIT have been arrested! When? Why?"

"They were picked up on Friday afternoon. They will be arraigned and charged in court on Monday. That is the good news," answered David.

"Why is that good news?" asked Neville.

"Because they will have a court hearing rather than simply being detained indefinitely. We expect that they will be granted bail until their case come to trial."

"What are the charges?" asked Justin.

"They will be charged under the provision of the Bantu Education Act. However so far there are no details concerning the specific charges."

The trial of Prof. Armstrong was set to begin only one week after the arraignment. Clearly the State prosecutor was anxious to mount a show trial as a warning to others. Justin was assigned to cover the trial for Campus News. He made notes on the salient features of the trial for publication. The charge read, 'Establishing and running an illegal school for Bantu persons'. As it turned out, and much to the delight of Justin, and indeed much of the university community, the defence lawyer made mince meat out of the prosecution's case. Granted, the case was poorly conceived and presented from start to finish.

In his newspaper report, Justin focused on the defence lawyer's cross-examination of the State's star witness a member of the police force.

Lawyer: In your testimony you stated that you witnessed the defendant arriving at the alleged school on Saturday 14th May.

Witness: That is correct. But he also arrived on other Saturdays as well.

Lawyer: Did you observe him on any other Saturday?"

Witness: No sir, but have been informed so by reliable sources.

Lawyer: That is hearsay and not permissible as evidence.

Prosecutor: Your honour, the State will provide evidence from other witnesses to the effect that the defendant was present at the school on numerous Saturdays.

Lawyer: You mean, I assume, the *alleged* school.

Prosecutor: I stand corrected.

Lawyer: Your honour, to save the court's time I will concede that the defendant was present at the alleged school on more than one occasion.

Judge: Thank you for that.

Lawyer: Now would you describe the physical structure of this alleged school.

Witness: The alleged school is held in a large hall attached to a Catholic church.

Lawyer: And what did you see or hear when you entered the alleged school?

Witness: I did not enter the alleged school.

Lawyer: So is it true to say that you have no idea of what was going on in the church hall?

Witness: I did peek in through one of the windows.

Lawyer: Ah! So you peeked in. And what did you see?"

Witness: I saw a lot of Bantu children sitting in groups. There were also a few white students in each group.

Lawyer: And can you tell us what they were doing?

Witness: They were obviously being taught and studying.

Lawyer: And how do you know that?

Witness: When I observed them entering the building they were carrying books.

Lawyer: And did you stop any of them to examine the books?

Witness: No, I did not. I wanted to keep a low profile.

Lawyer: So for all you know, these books might have been bibles or hymnals?

Witness: It is possible, but I do not think so.

Lawyer: We are not here to find out what you think, only what you know. Might they have been bibles?

Witness: It is possible.

Lawyer: Is it also possible that what you observed when you peeped in through the window were youngsters engaged in bible study or in prayer."

Witness: It is possible, but I do not think .... Okay sorry. It is possible.

Lawyer: Is it possible during the few seconds that you peeked in that you saw a white student leading the group in prayer?"

Witness: It is possible.

Lawyer: Do you know of any law that prevents persons from congregating to pray or to study the bible?

Witness: I do not know of any such law.

Lawyer: Do you ever pray in a group?

Witness: Yes, every Sunday.

Lawyer: It seems that it must be a perfectly legal activity. Your honour, I have done with this witness."

The prosecutor did his best to rescue the case, but for all extents and purposes it was sunk for good. The judge not only delivered a 'not guilty' verdict, but reprimanded the prosecutor for wasting the court's time with such a flimsy and poorly presented case.

Following this fiasco, the charges against both Prof. Armstrong and Mr. du Toit were dropped. However the State did have the last word. The passports of both men were confiscated—an action against which there was no appeal.

The weekend after the trial Justin accompanied Neville to Grand Central, where he had his first proper flying lesson.

The next week Justin visited the offices of the Institute for Racial Reconciliation to meet with Anton du Toit. "I am pleased the charges against you were dropped."

"In some ways it is a relief, but sometimes I wish I had been found guilty and jailed."

"You are not serious are you?" When Anton remained silent, Justin continued, "Is there something that I do not understand?"

"It hard to explain. Have you heard of Henry David Thoreau?"

"Yes."

"Then you may have heard of his perhaps most famous quote. 'In an unjust society the only place for a just man is prison.' It is not a quote that I find comforting. We do not live in a just society, and yet I am not in prison. What does that say about me? Am I not just enough? Is there more that I should be doing, but what? You can understand that if I were to be jailed, these doubts that gnaw at me would at least be resolved."

"I understand. But now I have to wonder whether I should be in prison. Actually you have given me an idea for an editorial in Campus News."

"I am sorry Justin. I really should not burden you with my angst. I assume you came to see me about the report."

"Yes, here it is." Justin showed Anton the first draft of the report on the mathematics curriculum various study groups were using around the country. "There are still a few groups that I have not heard from, but I suspect that there will not be much in the way of new information. Is this the kind of report that you wanted me to compile?"

Anton scanned through the report quickly. "I will look over it in more detail later on, but from what I have seen this is exactly what I was hoping for. Thank you very much."

"If that is the case I will have a final copy typed up."

"There is one other matter I wanted to raise with you. The confiscation of my passport has created a problem. As you know I was due to travel to New York to confer with the Foundation, and hopefully sign the final contract. I did enquire if someone from the Foundation would come here, but that idea proved to be impractical. The head of the Foundation is a black man and quite naturally he does not want to come here. Chances are he would not be allowed into the country anyway. Also the full board would need to give its approval and to fly eight persons here is an unnecessary expense. So I was wondering whether you would be prepared to go to New York in my place?"

"Why me? Surely someone from the Institute would be more appropriate."

"Firstly, we only have a small staff. However the main reason is that you are the only one with a maths background. And you are the only one who could answer questions about the report that you are writing. Of course I will be available by telephone at any time."

"What about signing the contract?"

"That will not be a problem. I will give you power of attorney. And I will give my verbal consent by phone." As Justin hesitated he added, "You would only be gone for less that a week. The Foundation will of course sponsor you air fare."

In the end, Justin agreed, as he knew he would.

When Justin joined the other house mates for dinner, it was obvious that some disturbing news had been shared. "What's up?" he asked.

Neville was first to speak. "The New Zealand rugby tour has been cancelled thanks to our idiot prime minister. New Zealand was already under pressure to severe sports ties with South Africa. However they did agree to go ahead with the tour, but to include Maoris, and what does our idiot prime minister do? He cancels the tour. This will be the end of all future tours."

"The other news is even worse," said David. "Richard Levine broke while in detention."

"Who is he? Asked Justin.

"The president of the South African Student Association."

"Oh yes! Now I remember. He is from Cape Town."

"Richard has apparently agreed to testify against his colleagues, who are being rounded up as we speak. He is to be the State's star witness in a showcase trial."

"What did they do to Richard?"

"We have no idea yet, but I would dearly like to find out. However he will be held in some secret location until the trial. But since this is to be a public trial, he will at least have access to a lawyer. Perhaps his lawyer will be able to find out how they broke him."

Dinner was a sober affair. Everyone was upset, but none more than Neville.

Ian had known Jenny for some time, but it was only once he joined the Student Council that he really began to appreciate her qualities. Where Jonty Webb had been a solid and dependable leader of the Student Council, Jenny proved to be a dynamo. Under her leadership the profile of the Council, and indeed the university as well, had emerged in remarkable ways. Ian could think of at least three aspects of campus life in which Jenny had played a major role. The protests against police torture, detention without trial, and apartheid in general had grown exponentially. Every Friday afternoon a protest was held just outside the university main entrance. Each week the numbers increased, and at this point students were being joined not only by faculty members, but also by the public at large.

A second initiative initiated by Jenny were the so-called 'These are my words' lectures, which were now held weekly. A year or so earlier, to quote any banned person or even to display his or her picture, had been declared unlawful by the government. The lectures that Jenny organised were designed to subvert this proclamation. The first one had been titled, 'These are my words, not those of Nelson Mandela'. The speaker had cleverly conveyed the gist of some of Mandela's speeches but in his own words. Each week a different banned person was featured. Strictly speaking these lectures did not contravene the law since no banned person was ever quoted directly. No speaker ever appeared more than once, and so detaining one of them did not put an end to the series. The lectures became hugely popular and were quickly reported on in the both the local and international press.

The third initiative by design received no publicity. When a person was detained, it was often the family that suffered most, especially if the person in question was the bread winner. Various organisations, such as the Black Sash, did what they could to support these families. However money was always hard to come by, and even more so when the government blocked overseas money from being donated to this cause. Jenny took it upon herself to set up 'scholarships' from overseas sources for trusted students, but this 'scholarship money' was subsequently donated by that student to a needy family. It was all perfectly legal.

Ian was still getting to know the other members of the Student Council. In his mind he had divided them into three categories: respected, admired, and likeable. Jacob Tremor fell into the respected category. He was a veritable workhorse. No call for a volunteer went unheeded by him. In any debate he could be counted on to take the most radical position. But Ian could not find it in himself to like him. He did not socialize with any of the others on the Council, and indeed appeared to have no friends on the campus at all. And he had no sense of humour. On the other extreme was Amy Adams, who one could not but help liking. She was on the Council representing the science faculty, and was herself a physics major. She was obliging and helpful, but seemed uninterested in politics, whether at the student or national level. At times when debates became overheated, she was the one to pour oil onto troubled waters. But what about Jenny? In Ian's opinion she could fit into each of the three categories.

One evening, Ian and Jenny were working late in the Student Council office. He glanced over to where she sat, hunched over her desk, pouring over a set of figures, probably the scholarship data. She had this endearing habit of chewing on the top of her pen when she was concentrating hard. Her dark, long hair, parted in the middle, reached the top of the desk, and every so often she pushed it way with an annoyed brush of her hand. Her face had a kind of elfin charm, which disguised her steely determination, as more than one of her detractors had found out to his or her misfortune. She must have sensed his gaze, because she looked up and gave him one of her dazzling smiles.

"I am good for about another hour's work, but first I need some coffee," said Ian. "Can I get you some?"

"That would be marvellous. I need to finish up these figures tonight."

Ian planned to use the coffee break to get to know Jenny better. In the short while that they had worked together he had come to like and admire her. But he was beginning to realise that his feelings for her went beyond that of a colleague or even a friend. However he was cautious by nature, and did not want to rush things. They chatted amiably for about ten minutes, and then resumed their work.

Over the next couple of weeks, Ian and Jenny saw quite a lot of each other. These were not real dates, Ian reflected, but the two of them were more than casual colleagues spending a few moments together. Jenny, too, was cautious by nature but it was possible, Ian realised, that their current relationship could well blossom into something more substantial. Jenny, he learned, was the eldest of three children, and she still lived at home with her parents in the well-to-do suburb of Parkview. The time might well come soon when he would be taken to her home to meet them.

The opening night of Macbeth went off without a hitch—in fact it was a roaring success. The theatre was packed and the performance was warmly received. The vice chancellor himself, and many of the university senate were present. Mr. and Mrs. Jansen had driven up from Sabie for the occasion. After the show, they took Julie and Neville out for a post-performance drink.

Neville proposed a toast, "To the outstanding actress of the show, Julie Jansen."

"I was only on stage for about thirty seconds."

"But that was the best thirty seconds of the whole evening."

Lord protect my daughters from these silver-tongued soutie rogues, Mr. Jansen thought to himself.

The cast was buoyed by the warm reception of the play, but also realised that there was now a long road ahead. Since Macbeth was a matriculation set book, many matinees had been scheduled especially for schools. They would be kept busy for the next month.

When Jenny got home one evening in time for the family dinner, she was surprised to find a strange car parked in the driveway. Her mother met her at the front door. "There are a couple of gentlemen here to see you." Her mother looked worried.

When Jenny entered the living room her father was arguing with the two strangers, "I will not allow you to interview my daughter without my being present."

"Who are these men?" she asked her father.

"They are from the Special Branch. That one is Snyman and the other one Prinsloo. I have forgotten their ranks, but that is not important."

"It's okay dad. I can handle them alone."

"No. I insist on being present."

It was Col. Snyman who answered for both of them. "It is fine with us if you remain. In fact it might be best if you do hear what we have to say."

"Very well. Have your say."

Snyman continued, "Miss Marsh, we have just come to have a friendly word with you, and not to take you away. We know what you are up to, and to put it bluntly you are playing with fire. I too have a daughter your age, and I would hate to see you get hurt. But you will have to stop what you are doing."

"I am not breaking any laws, and you know it."

"I am not speaking about laws. You are associating with communists and being used to further their cause. You come from a nice family and we would be sorry to see you get yourself into deep trouble. Just stop it before it is too late."

"What I am doing has nothing to do with communism. I am helping people and trying to make South Africa a better and just society for all. I see no reason to stop what I am doing. Anyone with a conscience would do the same."

"Girlie, you are young and naive. We came here in your best interest. This is your first and last warning. I hope that you will take heed. We will be watching you closely. Good evening, Mr. Marsh." With that the two men marched out.

"Thanks for sticking up for me, dad." Jenny was furious.

"Sorry pet. All I could think of doing was throttling that slimy bastard. How dare he come into my house and threaten my daughter."

"Dad, that is the whole point. These bastards, as you call them, can do whatever they like. As long as laws like the ninety day detention act are on the books, they can indeed do whatever they please. If we don't stop them, things will only get worse."

"There are some good people in the government. I am sure they do not know or approve of actions like this."

"Dad, or course they know and approve. They passed the act in the first place. That is why we are protesting."

"Well, you will have to leave it to others now. You will have to follow their advice. I could not bear to see them take you away."

"Dad, I appreciate your concern, but there is no way I am going to back down."

"Please be reasonable."

"I am. It would be unreasonable to back down in the face of fascist police doing the will of an unjust, minority government—one that you voted for. When good men do nothing, evil prevails." She immediately regretted reopening the issue of her father's support for the government, but it was too late to retract her words. She should have stuck to the one important issue at hand. Now the situation was spinning out of control.

"You don't need to quote your empty slogans at me. This is my house and you are my daughter. As long as you live under my roof you will do as I say."

"Fine. I will leave if that is what you want."

Mrs. Marsh, who had come into the room quietly after the police had left, was appalled at how quickly the argument had escalated. "Those police have upset you both. Let's stop talking about it right now and go and have dinner. When you have both cooled off, perhaps we can discuss things calmly in the morning."

Dinner was a subdued affair, with no mention made of the Special Branch visit and its aftermath. Jenny excused herself after the main course saying that she was not hungry.

Jenny did not sleep well that night. Shortly after dawn she heard the sound of a car starting up and went to the window in time to see her father disappearing down the driveway. Since she was up anyway she decided to go down for breakfast. Despite the early hour her mother was already in the kitchen. "Good morning dear."

"Good morning mom. Was that dad leaving just now?"

"Yes, he said he had a lot of work to do today."

"Was that the real reason?"

"I suppose not. He wanted to avoid getting into another argument with you. He thinks that I am more tactful than him, and that I should be the one to talk this out with you."

"Has he changed his mind at all or does the ultimatum still stand?"

"He didn't really say, but I am sure he will come around in time. But don't you think you could meet him halfway. Stop what you are doing for now, but maybe get active again more quietly. He would not need to know."

"So you are saying that I should go behind his back just so I can continue to live here?"

"That would not be right would it? No I take it back. It is just that I am so desperate to have this situation sorted out."

"I understand. I really do not want to hurt you, either of you. But I hope that you can understand that if I give up my fight for justice, I am no longer myself. If I chose to stay under dad's terms it would not be me, just a shell of my former self."

"Yes, I can see that. Your father does love you very much. You must know that. You are the apple of his eye. Its just that he can be rather stubborn at times. Maybe you take after him."

"Perhaps you are right about us being stubborn. If we continue to live under the same roof, we might well provoke an unbridgeable breach. I've been grappling with this all night. I think it best for all of us that I do move out. I will take what I can today and come back for the rest of my things when I have a permanent place to live."

"Oh Jenny. I cannot bear this." She was crying now.

"Mom, please don't cry. I will come and visit. I think that short visits are the only way we can prevent the total breakdown of our relationship, with dad I mean."

"But where will you go?"

"I can stay with friends until I find a place of my own."

Mrs. Marsh watched sadly as her daughter left about ten minutes later.

After his nine o'clock lecture, Ian walked over to the Student Council office. Jenny was sitting at her desk, and she turned quickly away from him as he entered and pretended to be reading a book. But she had not turned quickly enough to prevent Ian from seeing her tears.

"Jenny. Whatever is the matter?"

There was no use hiding anything from him so she poured out the whole story.

"Where will you stay?"

"Something will come up."

"In other words, you have no idea. Come and stay at our place until you find something more permanent." When he saw the look of horror on her face he added, "It looks much better now than when you last saw it. We have tried to clean it up."

"I couldn't impose on you. What would the others say?"

"They would say 'Good for you, helping a damsel in distress.' No seriously they would understand." She still said nothing. "I could move in with Justin and you could have my room."

"And leave me unprotected while surrounded by a bunch of randy jocks! No seriously, it would be bad enough to inconvenience you, but leave the others out of it."

"Then you could stay in my room. I will sleep on the floor and you can have my bed."

"Ian don't be such a gallant prude. If I do move in I am not going to put you out of your bed. Or sleep on the floor for that matter."

The matter was settled and Jenny moved in with Ian. A week later they both moved into a flat of their own.

The performances of Macbeth were proving to be a great hit, especially with the matriculants from schools all across the region. In most cases a school would make a block booking and bus in the entire matriculation class to see the performance. It was during the second week that trouble surfaced. Andy Kaplan was called in to meet the Dean of the Arts Faculty.

"Congratulations! I hear that your play is being very well received. I have heard some very complimentary comments. I certainly enjoyed attending the opening night."

"Thank you, prof."

"However I have to convey some rather disturbing news to you."

"What is it?"

"The Minister of Bantu Education has prohibited all schools under his jurisdiction from attending the performances."

"But that means about half of our future audiences will be absent. On what grounds has he made this ruling?"

"He says, and I quote, 'It is not in the interest of Bantu pupils to be exposed to seditious and humanistic influences.'"

"But Macbeth is a matric set book. How can he be against them seeing the play if they are required to read the book. It makes no sense."

"I agree. I suspect that it has nothing to do with the play but rather that he does not want them to be on our campus. Not with all the protests and other anti-government activities that are going on at the moment."

"Is there nothing that we can do?"

"We will of course issue a statement condemning this ruling, but you can be sure that it will make no difference. I am sorry, but there is not much else we can do."

That night over dinner Andy vented his anger. "I am damned if I am going to let some ignorant rock-spider ban anyone from experiencing great literature. The man is an utter toss. May his soul rot in hell."

"But what are you going to do?" asked David.

"What can I do? It's not as if I can just go to Pretoria and shoot the bastard."

"I was thinking more in terms of the play than of shooting someone."

"What if we took the play to Soweto?" suggested Justin.

"Do you think we could do that?"

"If you like I could go with you to some of the school principals and sound them out."

"But what about the scenery, the lights, the costumes, and all that?"

"I suppose it would have to be a pared down version, but it is up to you."

"Yes, I would like to take you up on your offer. Let's go as soon as possible. If we can work something out, I would still need to see if the cast are willing to do it."

Justin wondered how best to make good on his offer. He had briefly met a few of the high school principals in Soweto, but did not know any of them well. In the end he decided to approach the one that he knew best, a Mr. Mamabolo, and ask his advice. Consequently the next day Justin and Andy went to Soweto, where they were shown into Mr. Mamabolo's office.

"Good morning. It is good to see you Justin, but who is this young gentleman who is with you?"

"This is Andy Kaplan. He is the director of Macbeth, the play that we are putting on at the moment. Justin this is Mr. Mamabolo."

"Ah yes, I know about your play. I presume that is why you have come to see me."

"Yes it is. The Minister of Bantu Education has prohibited your students from attending the play."

"Yes I know. I have received a circular from the Department to that effect. So have all the other principals. Yes, I know all about it."

"We might be willing to come and perform that play here at your school, if that is what you wish."

"What I wish and what is possible are not the same thing. Thank you for the offer. It is very generous of you. But if I were to permit you to bring the play to my school, I would most likely be fired. I think that you will find that the other principals will give you the same answer. The Minister does not take kindly to being crossed."

"So there is nothing that we can do?"

"That is not exactly what I said. You have an English saying I believe, 'There is more than one way to skin a cat.' I am not going to give you any advice, but if perhaps you were to put on the play in a church hall, maybe the one where you hold your Saturday sessions or maybe some other venue, and it were open to anyone in the community, who knows if my students would go there or not. It would be out of my hands."

"That does sound like a possible solution. Thank you."

"Don't thank me. I have said nothing." Mr. Mamabolo wrote something down on a slip of paper. "Here is the person to contact if you want to use a church hall. Also, just so you know, we are required by the Department to record all visitors. So if you are questioned, you came here to offer a donation of library books."

Since they were already in Soweto, Justin and Andy went to the address that Mr. Mamabolo had given them. They were met by a Father Gebeda, who welcomed them and insisted that they join him over a cup of tea. It was a new experience for Andy, who found the tea milky and sweet, but not unpleasant. After they had explained the position, Father Gebeda responded, "You are of course welcome to the use of the hall free of charge. However we are fully booked over the weekends. I could let you have it on Friday afternoons."

"We still have to run this whole thing by the cast, but could we tentatively book the hall for the next three Fridays?" Father Gebeda agreed.

On their way back into town, Andy said, "If we hurry I will be able to meet with the cast before today's matinee."

"Do you think that they will agree to put on some performances in Soweto."

"Some may be hesitant, but I think most will agree. I am fairly sure that all the main characters will jump at the opportunity."

The meeting with the cast turned out much as Andy had predicted. There were a handful that were hesitant to go into Soweto, or who had other commitments. Andy was pleased at the backing he received from Donald Campbell, who played the role of Macbeth. "Actually this will a great opportunity for us all. Back in the days when Shakespeare himself was involved in the staging of his own plays there were no lights or fancy sets. Performing in a church hall will be as close as we get to replicating what Shakespeare's audiences saw. If you ever get to London, do go and see Shakespeare performed in the new Globe Theatre. There is no elaborate scenery. The focus is entirely on the acting, as it should be."

It was agreed that Macbeth would be performed in Soweto on the next Friday.

On Friday the cast piled into the bus that would take them to Soweto. Justin and Colleen were part of the group as they knew their way around Soweto, and in any case Justin wanted to cover the event for Campus News and Colleen wanted to keep an eye on Julie. Ian and Jenny also decided to attend sensing that perhaps their presence might be useful if anything unexpected occurred. Andy was grateful for their presence as the representatives of the Student Council.

As the bus turned off the Soweto Highway into Soweto itself, faces were pressed to the windows taking in the sights that most members of the cast had never experienced before. Word must have gotten around the township as people cheered and waved as the bus went by. However it was a different sight that greeted them at the church hall. A large crowd stood silently across the road from the hall. Parked in front of the hall were two police cars. Father Gebeda was sitting stony-faced in one of them.

As soon as the bus came to a halt, a member of the Special Branch entered it. "Who is in charge here?"

For a long while there was complete silence until Jenny stood up, "I am."

"You name?"

"Jenny Marsh. I am president of the Student Council."

"You are all under arrest. You will follow my car to the police station where you will be dealt with. Two of my men will ride with you just to make sure you do not try any funny tricks."

There was a shocked silence in the bus as it turned to follow the police car. Jenny whispered to Ian, "We have to do something."

"What better time to teach the cast some songs."

"Good idea."

Ian stood up and addressed the other students. "Time to sing some songs. You may know some of them and others may be new to you. Just sing along as best you can." With that he broke out in a rendition of 'We shall overcome.' It was followed by 'Where have all the young men gone?' and 'Go tell it on the mountain.' Soon any protest song that any one knew was thrown into the mix, and some others besides. By the time they reached the police station the students were in high spirits and the two policemen were stony-faced.

At the station they were all herded into a large room. At least they were not in a cell, Justin thought. After a few minutes the man who had met them at the church hall entered the room. "Do any of you have a permit to be in Soweto?" When no hands were raised he continued, "As I thought. You will all be charged with entering a prohibited area. You will be photographed, finger-printed, and then released with a warning. All except three. Step forward when your name is called: Marsh, McCall, and Roberts. Right. The rest of you follow the sergeant to have your portrait taken." No one thought his little joke was funny. Justin managed to catch Colleen's eye as they are ushered out and nodded as if to say all will be right. "You three will be our honoured guests for a little while longer." Still not funny. "There is a gentleman who is very keen to have a word with you, or in your case Marsh a second word."

The three sat around with nothing to do for at least an hour. The room was completely bare except for a table surrounded by six chairs, all bolted to the floor. The walls were painted a kind of washed out grey, as was the concrete floor. There were no windows and the light was provided by harsh fluorescent tubes. Eventually Col. Snyman strode into the room. "So we meet again Miss Marsh. You have chosen to ignore my friendly warning. That is too bad. And you two gentlemen, do not think for a moment that I have not had my eye on you. As I have already told Miss Marsh, you are all playing with fire."

"There is no law against performing a play for matriculation students," replied Ian.

"Ah, but that is where you are wrong. First you entered Soweto without a permit." Justin was on the brink of saying 'but we have been doing that for months' when we realised it would simply be digging himself deeper into a hole. "Second, you have incited Bantu persons to ignore a ruling made by the Minister of Bantu Education. Both of these are punishable offences. Do any of you have anything to say for yourselves?"

Wisely none of the three offered any comment, although there were plenty of observations that Justin wanted to utter. The African students that he had encountered during the Saturday sessions all agreed that in this kind of situation it was best to be docile and play dumb.

"You do realise that I could lock you all up and throw away the key. No one would even know where you are, and whether you are still alive." Still all three remained silent.

"This is going to be your last warning. Stop all your seditious activities. Lucky for you I am playing golf with the prime minister tomorrow, so I cannot have you buggering up my weekend. Next time you will not be so lucky. Now get out of here. I will have someone drive you back to campus."

They left silently.

"Don't bother to say thank you," was the parting shot that followed their departure.

Had Justin waited a few days to cool off before setting pen to paper, what he wrote might have been more temperate. His disposition was not softened by Andy, who was still raging on about 'cultureless hairybacks', 'ignorant cretins' and 'uncouth rock-spiders'. As it was, his bottled up rage at their treatment by the Special Branch boiled over into the written word. He penned an article for Campus News about the whole Macbeth fiasco, which while factual was nevertheless peppered with choice adjectives. He next wrote a scathing editorial in which he called the Minister of Bantu Education a 'mean-spirited racist', and had even choicer epitaphs for the Special Branch.

The shoe dropped two days after the publication of Campus News. Justin and Jenny were summoned to a meeting in the vice chancellor's office. Besides the vice chancellor himself, also present were the registrar, and a lawyer, Mr. Kent. No time was wasted on pleasantries. "Miss Marsh, what is your role in this mess?"

"I can vouch that the article is factual. I was in Soweto when we were arrested and I was also one of those interrogated by Col. Snyman."

"Did you have any role in writing the article or the editorial?"

It was Justin that answered for her, "Miss Marsh had nothing to do with either. I take full responsibility for them both. I did not even show them to her before publication."

"Mr. Kent, would you be so kind as to explain to these two the mess that they have landed us in." By way of explanation he added, "For your information, Mr. Kent is retained as the university's lawyer."

"The university has received notice from the Minister of Bantu Education that he intends to sue the university and the writer of the editorial for slander and libel. He will only desist from this action if he receives a full written apology to be published in newspapers which he will name, and a face-to-face verbal apology to be given in front of witnesses in his office in Pretoria."

It took some time for this information to sink in. "My advice to the vice chancellor is that he has no option but to comply and to issue the apology. The only good news is that the Minister of Police has declined to take part in the action. He wishes to avoid the publicity that it would invoke." Unlike the minister, Col. Snyman had not demanded an apology, but instead has opened a new file with the name Justin Roberts on the cover.

"What would happen if we refuse to apologise?"

"In my opinion the minister would make good on his threat. He would sue both you and the university."

"Yes, that is obvious. I mean what are his chances of winning the case. After all, he is a mean-spirited racist."

"That is your opinion. His lawyers, no doubt, would point out that he used the phrase 'in the interest of Bantu pupils' in his ruling. They would argue that since he has the best interests of African people in mind he cannot be a racist."

"What are the chances of the minister winning the case against us?" asked the registrar.

"It would depend on the judge assigned to the case, but I suspect most would be inclined to side with the minister. However, and this is purely my own opinion, I suspect the government does not care a hoot who wins this case. They would take the opportunity to drag it out for months, and in so doing both embarrass the university and deplete its finances. Winning or losing could also have severe consequences for you, Mr. Roberts."

"I am not sure I understand why that should be."

"If you lose, you will have to pay damages to the minister, and these could be considerable. But win or lose, there will be the costs of the case itself. Each side will most likely have to bear its own costs, and these are bound to be considerably more than any damages if awarded. Now when it comes to you, Mr. Roberts, we enter into some interesting legal areas. Are you being sued as a representative of the university, or as an individual in your own right? As the university's lawyer I would have to argue for the latter, in which case you would have to get your own council. Then it would have to be determined whether you are being sued as a minor or as an adult. How old are you by the way?"

"Twenty."

"Probably as a minor then, in which case your parents would be responsible for the costs that you incur. They would most likely have to sell off the family farm to pay your debts. Also I understand that you are scheduled for a trip to New York. If the trial dragged on you would not be able to go." The lawyer had obviously done his homework. "I will now leave it to you to come to a decision as to how you wish to proceed. Please convey your decision to me at my office no latter than tomorrow. If the minister does not hear from us by then he will opt to sue."

Jenny and Justin did argue heatedly for not issuing an apology, but while they might have held the moral high ground, the cards were stacked against them and they knew it. In the end they bowed to the inevitable and agreed to go along with the apology.

Mr. Kent took care of sending a written apology to the designated newspapers and setting up an appointment with the minister. On the appointed morning, Jenny and Justin were driven to Pretoria by the vice chancellor in his Mercedes Benz. No one spoke during the entire journey. It was only when they were exiting the car that the vice chancellor said, "Let me do the talking." Justin and Jenny were happy to comply. They were shown up to the minister's office, where they had to wait for about half and hour before being shown in. Their only greeting was a curt, "Let's get on with this."

"Minister, on behalf of myself and these students, I would like to apologise for any aspersion we may have cast on your good name. We do not agree with your action, which I believe was unfortunate, but we did not have the right to question your character." The old geezer does have some backbone after all thought Justin.

"I accept your apology." Turning to Justin he added, "Are you the young upstart who wrote that trash?"

"Yes sir."

"I would like to hear your apology."

Justin hesitated for a few moments and then said, "I apologise if what I wrote about you was not true."

The minister appeared to be dissecting this 'apology' carefully. Justin held his breath—had he gone too far? In the end the minister merely nodded and indicated that they should leave.

They arrived back on campus during the lunch break. Students watched with curiosity as Jenny and Justin extricated themselves from the car. Prof. Armstrong later wrote them a short note. 'Seeing the two of you being publicly released from your humiliation reminded me of the days when Romans paraded their captive generals through the streets of Rome.'

Following the visit to the Minister of Bantu Education, Justin was both angry and despondent. His depression worried Colleen, and she began to consider how she might perk him up. She remembered him saying on one occasion that one thing he enjoyed about flying was that it demanded so much attention that all other worries were pushed aside. She decided to see if he was at home.

Having exchanged their usual greetings she asked, "How far along are you with your flying lessons?"

"To be honest I have been neglecting them of late. I have completed about six hours at this point. I should be ready to solo around ten to twelve hours. Why do you ask?"

"You seem to love flying so much I hope that I could experience it sometime. Is there any chance I could go up with you one of these days?"

"Sure. Why not? It would have to be with an instructor. I know what. Let me see if I can rent the C172—it is a four seater—tomorrow. If so you could come up with us. It is time I took another lesson anyway."

"That would be great."

"Not to change the subject, but how is Julie doing? At the police station she looked as if she had seen a ghost."

"It did not take her long to recover. After a few minutes with Neville she was back to her usual self."

"That is good news. I will let you know about flying tomorrow."

Justin was able to secure the C172. As it turned out, Colleen was thrilled with her first flight in a small plane. It was every bit as exhilarating as Justin had claimed.

Under Jenny's presidency, the Student Council was meeting every second week. With all the protest activities that she had initiated, there was always a full agenda. Meetings, which started around eight in the evening, often went on until past midnight. Justin, who was not officially a member, was encouraged by Jenny to attend so as to be able to report the proceedings in Campus News. His presence also served to emphasize the connection between the paper and the Council.

Justin was in the process of packing away his papers as the final item on the agenda was disposed of, when Jacob Tremor spoke up. There was something about Jacob that Justin disliked. He was too eager, too rabid, too humourless, too extreme, too a lot of other things that Justin could not immediately bring to mind. "I move that this Council constitute a committee of the whole."

"What on earth does it mean?" whispered Justin to Ian.

"It means that this is no longer a meeting open to the public, and that the proceedings will not be minuted." Since the public seldom, if ever, attended these meetings the point seemed moot to Justin.

"Any seconds?"

The motion was duly seconded.

Jacob walked over to the office table in the corner of the room and removed the hand set of the telephone from its cradle.

"What on earth is he doing?" asked Justin, loud enough this time for others to hear.

It was Amy Adams, the physics student, who finally answered. "There is this myth that if the handset is removed, the Special Branch will not be able to listen in on our meetings. It is of course a ridiculous notion. If anything, lifting the handset opens the line making it easier to eavesdrop. In any case if they are listening in they must be bored out of the minds by now." It seemed to Justin that this ground had been covered repeatedly in the past.

Jacob took to the floor. "You remember how shocked we were at the news that Richard Levine, the president of SASA, had been broken, and will soon betray his colleagues. I have found out how they broke him. He cracked under solitary confinement. They did not even have to lay a finger on him."

"What has any of this got to do with us?" asked Jenny.

"I have been given access to something that might help us if ever we find ourselves in the same position. It is a test that the CIA has developed to determine how best to break suspects that they have in custody. If they know a person's weak spot, they do not have to waste time on ineffective methods."

"So how is this supposed to help us? I cannot see us trying to torture the Special Branch."

"The point is that if we know our weak spot, we could take steps to guard against it. Perhaps if Richard had put himself in solitary confinement before he was detained, he might have been in a better position to withstand it later."

Ian chipped in. "Or perhaps we could use that knowledge to mislead the interrogators away from our weakness. It would be like the Brer Rabbit story, where he begs his captors to give him any punishment except to throw him into the brambles, which was precisely what he wanted them to do."

"Yes well, as I was saying," Jacob did not like being interrupted, "it would be prudent for each of us to take this test."

"Tell us more about how this test works. Do we have to swot for it?"

"All you have to do is watch a series of short movie clips. Sensors are placed on your scalp and your brain activity is monitored. It is easy and painless. It takes about half an hour tops and it is free."

"How are the results displayed?"

"Your brain activity is recorded and then interpreted in the form of a written report. From what I have gathered so far three main categories of weaknesses have been identified. These are physical or social isolation, physical pain, and concern for others. Of course these are just the broad categories. The results are far more detailed."

"Is this test being administered by the Psychology Department?"

"No. The test has come into the possession of a free lance psychologist. I happened to come across him quite by chance. I guess it was our lucky day."

Since there were no more questions, Jenny adjourned the meeting.

As it turned out almost all of the of the Council members, Justin included, did take up Jacob's offer of the test. Most did so out of curiosity rather than fear.

The week before Justin's trip to New York, he met with Anton du Toit. "Everything that you will need for your trip is here in this folder. Let me go through the contents with you. Here is your return air ticket."

Justin looked at it carefully. "It seems that I am booked on British Air through London. I assumed that I would be taking the direct flight to New York."

"That flight is operated by South African Airways, and the Foundation will not deal with any company owned by the South African government. Anyway, I prefer not to endure that long Johannesburg to New York flight. London makes for a welcome break.

"You will be staying as a guest of the Foundation at the International House on Riverside Drive. Here is the confirmation of your booking and payment. I suggest you take a taxi from the airport.

You could take the subway but it is confusing at first. Here are some US dollars just to see you through. A daily stipend will be waiting for you when you check in at International House. Any questions?" Justin shook his head.

"Here is the final version of your report to present to the Foundation and this is a copy of the contract. The original version, which you will sign on my behalf, is in New York. All that remains is for me to wish you bon voyage. I assume that you will be able to make your own way to Jan Smuts airport. Oh! I nearly forgot. Prof. Armstrong would like you to drop in on him at your earliest convenience." With that they shook hands and Justine made his way back to the campus.

Once on the campus, Justin made his way to Prof. Armstrong's office. "Come in my boy. I was just making myself some tea. Will you join me?"

"I will. Thank you very much prof."

Once they had settled down to a warm cup of tea, Prof. Armstrong continued, "So you will be leaving for New York soon. When exactly? It is this coming weekend is it not?"

"Yes. I leave on the Friday evening flight for London and then on to New York the next day. I will return a week later."

"I have requested you to stop by as I have a favour to ask, two actually. The one is very easy, but the other may take quite a bit of your time in New York. Before I go on, I must impress on you that you must not feel under any obligation to undertake either of them."

"I am sure that I will agree, but tell me what they are."

"It is fortuitous that you are flying via London. I have in my possession some documents, some evidence, which—how shall I put it—is of rather a sensitive nature. I do not trust the postal system as almost all my mail is opened. If you will take these document to London for me, I shall have someone meet you at Heathrow airport."

"Sure, no problem."

"Not so fast. Justin, I want you to understand that if these documents are found in your possession you could be in a lot of trouble. On the other hand, it is what is brought into the country rather than what is taken out that most concerns the Special Branch. Do you understand?"

"Yes prof I do and I will. What is the other favour?"

"I am part of a group—a secret group—that is designing a new education system for the post-apartheid era. As you most likely know, many of the African countries to the north of us have had to revamp their education systems after they achieved independence. They have had to replace colonial structures with a new, universal education system. In mathematics, for example, many have tried to adapt some of the new ideas being implemented in schools of their old colonial masters. Some very interesting ideas are attempting to be implemented, but with what success we do not know. These countries are all closed to us. I have a colleague in New York, a Professor Sheffield, who is making a close study of these post-independence efforts in education in African countries to the north of us. I had hoped to spend time with him to find out what he has learned, but now that my passport has been taken away that is no longer possible. And he refuses to come here. Much of his research findings are unpublished, but he has agreed to make them available to me. I did phone him yesterday, and he will make them available to you, if that is something that you think you can do for me. I know it is a big ask. If you agree it might well take three or four days of your time in New York."

"It sounds very interesting and potentially useful. Do you really think there will be a post-apartheid era?"

"Without doubt. Without doubt. Perhaps not in my life time, but certainly in yours."

"What exactly do you wish me to look for in Professor Sheffield's research papers?"

"Try to get an overall understanding about the nature of the new curricula, how they are being implemented, what are the successes, and what are the failures. Anything that you think we might learn from when our time comes."

"I will do my best."

"Thank you my boy. I will be eternally grateful. By the way, Professor Sheffield is on the faculty of Columbia University, which is just a block or two from International House."

As Justin was leaving, he added, "I almost forgot. Here is the package to be delivered to London."

"How will I know who to give it to?"

"Don't worry about that. Once you clear customs, some one will approach you and say, 'Dr. Roberts I presume'." As he left Justin wondered if those words were a secret code or just a joke. It was always hard to tell with Professor Armstrong.

As Justin was leaving, Professor Armstrong experienced a pang of guilt. What right did he have to place these young, idealistic students in harms way? It was all very well to rationalise by reasoning that the good of the cause was more important than the safety any individual, but did that not put him on a level with the proponents of apartheid? It could be argued that students like Justin had made their own decision to join the cause, but would they in reality be in a position to refuse a request from a senior and well-respected academic? On the other hand, it was not as if he and his family had not had to sacrifice for the cause. The confiscation of his passport was a comparatively small matter. The previous year his eldest son had been detained, tortured, and had then left the country on an exit permit. His wife had been devastated by the loss. And although he had confidently told Justin that apartheid would end in his lifetime, if he was honest with himself he had his doubts. There were times like this when he questioned whether the sacrifices that he was making, and asking others to make, were really worthwhile. The government's hold on power seemed absolute and permanent. Resistance at times seemed so futile. He took out a file from a drawer in his desk and thumbed through the well worn contents once again. The file contained offers from prestigious universities in the United Kingdom, the United States, and Australia offering him lucrative positions at their respective institutions—full professorships, endowed chairs, and the like. It would be such a relief simply to live the life of an ordinary academic. It would also be an opportunity to reunite his family. Having looked through the contents of the file, he sighed and put it away again. Now was not the time to leave. He would battle on, for the time being at any rate.

EIGHT

JUSTIN DID NOT SLEEP WELL THE NIGHT BEFORE HIS FLIGHT TO NEW York. He had a series of disturbing dreams. When he arrived at the airport he discovered that he had forgotten his passport at home, so he had to rush back, but then it was too late to drive back to the airport, so Neville offered to fly him instead. As the small plane approached the airport, Justin's flight was taking off, so Neville said that he would just have to follow it. Luckily Justin had woken up at this point drenched in sweat. There was no point in trying to sleep any more, so he dressed and took himself to the kitchen for an early breakfast.

As he was finishing up, Neville walked in. "I see our world traveller is up and raring to go."

"Good morning to you too."

"I hear you will be flying in a Boeing 747. Lucky you."

"What is so special about it?"

"What is so special! Where have you been! It is the most advanced plane ever to take to the skies—and one of the largest. It has been dubbed a jumbo jet. Did you know it even has an upstairs section? It is so technologically advanced that it can practically fly itself. I even have a cartoon about it. Let me try to find it." He rummaged in his backpack. "Here it is." In the cartoon, the pilot of a small plane had inadvertently landed on the wing of a jumbo jet. The caption read, 'Hey. Anyone can make a mistake.'

Since he had already packed, Justin decided that he may as well attend his two morning lectures. Colleen had offered to drive him to the airport, but they would not need to leave until about four o'clock. After the lectures, and with time to kill, he made his way to the Student Council offices to take leave of anyone who happened to be there. Ian was there with someone he did not immediately recognise. "Hi Justin. You all set for your trip? You remember Lucky, don't you."

"Yes of course. Hi Lucky. Good to see you."

"Lucky came here to see you. If you hadn't shown up I was going to take him around to your place."

"Sure. I was thinking of going down to the cafeteria to grab something to drink. Would you both like to join me?"

"I am tied up here, but Lucky why don't you go along with Justin."

Once they reached the cafeteria, Justin ordered a Coke for each of them. "So how are things with you?" he asked.

"Not too bad. A little hectic actually. Since that article appeared the police seem to be keeping close tabs on me. I have also received a number of death threats."

"I am sorry to hear that. How about Thembi?"

"She is fine. The police do not seem to be harassing her. The Saturday sessions are a great blessing to her."

After some more small talk Justin said, "So why don't you tell me why you came to see me."

"Is it true that you are leaving for America soon? For New York?"

"Yes. Tonight actually."

"I have come to ask if you will do something for me."

"Of course I will if I am able. What is it?"

"Not many people know this, so please keep it to yourself. I am in the process of applying for asylum in America. I have a cousin who lives in New York. If he will sponsor me, my application could be speeded up. He is trying to find out what all is needed for him to be my sponsor. From what I can gather, he might have to provide a financial statement and a letter of intent. There might be other documents as well. So I am asking you to bring these documents back with you, since I do not trust the post. If you agree, he will bring these documents to you wherever you are staying in New York."

"Of course I can do that. I will be staying at International House on Riverside Drive. I am sure he will be able to find it."

"Thank you very much. I am most grateful. I hope you have a great trip. I will contact you when you get back. Hamba kahle."

Justin watched as Lucky made his way towards the door of the cafeteria.

Colleen arrived at the bachelor pad, as it had become known, just before four o'clock. Justin had already loaded his suitcase into his beetle and was ready to leave. He checked his carry on bag once more just to be sure, the dream of last night still haunting him. Every thing was in place—ticket, passport, toiletries, a change of clothes, and Professor Armstrong's package. He drove them to the airport, asking, "Do you want to come in to the terminal?"

"I am not good at goodbyes. I don't want to embarrass you or myself by crying. I will just drop you off and leave." And that is what they did, a quick goodbye kiss and then she drove off.

Justin checked in and received his boarding pass. Next he had to pass through passport control. He had to do all he could to prevent himself from shaking. Professor Armstrong's package seemed to be burning a hole in his carry on bag. However, he need not have worried. The passport control officer merely stamped his passport and wished him a pleasant journey. A half hour later his flight was called, and along with the other passengers, he walked out onto the apron and up the stairs into the 747, resplendent in British Air colours.

Although he had been forewarned, as Justin entered the cabin he still gasped in amazement at the size of the 747. It seemed to him like a miniature auditorium. He had to walk past countless rows until he finally came to his seat. He could not conceive that a monster this size would ever be able to rise into the air and fly. He had secured a window seat right towards the rear of the cabin, where the three seat rows gave way to two. Before take off, the cabin crew mimed the safety information, to which no one but he seemed to be paying any attention.

A short while later the aircraft began to taxi and then lined up for take off. The procedure was no different from what he had practised in a plane many magnitudes smaller than this one. The jet engines began to roar and Justin was pinned back in his seat. After what seemed ages, the rumble of the wheels ceased, the nose lifted, and they were airborne. Justin watched mesmerised as the lights of the city slipped slowly beneath them until they vanished altogether as the plane nosed its way into the inky black sky, studded with stars.

It was not long after the plane had reached its cruising altitude that the seat belt lights were turned off. Shortly thereafter a pretty stewardess with a pert smile leaned over towards Justin and asked if she could get him anything to drink. "A glass of wine please." She handed him a wine list, which he scanned for the only wine with which he was familiar, Lieberstein. It was not on the list.

"I am not familiar with these wines. I wonder if you could recommend one for me." He hoped he had come across as sufficiently sophisticated. Since the seat next to him was vacant, she knelt on it so as to better see the wine list that he was holding. "If you would like a red, I recommend that Bordeaux," she replied pointing. "It is my favourite."

"I will trust myself to your good taste. Thank you very much."

He sipped the wine when it came. 'Saints above! If this is real wine, what is Liebies?' The Bordeaux rolled smoothly off his tongue, leaving an exquisite after taste in his mouth. What had he been missing all his life? He asked for another glass to go with his dinner.

As the stewardess removed his dinner tray, she asked "Can I get you anything else to drink?"

"Do you have another wine that you would recommend?"

"I find that a light, and slightly sweet Rhine wine is the perfect after dinner drink. We do have a reasonably good Liebfraumilch. Would you like to try it?"

"Yes please."

Another wine, another sip of paradise. Justin finally drifted off into a wine induced sleep.

When he woke up, feeling somewhat groggy, it was day time and breakfast was being served. His wine mentor of the night before had been replaced by another stewardess. As the breakfast trays were being cleared up, the captain announced that they would begin their descent into London. As it turned out they were placed in a holding pattern, and Justin did his best to pick out familiar London landmarks. His maternal grandparents had been born in London, and although they had spent most of their adult lives in South Africa, they still referred to it as home. He had grown up on stories about London— the docklands, the Tower, London Bridge, and of course the River Thames. The monopoly set that he had played with as a boy had London names. Old Kent Road was the cheapest real estate, while Mayfair the most expensive. Now these magical places from his childhood were unfolding below him as the plane circled the city. He even managed to pick out of few of the better known features. The River Thames was easy to locate. That must be the Tower Bridge, and further along the river, Westminster. One of those open green spaces, must be Hyde Park, but which one? Old Kent Road and Mayfair would be much harder to pick out. Finally their plane was given clearance to land, and minutes later they touched down at Heathrow Airport.

As Justin approached immigration and customs, his heart was in his mouth. Professor Armstrong's package was uppermost in his mind, and he was convinced his face had guilt written all over it. He kept reminding himself that he was now in England and had nothing to fear, but rationality does not always win out. The immigration official noted that Justin was on his way to the USA and stamped his passport with a nod and friendly greeting. At the customs check point he simply walked through without being stopped. His relief, however, was short lived. His next task was to hand over the package, and he had no idea how that would play out. He began to walk uncertainly towards the shopping mall and food court. All at once he became aware of a man walking lock step beside him. He heard a voice say, "Go into Wimpy's and order something," and then he was on his own again. He kept walking, and sure enough before long he came to a sign for Wimpy's. It seemed to be some kind of cheap hamburger joint. He went in, ordered a cup of coffee, and found an empty table at which to sit. The coffee was undrinkable, but he pretended to sip it anyway. After a couple of minutes, a man slid into the other seat at his table. "Sorry to send you to a ghastly place like this, but it is always busy and a good place not to be recognised. Also, I had to first make sure that you had not been followed from the plane. You can let me have the package now." Justin handed it over thankfully. As the contact left he added, "Give me a couple of minutes before you leave here. I suggest you check into your New York flight as soon as you can."

Having been relieved of the package, Justin felt that a load had been lifted from his shoulders. As he thought about it, he realised that he was just not cut out for a life of deception. How had he got himself into this fix? At the beginning of the year he had envisaged a clear path to his career goal of becoming a lawyer. However against all expectations, here he was sitting in London as some kind of secret agent. Or if not a secret agent, at least a smuggler. Moreover, he was up to his neck in political activities back in South Africa. How had this all come about? What might he have done differently? It was not as if he had set out to become an activist. Anyway, with the package safely out of the way, perhaps the coffee might taste better. It didn't. Justin tried to finish the coffee, but even having been conditioned by Neville's cooking, he failed at the task. He paid and left to find the gate for his flight to New York.

The New York flight, also a 747, was fully booked. Justin had a seat in the middle section and thus was not able to look out of a window. The arrivals hall at JFK was hot and crowded, and the queues slow moving as several 747s had arrived at much the same time. The airport had not yet adapted to the age of jumbo jet travel. The staff whose job it was to help passengers find the correct queue were rude and pushy. After an hour of waiting, Justin finally reached the immigration official and had his passport stamped. In the customs hall his suitcase was thoroughly searched before he was able to exit into the steamy heat of New York. He recalled the last piece of advice Professor Armstrong had given him. "New York will be hot and muggy this time of year. Wear light clothes. New Yorkers are rude and pushy. Don't take it personally. When talking to strangers, don't admit to being from South Africa. It is a way to avoid some unpleasantness. We are regarded as the polecats of the world."

Justin climbed into the cab at the head of the line and gave the address of International House. It turned out that the cab driver was originally from Jamaica, and was both friendly and chatty. "Is this your first time in New York?"

"Yes. First time in America as well."

"I am sure that you will enjoy it. Where are you from?"

"Sydney, Australia."

"No kidding. Have you been following the test match between Australia and the West Indies? It is turning into a cliff hanger."

"No, I have just come from England and was not able to keep up with it. Perhaps you could fill me in." The cabbie happily complied. Thanks to Neville, Justin did recognise a few of the names of the Australian cricketers and was able to keep up his bluff about being Australian by making the occasional comment. Between his descriptions of the ongoing cricket match, the cabbie pointed out the various landmarks for which the city was famous. Justin was relieved when they finally arrived at International House where he paid the cabbie off and thanked him profusely for catching him up on the test match.

Once checked into his room, Justin considered going out again to explore his surroundings. However, despite the fact that it was only six o'clock in the evening, he was very sleepy. Then the realisation struck him. It was already midnight in South Africa. No wonder he was ready for bed. He fell asleep immediately, but woke up at three o'clock in the morning while it was still dark outside, and could not go back to sleep. So this is what people meant when they talked about jet lag.

As soon as it was light, he went down stairs, where the night porter was still on duty. "Is there anywhere around here where I might find a bite to eat?"

"It is early, but you might find a few places open on Broadway."

"Which way is Broadway?"

"A couple of blocks that way, away from the river."

Justin found Broadway with no difficulty, and was grateful to find one of the delicatessens open. Having sated his hunger with whatever meal it was, he made plans for the rest of the day. According to a map that he had purchased, Central Park began about ten blocks from where he was eating. He decided to walk to the park and then through it all the way to its south end. He spent the day as a typical tourist. Being a hot summer Sunday, the park was full of people playing games and simply relaxing in the shade. He was in no hurry, and sat down on benches a number of times simply to take in his surroundings, all of which were so new to him, and to enjoy watching New Yorkers. From the Park, he continued south along Fifth Avenue, and on impulse went to the top of Rockefeller Center to savour the view of the city spread out before him. Further down Fifth Avenue he came to Washington Square, and from there to Greenwich Village, where he ordered an early dinner. In his encounters with people along the way—lunch in the park and dinner in the village—he kept up his pretence of being from Australia. It was becoming second nature at this stage. He kept hoping that he would not run into any real Australians, who would spot him for a fake right away. After dinner, he took the plunge and successfully found his way back to International House using the subway.

His meeting with the Foundation was not scheduled until Tuesday, so he had another free day at his disposal. So as not to be late for that meeting, he decided to make sure he could find his way there, and perhaps even announce his arrival. The Foundation's headquarters were not far from where he was staying. He walked through the campus of Columbia University to Amsterdam Avenue and then turned to his right to find the Cathedral of St. John the Divine. The Foundation was located in a building across the avenue from the cathedral. He found the building and noted that the Foundation's offices were on the second floor. I may as well go on up and see where they are, he decided. Immediately off the stairwell was a desk with a smartly dressed receptionist. Justin had intended simply to find the location of the Foundation, but was stopped in his tracks. "Can I help you sir?"

"I have a meeting here tomorrow, but I thought it best to make sure that I would be able to find my way here."

"Are you from South Africa?"

"No. I am from ... uh yes. I am Justin Roberts."

"Great. We are expecting you. Did you have a good flight? Is your accommodation satisfactory?"

"The flights went well, and the accommodation is much better than what I am used to. Thank you for arranging it."

"I have just been making copies of your report for the board members. You must have spent a lot of time on it. By the way, I love your accent."

"I found it very interesting work. I hope the report will be useful."

"Is there anything else I can do for you? A cup of coffee?"

"No thanks."

"Directions to some place?"

"I am finding my way around fairly well. Yesterday I walked through Central Park from top to bottom and then made my way on down Fifth Avenue as far as Greenwich Village."

"Good grief! You walked through the north end of Central Park! You could have been killed. People are mugged there all the time. Didn't anyone warn you?"

"I didn't ask anyone."

"Well let me give you a few tips. Do not, I repeat do not even think of going into Morningside Park. Riverside Park is mostly safe, in the daytime anyway. Stay away from it at night. Where are you going from here? Some streets are safer than others."

"There is someone I need to be in touch with at Columbia University. I think I will go there now. I know where it is as I cut through the campus on my way here. I will go back up along Amsterdam Avenue."

"Very well. That is your safest route. I will see you tomorrow. The meeting is scheduled to begin at ten."

The campus of Columbia University was not at all what he had expected. As a prestigious Ivy League university, he had envisaged a campus of open spaces, broad avenues, and leafy trees. The buildings were impressive, but cramped together with almost no space between them. He was mildly disappointed. He was also surprised that the campus seemed devoid of students, but then he remembered that this was the summer break. It was not difficult to locate Professor Sheffield's office, but he hoped that he would find him there. He knocked on the door.

"Enter."

"Good morning professor." If the campus had disappointed, Professor Sheffield did not. He epitomised the image of a college don. He had greyish hair which covered his ears and sported a fully formed salt and pepper beard. Despite the heat he was wearing a tweed jacket, and a pair of horn-rimmed glasses completed the image.

"Good morning. Do I know you?"

"I am Justin Roberts. Professor Armstrong asked me come and see you."

"Right. We spoke on the phone last week. I was sorry to hear his passport had been revoked, but in some ways I am surprised it took so long in coming. Anyway it is good to meet you. Armstrong has spoken very warmly about you, and all you have done to help him. I hope that I can be of some assistance to you and of course to him."

"Did he tell you why he asked me to come and see you?"

"Yes he did. And I must admit I am impressed by the foresight of the group of which he is part, drawing up a blueprint for education in post-apartheid South Africa. It is both far-sighted and optimistic."

"He told me that you are researching the new education policies and practices in many of the post-independence African countries, and that he hopes to learn from you how these efforts have unfolded. He asked me to learn as much as I can from your research and then to report back to him."

"I am not sure he realises what a formidable assignment he has given you."

"How do you mean?"

"My younger untenured colleagues are under enormous pressure. They are expected to publish five or often more papers annually. I am free from that kind of pressure, not that I have slacked off on the research front. The phenomena that I am studying evolve over decades not years. Educational policies and practices in these developing countries are continually in a state of flux as reality clashes with aspirations. My younger colleagues are forced to publish a paper or two after one quick visit to just one of these countries. However what they find today may have changed by tomorrow. I have the luxury of taking a long term view. To get the full picture one would have to trace developments over a span of say fifty years. I have been collecting data for ten years now, but with old age catching up I will likely have to publish my results in another ten years. So I will have to be content with twenty rather than fifty years of change and development.

"The reason that I am telling you all of this is that I have accumulated ten years worth of data from eight different countries. These data include surveys, interviews, policy documents, evaluation studies, video recording of classroom lessons, field notes, and so on. None of these have been published yet, although naturally I have made some tentative conclusions from the evolving data. The problem is, how can you best benefit from all that is here. I assume you will not be in New York for very long."

"I am only here for this week, and I will have to spend some time at the Foundation, where I am standing in for Professor Armstrong. Do you have any suggestions as to how best I might proceed?"

"Well that is a tall ask, but let me think. First of all, I suggest that you concentrate on only two or at most three countries, not all eight. Nigeria, Kenya, and perhaps Liberia might be your best bets. Second try to get familiar with only a sample of the educational spectrum. I believe that in Soweto you are focusing on secondary mathematics and science, so it might narrow things down considerably if you traced their development over a ten year period in just a couple of countries. Third, narrow your search to certain types of data, for example policy documents, evaluation reports, and perhaps a limited number of interviews."

"That all makes sense. Thanks."

"Good. In that case I can have my research assistant locate all the relevant research files for you. Let me make a few more suggestions. Do not get hung up on the first post-independence years. In the euphoria following independence there seemed to be a belief that all things were possible. Generally speaking you will find that some very lofty and ambitious goals were set in the early policy documents, which took little account of the context in which they would have to be implemented. As time went by it was realised that these goals could not be met in schools with no or limited resources and teachers with only the bare minimum of training. So you will find an interesting evolution of policy as evaluation reports became available. I think you might find some valuable lessons here for post-apartheid South Africa. You should also look carefully at where these newly independent countries sought inspiration for their new curricula. In science education, for example, Nigeria looked to Scotland, Kenya to England, and Liberia to the USA. The admiration that they displayed for the education systems of their former colonial masters is somewhat ironic. As you might imagine adopting foreign curricula, or should I say adapting, did not always work out well. An interesting question is, 'Where will South Africa look when it comes to revamping its curricula?'"

"On the logistical side of things, you obviously cannot remove any of my documents, so you will have to take copious notes, and then incorporate them into some kind of coherent report. There is one exception. Have you heard of a Xerox machine? No. It is a marvellous invention. You can take any piece of paper and it will make an exact copy. The Department does have one, but our esteemed head does not like it to be over used. For something that would be difficult for you to copy, say a diagram, I can have my research assistant make you a copy. But please keep these requests to a minimum. Come with me and I will show you where you can work. It is up to you to decide how much or how little time you spend here."

Justin followed Professor Sheffield down the corridor to another room. There was one window that looked out over the main quadrangle, and a long table running the length of the room. Each side wall was filled with shelves stacked with hundreds upon hundreds of lever-arch file folders, each carefully labelled. Working at the table was a young black man whom the professor introduced as his research assistant. "Justin this is Victor Maraga from Kenya. Victor, this is Justin Roberts. He is from South Africa, but he is okay. You will please assist him with anything he needs. I will leave it to him to explain what he is doing here. Justin, let me get you some data to start you off."

Professor Sheffield walked over to the shelves and picked out two files, one labelled 'Nigeria, Policies 1-5' and the other 'Nigeria, Evaluation Reports, 1-5'. "These are overall policies, but buried in them you will find out what you want to know about mathematics and science education. One more thing. I do not want you to take down any of these files by yourself. If there is something that you need to read, ask Victor and he will get it for you. Besides he knows where everything is kept. I need to go now, but good luck. You can come and go as you please. The room is open until about six at night. If you want to work at night, get Victor to give you a key. I will drop in from time to see how you are getting on. If you have any questions or concerns, don't hesitate to come and see me."

There was an awkward silence after the professor left. Eventually Justin said, "So you are from Kenya." He could not have said anything more stupid.

"Yes."

"I have never met anyone from Kenya before."

"I have met a number of South Africans." It did not sound like a compliment to Justin.

"Look, I am sorry if the prof has palmed me off on you. I did not ask him to."

"The prof must think it important. Why don't you give me a quick run down on why you are here."

Justin did his best to explain the purpose of his mission.

"Now I can see why the prof wants to help you. I am amazed that there are some people in South Africa with so much foresight. I think what you have described is a very important project."

"Can you tell me a little about yourself?"

"I was recruited by the prof about six years ago to be his guide and translator in Kenya. I had just completed my B.A. and was looking for some kind of work. He must have seen some potential in me since he arranged a scholarship for me here at Columbia. I first did a masters and am now writing up my Ph.D. thesis."

"What is the topic of your thesis?"

"I am analysing some of the data prof collected in Kenya. I am looking at the educational policy changes over the ten years since independence, and delving into the possible causes of these changes. An underlying cause of most of these changes can be traced to the gap between the intended and enacted curricula. I am sure there are many lessons that you can learn from our experience, and I will be glad to share my findings with you. Looking back I wish we had taken the time like you are to think through some of the challenges facing our education system before plunging headlong into reform."

"I will be grateful for any insights that you can give me."

"Sure thing. Look I have to run a few errands now, but would you like to have lunch together?"

"That would be great."

By the time lunch time came around, Justin had gleaned most of what he wanted from the two files that Professor Sheffield had given to him. For lunch Victor took him to a small pizza parlour on Broadway where they split a pizza and shared stories about their respective countries. With the initial tension between them now dissolved, they discovered that they had much in common.

Back in the office Justin asked, "Does the 1-5 on these two files imply the first five years of research?"

"Yes exactly."

"Then I should probably look through the next years. Could you get them for me?"

"Yes, certainly." Victor pulled two files off the shelves labelled 'Nigeria, Policies 6-10' and the other 'Nigeria, Evaluation Reports, 6-10'. Once he had finished with these he asked Victor for the files on Nigerian interviews and field notes. Around five o'clock Victor left, bidding him close the door when he was finished. "It will lock automatically. See you tomorrow."

"I have a meeting at the Foundation in the morning, so maybe tomorrow afternoon. If not Wednesday morning."

Justin finally packed things up around six thirty, had a quick dinner at a deli on Broadway, and then returned to International House. The porter greeted him with a message. "A gentleman came by asking for you. He said he will return tomorrow around five thirty, and hopes to see you then. He did not leave any other kind of message."

Justin racked his brains as to whom it might be, and then remembered that Lucky's cousin was slated to make contact with him.

Afraid of being late, Justin actually arrived ten minutes early for his meeting at the Foundation, where he was greeted by the same smartly dressed receptionist. "Good morning Justin. I hope that you slept well. I am glad you are a little early. The chairman would like to meet you before the meeting begins. Please come with me."

They walked down a plushly carpeted corridor lined with what Justin took to be original paintings of landscapes. She knocked on a door at the end of the corridor and entered without waiting for an invitation. "Justin Roberts is here, sir."

"Thank you Marlene. Please bring us each a cup of coffee. How do you like yours Justin?"

"With milk and sugar."

"Must be a South African custom. You cannot even stand having your coffee black."

Justin was taken aback, unsure of how to respond. He looked anxiously at the chairman who was by far the largest and blackest man he had ever encountered. He stood there just staring at the man unable to think of anything to do or say. Then suddenly the chairman's face broke out into a huge grin. He wrapped his enormous arm around Justin's shoulder, saying, "Just kidding my boy. Just kidding. It is great to have you here. I have read your report, and I must say it is comprehensive and well written. Not like some of the trash that gets sent to us. Thank you for your effort. I don't suppose du Toit or Armstrong paid you a dime to write it?"

"Not a penny, sir."

"I guess they have to do things on a shoe string. Before the meeting begins, I would like to ask you a little more about this project that you are involved with in Soweto."

As they sipped their coffees, Justin did his best to answer the chairman's questions. Having satisfied himself, the chairman continued, "Come with me to meet some other board members. They have some questions about the report and the wording of the final contract. The full board will meet on Friday morning for the formal signing of the contract, which will be attended by the press."

Justin answered all the board's questions as best he could. Once all the points raised had been clarified, the chairman said, "As I understand your recommendations, you say that there is no need to develop any mathematics text books or other curriculum materials. These already exist, either from local or foreign sources, and that study groups around the country are already using these. However there is a huge shortage of these materials. You suggest that we could help by supplying these materials. However you do go on to suggest that the work of these groups might be enhanced by the development of study guides to assist with pace and sequence of the content. Is this a fair summary of the recommendations in your report?"

"Yes sir. That sums it up nicely."

"Then there are just a couple of questions about the contract between du Toit's project and the Foundation. I was speaking to him before you arrived on the phone. He does not want the word 'school' to appear in the wording of the contract. I am not sure why since you are essentially running a school aren't you?"

"If what we are doing is seen as a formal school, it would be illegal and we would likely be arrested. At Professor Armstrong's trial the prosecution could not prove that what we are doing constituted a school. To have the word 'school' in the contract would be a gift to the prosecution in any future trail."

This explanation was met with a stunned silence. "You mean to say you could be arrested for teaching mathematics!" Justin simply nodded. And then added, "Actually we were arrested for trying to put on a Shakespeare play for school children in Soweto, but were not charged—just released with a warning."

There was another stunned silence, finally broken by the chairman. "I would like to thank Mr. Roberts for his report and what he is doing in South Africa. What he has told us goes to show how important it is that we support brave people like du Toit and Armstrong, and of course their volunteers. We look forward to seeing Justin again on Friday when he will sign the contract on behalf of du Toit, who as you all know could not be here."

On the way out he said to Justin, "Do you have any decent clothes to wear for the signing ceremony on Friday?"

Justin was embarrassed to admit that he was wearing his best clothes at the moment. "Do me a favour and buy yourself a decent jacket and tie for the occasion. Make that a shirt as well. What the hell, maybe some trousers too. Marlene, give this guy $50 from petty cash so that he can look presentable at the signing." With that he extended his hand, and without thinking, Justin responded with the African handshake—shake, grip thumbs, shake again. He looked at Justin with surprise, "I guess you really are an African after all."

Justin decided to spend the afternoon back on campus working on his report for Professor Armstrong. Before going onto the next country he needed to make sense of all he had learned about Nigeria. After a couple of hours work, he was satisfied that he had created a halfway decent summary of all that he had learned. He arrived back at International House in time for his meeting. His guess had been spot on—it was Lucky's cousin. "You must be Justin. Lucky has told me all about you. By the way, my name is Frank."

"Pleased to meet you."

"Here are all the papers Lucky will need for his asylum application."

"I will give them to him when I get back."

"I appreciate your help in this."

"If you don't mind my asking, how do you know Lucky? You do not even have a South African accent."

"I have lived in New York since I was two. My parents fled South Africa in the 50's, so I have never actually met Lucky. We are related in some way or another—one of those extended African family relationships. There is no word in English to describe our actual relationship, so to make things easy we refer to one another as cousins. Look, I am in a bit of a hurry today, but I was wondering if you would like to go out with me tomorrow night."

"That would be great. Do you have anything specific in mind?"

"Have you been into Harlem yet?"

"I don't think so."

"There are some great restaurants and night clubs. Harlem is just down the road from here. It would be a pity if you left New York without experiencing Harlem. I will meet you here around six tomorrow evening."

"Thanks. I look forward to it. Could I invite the guy who is helping me with my research? He is from Kenya."

"Sure thing."

Justin worked all morning on the data that had been collected from Kenya since independence. During the lunch break he invited Victor to join Frank and himself that evening. Victor was somewhat taken aback, "You have only been here a couple of days, and already you are heading into Harlem. You do get around, but I hope you know what you are getting into. Yes, I would love to join you. How do you know this Frank guy?"

Justin explained his connection to Lucky and hence Frank.

That evening the three of them met outside International House and made their way down to the heart of Harlem. Justin could not help but notice that his was the only white face in evidence. As they entered the bar, or was it a club, chosen by Frank, all conversation stopped. There was an ominous silence as they made their way into the bar, all eyes fixed on Justin.

"Holy shit, we're toast," whispered Victor to Justin. He tried to edge the trio towards a booth in the corner of the room.

"No way," hissed Frank. "That is what they expect us to do. We are going to sit right out in the open at the bar counter." And that is what they did. Justin sat down and fixed his eyes on some spilt beer on the counter top, conscious of the fact that every pair of eyes in the place were fixed upon him. This is exactly the reverse of what would happen if an African walked into a bar in South Africa, except of course they were forbidden to even enter. How was this going to end? At least no one had yet tried to drag him outside and beat him up, which is what would have happened to an African back home. Eventually the barmen sidled up to the trio saying, "Well Frank, what trouble have you dragged in here tonight?"

"These, my friend, are my African brothers."

"Even this honky?"

"Especially this white guy, who is one of us, and my honoured guest. He has risked his life to help my cousin back in South Africa." A bit of an exaggeration thought Justin, but this was not the time to set the record straight.

"In that case you are all welcome. The first round of drinks is on the house."

As if by magic, the whole atmosphere changed in an instant. The buzz of conversation resumed and during the evening a number of customers came up to introduce themselves and shake Justin by the hand. Later on the band arrived, and Justin was introduced to soul music for the first time in his life. During a break in the music, the three of them retired to a booth so as better to be able to converse. Frank wanted to hear all he could about the latest news from South Africa, and in particular what Lucky and Justin had been doing in Soweto. Justin filled him in as best he could, including the circumstances that had brought him to New York.

"So basically what you are doing is helping students in Soweto to gain qualifications in mathematics and science."

"Yes, as are other similar projects around the country. Hence the need to develop study guides."

"It is admirable, but is it enough?"

"What do you mean?"

"You are helping students to better understand mathematics and science. But are you helping them to develop a vision of what to do with this knowledge? Do they, or for that matter you, ever think about how they might use this new knowledge to benefit society? Is this new knowledge giving them a purpose in life? Does it make them dream about a better future?"

"You know, I never thought about it that way. What do you think we might do to address these questions of yours?"

"Have you ever considered what you might provide them with to expand their thinking? Not just to increase their understanding, but to ask themselves what they will do with this new knowledge?"

"To be honest, I have never thought of that. I suppose there are sources we could point them to. Do you have any suggestions?"

"Have you ever heard of Martin Luther King's speech about 'I have a dream?' You might expose them to it and then challenge them to think about what their dream might be, for themselves as well as for their country."

"I can see how important expanding their thinking could be. To be honest, mostly what we are doing is to help them pass examinations. Any other potential sources?"

Victor joined the conversation for the first time. "Have you ever heard of the Arusha Declaration?" Justin shook his head.

"It is essentially the dream, or even blueprint that Julius Nyerere set out for an independent Tanganyika. It is quite an inspiring vision for his new country."

"I would like to read it. Do you have a copy?"

"Yes. I have some spare copies, so I can give you one."

"Thanks. You are both giving me some wonderful ideas as to how we might make our project more relevant. Do you have any ideas for other sources?" But at that point the music started up again and further conversation was impossible.

Justin decided that the next day, Thursday, would be the last time he worked on the research for Professor Armstrong. He worked on the Kenyan data all morning and used the afternoon to compile what he had found into a report. Victor proved to be a great help. Not only had he gathered some to these data himself, but he also had an insightful understanding of that country's educational system. Justin felt that he had done all he could by late afternoon, and turned his attention to his next task.

"I need to buy some new clothes for tomorrow's signing ceremony. Do you have any suggestions?" Victor gave him the names and addresses of a couple of possible shops. Before leaving the campus, Justin went to Professor Sheffield's office to take his leave and thank him for all his help. "I was just on my way to find you Justin. My wife and I would like to invite you around for dinner tomorrow night. We also have tickets for the opera if you would care to join us afterwards. Have you ever been to an opera?"

"No sir. They are performed occasionally in Johannesburg, but I have never been to one."

"Well it will be a new experience for you. The Metropolitan is one of the great opera houses in the world, and tomorrow night they are performing one of the best known operas of all time, Carmen."

"Thank you sir. I look forward to he evening."

"Come by our place for drinks around five thirty. We live on Riverside Drive not far from International House."

While getting dressed for the signing on Friday morning, Justin realised that he should have taken more care when buying his new clothes. He now realised that American sizes differed from those with which he was familiar. He had not tried on his new clothes at the store, but had simply held them close to his body. Shopping for clothes was not his favourite activity. As a result, everything he had bought was just a little too large for him. It was too late to do anything about it, so he finished dressing and set off for the Foundation, hoping that no one would notice that his clothes were slightly on the baggy side.

When he entered the Foundation's premises, Marlene gave him a cheerful good morning and tried not to laugh out loud. The Chairman, too, seemed a bit more jovial than usual, and if he noticed Justin's clothes, did not comment on them. The ceremony went off well, although some of the speeches might have been a little shorter. Justin was relieved to find that his name was not listed as one of the speakers. At the appropriate time he signed the contract on behalf of the Institute for Racial Reconciliation. The ceremony was followed by a well catered buffet lunch.

Dinner at the Sheffield residence was a congenial affair. At first Justin was taken aback somewhat to find that Mrs. Sheffield was from Zambia. It was the first time he had encountered an interracial couple, and it was a little unnerving at first. But after a few minutes it all seemed so normal, making his own country's prohibition seem ludicrous. Why should people of different races not be allowed to marry? The Sheffields seemed to be a normal and happily married couple. The meal itself comprised of some delicious, if somewhat spicy, Zambian dishes.

The opera turned out to be the highlight of the evening. Justin was not sure what he had expected, but the exhilarating music, the artistry of the singers, the colourful costumes, the thunderous applause at the end of each act, made for an unforgettable experience. He knew that he was hooked on opera for life.

At Professor Sheffield's suggestion, Justin spent his last day in New York as a typical tourist, taking the Circle Line cruise, visiting the Statue of Liberty, and spending some more time in Central Park and the Metropolitan Museum. He was booked on the late evening British Air flight to London, where he spent all his time at Heathrow, since there was not enough time between his flights to go into the city, but more time than one wishes to spend at an airport. The second flight saw him back at Jan Smuts airport early on the Monday morning. The only advantage of two evenings in a row in a jumbo jet was that he had adequate time to sample many fine, and to him new, wines.

Disembarking at Jan Smuts, he experienced a sinking feeling in his gut. He was home again, but home was the land of apartheid and police torture. He was experiencing what others had already expressed to him, that dread of being back. It was only on his return that he realised how care-free he had felt while out of the country. At least he would no longer have to keep his wits about him, deciding when and when not to pass himself off as an Australian. At the immigration control point he was questioned endlessly about his trip to New York—what he had done there and with whom he had met. It was not a welcome-back-home kind of encounter. At the customs counter his hand luggage was search meticulously—every item was removed and inspected thoroughly. The book that he had been reading on the plane, the Gulag Archipelago by Aleksandr Solzhenitsyn, was seized upon eagerly. The customs official could not believe his eyes when he could not find the title on his list of banned books. It even had a red cover, for heaven's sake. Justin considered trying to explain that Solzhenitsyn was both a Soviet dissident and a Nobel Prize winner, but he was sure the effort would be wasted. In the end the official grudgingly returned the book convinced that somehow he had been tricked. To make matters worse, his suitcase had been lost. The British Airways agent assured him that his suitcase had been put on his flight in London. "Many of our passengers fly on to Durban or Cape Town for vacations. Perhaps your suitcase was put on one of those flights by mistake. It will be delivered to you when found."

But the best part about being home again was still to come. There Colleen was waiting to welcome him home. It was wonderful to see her again.

The missing suitcase was duly returned the next day, but all the documents for Lucky were missing.

NINE

On the Saturday after his return from New York, Justin and Colleen joined the group that went out to Soweto. He dreaded telling Lucky that the papers from his cousin Frank had been misplaced. He racked his brains with all his might, but could not come up with any explanation as to how or when he might have lost them. Did he leave them on the desk in his room at International House? Surely not. He had checked the entire room very carefully before leaving. What could have happened to them?

He had barely stepped out of his car when a distraught Thembi came running up to him. "Have you heard the news?"

"No. What news." Clearly whatever the news, it was not going to be good.

"Lucky is late."

"No! What happened?"

"He was hit by a car." That was all she could get out. Colleen put her arm around her while she cried on her shoulder. "I am so sorry. How terrible. Come inside and tell us all about it."

Once she had composed herself she continued with her story. "He was walking home on Thursday evening. While he was crossing the street a car came shooting around the corner and hit him. It did not even stop. Several bystanders tried to help him, but by the time an ambulance arrived he was already late."

"I am so sorry. Was the driver ever caught?"

"No. The police have not placed much priority on the case. No one got the licence plate number, and they doubt whether the driver will ever be caught."

They sat in silence for a while.

"There is one other thing. The family would like Justin to be one of the speakers at his funeral."

"Why me?"

"Lucky was always saying that you and he would build a new South Africa together. We think he would have wanted you to remember him at his funeral. You must come too Colleen."

"I would be honoured, but I have never done anything like this before. I am not even sure what the protocol is like at a funeral."

"I will be there to help you. The funeral will be next Saturday morning at the sports stadium across the road from here."

Justin and Colleen arrived at the venue for the funeral in plenty of time, but the stadium was already filling up. It was one of those clear but chilly Highveld mornings, and smoke from coal stoves still hung in the air. The mourners sat on the bleachers while the invited guests and speakers were seated on a temporary platform facing the bleachers. They were met in the parking lot by Thembi, who guided them to their seats on the platform.

"First come and meet Lucky's parents," and with that she made the introductions. His father spoke for the family, "It is good to meet you even if in these sad circumstances. Lucky always spoke highly of both of you. We will miss him terribly, but it is of some comfort that he has friends who will continue to fight for his vision of a new South Africa. Thank you, too, for agreeing to be one of the speakers."

"It is my pleasure, sir, and I am sorry for your loss. Lucky was a wonderful person. We will all miss him."

Thembi showed them to their seats and handed them a programme. Justin noted that he was the third speaker on the list. "I will sit right behind you and translate as some of the speeches will be in Sotho and some in Zulu."

Justin gazed out at the crowd sitting before him. It was uncharacteristically quiet and expectant. He could not help but notice that his and Colleen's were the only two white faces in the entire stadium. Many were staring at him with curiosity, but no hostility, written on their faces How would they react to his being one of the speakers? Was he intruding in a space where he had no right to be?

After about ten minutes a hearse drew up in front of the platform and six pall bearers lifted a coffin from it and gently laid it to rest on two supports. The coffin was draped in cloth of three colours, black, green, and yellow. Absolute silence had descended on the crowd. And then, as the pall bearers stepped aside, the crowd as one broke into a rendition of Nkosi Sikelel' iAfrika, their voices harmonising as the notes drifted up into the winter sky. It was a magic moment. Justin glanced over at Colleen, and saw that tears were streaming down her face and he held her hand tightly.

After the anthem, and while the master of ceremonies was making his way to the podium, Justin asked Thembi, "What is the meaning of those colours in the coffin?"

"Those are the colours of the African National Congress. Lucky was a dedicated member. Did you not know?"

"I had no idea. The ANC is banned after all." Before he could say any more, the master of ceremonies introduced the first speaker.

Although the speech was in Zulu, Thembi provided a summarized version for Justin and Colleen. Justin had never before in his life given a public speech, and he tried to pick up a many hints as possible from the first speaker. He noticed that it was not so much the words themselves that seemed to count, but how they were delivered. He realised quite quickly that in this setting a speech was not a one way affair, but rather an interaction, even a dialogue, between the speaker and the audience. At the end of almost every sentence the speaker would pause and wait for a reaction from the crowd. It was unlike anything Justin had ever witnessed before. After the first speech, which lasted some fifteen minutes, the master of ceremonies announced a hymn. Justin did his best to join in. Although the tune was familiar, the words were in Zulu. The second tribute was in Sotho, and again Thembi provided a translation. Another hymn was sung, and then it was Justin's turn to speak. After a glowing introduction he felt even less competent to speak. How would the crowd respond to a speech in English delivered by a white man? Would he be able to interact with them as had the previous speakers? In the end he took a deep breath and launched into his tribute. Fortunately he had not written out his speech as he now realised that in this situation to read a speech would not go down well. Instead he spoke from the heart and with emotion. He recounted how he had met Lucky, heard about his exploits which had led to is arrest and torture. He told how they had worked together in the mentorship programme. The more the crowd responded to his words, the more his rhetoric soared as he became one with them, all differences seemingly to have been dissolved. He even ended with two of the few Zulu words that he knew—hamba kahle Lucky my friend.

Five more tributes followed that of Justin, each being interspersed with hymns or anthems sung by various school choirs. The energy in the crowd increased as the event unfolded—a kind of energy that neither Justin nor Colleen had ever experienced. And yet they felt as one with the other mourners, their white skins somehow merged in the sea of humanity.

As the strains of the final hymn faded from the stadium, the coffin was loaded back into the hearse. Thembi tapped them on the shoulder and motioned for them to follow her. "We will now go to the home of Lucky's parents. It will be best if you drive there. I can come with you to show you the way."

By the time that they arrived the place was already crowded. A bucket of water was situated outside of the gate. "Give your hands a quick wash in the water. Watch how other are doing it. It is known as a ritual cleansing." Having duly washed their hands, they were shown to the rear of the house where a large markee had been erected, inside of which were tables groaning with large pots of food. To their embarrassment they were ushered to the top of the queue and urged to fill up their plates. However none of those waiting seemed to mind, and indeed called out their thanks to Justin as he made his way to the table of food.

Justin and Colleen filled their plates, and then looked for a place to eat. They were quickly offered two hastily vacated chairs, which they accepted rather than make a fuss. While they ate, a constant stream of people came over to talk to them and thank them for their participation. Quite a number of them Justin recognised as students from the Saturday mentorship programme, but others were total strangers. It was some time before they could finally take their leave and drive home.

Both Justin and Colleen were in a pensive mood on their way home. Neither attempted to start a conversation, and so they rode in silence—not awkward one, but rather the kind of mutually agreed upon silence between kindred spirits. Their experience at the funeral had given both of them much to think about. When they arrived at Colleen's flat she asked Justin to stay for a while. "There is so much I want to say—to process in my mind. I have never had an experience anything like what we had today."

Colleen brewed them each a cup of coffee. It was only when her cup was half empty that Colleen spoke for the first time. "I am not sure what I want to say. I am trying to sort out my feelings. Maybe if you simply allow me to ramble on you can help me express what I dimly feel."

"I can try. Perhaps we both need to sort out what today means for us. So go ahead."

"It seems that today was some kind of turning point for me. It did something for me that I am still trying to understand. It is not as if this was my first time in Soweto, or the first time that I have interacted with Africans. We do that every Saturday. But on those occasions we are bound more or less by our roles—teacher and student, giver and receiver. We are the white benefactors. But today it felt different. It was as if we were part of the community, and were accepted by the community as such. We were treated with such warmth. It seemed to me that perhaps for the first time we were not seen as white, but as fellow human beings bound together by grief. It suddenly struck me when you were talking about Lucky's vision for a new South Africa, that we were experiencing your words right at that very moment. I may not be making myself very clear. I am still trying to put in words what I feel."

"I think you have expressed your feelings very well. Now that you have said it, I realise that you have captured my feelings as well."

"I think we have experienced something that will be with us for ever. And it will not be easy. For example, I will never again be able to endure those conversations that always seem to crop up when whites get together and start talking about how 'they are no more than savages' or 'how uppity they are getting'. Will I now argue back, or simply walk out? I just don't know. And what about my father? His belief's and what I am now becoming are incompatible. Sooner or later there is bound to be some kind of confrontation—perhaps a permanent estrangement." They were both silent for a while, and then she continued. "I think of my mother. She does not share my father's views, but she does not stand up for her own. She would rather keep the peace. I guess it is so much easier that way. But if I were to be like that I would lose you. I would lose myself." There were now tears in Colleen's eyes. Justin put his arms around her, but had no words of comfort.

It had been a busy two weeks since Justin's return from the United States. He needed to deal with his report back to the Institute of Racial Reconciliation, his discussions with Professor Armstrong on his research findings, and to make up the backlog of his own studies. He also knew that they both needed a break and time to recover from the emotional draining of Lucky's funeral. And so he and Colleen decided to spend the day after the funeral in the Magaliesberg mountains. They invited Ian, Jenny, Neville and Julie to spend the day with them.

They left early in the morning just as the sun was rising. It was a clear but chilly late winter day, with wisps of fog still clinging to the ground. They all managed to squeeze into Ian's car, and it took them just over an hour to reach the farm on the southern slopes of the range, where they were able to park. The Magaliesberg range stretches east-west with a steep and forbidding southern approach and then a gently descending northern slope. The latter is etched with numerous mountain streams and pools. The six of them panted up the steep southern slope in the shadow of a buttress known as the Dome, a favourite with climbers. About three quarters of the way up stood a small, lone tree which they had dubbed on previous excursions as the 'Last Gasp Bush'. It meant that the summit was now within their reach, which once attained left them an easy downhill hike to the Dome Pools. As they descended, a mountain reedbuck broke cover and darted away, while baboons barked their warnings to one another.

By the time they reached the pools the sun as well into the sky, and the morning chill had given way to a pleasant mid-morning warmth. Hot from their hike, the first order of business was to strip off and dive into the cool but refreshing water in the pool. Once cooled off, which did not take very long, they stretched out on the rocks to warm themselves in the sun. It did not take long for the conversation to turn to Justin's trip to New York. Neville wanted to hear all the details of what it was like to fly in a 747. Unfortunately most of what Justin could remember entailed the various wines that he had sampled while in flight. Julie wanted to know all about New York City. Was it as hip as people claimed? What did they wear and what did they do? Ian and Jenny were keen to find out what he had done there and glean his impressions of life in a different country and culture. Justin did his best to answer all their questions. The most difficult one eventually surfaced. "Did you learn anything that might impact our efforts here?"

Justin carefully considered how best to answer. "I learned quite a lot about how maths and science have been taught since independence in both Nigeria and Kenya. I think that there are a number of ideas that we could introduce about the way to approach these subjects even within the constraints of the given syllabi."

"Such as?

"Well to teach for understanding and problem solving rather than simple rote memorisation—to encourage mathematical and scientific thinking."

"Yes, I see how we could incorporate some of that."

"I was also faced with a challenge by Lucky's cousin while we were having some drinks in a club in Harlem. In essence he asked what was the purpose of teaching maths and science without being conscious of a broader perspective. He probably phrased it better than this, but I hope you get the drift."

"You mean getting students to think about how their learning maths and science can contribute to the building of a more just society?" suggested Jenny.

"Yes exactly. You have hit the nail on the head."

"Do you have any ideas on how to do this?"

"Perhaps we could compile some kind anthology—a set of readings—which we could hand out during our Saturday sessions."

"That would be a good and doable start. Any idea what to include?"

"I did come across a couple of thought provoking manifestos. One was the 'I have a dream' speech by Martin Luther King. Do you know it?"

"I have heard about it but never actually seen the contents."

"We could introduce it with a challenge such as, 'This is King's dream for America. What is your dream? How do you see what you are learning might contribute to a better South Africa?'"

"That is a brilliant idea." Ian too was getting caught up in the idea. "Any other reading that you might have in mind?"

"I was given a copy of the Arusha Declaration. Ever heard to it?" The others all shook their heads. "It is the vision set out by Julius Nyerere for his newly independent country, Tanganyika. I found it to be a very inspiring document—very idealistic."

"I would like to see it."

"I will show you my copy."

"Thanks. Any other ideas for our anthology?"

"Some of the curriculum documents that I read laid out a clear statement of how mathematics and science should be harnessed into the broader goal of nation building. I think that they would make for suitable readings. I did copy some of these statements."

Jenny was now all for action. "As soon as we have time, by which I mean tomorrow, I think that we should start composing our anthology. We can hand out copies every Saturday. Let's call it 'An Anthology for Mathematics and Science Education'." And thus the idea was born while sitting in the sun on rocks next to the pool of sparking, clear water.

Julie brought them all back down to earth. "If we are going to have a braai, we had better go out and find some fire wood." Which is what they did. Whether it was the smell of meat being grilled or simple curiosity, Justin could never be sure, but for the next hour or so a troop of baboons watched them from the safety of the cliffs above the pools. It was good to be back in Africa.

On their way home to Ian and Jenny's flat, they stopped at a Greek café to buy a copy of the Sunday Times. While Jenny, Julie, and Colleen retired to the kitchen to fix up a late supper, Ian, Neville, and Justin poured through the newspaper, calling out the main news items to the girls in the kitchen. It was Ian that spotted it first. "It looks as if the trials are finally going to get under way."

"What trials are those?" asked Colleen.

"Almost the entire student leadership in the Cape Town area has been rounded up during the past few weeks. It has just been announced that they will be charged with treason and given a public trial."

"If the rumours are true, Richard Levine will be the star State witness," added Jenny.

"Remind me again, who is Richard."

"He is the president of the South African Student Association. He was detained some months ago and cracked under police torture."

"Here is another interesting item. A parliamentary commission has been formed to investigate the activities of the Institute for Racial

Reconciliation and other organisations. Its official name is 'The Commission of Inquiry into Certain Organisations', but it is referred to here as the Slabbert Commission after the man in charge—a Nat member of parliament."

Justin's head shot up from the comic page. "Read that again." Ian read the whole news item aloud.

"Do you think you will be involved?" asked Colleen. "After all you went to New York on behalf of the Institute."

"I doubt it. I am not even a member and know almost nothing about the Institute itself. It was by sheer coincidence that I even got involved with it."

"Well, let's hope you are right."

On the following Wednesday morning Justin, David, and Tony were in the kitchen of their house when a police vehicle drew up by the front gate. David departed hastily saying, "Tell them that I am not here," and disappeared out of the back door and through the gate into the back alley. Tony went to answer the front door, revealing two policemen in uniform.

"We are here for a Mister Justin Roberts. Is he at home?"

Tony did not know what to do, but was spared from making a decision when Justin joined him saying, "I am Justin Roberts. How can I help you?"

"We are here to serve you with a subpoena. You are required to appear before the Slabbert Commission on the date and time stipulated."

Justin took the envelop without saying anything more.

Later that day he walked over to the offices of the Institute for Racial Reconciliation in the hopes of finding Anton du Toit. He was immediately ushered into du Toit's office. "Good to see you Justin. What can I do for you?"

"This morning I received a subpoena requiring me to testify before the Slabbert Commission concerning the activities of the Institute."

"I am sorry to hear that. My staff and I all received a similar subpoena yesterday, but I cannot understand why you received one. You are not even a member."

"What should I do?"

"That is up to you. We here at the Institute are still debating whether or not to comply. But there is nothing you could do or say that would harm the Institute, so you may as well testify. If you ask me, serving you with a subpoena is plain harassment and nothing more. What day are you supposed to appear?"

Justin told him.

"That is the same day as us. If you would like to ride over to Pretoria with us you are welcome."

"Thanks. I will let you know if I decide to accept your offer."

That night Justin called a meeting with Ian, Jenny, and David. He explained about the meeting and his conversation with du Toit. "So I need to decide whether to testify or to refuse to comply with the subpoena. What do you guys think?"

Jenny was quick to reply. "I think that none of us should legitimise this farce by appearing before the Commission. They will not learn anything new from you if you do choose to appear. The only purpose of the subpoena is to harass and intimidate you."

"That was quick. What do you think, David, Ian?"

"Let's not be too hasty," responded David. "There may be pros and cons. I suspect that I might be served with a subpoena soon, and I shall refuse to testify. But then I know much more than you do Justin. It might be worth our while to learn more about the process. If I understand your subpoena, you are to appear to testify about the Institute of Racial Reconciliation, but not any of the other listed organisations. It seems odd that they have even bothered with you—no offence—since you are not a member. But it means you have nothing to give away as long as you only answer questions about the Institute."

"Ian?"

"I am with Jenny. I think that on principle we should refuse to comply. On the other hand, sometimes tactics are more important the principles. It would be useful to find out first hand how this Commission will be operating. I expect many of us are going to be dragged into this mess sooner or later. Once the Cape Town trials are over I imagine they will be coming for us next. The Institute is just the first of a number of organisations to be investigated. In the end it is your decision, but speaking for myself I will not think less of you whether you decide to testify or not."

The others nodded in agreement.

"Does any one know what the penalty might be for refusing to cooperate?"

"As far as I know that has not been spelled out at all. That is just one more thing that we need to find out."

"Any more thoughts?" None were forthcoming. "This is something with which I will need to wrestle during the coming weeks. On a brighter note," Justin continued, "our 'Anthology for Mathematics and Science Education' will be ready for distribution this Saturday.

During the following weeks, Justin agonised over the decision, to testify or not to testify. Although not spelled out explicitly most of his colleagues seemed to be against his testifying. He would be a seen as a hero if he refused. But was he prepared for the consequences, whatever they might be? If only he knew what the punishment was likely to entail. On the other hand his testimony could do no harm to the Institute, and he could gather some valuable insight as to how the Commission operated, which might benefit others. One day he would be dead set against testifying, but on the next he felt differently. He constantly vacillated between the two options.

The one bright spot during these weeks of indecision was the Saturday programme in Soweto. The Anthology had been handed out as planned, and had been met with surprise and interest. However by the second Saturday the demand for it far outstripped the number of copies that had been brought. Everyone it seemed wanted a copy, not only for themselves, but for friends and relatives. By the third Saturday the demand still outstripped the even augmented supply. It was satisfying to see an idea come to fruition so quickly.

Nevertheless, the question of whether to testify would not go away. Justin wished he could ask Anton du Toit whether or not he was going to testify, but that would be presumptuous. In the end he came up with a plan. He called the Institute and asked du Toit whether the offer of a lift to Pretoria was still open. When du Toit confirmed that he would be driving to Pretoria to testify, Justin took the plunge and said that he would appreciate a ride there as well. "Very well. Meet us at the Institute at eight in the morning."

When Justin arrived at the Institute on time, only Mr. du Toit was present. "Good to see you my boy. Let's get under way."

"What about the others?"

"We have decided that the rest of the staff will refuse to testify. However I wish to find out more about how this Commission operates. Also I have a plan on how to deal with them. Get in the car. Let's be off."

Before they could climb into the car, Colleen appeared. "I am coming with you."

"How did you know where to find me?"

"I have my sources. Anyway are you going to let me in or not? If not I will simply follow you in my car."

"You have a good woman there Justin. Let her in."

"But what will you do while we testify? The hearings are closed to the public."

"I will just browse around Pretoria while I wait for you."

The Old Synagogue, just off Church Square in Pretoria, was the venue for the Slabbert Commission hearings. It had most likely been selected for its symbolic value since the infamous treason trials had all taken place in this building. Justin and Anton du Toit were checked in at the front desk by a young female receptionist, and having been searched for weapons, were shown into the waiting room. Here they sat for about an hour although it did seem that they were the only ones due to testify that morning. Forcing them wait was probably just to make a point that they were at the mercy of the Commission. Finally the same receptionist appeared and asked du Toit to follow her. Not long afterwards she returned and ushered Justin into a separate room. So, Justin surmised, they were to be questioned separately.

The room was sparsely furnished. Seated behind the only table in the room were three men, all wearing almost identical suits and ties. There was not a hint of warmth in their wooden faces, as the one in the middle motioned Justin to sit down in the single chair facing them. Whether it was bravado or something else, but something made Justin decide not to play their game. Instead of sitting down immediately, he slowly turned through three hundred and sixty degrees, carefully taking note of his surroundings. There was a single door and nothing else in the wall behind the three men. The wall, as were all the others, was panelled with a dark wood from the floor to about three quarters of the way up to the ceiling. It was a high ceiling, at least four metres by Justin's estimate, and made of moulded iron. The wall to his right had one small, high window which enabled him to see the jacaranda tree outside, which was in full bloom. The wall behind him only contained the door through which he had come. The fourth wall was devoid of anything except the dark panelling. If there had once been pictures on the walls, they had been carefully removed. The room by design was as bleak as possible.

Once Justin had sat down, the man in the middle introduced himself. "My name is van Tonder and these other two gentlemen will be assisting me with our inquiries." Justin knew that van Tonder, who was also a member of parliament, was the deputy head of the Commission. That meant that du Toit was probably being questioned by Slabbert himself. It made sense since Justin was clearly the lesser of the two in terms of importance. He wondered who the other two men were since they had not been introduced. In the absence of names, he mentally dubbed them as Tweedledee and Tweedledum.

It was van Tonder who started the proceedings, "For the record, please state your name."

"Justin Roberts."

"Do you have any idea as to why you have been called to testify before this Commission?"

"None what so ever."

Van Tonder nodded at one of the other men to take over. It was Tweedledee. "Are you a member of the Institute for Racial Reconciliation?"

"No, I am not."

"Did you recently sign a contract in New York on behalf of the Institute?"

"Yes I did."

"Since you are not a member, why were you authorised to sign the contract?"

"I do not know. I found it strange too. You will have to ask Mr. du Toit that question."

"Did it occur to you to refuse to undertake the trip to New York and to sign the contract?"

"Not really. Who would throw away a chance at an all expenses paid trip to New York."

The other man, Tweedledum, took over. "Are you familiar with the contents of the contract?"

"Only in the broadest terms."

"Go on."

"I gather it was to provide funding for study opportunities for under-privileged students. That is about all I know. I did not read through the contract since Mr. du Toit was satisfied with its terms."

"Why then did Mr. du Toit not sign the contract himself?"

"I am sure you know the answer to that one. You prevented him from going to New York."

"How to you know Mr. du Toit?"

"I only know him as the head of the Institute for Racial Reconciliation."

"Did you bring anything back for him from New York—money or any kind of package?"

"No. Only a copy of the signed contract."

"What else did you do in New York?"

"I have told you what I did on behalf of the Institute. Whatever else I did is personal and has nothing to do with my mission for the Institute."

Tweedledee took over again. By now Justin was sure that the two men were from the security police and that van Tonder was just there to legitimise the proceedings. Tweedledee began to read some information about education in Kenya. Justin's blood turned cold as he suddenly realised that he was hearing an extract from the report that he had written based on Professor Sheffield's research. "Who gave you this information?" asked Tweedledee.

"The terms of reference under which this Commission operates is to investigate certain organisations, including the Institute for Racial Reconciliation. Since the information on Kenyan education that you have just read has nothing to do with the Institute, I find the question inappropriate and decline to answer."

There was a long shocked silence. Justin berated himself. Would it really have done any harm to answer the question? It was all public knowledge anyway. Any moment now, he was sure, the door behind the three men would open, a couple of policemen would enter and drag him back out of the room, and he would not be heard of again.

Eventually van Tonder broke the silence, "It is up to us to decide what questions are appropriate."

"That may be, but it is up to me to answer them, and I will only do so if I am convinced that they are appropriate."

There was another long silence. This time Justin was sure that he would be detained. In the end it was van Tonder who spoke again. "You misunderstand us. We are interested in what you have found out about education in Kenya and Nigeria. Perhaps there is something valuable that we might learn from you. We were just hoping for a friendly conversation."

"I appreciate your interest, and yes I think there is much we in South Africa could learn. But this is not the right occasion. I am here against my will to be interrogated about the activities of the Institute. I would happily have a friendly conversation with you about education, but in a different setting."

There was another long silence. This time you have really done it he thought. They tried to save face and you turned them down. Since I am likely in for the high jump, I may as well take the offensive. "I would like to know how you got a copy of my private research information."

It was Tweedledum who answered, "It was easy since the papers were in your suit case when you returned from New York. We also took the documents for your friend Lucky since we knew he would not be needing them. We hoped we might find a Playboy magazine so that we could charge you, but our luck was out. Perhaps you are a pansy boy—a moffie."

Justin realised that he was being baited, but it was all he could do to keep his temper. He stared at the floor as hard as he could, biting his tongue and saying nothing. The ball was now in van Tonder's court. Justin was sure he would not leave the building a free man.

Finally van Tonder said, "We have taken enough of your time, Mr. Roberts. You may go now. Thank you for your cooperation." Without a word, Justin rose to his feet and made his way to the door. His knees felt weak and he hoped he was not shaking. It was Tweedledee who made the parting shot, "I am sure we will be seeing more of you Mr. Roberts. You are not as clever as you think."

Justin wanted to put as much distance between himself and the Commission, so he walked to where they had parked the car. He hoped Anton du Toit would think to look for him there. However when he reached the car, du Toit and Colleen were already waiting for him. "Glad you found me my boy. Let's get going."

"How come they finished with you so quickly?"

"It was an interesting experience, but first some lunch is called for. I know of a nice, small restaurant over in Sunnyside, where we shall now retire. I will fill you in over lunch."

They drove out of the centre of town on Church Street. The jacaranda trees were in full bloom, painting the entire city a glorious purple. It was a sight for which Pretoria was justly famous, despite that fact that jacarandas were not indigenous. Once they had passed the majestic Union Buildings, they turned off and headed into the heart of Sunnyside and located the restaurant.

Although Justin was still too upset to be hungry, he did order a cheese sandwich. Colleen chose a salad, but Du Toit, on the other hand, ordered a full and sumptuous lunch. "So how did your session go my boy?"

"It was not too bad at the beginning. There was not much I could tell them about the Institute. But then it turned out that they had searched my suitcase and found my notes on Professor Sheffield's research and the documents to support Lucky's asylum application. That is when things began to go downhill. I refused to answer questions on the research notes and they admitted that they knew Lucky was dead. Do you think that they engineered the accident?"

"It is quite possible. I would not put it past them, but I guess that we will never know."

"And then because they did not find a Playboy in my suitcase they implied that I was a moffie."

Du Toit laughed, while Colleen leaned over, gave Justin a kiss and ruffled his hair saying, "You are my favourite moffie. If that is the worst that you will ever be called, count yourself lucky."

"I guess." Wanting to change the subject he asked, "So how did the session go with you?"

"Not badly at all. As I mentioned before, I came prepared. It was actually Slabbert, and not one of the police goons, who asked the first question. I then took out copies of the annual reports covering the past twenty years and said, 'The answer to your question can be found in the Annual Report number 24. Shall I read it to you, or would you rather read it yourself?' Slabbert said, 'Read it.' So I started reading it until Slabbert said that that was enough. I was able to answer each subsequent question with 'The answer to your question can be found in Annual Report number whatever. Shall I read it to you, or would you rather read it yourself?' The only difference was that I was not asked to read from any of the reports again. In other words, my boy, I was able to make complete fools of them. I only wish the press had been allowed to be present. They did not have one question to which they could not have found the answer by reading the past annual reports. And so they requested that I depart their nefarious gathering lest I spoil their day even more. Come my boy, you have hardly eaten anything. At least share a glass of wine with me." Justin did not refuse.

"So why have they gone to the trouble of setting up this Commission if they are not really looking for information?"

"The government's goal is to declare a number of organisations such as the Institute as falling into the 'affected' category. It means that their activities will be restricted in a number of ways. For example 'affected organisations' will not be allowed to receive funding from overseas sources. The Commission is simply a farcical attempt to legitimise what they have already decided to do.

"But tell us Colleen. What exciting adventures did you have in our nation's glorious capital?"

"I guess not nearly as exciting as yours. I spent most of the time on Church Square feeding the pigeons. It is really quite an attractive part of the city. I did stroll down Church Street as far as the Kruger House, but I did not go in. I could just imagine the old sod sitting on his stoep and meeting with his fellow boers."

"It was a pity you did not go in. There is much that you might have learned. But never mind. Let's hit the road for the rarefied atmosphere of Johannesburg."

Despite the lunch along with du Toit's levity and cheerful conversation, Justin was still agitated by the time they got home. The whole episode had left an ugly taste in his mouth. Clearly difficult times lay ahead and he despaired for the future. Was now not the time to get out and start a new life in another country? It was the perennial question that all Justin's friends seemed to ask of themselves from time to time, especially when the situation seemed hopeless. Would Colleen be willing to leave her family behind?

Meanwhile for her part Colleen was determined to lift his spirits. A bottle of good wine, which they polished off together, certainly helped. By the end to the evening he had dispelled any lingering notion that he might be a moffie.

TEN

JUSTIN'S TRIP TO PRETORIA HAD MADE HIM ANXIOUS IN ONE unexpected way. There was an old student adage that went 'unless you have started to swot for the finals before the jacarandas start to bloom, it is too late.' Granted the jacarandas bloom in Pretoria before Johannesburg, but even in the latter city the purple flowers had begun to show themselves—just not in the same profusion as in Pretoria, but there nevertheless. His studies of late had certainly taken a back seat to his other activities, and now it was time to refocus. However it was easier said than done. There were still the Saturday coaching sessions in Soweto which needed to be wrapped up. Also Ian and Jenny were pressing him to stand in the upcoming Student Council elections and he was finding it difficult to say no.

Dinner on the following weekend was slated as a celebration of success in the Student Council elections. It was also the final weekend before the exams got under way. Neville, Ian, Justin, and Jenny all gathered in Colleen and Julie's flat. Neville had sprung for four bottles of Nederburg, a wine which was normally priced beyond their reach. The party had just got under way when they were joined by Tony Forester and Patricia Case, who along with Justin were newly elected members of the Council. Neville was the new chair of the All Sports Council. It was inevitable that sooner or later the conversation would get around to the upcoming exams.

"So Justin, are you ready."

"Not in the least bit. What with my trip to New York and then the Slabbert Commission, my studies have suffered somewhat. I am going to have to do some heavy duty swotting."

"How did it go with the Commission?" asked Patricia. "I have not seen you since you had to appear." Justin filled in the details as succinctly as possible. It was not long before the conversation drifted back to the dreaded topic of the upcoming exams and how to cope with them. It seemed that no one in the room felt ready. It was Neville who provided the surprise of the evening. "I have decided not to swot for them."

"Why ever not?"

"Because they are a waste of time—a farce in fact."

"Pray continue. Tell us more."

"Well look at all of you. You are all trying to figure out what will be asked in the exams, and then preparing your answers."

"Of course. It is called spotting. We all do it."

"Exactly. So the exams do not measure what you know, but only how well you have guessed. You might have all kinds of knowledge, which will never be tapped by an exam. That is why I think that they are a waste of time."

"So what is your solution?"

"We need to develop some kind of helmet with electrodes that you fit onto your skull. You then turn on a switch and it simply measures everything that you know. Simple and painless. No more spotting and no more swotting. It credits you with everything you know."

"In your case there might be too much for it to measure when it comes to seducing girls."

"Come on. I am serious guys. Think of all the angst and pain it would relieve."

"So how far have you come along with your invention?"

"I know exactly what it needs to do. I just need someone to work out some of the technical details."

"I don't suppose that it will be ready in time for this year's exams."

"No. That is a problem."

"Aren't you repeating some first year subjects for the third time as it is?"

"Yes, but each year I learn some more. If all of that could be measured by my helmet I would be home, cut and dried. Top of the class."

There was not much more to be said about the upcoming exams after Neville's ambitious idea. It was a great idea—impractical, but a great idea nevertheless. The end of year exams were dreaded by students across the board. They started late in October and stretched out through most of November. This coming Friday, Justin mused, he would be joining hundreds of nervous students outside the examination hall waiting to be let in. The hall itself was vast and impersonal with rows of desks stretching from the front to the doors in the rear. Each row was dedicated to a different subject so as to prevent cheating by looking at ones neighbour's answers. During the three hour ordeal invigilators would stroll up and down the rows, making sure no one was attempting to cheat. Justin was grateful for his schedule. He had one exam in the first week—an easy one. All the others were in the final two weeks, giving him time to prepare for them.

While Justin was day dreaming about the upcoming exams, the conversation drifted on to plans for the summer holidays. Most were either going home or down to the coast. Neville was planning to work on his commercial licence. "I need to build up another two hundred plus hours, so I plan to fly around the country some. If any of you would like a ride some place just let me know. It will be my pleasure. Are you going to do any flying Justin? You seem to have ignored your lessons of late."

"Yes, flying along with everything else. But I should pick it up again. After the new year I will be spending some time down in the Lowveld with Colleen, but I will see what I can fit in."

As the party was breaking up, Jenny chipped in with a reminder. "Don't forget the Student Council meeting on Wednesday night. It will be a joint meeting between the outgoing and incoming council members, as well as the final one of the year.

Patricia, who along with Tony, had become the stalwarts of the Soweto project chimed in with one more reminder, "Our final session will be on this coming Saturday and we should all try to be there. It is supposed to be a secret, but the students whom we have been coaching are planning a surprise thank you party."

"That is so generous of them," said Justin. "I will certainly be there." Others nodded in agreement. "It will also be an opportunity to offload the last copies of the Anthology."

The final Student Council meeting of the year was mercifully short. Past meetings had often lasted well into the wee hours of the morning. However, with the end of the year in sight and exams already under way, there was not much in the way of new business. The main order of business was to appoint the new executive which was duly accomplished with no surprises. Jenny was to be President, Ian Vice-president, Tony Treasurer, and Justin Secretary.

The meeting was about to be adjourned when Jacob Tremor asked the chair for permission to make an announcement. "A month or so ago many of you opted to take the test to see how well you might stand up to torture. The results are available. If you would like to see your own results, simply let me know and I will set up an appointment for you."

"I still think the whole thing is a bunch a baloney," said Amy Adams. "There is no real science behind the test—zero validity if you ask me."

"Well no one did ask you since you did not take the test. Anyway, I though you scientists were supposed to be open to new ideas and not just to reject them without at least subjecting them to experimentation."

"Science moved on from alchemy and other forms of mumbo-jumbo a long time ago."

It was the kind of exchange which could rapidly deteriorate into something nasty and so Ian interrupted to defuse the situation. "Jacob may have a point. The news coming out of Cape Town is distressing. It seems Richard Levine has spilled his guts to the Special Branch. It seems that he has given them all the names of his collaborators, who are being rounded up as we speak. The rumour is that he broke after just a couple of weeks of solitary confinement. They did not even have to rough him up a little."

"So how would knowing how he would react to torture have helped him?" asked Tony.

"I don't really know. Perhaps there might be things that one could do to prepare oneself for something like solitary confinement."

"If nothing else, if he knew he would crack he might have thought twice about joining the African Resistance Movement," added Jenny. "If he had not joined, he would not have known the names of its members."

These were sobering issues. Justin decided that he would ask to see the results of his test.

The streets of Soweto, once so exotic to him, were now familiar territory. Dusty, shabby, but as always teeming with life. As he gazed through the window, Justin wondered when he would come this way again. He would miss the times he had spent here with the Soweto students. They were so keen to learn, and so appreciative of the slightest help offered to them. Perhaps next year the project could start up again.

"Now remember," Patricia said as they were disembarking from the bus, "the party is supposed to be a surprise. At least do your best to look surprised." The hall was festooned with coloured streamers and balloons. The Soweto students were standing in a group resembling an informal choir. As the tutors entered there was clapping, cheering, and ululating. Suddenly one of the students stepped forward, raised his fist, and shouted "Amandla". The rest of the group responded with "Ngawethu". This was repeated three times. Then soaring above the noise of the crowd came a solo female voice singing, "Nkosi Sikelel' iAfrika". She was immediately joined by the rest to the students singing the remainder of the anthem in a haunting harmony. Justin glanced at Colleen and saw that there were tears in her eyes. His own were also a little moist. It was one of the memories that he treasured most during his years in exile.

After the anthem, everyone took to their seats and a number of the Soweto students rose one at a time to express their thanks. Justin was struck by their colourful command of language and their mastery of rhetoric. Their praise was far in access of anything the tutors had done or earned. While his white friends may simply have said, 'Hey thanks you guys', the Soweto students were extravagant and effusive in their remarks. Tony then replied on behalf of the tutors with thanks for the event, but his speech was a pale imitation of what had gone before.

Speeches over, it was time for lunch. Near the hatch to the kitchen, a table had been covered with a white cloth and was laden with food—boerewors, pap, and a rich tomato/onion sauce. The tutors were served first and then everyone else tucked in. "A typical South African meal," commented Colleen to Justin. "My father would thoroughly enjoy it if he were here."

"The food, but perhaps not the company."

"Actually I think he would enjoy the company as well. He likes being with young people, and I think he would find it interesting to talk to some young Africans. He doesn't hate them you know although he does believe in separate development."

Before Justin could reply there was a disturbance at the front door. Two policemen in uniforms strode into the hall. Justin noticed that a number of students quietly slipped into the kitchen and then out the back door. They would be able to melt into the back streets of Soweto, an option not open to him. "That's funny," whispered Ian, "they are regular policemen, not Special Branch. I wonder what they want." It did not take long to find out.

"We are looking for three persons, Ian McCall, Jenny March, and Justin Roberts. You will come with us." There was not much that they could do other than comply. A deadly hush had fallen on the party. A police van was waiting outside the front door and they were bundled into the back where there was already a black policeman. Once they were under way, it was Jenny who asked the policeman with them, "Do you know where we are being taken?"

"To Orlando police station."

"This is very strange," muttered Ian. "The regular police normally only busy themselves with real crime."

"Who are the guys up front?"

"Sergeant Joubert and Constable Meiring." Their minder was clearly not comfortable speaking to them, and so the rest of the journey was made in silence. It was no more than a ten minute drive to the Orlando police station, where they were escorted inside. It was a typically soulless room furnished with government supplied desks and chairs. A portrait of the Minister of Justice scowled at them from the far wall.

"Do you recognize this book?" asked Joubert holding up a copy of the Anthology.

"Yes."

"Do you admit to giving it out to residents of Soweto?"

"Yes. Where did you get it if I may ask?"

"That is none of your business, but if you must know some of your students are my informants. Now to the matter at hand. I will be charging you with the possession and distribution of communist propaganda to Bantu persons." He took out the charge sheet and began writing. It took him a while and Justin was even tempted to offer help, but refrained. Once completed, he signed the charge and handed it to Meiring for his signature. "All we need now is the authorisation of the station commander. This will be a real feather in the cap of Orlando police station. We will show those Special Branch types that we are just as good as them." He disappeared into the commander's office, only to reappear a few minutes later. "Colonel Smit wants as all in his office."

The commander's office had a different feel about it. For a start there was no portrait of the Minister of Justice. Besides that an attempt had been made to give the room a personal touch. The official issue

chairs had been covered with a colourful material and there was a
vase with flowers on the desk. The walls were covered with personal
photos—mostly of Colonel Smit himself. There was one that made
Justin do a double take. It was of a group of senior officers in soldiers'
uniforms with General Jan Smuts in the centre. It was presumably
taken in North Africa during World War II. This might be an
interesting meeting mused Justin.

"So Sergeant, if we file charges, do you realise that there will have
to be a court case? That they will not be detained under the ninety
day law if charged?"

"Yes, I do realise that sir."

"As arresting officer, do you realise that you will be the main
witness for the prosecution."

"No problem sir. It should be an open and shut case. They have
already admitted their guilt."

Colonel Smit addressed Ian, "Have you admitted to the charge?"

"No sir. We admitted to distributing the booklet which is in front
of you."

"Which is clearly communist propaganda," chimed in Joubert.

"So you are confident that you could prove that in a court of law?"

"No doubt at all, sir."

"Are you sure that a defence lawyer would not be able to pick
holes in your case?"

"I am confident, sir."

"Okay sergeant, just to be sure, let me play the role of a defence
lawyer just to give you an idea of what it might be like. Are you ready?"

"Yes sir."

"Sergeant Joubert, in your testimony you claim that the booklet
in front of us contains communist propaganda. Am I correct?"

"Yes, your honour."

"Let us take the first section. It's title is 'I have a dream'. Who
wrote it?"

"A man called King."

"Where is he from?"

"Well I am not too sure. I would assume Russia, but then King is not a Russian sounding name. Maybe his real name is something else and he just uses the name King when he writes."

"I see. And could you point out the sections in the article which you consider to be communist propaganda?"

"That is easy sir, I mean your honour. It talks about black children and white children being equal, which would undermine our whole way of life. Clearly communist propaganda."

"I see. If I might inform you Sergeant, the author of the article is the Rev. Martin Luther King, who happens to be an American, and a man of the cloth. You might also like to know that the Declaration of Independence, which gave rise to the American Revolution, states clearly that 'All men are created equal'. So do you still believe that equality is a communist ideal?"

"Now you have me really confused sir," said Joubert, all pretence of play-acting gone. "Are you telling me that America has also turned communist. I never realised that."

"No you blithering idiot. I am telling you that equality is a universal ideal which has nothing to do with communism. I am telling you that there is not a single pro-communist word in the whole of this booklet. I am telling you that if I had allowed you to file this charge, not only would you have made a complete ass of yourself on the witness stand, but this station would have been the laughing stock of the whole country. Now get out and leave us alone for a while. I need to repair the damage that you have done."

"Thank you sir," said Jenny.

"Not at all. It is I who should be apologising to you. Please excuse Sergeant Joubert. He is a sad case. His father is in the Special Branch. He too would like to be there, but his application was turned down. The powers that be realised that he is simply too stupid. My guess is that he pulled a stunt like this hoping to gain favour with the Special Branch. He is too dim to realise that the Special Branch does not charge and try people—it simply picks them up and then they disappear or turn up dead."

It was the kind of admission none of them expected to hear from a policeman. No one knew what to say next. In the end Justin pointed at one of the photos on the wall and asked, "Are you there in the group with General Smuts?"

"Yes. I am second from the left. It was taken at El Alamein. A famous battle in North Africa which I guess none of you are old enough to remember. Yes, I am a Smuts man—one of the few left. Perhaps the only one left in the police force."

"With your views and background, it must be difficult for you to be with the police." A comment, or perhaps a question, from Jenny. Smit took it to be the latter. "I stay to keep my pension. I only have just a couple of years to go. I suspect that they sent me here to Orlando as a kind of punishment. But actually I quite enjoy it. They do not expect me to solve any crimes, just to fly the flag. I would like to think that I have done some good for the community. By the way, I do admire what your group has been doing for the students here in Soweto."

"You put on quite a star performance there as a defence lawyer," said Jenny with a smile. "Perhaps you should have gone into acting."

"No. I cannot see myself on the stage, but thanks for the compliment. I guess you would like to get back to your companions. I will have Meiring drive you there."

The devastating news coming out of Cape Town was a severe distraction to all for preparing for the exams. Not only had Richard Levine given up all the names of his associates in the African Resistance Movement, but he had agreed to testify against them in exchange for his own amnesty. Political trials were a rare event in the country at that point in time, and so there was a lot of public interest. However the trials were scheduled for the month of December, a time when most South Africans were enjoying the summer holidays. Nevertheless, Justin and his friends had their ears glued to the radio, despite its bias, during the times that that there was live coverage, and later read the newspaper accounts for what they considered a fairer coverage.

The prosecuting team handled their star witness carefully. For the most part they would describe an event and then ask Richard whether what had been said represented the correct state of affairs. For the most part, all he had to say was 'yes'. The defence tried in vain to shake his testimony, but all he would say was 'that is what happened' or 'what I said is true'. One after another his associates were either sentenced to life in prison or to death. He had been the best man at the wedding of one of those thus sentenced. It was only after the sentencing on the final day of the trial that he rose from his seat and shouted out, "I hate Apartheid. I hate what you have made me do. Long live a free South Africa."

It was never clear whether he thought that this final outburst might win him sympathy with his friends. But as he left the court house, every one of his former colleagues, those not betrayed, turned their backs on him. He tried to apologize, to explain, but everyone of them simply walked away. Nor did he find any sympathy from those with whom he had cooperated. One judge, uncharacteristically frank, commented, "To refer to him as a rat is hard on rats."

He walked back to his digs a lonely and broken figure. The next morning his decapitated body was found on the railway line between Rondebosch and Rosebank. He had left a note behind in his flat. '*The suddenness, speed and near-comprehensiveness of the disintegration of my will and ability to resist interrogation in solitary confinement took me totally by surprise. I just caved in. I have often wondered why we do not know how we will react. Is it because we do not know ourselves sufficiently well? Please forgive me. I cannot forgive myself.*'

The events in Cape Town caused shock waves to reverberate throughout the student community and the anti-apartheid movement in general. It was one thing to condemn the actions of Levine, but the uncomfortable questions remained, 'What would I have done in his situation? What would it take to break me?' Justin was not immune to these nagging questions. He could not rid his mind of Levine's final realisation, '*Is it because we do not know ourselves sufficiently well?*'

He decided to immediately take up Jacob's offer and to find out the results of the test on withstanding torture that he had taken.

The address given to Justin was different from where he had taken the original test. It was an office building in a seedy part of Hillbrow. He walked up the stairs to the third floor and knocked on the door marked Psychological Services.

"Come in." He entered a sparsely furnished room. It was not what he had been expecting. For a start, there was no receptionist—or even space for one. The sole furnishing consisted of a desk and two chairs. No filing cabinets, no book shelves with books, no diplomas on the walls, no carpet. It looked like a half dismantled stage set after the final performance.

"I am sorry. I appear to have come to the wrong room. I was expecting to meet Dr. van Aswegen."

"This is the right room. Dr. van Aswegen had to go to Cape Town on urgent business. I am his colleague, Dr. van Rooyen. We work closely together. You must be Justin Roberts. I was expecting you." With that he shook Justin's hand. "Good to meet you. Take a seat. You have come for the results of your test."

"Yes, that is why I am here. Are you sure I shouldn't wait for Dr. van Aswegen?"

"If you wish. But he and I work closely together and have both administered the test numerous times. I have your results right here. But if you would rather wait, that is fine with me. It might be several weeks before he gets back."

"No. If you are familiar with the test, let's go over my results."

"Very well then." He took a file out of his brief case and studied the contents for a moment.

"As you recall, the test is designed to identify areas where you might be susceptible to torture. What might work on you and what might not. We look for three main categories of weaknesses—physical or social isolation, physical pain, and concern for others.

"Taking the first of these categories: you registered very little distress at the suggestion of physical or social isolation. In other words, if you were to be put in solitary confinement you would most likely withstand it. A few people, and you appear to be one of them, are remarkably self-contained. You can live with yourself, and do not depend on interaction with others to remain sane. I must caution you however that the test is not one hundred percent reliable. If I were you I would test myself. Have you ever gone for a week without talking to another person, without even seeing another person? If not, it is something that you might want to try. It is good to know the boundaries of your defences."

Levine's words, '*Is it because we do not know ourselves sufficiently well?*' echoed in Justin's mind.

Van Rooyen continued, "Next, let's look at the second category. You registered little distress at the suggestion of physical pain—real old-fashioned torture in other words. It is an unusual finding, but it is possible that you could stand most kinds of pain that might be inflicted on you. Again I caution you about the reliability of the test, but there is not much else one can do about it. I certainly advise you against torturing yourself just to find out. The best you can do is to strengthen yourself mentally. Imagine yourself being tortured in different ways and then try to block out the imagined pain. Any questions?"

Justin shook his head. Is this really happening? Am I living in a country where one needs to figure out how to deal with torture? It all seemed somehow unreal.

"Finally, let's consider the third category. The images of another person being tortured did distress you. More than most other people in fact. It suggests that you have a high degree of empathy for others. It might be a laudable characteristic in general, but it would give a person trying to break you a means to do so. I will not ask you about your family, but if you are going to get yourself into a situation where you might be detained and pressured, first consider your relationships with those close to you. They could be your Achilles Heel."

Justin felt deflated and simply stared at the floor.

"Do you have any questions for me? Have I explained your results clearly enough?"

"No questions thank you. You were very clear. Do I get to keep the results?"

"Certainly. Here they are. Well good luck to you whatever you are up to."

Justin thanked him and left the room.

Time had stood still, all other activities suspended, during the period when the full impact of the exams took hold. Sitting at his desk swotting and sitting in the examination hall sweating out answers to questions had became the be all and end all of Justin's existence. He was not alone in this, with the exception of Neville. However after the last exam had been done and dusted, normal life resumed.

The first big event was Justin's twenty first birthday party. It was the age at which a small inheritance from his grandfather became available to him. It was only five thousand rand, but that kind of money can go a long way when you are a student. He and Colleen decided to spend some of it on a party for all their friends. It had not been an easy year, all things considered, but there was also much to celebrate. Ian and Jenny announced that they had decided to get married, and to do so as soon as possible. Neville had been chosen to play for the Transvaal B cricket team. Andy Kaplan had landed a role in PACT's production of 'Who's afraid of Virginia Woolf'. David Cohen had not yet been arrested. The celebration lasted through the night. As people began to drift off, Neville said, "I hear you are planning to get rid of that decrepit old Volksie of yours. What will you replace it with?"

"I have not decided on anything yet."

"Let me give you some advice. Buy a Peugeot 404."

"Why? What is special about it?"

"It is one tough vehicle. It has won the East African Car Rally for a number of years in a row. If you are planning to go bundu bashing in the Eastern Transvaal next month, it is just the car for you. It will go almost anywhere that Jeep can, and it looks much classier."

"Thanks for the tip. I will look around."

The lazy days of summer. The house mates and their friends made the most of it. They would be returning to their families for Christmas. Even Jenny would be spending the day with her estranged family, but only the day. But before then the group of friends had three glorious weeks of summer to enjoy with no lectures, no exams, no politics, no meetings, and no commitments of any kind. Jenny organised a trip for them all to the amphitheatre of the Drakensberg mountains. They ascended by the chain ladder and spent a couple of nights in the derelict mountain club hut high above the Tugela falls. Here they saw a different version of Jenny. On campus she was the fearless and resolute leader of the student protests. She could be ruthless and uncompromising, but here in the magnificent surroundings of the Berg, a different version of her emerged. She cooked dinners for them all, led them in sing-songs (protest songs were not excluded), and told funny stories of her childhood. She and Ian discussed their upcoming wedding and what they hoped for in their married life together. Justin had always been in awe of Jenny, perhaps a little afraid. He admired her, but found it hard to relate to her drive, her passion, and her dedication. But here an entirely different Jenny was on display—a vivacious and fun-loving girl. After two relaxing days, they were all sorry to leave the lofty mountain heights and return to the city.

Ian organised a couple trips to the Magaliesberg. Here too they enjoyed joking around and sharing childhood memories as they splashed around in the crystal clear pools or sunned themselves in the harsh African sun.

They all turned out at the Wanderers to watch Neville play his first match for the Transvaal B cricket team in a match against Natal B. In the first innings he was out for a duck. However in the second innings he scored a breezy ninety seven. He might even had reached his century had he not tried to reach it with a six.

Neville used his seemingly endless contacts to find a car for Justin. It was a low mileage, apple green Peugeot 404. Justin fell in love with it at first sight. He was sorry to lose his trusty old Volksie. It had done him well, but there was not much life left in it. He looked forward to driving it down to the family farm for Christmas and then on to the Eastern Transvaal.

When he was not having fun with the gang, or spending time alone with Colleen, Justin worked on his flying lessons. He achieved his first major mile stone—his first solo flight. It was confined to the airport's circuit, but nevertheless it was a thrilling moment. Flying was really getting to be a joy. He loved maps, plotting routes on them, and learning how to compensate for the winds at different altitudes. He was beginning to feel like a real pilot. Another reason he enjoyed flying was that it demanded an absolute concentration and his full attention. Everyday concerns had to be put aside as he handled the controls of the plane.

Besides his own lessons, he accompanied Neville on a number of flights. Neville was doing his best to clock up enough hours to become a commercial pilot. They flew together to all corners of the Transvaal, and even down to Natal on occasions. Neville let him handle the controls on many of these flights, and even to plot their routes. Since Neville was not an instructor, none of this counted towards Justin's progress, but the experience was nevertheless invaluable.

The flight Justin enjoyed the most was the one along the edge of the Drakensberg. The first land mark that came into sight was the Tugela Falls. He could even pick out the mountain club hut where they had stayed during the previous week. Neville did a right hand three sixty degree turn above the falls. Justin, sitting in the right hand seat had a perfect view of the magnificent vista. It seemed another group of hikers was using the hut, who waved at them as the aircraft swept by. It was breathtaking. One moment they were about five hundred feet above the ground, and then, as they crossed the escarpment edge, the ground dropped away as if swallowed by a black hole.

"I would like to take a look," said Neville. "Do you think you can manage a three sixty degree left turn?"

"Sure thing."

"Okay. Make sure that you don't lose any altitude and keep the turn at thirty degrees with the left wing tip pointed at the hut."

As Justin eased the plane into the left turn, Neville gazed out at the landscape below, but with a surreptitious glance at the instruments every couple of seconds, just to make sure Justin was maintaining bank angle and altitude. Suddenly he burst out, "Holy, Moly. LOOK! No don't look, just keep flying the plane. There are a couple of topless babes down there by the stream."

Tempted as he was, Justin did not try to sneak a peek, and completed the turn as instructed, but did gain two hundred feet. "Not bad. Better to gain rather than lose altitude when you are close to the ground." They continued the flight along the edge of the escarpment following the curve of the amphitheatre. They cleared Cathedral Peak and passed over Didima. Next came Giants Castle and Bannerman pass. A year earlier Neville, Ian, Tony and Justin had climbed this pass and spent the night in caves at the top. Finally, as Sani Pass came into view, Neville swung the plane towards the east and headed for Howick, where they landed and stretched their legs before heading home. The flight along the escarpment, the Barrier of Spears in Zulu, remained a memorable experience for Justin.

Just before leaving for Christmas he flew his first cross-county flight with his instructor. It was a fairly easy three-legged route; Grand Central to Swartruggens to Pilanesberg and back to Grand Central. He plotted the route on his map and selected check-points along the way. Before leaving, he factored in the wind and estimated his arrival at each point. As it turned out, he crossed each check-point within less than thirty seconds of his estimated time. His instructor, who was not given to compliments, was very pleased with the flight. One reason that he was able to perform so well on his first cross-country flight was the experience of flying with Neville.

It was the day before he was due to leave for home that a couple of policemen arrived at the house. "We are looking for Mr. Justin Roberts." Justin, who had answered the door replied, "You have found him."

"We have a warrant to confiscate your passport. You will hand it over to us immediately."

"What is the reason for taking away my passport?"

"The minister does not have to give any reason. Just hand it over."

As soon as they had left, Justin rushed around to Ian and Jenny's flat. They too had had their passports confiscated. "What is going on here? Why have they done this?"

"It could be for any number of reasons," replied Ian. "But given that it is just the three of us, I suspect that this might be the revenge of Sergeant Joubert. He was really humiliated when he tried to arrest and charge us with being Communists. And his father is in the Special Branch."

"Yes, I suspect you may be right."

"Or maybe it is the Special Branch's own reaction to the Anthology."

ELEVEN

As was the case with most of the group of friends, Justin spent Christmas with his family—in his case on the family farm near Standerton. Traditionally it was a large family affair. Both of his parents came from large families, and so every Christmas hordes of uncles, aunts, and assorted cousins descended on the family farm. The celebrations were always held, weather permitting, around the swimming pool with its deck chairs, beach umbrellas, and of course braai facilities. One of his cousins, he was not sure which, had brought along an English boyfriend whose pasty skin contrasted sharply with all the other sun-bronzed bodies. The boyfriend could not get over the idea that Christmas could be celebrated around a pool, wearing bathing suits, rather than bundled up against the cold. He insisted on having his photo taken as he dived into the pool, so as to have something to boast about when he returned home.

Justin did his best to participate in the festivities. He was acutely aware of the surreptitious looks he received from time to time when the person concerned thought that he was not looking. No one in the family had ever been arrested, interrogated by the police, or had their passport confiscated. Everyone was polite enough to completely avoid any mention of the 'dishonour' Justin was bringing to the family's good name, but that only served to heighten Justin's feeling of isolation and estrangement. Controversial topics were studiously avoided, and conversation was mostly confined to family gossip and sports, neither of which held any interest for Justin. He found himself wishing that someone would consider ribbing him with a comment such as 'have you been fitted for your prison outfit yet?' Any such lame remark would have been better than the conspiracy of silence.

He wondered how Jenny Marsh was coping. She had agreed to spend Christmas eve and day with her family—the first time since leaving home after the confrontation with her father. But mostly he thought about Colleen, and schemed how soon he could take his leave from this uncomfortable gathering of the clan, and head for Sabie. His thoughts were also occupied by his decision to find out what his reaction might be to a self-enforced period of solitary confinement— although in truth it would be more solitary than confined.

Justin finally took his leave from the family gathering on the day after New Year. Cousin Heather had somehow persuaded him, against his better judgement, to stay on for the annual New Year's Eve dance at the local country club. He had been hesitant at first with last year's dance still fresh in his mind. It had been one of those years when the rains had failed and the crops were drying up. Even before the dance everyone was on edge and short tempered, and the result had been an almighty free-for-all brawl at the dance itself. Weeks of frustration were vented on each other with vengeance. This year the rains had been good and the dance went off without a hitch.

His spirits soared as he exited the rough farm track and accelerated along the open road that eventually would take him to Sabie. He had the road mostly to himself. Perhaps most of the other would be drivers were still sleeping off the effects of the New Year celebrations. His new car was a dream to drive, smooth and quiet. However his pleasure was tinged with nostalgia for his faithful old VW bug. He and Colleen had watched together as its new owner drove it away, never to be seen again. Because of its bright yellow colour, Colleen had christened it Buttercup, a name which stuck. She had accurately described it as both temperamental and cheerful. He would miss it.

Meanwhile the rolling hills of the Eastern Transvaal Highveld slipped by mile after mile. This was the heart of the so-called maize triangle. The landscape from one horizon to the other was filled with acres of green mealies, tall and healthy from the recent good rains, and with avenues of blue gum trees. It was the country that he knew so well.

Presently he passed through the town of Bethal, so typical of those in this area. So similar to the town where he had first gone to school and where his family did business. The main street was lined with shops. Those owned and run by Indians were on the edge of town, and the bigger chain stores, such as OK Bazaars, near the centre. Some of the Indian stores were already closed for ever. Justin recalled that the new government policy was to deny them the right to trade in the town itself, and that they were being forced to move. He remembered as a four-year old shopping in the OK Bazaars with his mother. It was a large, impersonal, and intimidating place for a four-year old. But then they started shopping at one of the Indian stores in town, Abdullah's Market. The reason, his mother explained to his father, was that the prices there were more reasonable and the quality just as good. It was the best she could manage with their shrinking budget. For Justin the change was a boon. Abdullah himself always greeted them at the door as if they were his most valuable customers, and then slipped Justin a roll of his favourite wine gums when his mother was not looking. But times were hard. When his family had first started farming in this area they had begun from scratch, and the drought made things even worse. At night Justin would hear his father and mother discussing what to do. Once their savings ran out there seemed to be no option but to abandon the farm and try to find work in the city. However in the end it was Abdullah who had extended them credit, which allowed them to buy food and clothes, thus saving them from starvation and having to abandon the farm. Perhaps up to half of the farmers in this district during the long drought years had been helped in this way by the Indian shop owners. Now the people that they had helped in the past were driving them out of town.

The central square of the town was dominated by the imposing Dutch Reformed church on the one side and the Post Office on the other. The far end of town was dominated by large storage silos and a handful of farm supply stores and farm equipment dealerships. And so back to the open road.

The next major town was Middelburg, where Justin joined the Pretoria–Delagoa Bay highway. Belfast came and went as did Machadodorp—the road did not pass through either of these towns. Next came Waterval Boven where the road dropped from the Highveld down to the Lowveld. Justin noticed some rock climbers on the cliff near the waterfall and decided to stop and watch them while he ate the lunch that his mother had packed for him. He had once considered taking up rock climbing and had even made one ascent. It was on the Dome of the Magaliesburg mountains, but on that same day a friend of his had fallen to his death. He never climbed again. As he ate his lunch, two figures carefully made their way up the cliff face and eventually reached the top. A goods train slowly ground its way up the incline from Waterval Onder to Waterval Boven.

As he resumed his journey, the maize fields of the Highveld gave way to the orange, banana, and mango orchids of the Lowveld. Between these cultivated areas lay a profusion of lush tropical vegetation, dominated by stately acacia trees. The gardens of plots along the highway sported colourful arrays of tropical flowers such as bougainvillea and poinsettia. It was a different world altogether.

Once he turned off the highway to make his way to Sabie, anxieties began to crowd his mind. How would he be received in the Jansen home? How much about this arrest and testimony before the Slabbert Commission had they heard? And then there was Colleen. He might have mentioned his decision to test his ability to withstand solitary confinement, but he had not told her when and where. How would she react to his plans? There was only one way to find the answers to all these questions, and that was to keep going.

The next morning Colleen and Justin set off early to spend some time together and to explore the surrounding countryside. They drove in silence for a while, neither of them quite sure where to begin the conversation. In the end it was Colleen who broke the silence, "Why were you so keen to get out of our house?"

"I wanted to spend to spend some time with you. It has been weeks since we were last together."

"I missed you too. But there is more to it than just that, is there not?"

"Yes I suppose there is. What do your folks think about our relationship? Have they said anything to you about us?"

"Did they say anything last night to you that made you feel unwelcome?"

"No. Not at all. They could not have been more welcoming and friendly. Which, perversely, is why I am worried. Not a word was said about my being arrested or having my passport confiscated or called to testify before the Slabbert Commission. The silence was deafening. Do they even know?"

"Oh yes! They know all about it. My dad grilled me when I first came home. He seemed to know more about you than I do."

"That sounds ominous. Where does he get his information?"

"You know for some time I have suspected that he is a member of the Broederbond. That would give him access to all kinds of information. Of course, if he is a member he would have to keep it a secret, even from his own family."

"I never thought of that."

They drove on in silence for a while, drinking in the sights of the forest and the mountains. After a while Colleen asked, "So where all would you like to go today?"

"I hoped you would show me some of the more out of the way places—off the beaten track so to speak."

"Of course. There some wonderful places that almost no one knows about. They may not be as spectacular as some of the more famous sites, but I like them better. I can be almost sure that no one else will be there at the same time."

"These sound like just the kind of places that I have in mind."

"For what?"

It was now or never. "Do you remember the test that I took to see if I could withstand solitary confinement?"

"Yes. What about it?"

"I think that I might have mentioned my plan to actually see what it would be like to be totally isolated for about a week. Not to speak to or even see another person."

"Well you did not mention it to me. Tell me more about this plan of yours."

"I am thinking of spending at least a week by myself in some of the more remote places around here. I want to see how I will react to complete isolation. I was thinking of setting out tomorrow or perhaps the next day."

A frosty silence ensued. "Look I will not try to talk you out of your plan, although to be honest I do not understand what you hope to achieve. But your timing is off. How do you think I could explain to my folks that my boyfriend expects to be detained and put in solitary confinement? Do you really think that that will endear you to them? No. Rather spend some time here together as I assumed was your intention. Then if you must, go off and be by yourself."

"I am sorry to have sprung this on you. But you are right. Let's enjoy the next couple of weeks together. I will do my solitary bit next, and after that it will be time to go back and get ready for the new term."

"Right. For a start let me show you some of my favourite, secret places."

For the next couple of hours they explored some of the hidden gems in the forests that surround Sabie and Pilgrims Rest. For the most part they drove along seldom used tracks that more often than not paralleled small, clear streams. When these tracks were no longer drivable, they would get out and walk. Often, if they followed the stream long enough they would come to a small waterfall. Their progress was tracked from time to time by troops of vervet monkeys, chattering with excitement and calling to one another, warning of these strange intruders. At one of the waterfalls they sat down to rest for a while, watching various birds come and go. There was, it seemed, a resident malachite kingfisher that appeared to be content simply to sit on a branch and study the water in the pool. Perhaps the fish were all in hiding. An outraged grey lourie screeched at them to 'go away'. Colourful crested barbets were plentiful as they searched out the wild fruits of the area. Now and again the plaintive cry, a series of descending notes, of an emerald spotted wood dove could be heard. These were the sights and sounds of Africa.

As the day grew warmer, Colleen had a suggestion. "Do you remember that last time I showed you around I mentioned my favourite swimming pool? We did not have time to go to it then. Let's go there now. We can have lunch there and cool off in the pool."

"Great idea. Show me the way."

It took them about a half hour's drive to get to their destination. The forest had given away to a more open grassland, studded by the occasional bush. "Turn down that track just ahead on the left. It ends in about one hundred metres. We can leave your car there. We will have to walk the rest to the way."

Justin complied with Colleen's instructions and minutes later they were walking through the veld with their lunch in a day pack. "Where are we going? I cannot see any sign of a pool."

"The upper reaches of the Treur River lie in a valley just beyond that koppie. It will take us less that twenty minutes to get there. The pool is a hidden gem. As you can see there is no path to it, and only a few of us locals know about it."

Sure enough, twenty minutes later Justin stood on a rocky outcrop on the edge of a small cliff overlooking the river below. The crystal clear water of the river threaded its way downwards from one rock pool to the next, some not much bigger than a bathtub, while others were larger and deeper than the average home swimming pool. Colleen pointed to the largest one. "That is my special pool. We can make our way down to it by means of a cleft in this cliff. Follow me."

The scramble down to the pool was not too difficult. There were a couple of rock faces where toe- and hand-holds had to be found, but these were not challenging. Before long they were on the rocks by the side of the pool. By now the sun was at its zenith, and both of them were hot and sweaty.

"Let's cool off in the pool before eating lunch," suggested Colleen.

"I did not think to bring my swimming costume." Even before he had finished the sentence, he knew how ridiculous it sounded. He knew exactly what Colleen's response would be. Had he said it out of guilt? All the way to the pool he had had images of Colleen's fabulous naked body diving into the water. Now that it was about to happen, was he trying to cover up his thoughts?

"Don't be silly. Why would we need costumes? Here we are children of nature." With that, Colleen quickly stripped off her clothes and dived into the pool. "Hurry up and join me. If you are that shy you can leave on your underpants." Justin pulled a face at her in defiance, stripped off and joined her in the pool. It was a lot colder than he had expected. It took his breath away. They frolicked for a while, splashing one another. But the cold quickly forced them from the water and they found relief by stretching out on the warm rocks in the hot sun.

It did not take too long before they were hot again, and seeking shelter in some shade, tucked into their lunch. Perhaps it was just the surroundings, and of course the company of a gorgeous water nymph, but to Justin a boerewors roll had never tasted better, especially when washed down with a cold beer. After lunch, they repeated the cycle of swimming and then warming themselves in the sun. As Colleen was chasing droplets of water down Justin's back, she spoke. "You know what I would like to do next?"

"No. Tell me."

"I would like to go and spend time on my special rock. The one I took you to last time. The one where we kissed for the first time."

"I remember that rock well, and especially the time that we spent there together. You told me that it is the place where you go to celebrate, or sometimes to grieve."

"Yes. And also to think things through."

"If that is where you would like to go, of course let's do it."

With that they got dressed and set off for the rim of the Blyde River Canyon.

Justin immediately recognised the rock when they were about half a kilometre from it. The rock was indelibly stamped in his mind. The event that had occurred there some six months ago had irrevocably changed his life.

Once they reached the rock they made themselves comfortable, holding hands and gazing down at the river below. It was completely quiet, except for the distant roar of the river as it rushed over the several cataracts. Whatever it was that had brought Colleen here again remained unspoken, perhaps even unthought. Finally, to break the silence, Justin asked, "Is it the Treur or the Blyde river that we see below?" even although he knew the answer. He just felt that he had to break the silence. They had come here for a purpose.

"It is both."

Colleen was still not ready to voice that which had brought them here, and so they continued to sit in silence. As the sun began to sink in the West, they watched the shadow creep up the far wall of the canyon. Justin eventually tried again. "When did you first come here?"

This time Colleen did answer, but only after a long silence. "It was the time that our dog died. I was about ten years old at the time. He was a little terrier mix called Scruffy. My mother brought me here and we buried him somewhere not too far away, but I could never find the exact spot again. After we had buried him we came and sat on this rock. I must have cried for hours while my mother simply held me tight. Later in life, after I have gotten my driver's licence, I would come here alone whenever I felt the need."

Again they sat in silence.

"So why have we come here this time?"

"First I need you to hold me tight." Justin leaned back against the rock while Colleen nestled in between his legs, her back against his chest, and with his arms around her waist.

"I am not trying to talk you out of spending a week on your own. In fact I really think that you ought to go ahead with your plan. But do you really believe that you might be detained and tortured or put in solitary confinement? If so, will it come between us?"

"Nothing can come between us. But to the first part of your question, a year ago I would not have believed that it could happen in this country, or to me for that matter. But now I am not so sure, especially after what I have already experienced."

"Are you really sure that the Special Branch are doing these things? I have asked my father and he assures me that the Special Branch would never stoop to torture. He knows many of the top brass, and he assures me that they are all upright Christians—most are even elders in their respective churches. He is positive that these rumours of detainees being killed or tortured are nothing more than anti-government propaganda. He maintains that we are in a do-or-die struggle against godless communism."

"I would like to believe your father, I really would. But I know of many people who have been tortured, or rather David does. We do know what happened to Lerato's brother. Then think of all the people who have died in detention. The police usually say that they slipped while taking a shower, but really how credible is that? Also do you remember the Timur case?"

"Is he the guy who jumped out of the seventh floor window?"

"Yes. Except there is a witness who saw him being pushed out. She was a secretary in an office across the street."

"So why did she not come forward?"

"Seems she was too scared. And now she has disappeared—fled the country most likely. Or worse."

"How do you know all this?"

"David was there when she divulged what she had seen. Then the next day she was gone. I hope she did flee rather than being picked up by the Special Branch."

"How come does David seem to know so much? And where is he? I have not seen him around for some time."

"He does seem to move in clandestine circles. With him I have always felt it best not to ask too many questions. He seems to come and go quite a lot, but of late I have not seen much of him either. I have no idea where he is. He is often gone for a couple of weeks at a time, and then one morning there he is having breakfast with the rest of us. But whatever he is up to, I do believe that he is a man of integrity. I do believe he is truthful, and that he wants to see justice and equality for all in this country."

"I guess what really worries me is where you might be headed. Will you eventually be like David—disappear for weeks on end and get up to God knows what? Will you end up on the run from the police and have to flee the country? Or even worse, be tortured or killed"

"That is not my intention at all. But on the other hand can I—can any of us—close our eyes to the injustices in this country? Do you remember that editorial that I wrote based on the quotation 'The only place for a just man in an unjust society is in jail'. I still think about it often—it somehow haunts me. The last thing that I want is to end up in jail, but on the other hand I cannot ignore what is going on around me, around us. I do not see myself as a martyr, so perhaps I just need to keep doing enough to ease my conscience, but at the same time not enough to put myself in the sights of the Branch. At heart I am probably a coward. This is probably a poor answer to your question, but I don't know what else to say."

"You have said plenty. That editorial that you wrote—I remember it well. Do you think it only applies to you or to me as well? Should I be preparing myself for a possible detention?"

"No, I do not want you involving yourself."

"Why? Because I am a girl? Do you think only guys should be concerned about justice?"

"You have me there. In some ways I guess I am a chauvinist. I could not bear to see you hurt in any way. I do care about you deeply."

"And I you." After a pause she added, "I think we have talked about this enough, for one day at any rate. What I need now is for you to kiss me long and hard. After that we had better make our way back home."

They did not talk much on the way home, each wrapped up contemplating on what had been spoken on the rock. Colleen did have one final request. "Let's enjoy the next weeks to the full and not revisit what we talked about today."

The following weeks were probably the happiest of Justin's life, idyllic hours spent with Colleen. During his years in exile he would often try to replay them, day by day and hour by hour. As time went by, some of the details, some of the days themselves, would merge and reappear in different guises, but he could always remember the most salient features. The second day was more or less a repeat of the first, except the first thing that he did was to buy a map of the area at the local book store. Colleen pencilled in the various out-of-the-way places to which she had taken him. Unlike the first day, they spent much longer at her favourite pool, making love as the sun warmed their bodies. Unlike the first day, they did not return to her special rock.

They spent at least two, or was it three, of the days in the Kruger Park. They would rise early in the morning so as to arrive at the Park at the moment the gate was opened for day visitors. It enabled them to enjoy the sunrise in the Park—the time when the nocturnal animals retired for the day, while the others stirred themselves for what the new day was about to offer. Unlike many of the visitors to the Park, Colleen did not occupy the days in search of the big five. She much preferred to pick one spot and spend hours observing and absorbing the subtle changes from one minute to the next. It might be the arrival and then departure of a frankolin, or the arduous progress of a dung beetle. She often chose spots that were not popular with the average visitor—the much visited hides by a water hole. She usually favoured a small lay-by along the Sabie River road, or by a minor water hole. As she explained to Justin, "I come here for the total experience, and not just to see a particular animal such as a lion or elephant. I need to feel one with the whole bushveld in all its variety and glory. To me, observing a dung beetle is just as thrilling as seeing a lion or a leopard." Occasionally a car would pull up along side them with the inevitable question, "What do you see?" When Colleen pointed to a bird or a beetle, the car would quickly depart.

It was after several hours of quietly sitting in one spot, observing the occasional animal coming and going that Colleen broke the silence. "I know we agreed not to talk about this again during these days, but I keep turning over a question in my mind. Could I leave this all behind? Could you leave this all behind?"

"What do you mean?"

"If the option were to stay and be detained and tortured, or to leave the country, what would you chose?" She could not have put it more bluntly. It was a question which probably occupied the minds of many of their acquaintances, but which most avoided answering.

"I have always assumed that I would never leave, and then proceed to shut out any thoughts of the consequences. It has always been easier not to answer your question."

Colleen persisted. "What if the choice were between my being tortured and us leaving the country. What would you choose then?"

"In that situation I would see no option but to leave together. But what about you? Could you really leave your family? You all seem so close. And could you really leave this bushveld paradise around us for ever?" It was the first time, Justin reflected later, that there was an acknowledgement that their future lives were entwined. It was a time when they still had dreams and hope, not just memories and regrets.

"Touché. To be honest, I cannot see myself ever leaving. Perhaps I will just have to convince myself that the things you fear will never come about." And so the questions raised by both of them continued to hover in the air not fully resolved, but not totally ignored either. Perhaps, Justin thought, it was best that way, for now at any rate. Enjoy this time together and let the future take care of itself, come what may.

Other vivid memories of that week included time spent with Colleen's family, her father in particular. One evening after dinner, while sitting around outside Mr. Jansen suddenly asked, "Did Colleen tell you about her Christmas present?"

"No. So what did you get that is special?"

"Dad, you tell him. You can probably explain it better than I can."

"We, her mother and I, gave her a brand new recording of the Ring of the Nibelungen. From what I have read, it is now considered to be the definitive recording. Birgit Nilsson sings the role of Brunnhilde, and it is conducted by Sir Georg Solti. Have you heard of Birgit Nilsson?

"No sir. I am afraid not. Is she from a 1950s band?"

Mr. Jansen shock his head sadly. "Well, have you heard of the Ring of the Nibelungen?"

"Again I must confess my ignorance."

"The Ring, as it is often called, is surely one of the greatest artistic achievements of all time. Its creator, Richard Wagner, dubbed it a musical drama, but it can just as well be called an opera. It is the story of gods, giants, and dwarfs, all based on Norse mythology. It deals with universal themes such as love, greed, lust for power, and betrayal. The story unfolds during four individual operas, although together they make up a whole. If performed back to back, the whole production would run to some fifteen hours. It is a mammoth undertaking to stage, one which is only tackled by a few of the great opera houses of the world. Birgit Nilsson is considered the greatest soprano of our time."

"It does seem a bit long. Doesn't the audience get rather tired?"

"It is never staged on a single day. Usually the four operas are spread out over the course of a week. I will be teaching Colleen during the coming days how to appreciate its genius. Perhaps she will share some of what she learns with you."

"I will look forward to that. You know while I was in New York I was taken to see an opera and I did enjoy it very much. So anything that Colleen can teach me will be much appreciated."

"You saw an opera in New York! At the Metropolitan Opera House! It is one of the most famous in the world. What a privilege!

How I envy you." Justin realised that his shares had just increased several fold. He had never seen Mr. Jansen so animated.

There was another memory that remained burned in Justin's mind. It was the last afternoon of Justin's final day with Colleen's family, when Mr Jansen said, "Come with me to the club for a quick beer. It would be good for us to get to know one another better." Justin's heart sank. There was no way he could refuse. It was an order not a request.

As it turned out, it was quite a pleasant encounter. Mr. Jansen did most of the talking. He spoke about his student days and how he and his wife had first met. He talked about the various positions he had held, and how these had led to his being the principal of Sabie High School. He talked about his hobbies and his love of music, especially opera. It was only while enjoying their second beer and in the final minutes before they returned home that the purpose of this meeting became clear.

"My wife likes you, and I trust her judgement. She thinks that you are right for Colleen, and I can see for myself how happy she is, and how much she loves you. But what concerns me is that from what I am told your actions are playing into the hands of our country's enemies. I am sure that you mean well, but is seems to me that you are playing with fire. Can you explain yourself to me?"

Justin realised that he needed to proceed carefully. He did not want to antagonise the person who might well be his future father-in-law. On the other hand, it would be a mistake to take the coward's way out and betray his own values. Such a course would not earn Mr. Jansen's respect. "I am not sure what you have heard about me, sir, but every thing that I have done, that I am doing, is to try to make South Africa a better place for all its citizens. Do you have any specific problems with anything that I might have done?"

"I have many. But take for example the way that you have spread lies about the police who are only doing their duty in trying to protect our country from a communist take over."

"Are you perhaps referring to the article about police torture in our student newspaper?"

"Yes, exactly. There is no way that our police would engage in such detestable actions."

"That is where I beg to differ, sir. I have spoken personally to students who have been tortured, and seen their wounds for myself. We made very sure of our facts before publishing that story."

"And you are sure?"

"I have no doubt. Also sir, you are an intelligent man. Do you really believe that so many detainees have died slipping on a piece of soap while taking a shower? Or is it something that you have to make yourself believe?"

Mr. Jansen looked down at his drink, but said nothing, so Justin decided to plunge on. "I have a colleague who has a witness to the police murdering a detainee by throwing him out of a seventh floor window. Personally I believe it would be wrong of me to remain quiet in the face of these crimes. It would make me complicit."

Justin wondered if he had gone too far, but eventually Mr. Jansen spoke. "Perhaps you are right. Maybe I have convinced myself that these things are not happening, because that is what I need to believe." He looked down at his drink again.

Justin decided to press on. "Sir, if you were a black man, would you settle for the government's version of separate development, or would you fight for the same rights and privileges that us whites enjoy?"

"You are right. If I was black, I would be in the forefront of opposing the government. But I do need you to understand that we in the government are not as stupid or as uncaring as you may think. There are many of us who know things cannot continue as they are. We know that in the long run the policies of separate development now being propagated are doomed to fail, and that they are not just. That they cannot be justified on biblical grounds. But right now, the so-called liberation movement has been high-jacked by the communists. If the communists do succeed in taking over our country, the blacks will have even less freedom than now—and I guess most of us whites will have our throats slit. Once the communist threat has been dealt with, we will have the time to make the changes that need to be made."

"I understand where you are coming from, sir, and I appreciate your talking to me like this. I am just not sure the best way to prevent a communist take over is to use the methods used in communist countries."

"You may have a point there. Listen, it is getting late and we need to get back in time for dinner. I would like to say one more thing before we go. You may not have realised it, but I do like you and I admire the way you stick up for your principles—and for your principles themselves. I am happy that my daughter has found you. But I want you to know that I love her dearly, that she is precious to me, and that if you do anything to hurt her I will hunt you down and strangle you with my own bare hands." It was spoken with a ghost of a smile so as to soften the words, but Justin had no doubt that the intent was meant.

"Sir I will never do anything to hurt her. Thank you for the drinks and for talking to me."

Justin left the Jansen family the next morning. Colleen was the only one who knew what he intended to do during the coming days. He stopped at the super market in Sabie to stock up on some last minute supplies, and then armed with the map that Colleen had made for him, headed into the forest. He drove up one of the tracks leading into the forest as far is he could drive and then spent the rest of the day hiking up each of the small feeder streams that ran into the one where he had left his car. The going was often tough as there were no trails to follow. At times he was forced to wade in the streams themselves, which was not that difficult seeing as that for the most part they were no deeper than about twenty centimetres. At times he heard some small animal crashing though the undergrowth, startled by his approach, but he did not see any. Birds, on the other hand were his constant companions. While he missed having Colleen beside him, it was no hardship to be alone in these surroundings. In some ways he revelled in the solitude and the sense of utter peace that it brought him. The day went by quickly, and as the sun began to set he returned to his car and got ready for his first evening alone. It seemed strange now to have no one else with whom to share his experiences of the day. He could not even think of a time when he had eaten dinner alone. He sat on the folding camp-stool that would serve as his only chair for the coming days as his dinner cooked on a small fire. Once it was ready ready he ate it slowly, thinking of what he might be talking about if Colleen were with him.

Dinner finished, and with the full onset of night, Justin was faced with how to proceed. His gas lamp cast a small pool of light, but not enough to read by. In any case, from what he had been told, detainees in solitary confinement are denied books, and so he had not brought any with him. He had no idea what to do with himself. There was no one to talk to, no radio to listen to, nothing to read, and by now he was surrounded by an absolute darkness. He tried to fight down his rising panic. He had never felt so alone in his whole life. There was not a single person in the whole world who even knew where he was. Get a grip on yourself he advised, but easier said than done. With nothing else to do he decided to head for bed at this early hour. His new car had reclining seats, and this is where he would be spending his nights. But sleep did not come easily. His mind was the enemy of sleep. He tried to banish all thoughts from his mind—to keep it perfectly blank. But that did not work out for him. Thoughts kept intruding. As he lay there he finally realised what would be his biggest challenge—what to do with his mind. How to keep it occupied. How to keep insanity at bay. It was while he was listing his options that he finally slipped into a fitful sleep.

His night of discontent was dispelled by the dawn of a new day. He had now spent nearly twenty four hours with no human contact. He could notch up his first day. After breakfast, he drove to another of the locations mapped out by Colleen, and spent most of the day making short hikes from the spot where he had chosen to spend the night. Again the beauty of the surroundings lifted his spirits. The area seemed to be one favoured by several troops of monkeys, and he found their presence comforting. That evening, as he was preparing his dinner, he confronted two obvious facts detracting from his experiment. Here in these idyllic surroundings, it was not only the birds and the monkeys that sustained him, but also the spirit of Colleen. This was her special place and he could sense her presence. As a detainee, he would not have the option of this environment, where he could fill his mind with the wonders it contained. He would have to survive without the stimulus of the untamed forest. He would have to endure in a place which was not imbued with Colleen's spirit. In order to really test his ability to withstand solitary confinement, he would need to change his plans. He studied the map. He would have to find a place where he would not only be isolated, but somewhere without the lingering memory of Colleen. After some contemplation he found it. Mariepskop stands on the eastern side of the entrance to the Blyde River Canyon, and commands an unparalleled view of the Lowveld stretching north all the way towards the Limpopo. For this reason it had been chosen as a site for a radar installation. If one took the road towards the top of the peak, about halfway up a side road, or more likely a four-wheel drive track if the map was accurate, dropped back down to the river itself. It seemed as isolated spot as he could hope to find. He had asked Colleen about it but she had never been there and knew nothing about whether the track was even drivable. He decided to move there the next day.

Now that the light was fading, and dinner was over, panic again threatened. Rather than turning in, he heaped more wood on his camp fire and tried to find ways of occupying his mind—to keep the terrors of nothingness at bay. At first he tried to play a game of chess in his mind. He had read about people who could play whole games this way. However, try as he might, he could not remember all the positions of the pieces on the board after about four moves. He tried several times before giving up and admitting to himself that chess would not be the best distraction to occupy his mind. But at least he had killed over an hour of the long night ahead. Next he tried to recall, and recite word for word, all of the Shakespeare sonnets that he could remember, and continued to do so after he had climbed into his sleeping bag. It was these sonnets that eventually led him to sleep.

He woke up the next morning somewhat refreshed. He had notched up the next milestone—forty eight hours without speaking to or even seeing another soul. It did not feel so utterly strange any more. After breakfast he packed up his car and set off the spot that he had chosen. He would have to drive through the town of Graskop, but he was resolved not to stop or to talk to anyone on the way through. Kowyns Pass took him down to the Lowveld proper, and from there he found the road up to Mariepskop. The track down to the river was every bit as rough as he had feared, but he trusted his Peugeot to make it down. Coming back up would be an even bigger challenge. The track ended when it reached the river, and it was here that he instituted his new regime. He collected four large stones and arranged them as to make a rectangle next to his car. The car would be his bunk, and the stones marked the boundaries of his 'cell'. He would not leave this 'cell' except for any necessary bathroom breaks. Even this break might be something of a luxury as he suspected detainees in solitary confinement were not even permitted this concession. He placed his camp-stool in one corner, and began the new phase of his solitary confinement.

At this point he would employ some nascent strategies to maintain his sanity in isolation. First he would devise a routine and stick to it religiously. Second he needed to find ways to keep his mind occupied and active. At some point he might experiment with some meditation techniques enabling him to clear his mind of all thoughts. But for a start, at any rate, he would need to keep his mind engaged. Third, he would keep his body in shape. He would practice a regime of exercises which could be accomplished within the confines of his cell. It was time to begin. He would sit on his stool and engage his mind in some chosen activity for one hour, followed up by thirty minutes of exercise. The snag was, he suddenly realised, detainees would not be permitted watches. The first step then, would be to set up a kind of crude sundial clock, which is what he did. The shadow of a nearly bush would creep over his cell during the course of the day. He made marks on the ground which he hoped approximated hours. How to occupy his mind now for one hour? He decided to recreate a Shakespeare play, starting with one that he knew reasonably well, Romeo and Juliet. He did not remember off hand all the lines in the first scene, but he could recall the gist of it. The first few lines came easily, but then he was stuck. After some thought he solved the problem to his satisfaction. He would make up his own lines in the style of Shakespeare, and which were true to the plot of the play. The task engaged him for at least the first hour, or maybe even longer. Each line, as it was recalled or recreated, was committed to memory. As new lines were added, he would go back to the beginning reciting the whole scene to as far as it had been completed. By the end he was quite pleased with his effort. The dialogue in the fight sequence was no doubt much shorter than in Shakespeare's version, as was much of the other dialogue as well. But he had fitted in all the main characters, as well as the essence of their various monologues. The Prince, Montague and his wife, Benvolio, and Romeo—they were all there, and now committed to memory. Time had passed by quickly.

Next he put himself through a series of physical exercises— those he could remember from his school days. While exercising, he kept going over the scene from the play that he had devised and memorised. He next tried to recreate and memorise the second scene—the one which introduces the Capulets, and the fatal attraction between Romeo and Juliet. Half the day was now over and his mind had been fully engaged and his body exercised. Although it was early days, it did seem possible that he could cope with being confined alone in a cell.

For the third mental session Justin decided to try something new. What would it be like to create a painting in his mind? It was worth giving it a try, perhaps beginning with a local landscape. He began by envisaging a blank sheet to paper, and the taking a virtual pencil he carefully drew the outline of a mountain range. Next he drew in some features on the slopes of the mountain, trees, bushes and grass. Of course he realised, there should also be some rocks. And what about the sky? Clouds or clear? When the sketch was complete, it was time to add colour. Water colour or oil? He decided on water colour as he had never painted with oil. Do not rush it. He decided to start with the sky, but first mix the paints so as to get the right blend of colours. Once he was satisfied with the colour, he painted it onto the sky, one small brush stroke at a time. He decided that the sky needed some clouds, and made up a mixture of white and grey paints, and then added some clouds to his sky. Next he mixed up some colours for the rocks—different colours for different rocks and added these to his painting. Looking up he was surprised to see that the sun had set behind the canyon rim behind him. He had been so concentrated on his imagined painting that time had slipped by unnoticed. He would work on his painting again tomorrow, but now it was time for dinner. It would be nothing fancy. Dinners would consist mostly tinned food warmed up on a small fire. Nevertheless he was pleased at how he had been able to while away the hours by keeping his mind engaged. He allowed himself a 'bathroom break' down near the river. That night he sat cross-legged on his bed and attempted to clear his mind of all thoughts while meditating. However he was only partly successful. Unwanted thoughts kept intruding on his mind.

The next four days unfolded as planned. He kept strictly to his regime of mind engaging activities interspersed with physical exercises. On the second day, he finished the painting that he had already begun, and created and memorised another two scenes of his version of Romeo and Juliet. As the days progressed, he also began to add new mental exercises. Drawing from his mathematical studies, he envisaged various ways of proving certain theorems, and also devised a number of the type of geometric problems that so often occurred in the matriculation examination. He re-enacted times he had spent with Colleen, such as the visit to her favourite pool. It had taken them twenty minutes to walk to the pool, and in his re-enactment he forced his mind to take just as long to make the journey. By the end of the fifth day spent in his 'cell' he had convinced himself the he had the mental discipline and resources to withstand solitary confinement. By this time he had painted two additional landscapes and a portrait of Colleen. He had also completed two acts of his version of Romeo and Juliet. Finally, by the third night, he had been successful in his attempt to completely clear his mind whilst meditating. It was time to rejoin civilisation.

The track leading out of the canyon had been made even more treacherous by the overnight rain. Nevertheless his trusty Peugeot made it out, albeit with frequent slipping and sliding. At the point where the track joined the Mariepskop road, it levelled out, and here the rain water had collected into a huge mud puddle. An army jeep had slid off the road and was stuck in the mud. Four or five soldiers were busy trying to push it out. He was sure to get stuck as well, but now was the time when there would be help. With that in mind, he gunned his car's engine and hit the mud puddle as fast as he could. To his surprise, and that of the watching soldiers, he somehow slid through the mud, and gained traction again on the surface of the road.

Some five hours later he and one very muddy car arrived back at the digs that had been his home for the past year.

Colleen had enjoyed the days that she had spent with Justin every bit as much as he had. They certainly ranked as the best days of her life to date. She reflected on the boyfriends with whom she had spent time during her first year at university, before she had met Justin. There had been many of them and certainly she had had a lot of fun. But that really was all it was. She would met someone, they would have some fun times together, and then part again with no regrets on either side. With Justin it was all so different. They had not enjoyed the kind of fun to which she had become accustomed—no dancing or wild parties. Yet the time that they had spent together was infinitely more rewarding and meaningful. Thinking back she could not recall a single former boyfriend with whom she could envisage spending the rest of her life. Now she had found that person in Justin. The trouble was that a rocky path lay ahead of them. The fact that at this very moment Justin was preparing himself to endure the torture of solitary confinement bothered her far more than she had let on. And to be realistic, far worse things might happen to him. Some people simply disappeared or turned up dead. Realistically, what kind of future was there for their relationship? Could Justin be persuaded to tone things down? Did she even want that of him? She knew that these were matters to which she needed to give some serious consideration, and what better place to do so than her special rock where she could be alone with her thoughts.

The next morning she told her mother of her need to spend some time alone and that she would be going to her rock. "When I get back, I would like to spend some time with you."

"I understand, my skattie, and I will be here for you when ever you are ready to talk."

The drive to the Blyde River Canyon through the verdant vegetation of the escarpment was like a healing balm to her troubled mind. On arriving, she parked her car and walked the remaining distance to her rock. She thought of the times past when she had come here, and how the magnificence of the scenery had never failed to bring her some comfort. And then the last time she had been here was with Justin when she had told him how much she loved him. Now she needed to sort out her misgivings and to make some far-reaching decisions. She had a mental list of questions that she needed to find answers to, or at least to come to some kind of tentative understanding. *Did she wish to continue the relationship with Justin?* That was a seemingly easy one, but the consequences had to be faced anyway. *Should she try to get Justin to play it safe? To stick to the less visible forms of resistance?* Certainly there were pros and cons here. *Should she herself become more active, and so more of a target. Become more like Jenny? Was she really cut out for that kind of activism?* She would really have to come to grips with her inner self to answer these ones. *What would or could she do if Justin were detained and tortured? Could she bear it?* A related question. *What if Justin went into exile, forced or voluntarily? Would she join him?* And of course there was the final nagging question. *What consequence would these answers have for her family?*

She sat on her rock for hours, engaging with one or more of the questions, letting her mind wander, and the re-engaging. She did not take the questions in any particular order, but let her mind dwell on the one that seemed most pertinent at the time. Slowly one question would become resolved, or at least partially so, and then she contemplate the next. By mid afternoon she had reached the point where she felt it was time to talk matters through with her mother.

Mrs. Jansen and Colleen chose to sit in the patio under the bougainvillea at the bottom end of the garden. A pot of tea, two cups, and a plate of Marie biscuits were on the table between them. They sat in silence for a while until Mrs. Jansen said, "Well skattie, what do you have on your mind?"

"Well, mostly about Justin I guess."

"What a surprise. I never would have guessed." When Colleen saw her mother's face, she burst out laughing. "Yes! What else could it be about, but it is not just about Justin. It is more complicated than that. I'm not sure quite where to begin."

"Perhaps just start with Justin."

"He is like no other boyfriend that I have ever been with. I do love him very much. But I also like him, which is not quite the same thing. And I respect him. He is the only person I have known with whom I would like to spend the rest of my life."

"So far I do not see anything too complicated. Everything you said has been pretty obvious to me. And even to your father for that matter."

"Okay, this is where it gets complicated. I will try to explain, but where to begin. Okay, how about this. Do you know where he is right now?"

"He went back home, didn't he?"

"No, he is somewhere alone out in the bush trying to see if he can withstand solitary confinement."

"Why on earth would he do that?"

"You must have read about the Richard Levine case."

"Is he the ex-president of the South African Student Association who was the State witness and who then killed himself?"

"Yes. But the point is he was broken by the Special Branch by being put in solitary confinement. He simply could not withstand it. So Justin and his colleagues have been advised to find out how much torture, and what kind of torture, that they might be able to withstand. As you know, Justin has already been arrested and had his passport confiscated. So it is quite possible that there is worse to come."

"But skattie, we are not an uncivilised country. We do not torture people."

"But mom, we do. Richard Levine is not an isolated case. In Soweto I have met and talked to people who have been tortured. Okay, these were Africans. But recently whites have also been targeted. Just a few weeks ago two different white women were assassinated using a parcel bomb. So it is not impossible that something might be done to Justin."

"If you are right this is very disturbing. Are you going to do something about it?"

"This is where I am most conflicted. I could try to get him to stop doing anything that might land him in trouble. I am sure he loves me enough that if I insisted he would comply. But then what? Would he despise himself as a coward? Especially if his friends are detained and tortured. Would he then begin hate himself? Might he then start to hate me because that is what I made him become? But if I don't get him to stop, I might lose him anyway. You can see why I am so confused."

Colleen noticed that there were tears in her mother's eyes. "Mom, I am sorry. I did not mean to upset you with my troubles."

"It is not your troubles. It is an old wound that has just been opened." She was silent for a while. "I am going to tell you something that few people know, but is perhaps relevant to your situation. But you must keep it to yourself." Again there was a long silence. "When the war broke out—world war two that is—I was engaged to a wonderful man. He was handsome, witty, kind, loving, and above all else idealistic. I was madly in love with him. Think of him as my Justin."

"You are not talking about papa are you?"

"No, it was before your father. My Justin was appalled by the rise of Nazism and decided to join up. Perhaps you might not know, but there was no draft in South Africa. Everyone who chose to fight was a volunteer. He could not stand aside and let evil triumph. Every shred of my being wanted to cry out and beg him not to go. Let others do the job. But in the end I decided to keep my torment to myself and said nothing. And so he did join up, trained as a pilot, and went to war."

"What happened?" But already she knew.

"He was shot down in killed within weeks of arriving." By now she could no longer control her tears. "If I had insisted, maybe he would not have joined up. But I know he would have hated himself, and me as well most likely. Either way I would have lost him, but his way was probably best, but maybe not."

Colleen put her arms around her mother and hugged her. "Does papa know this story?"

"Yes of course. He has been a loving husband, and given me three wonderful children. It has been a happy marriage despite that fact that he never was or will be the true love of my life. And I would like to think that I have been a good wife to him. I have always been faithful, unless you count the ghost of the past." Again there was a long silence. "So you see, your choice is not very different from the one I had to make. And only you can make it."

Colleen was stunned by this revelation. For a while neither of them spoke. It was Colleen who began hesitantly at first. "You have helped me make up my mind. Justin is the love of my life, but I will not hold him back or try to keep him for myself. I will support him in all that he does. But there is more to it than that. If I commit myself to Justin, it is not just to him but also to his ideals and to what he does.

If he does things that might get him arrested, I will do them too. I know that if I were to be arrested it would bring shame and disgrace to the family, especially papa."

"But I would be proud of you."

"Thank you mom. Also, if Justin is forced into exile, I will go with him as well. I would miss you all terribly, as well as this country, but that is what I would have to do." This time there were only some muffled sobs. Finally Colleen continued, "Think of me as Ruth. What did she say? Something like 'Where you go, I will go. Where you lodge I will lodge. Your people shall be my people.' I remember once papa told us that Ruth was a model of the ideal wife."

"Yes, but you realise don't you that she made the pledge to her mother-in-law, not her husband!" This wry comment broke the tension and they both burst out laughing. "Kom skattie, dry your tears. We need to go back inside. But let's keep this to ourselves for now. But I do have one favour to ask. Please stay with us as long as possible before going back to start the new academic year. It might be our last opportunity."

"Yes, I will. It is the least that I can do."

TWELVE

BY THE TIME JUSTIN RETURNED, THERE WERE ONLY THREE WEEKS LEFT before the beginning of the new academic year, and there was much to be done. The first order of business was dealt with promptly, that of where to stay. The demolition of their house had been postponed once again, and Tony Forester quickly secured a lease for another six months. Much of the time was spent on the reunion with friends, and catching up on all the holiday news. A welcome back party was arranged at the house, attended by all and sundry. However to Justin's great disappointment, Colleen had still not returned. He hoped that she was not mad with him for having spent time alone. The first surprise was that Neville showed up at the party with a new girl friend. The absence of Julie did not seem to phase Neville. He happily introduced his new girl friend to all present, "Isn't she just the greatest!"

Andy was also over the moon, but for a different reason. He had secured a contract with the Performing Arts Council of Transvaal. He would be the assistant director for one of its productions, and had also secured a small role in another.

"What about our Shakespeare production?"

"I will be able to manage that as well. Hamlet is the matric set work this year, so we will be staging it as usual."

"I hope you don't end up getting arrested again this year."

"I wasn't arrested, just given a warning. If those rock spiders interfere with my production this year they will be sorry."

"What will you do?"

"I am still figuring that one out. Maybe I will make the Minister of Education the villain in the play."

When prodded, Justin reluctantly recounted how he had spent the final week of his vacation. It seemed no one knew how to respond to this rather unsettling information. It was Neville who then managed to put his foot in his mouth. "If I were to spend a week in solitary confinement, I would choose a desert island with a wet bar and at least a couple of buxom bar-maids." His new girlfriend gave him a sour look. In an effort to recover some ground, he added, "You would be one of the babes." Her look only became more sour. Justin surmised that this new relationship was not going to last very long.

The highlight of the party was when Ian and Jenny announced that they were going to get married.

"Congratulations! When is the deed to be done?"

"We have not yet set a final date. Perhaps during the first week of term—sooner if we can make the arrangements. You are all invited of course."

The party continued well into the night. The final surprise was the arrival of David. "I hope you cretins have left some beer for me."

"Sure. Help yourself. The beer is in the tub with ice over there."

"So where have you just rocked in from?"

"Here and there. Nowhere special. Just a few details to attend to."

"Well I hope that you did not bring the Special Branch with you."

"Rest assured, they have no idea where I am. Perhaps you noticed that I came in though the back gate." No one asked any more questions of David after that.

At the first opportunity to use a phone, Justin called Colleen. Having been assured that all was well with her, and that he was not in the dog box, he asked, "What happened between Julie and Neville?"

"She dumped him. You must admit, there were no long term prospects for her with him. He is kind of shallow."

"Perhaps, but he does have a good heart."

"Yes, but it is the rest of him that I worry about."

Justin decided to use some of the time before the new term began to continue with his flying lessons, and consequently drove out to Grand Central. "Long time, no see," was his instructor's greeting.

"I know. I have been down in the Lowveld on vacation."

"So how much flying would you like to do now?"

"I would like to rack up a number of hours before the term starts. What all do I still need to do to get ready for taking my final test?"

"Right. let's make a plan of action. There are a couple of the more advanced manoeuvres that I still need to work on with you. In particular how to recover from a spin, and more importantly how not to get into a spin in the first place. We should also work on your steep turns. Then you will still need to do two solo cross country trips, but first you need to brush up on your emergency landing techniques."

"Sounds like a good plan. What first?"

"Let's go up together today and introduce you to spins. Most of the other stuff you can work on in your own time."

It felt like old hat now, to go through the start procedures, obtain clearance for take off, do the run up at the end of the runway, and then to head on out to the practice area. Once they had gained altitude above the practice area, the instructor said, "I will take you through your first spin. This is how we will do it. Keep your hands and feet on the controls so that you can follow me. First full throttle and nose up until the plane stalls. As the stall begins, kick the right rudder."

Justin's stomach hit his throat as the right wing dropped like a stone and the nose pointed straight towards the ground, which seemed to be rapidly spinning around the nose of the plane. In addition, the ground was approaching the plane rapidly. After a couple of spins, the instructor said, "Now I need to get out of this spin. Pull back the power. Right. Now full left rudder until the spinning stops. Now pull out of the dive by pulling back on the yoke. As the plane levels out, apply power again."

Justin was sure that he was as white as a sheet. "Well done for the first time. I have had a number of students panic and freeze. You kept your head and followed my movements well. We will try it again, but this time you will handle the controls alone, but I will be with you all the way. Do you think that you can remember the sequence?"

"Yes I think so."

"Climb to altitude again and then go into a spin."

Now that he knew what to expect, Justin quite enjoyed the experience. There is nothing quite so mind-boggling as seeing the earth below spin around the nose of your plane as you plummet towards it. What at first had been terrifying was now exhilarating. The manoeuvre certainly pumped him up with adrenalin.

"Unless you plan to become an acrobatic pilot, you will most likely avoid doing spins. Our main lesson today will be on how to avoid spins. The beginning procedure will be much the same—put the plane into a full power stall. Just when you think it might spin— when one of the wings seems it might drop—push the yoke full forward to get out of the stall." They practised recovery from incipient spins a number of times. Finally the instructor had Justin do a number of steep turns, until he could do so without losing or gaining altitude.

Once back on the ground the instructor outlined a plan for Justin. "You are close to getting your license. Keep working on those manoeuvres that we discussed. In the test you will not be expected to execute a spin—just to recover from an incipient spin. Once you have reached around forty hours, let me know and I will run you through a couple of mock tests." As an after thought he added, "Once you start classes again, why don't you follow Neville's example. He used to come out here at dawn, which is actually a wonderful time of day to be up in the air. It is usually silky smooth with little or no turbulence. This time of year we leave some of the planes parked out on the apron and you can collect the key from the box by the door. I will let you have the combination. That way you can fly whenever you want and still be back in time for your classes."

Justin returned home feeling pleased with himself.

Although it was over a week before the official start of the new academic year, Jenny scheduled the first meeting of the Student

Council. It was partly to hit the ground running in what promised to be a difficult year, but to be honest with herself, it was also to clear her calendar for her upcoming wedding. The meeting began with a social pot luck, to which no one had brought anything that was remotely appetising. Neville's contribution was the only one that met with any approval. Since alcohol was banned on the campus, he had smuggled in some beer disguised in two-litre ginger beer bottles. Mostly the pot luck provided the opportunity to catch up on each others' news. Jenny announced her upcoming wedding to Ian, and invited all present to attend. Neville, tactless as always, asked, "Will your parents be coming?" Justin kicked him on the shins. Jenny did not seem fazed by the question, and answered, "I am not sure. I am sure my mother will make it, and she might even be able to persuade my father to relent." Then to change the topic, she went on, "Justin, why not tell us your news?", which he did. Once he had finished, Ian commented, "So now he knows that he will be able to survive solitary confinement should the need arise."

"Strictly speaking that is not quite accurate," observed Amy Adams, the physics major. "All that he knows is that he can survive for one week, provided he is confined in an outdoor, scenic setting." Sometimes she could be excessively blunt and a pain in the backside, but Justin did value her analytical mind, and so made no move to reply.

Once what had passed as food had been polished off, and all the ginger beer bottles were empty, Jenny called the meeting to order. "We have a lot to cover this evening, so let's get started." Members of the Council took their places around the table and the meeting got under way. "Before we start with the actual agenda, let me fill you in on the disturbing news regarding our national student organisation. I am sure most of you already know most of the details, but let me tell what I have been able to pick up. It seems that the Special Branch used the holiday period, when the universities around the country were all closed, to smash the national organisation. Those who did not flee in time have been detained. Effectively there is now no national organisation."

"Do we know if those who tried to flee made it to safety?" asked Tony.

"I have not heard anything," replied Jenny. "Has anyone heard something?"

"It is just hearsay, but I heard a rumour that Smith made it to Botswana and Pretorius to Swaziland. We might get more news in the coming weeks."

"The police are refusing to divulge the names of those detained, so it might be months before we eventually find out who is safe and who is in detention," added Ian.

"Is what they are doing even legal?" asked Amy. "From my understanding even detainees have certain rights."

"They used to, but following the report of the Slabbert Commission, those belonging to the organisations that were investigated now have no rights at all."

"It is a serious situation, and we will return to it later in the meeting. But first I would like to get some of the routine matters taken care of. Each of the thirty odd clubs on campus have submitted the budget requests for the coming year. Our treasurer, Tony, has gone through all of them and we will need to make some cuts here and there. He will table them one at a time for approval, and if there is no dissent it should not take too long." Her prediction proved correct, and in less than half an hour the budgets had all been disposed of.

"The next item should also be fairly routine. Two new clubs wish to be recognised, and have their constitutions and budgets approved. One is the Synchronised Swimming Club and the other the Conservative Students Club. Their proposed constitutions are in front of you. Take a quick look at both of them."

Ian was the first to break the silence, "I am okay with the Synchronised Swimming Club. The constitution seems straight forward and the budget reasonable. However I do have some questions about the Conservative Students Club."

"Okay. Let's deal with them separately. Do I have a motion to accept the constitution and budget of the Synchronised Swimming Club?"

"So moved."

"And seconded."

"All in favour?" All present raised their hands.

"Right, the motion passes unanimously. Now let's get back to the Conservative Students Club. Ian?"

"I am looking at their mission statement. It reads 'Our mission is to provide a voice for conservatively minded students on our campus.' I think it is too broad. For example it would enable the Nationalist Party to operate openly on the campus, thus ignoring the ban on all parties on university property. On the other hand, I do believe that we should not deny them a voice."

"Why not? I would have no problem with simply turning down their application."

"To me it is a question of what we stand for—freedom of speech. Who was it who once said, 'I disagree with what you say, but I will defend to the death your right to say it' or something like that?"

Justin came to the rescue. "We studied that phrase in Intro to Philosophy. Apparently Voltaire maybe said something along those lines, but the actual wording is a paraphrase from a biographer, Evelyn Hall, of what she thought Voltaire had said or perhaps just thought."

"Thanks Justin. Well that phrase does sum up my thoughts on this situation."

"Didn't a similar situation arise in Cape Town last year?" asked Tony.

"Yes. A Conservative Students Club was approved. However radical students packed the first organisational meeting and elected their own members as the office bearers. Needless to say the conservative voice was not heard from after that coup."

"Not exactly fair play. I am sure Voltaire would not have approved. But what should we do with this application before us?"

"I have a suggestion," said Ian. "I propose that we ask the applicants to expand the mission statement to the effect that the Club would not act as the mouthpiece of nor promote the activities of any political party. We will then consider the application at our next meeting." A motion to this effect was duly proposed and passed.

"Now we come to what is perhaps the most important item before us. We are all aware of how the political situation is deteriorating and that resistance is becoming more and more difficult and dangerous. In the light of the government crackdown, I believe we need to step up our efforts. I would like everyone here to come up with suggestions. To get the ball rolling, I propose that we continue with the series of weekly talks under the heading 'This is my voice, not that of ...'. They have been very well attended in the past, and have been reported on in the press. For a start we could focus on the writings and sayings of some of our detained leaders. I have already approached a couple of possible speakers."

Tony was the next to respond to Jenny's request. "We should also continue with the Friday vigils."

"Definitely," responded Justin, "but let's hold some of them off campus—maybe in front of the police headquarters."

"We would never get a permit to do that."

"Quite so. We would do it without a permit."

"In which case we would all be arrested."

"Exactly. Imagine the adverse publicity with the police trying to arrest up to one hundred peacefully protesting students with say half of them girls. It would be a nightmare for them."

Jenny intervened. "Great! Let's just keep the ideas rolling. Some may not be practical, but let's hear them all."

"How about we erect a large bill board by the main gate where we keep a tally of the number of persons in detention, and the number that have died."

"Great idea. Any more?"

"How about we use theatre and concerts as a means of protest. Look how folk singers in America are protesting the Vietnam war. Also we could see if Andy Kaplan would be prepared to stage any plays about injustice, either on or off campus. After his brush with the law last year I am sure he would be more than willing to strike back."

The ideas continued to flow until a discordant note was sounded by Jacob Tremor. "With all due respect, you guys sound like a bunch of kids at a Sunday school picnic. Do you really think that the government is going to fall to its knees, or even shake in its boots, just because you sing a few mildly critical songs, or sit down quietly in front of John Vorster square?"

"So what do you suggest?" asked Ian not attempting to hide his annoyance.

"Do things that will really get the attention of the government. There are people who are planning to blow up police stations, shoot cabinet ministers, sabotage railway lines, and so on. If you want to make a difference, these are the ones that you should be working with. Stop kidding yourselves that non-violent protest is going to make the slightest difference."

"Hold it right there, Jacob," Jenny stepped in. "You can do whatever you like in your private capacity, but as an official body of the university, there is absolutely no way that we will get involved with, or even condone, violent action. You are totally out of line to make these suggestions at our meeting. In future, please desist from all such talk."

"Don't even a few of you have some guts? Any one who is with me raise your hands."

"Jacob, I have already told you, not here, not now, not ever. Now stop it at once."

"Just as I suspected. You are all nothing but an incompetent bunch of armchair revolutionaries. A pox on all of you." And with that he stormed out of the meeting.

After a shocked silence, Jenny coolly proceeded as if nothing had happened. "There is one more important matter that we need to discuss. At the beginning of this meeting, we heard about how the entire leadership of our national body has been decapitated. They have either been detained or fled the country. An emergency meeting of all Student Council presidents of the English speaking universities has been scheduled in Cape Town. Normally I would go, or failing that Ian as our vice-president. However, as our wedding plans have now been finalised and there is still much to do, there is no way either of us can make it. So we need to nominate someone to act on my behalf."

Ian jumped in, "I nominate Justin." It has already been arranged, was Justin's first thought.

"Any other nominations?"

"Let's send Jacob."

The laughter that followed helped, to some degree at any rate, to dispel the tension caused by Jacob's outburst. Once it had died down, Jenny said, "No, seriously, any other nominations?" There were none. "Okay, so I guess the honour is all yours Justin. Can you make it? We can fly you down."

"Yes, I suppose that I can make it."

"You can fly yourself down."

"No. I don't have my license yet. As a student I am not allowed to land at busy airports such as Jan Smuts or D. F. Malan. Or to fly that far from home base."

"So Neville, why don't you fly him down?"

"I would do so gladly, but I have been selected as twelfth man for Transvaal, so I have to stick around."

"Actually, if it all the same with you, I think that I would rather drive down anyway."

All business taken care of, Jenny declared the meeting adjourned.

Justin spent the weekend after the Council meeting at home. His mother spoilt him with all his favourite foods, while his father had taken pride in showing off all the new improvements he had made to the farm. It was not often that they had had the opportunity of late to spend any quality time together.

In the week that followed he had managed to go flying on three occasions. The one had been his first solo cross-country flight, a triangle with the first leg to Potgietersrust, the second to Witbank, and then finally back to Grand Central. All had gone perfectly—all his estimated times of arrival promptly met. On the other two occasions he had practised the agreed upon manoeuvres. He now had thirty three hours to his credit and the end of his student pilot days was in sight. Most of the rest of the time was spent with Colleen, who had by now returned from Sabie.

On one of the days they had hiked up to the Dome pools and spent the day sunning themselves, cooling off in the pool, braaing some boerewors, and sipping wine. The more time he spent with her the more he began to appreciate her winsome ways. He could not quite put is finger on it, but in some way their relationship seemed to have become deeper and more meaningful—that they were destined to spend a lifetime together.

During the evenings they managed to take in two films, but most of the time they simply spent in her flat in one another's arms listening to music. Colleen made good on her promise to introduce him to aspects of the Ring of the Nibelungen—at least as much she had been able to grasp from her father's tuition. They did not get further than Das Rheingold, the first of the four Ring operas. It was the prelude, along with Colleen's explanations, that had made the greatest impact on Justin. Classical music was new to him, and yet he found that what he was listening to somehow resonated in ways he did not quite understand. Yes, the music did tell a story, paint a picture, but it also evoked emotions that he had not experienced before. The prelude begins with a soft, drawn out sounding of just one note, low E flat, joined later by B flat. "It evokes the primordial beginning of time, but also the depths of the River Rhine," explained Colleen. Next, superimposed the these base notes come the rising arpeggios suggesting emergence from the depths of the river towards the surface. These became more and more insistent as the pace quickens. Next the triplets of waves join in as the surface is reached and the pace quickens yet again. Finally the whole picture is completed as the three Rhine Maidens join in and the prelude is resolved, reaching its climax. And it was not only the prelude—there was also the majestic strains that accompanied the gods to their new home in Valhalla. Somehow the music that Colleen had introduced him to had got under his skin in a way that left him both puzzled and elated, striking a chord in his very being that he did not know even existed. He could not shake it off.

Justin delayed his departure to Cape Town so that he could attend Ian and Jenny's wedding. It had turned out to be an interesting affair, to put it mildly. It was held in the church attended by Jenny's parents, although it had been sometime since Jenny herself had last graced its doors. It turned out that no one had seen fit to appraise the minister that the congregation would be multi-racial. In Jenny's mind, such a gathering was completely normal. Consequently there had been a scene when the ushers tried to turn away some of the African guests. It was only when Ian and the minister intervened that the matter was resolved. "Why did you not tell me that there would be non-white guests?" asked the minister in an annoyed voice. "Since the official position of the church is one of opposition to apartheid, we did not see it as an issue. It did not even occur to us that it might be a problem," explained Ian. "Yes of course that is our policy. It is just that we are not used to seeing it in action. We were caught off guard." To Ian this seemed a somewhat lame excuse, but he let the matter pass. Things could have gone badly, and he was relieved that Jenny's father had relented at the last minute and agreed to give her away. The remainder of the service went smoothly despite the grim look on Jenny's father's face as her gave her away. Jenny was a radiant and vivacious bride, stealing the whole show. However it was one of the bridesmaids, Colleen, who had held Justin's attention.

Finding a venue to host a multi-racial wedding reception had been much more of a challenge. In the end, Prof. Armstrong had graciously agreed to make the grounds of his home available, and that is where everyone retired at the end of the service. Justin was the master of ceremonies, and Ian had excelled himself when giving the traditional bridegroom's speech. He graciously thanked both his and Jenny's parents. The part that Justin remembered best was when Ian, pointing to the multi-racial gathering, said that he and Jenny hoped that this was kind of gathering might be a precursor of the new South

Africa. Justin was pleased that after the speech the guests had mingled so naturally, even although for many it was likely the first multi-racial gathering that they had attended. To be honest though, he did not pay as much attention to the speeches as he should have. His thoughts kept turning to what form Colleen and his wedding might take. Talk of putting the cart before the horse. He had not even plucked up the courage to propose to her.

THIRTEEN

THE DAY AFTER THE WEDDING JUSTIN FOUND HIMSELF HEADING FOR Cape Town on the N1 south. It was a Sunday, and consequently the traffic was light and he was making good time. It felt good to be on the open road again in his new car. By mid-morning, Justin was in the heart of northern Free State, where the country side was as flat as a pancake. Fields of maize stretched as far as the eye could see. His plan was to stop off in Bloemfontein for a quick lunch and to top up his petrol tank. Then he would proceed to spend the night on a farm in the Karoo with some distant relatives. As he approached Bloemfontein, he noticed that the sides of the road were lined with cars—dozens, no hundreds of them—all facing the road. It took him some time to realise what was going on. It was Sunday, and there was nothing else to do but to watch the traffic on the N1 and to read the Sunday newspapers. Every shop and restaurant in town was closed. All organised sport was forbidden. Even a game of tennis on a private court, while not prohibited, would be frowned on. Watching the traffic was apparently the one thing that was still allowed. It was with some difficulty that he eventually found a Greek café which was still open and where he was able to buy some bread and fruit—not the kind of lunch that he had envisaged.

By late afternoon he pulled into the hamlet of Richmond. From here he would need to take the dirt road to Middleburg, and then look for the turn off to Mooivlei, his destination for the night. He pulled up in front of the sturdy farm house, and before he could even get out of the car, Tannie Marie came flying down the stairs. She was the second, or was it third, cousin of his mother. As a family, they had on a couple of occasions spent Christmas here, along with scores of other relatives. Why she, alone among his many aunts, was known as 'tannie' was a mystery. "My skattie, how nice to see you again." She enveloped him in a bone-crushing hug. "My how you have grown— what a handsome young man. How long has it been? Five years at least, maybe more. Come on in. We will have some drinks on the stoep, and by then dinner will be ready. I hope you are hungry. You must be after such a long trip. Come along. Let me show you to your room, and then come and join us on the stoep."

After a quick wash, Justin joined the family on the stoep. The sun was setting behind the western hills, painting the landscape with a golden hue. The vlei, after which the farm was named, stretched out before the house. Here the grass was green, unlike the grey, stunted karoo bushes which dotted the stony hills. Sheep in their hundreds dotted the vlei. A couple of farm workers were busy rounding them up with the help of three hard working black and white border collies.

"Koos, look who the cat just dragged in."

"Welcome to Mooivlei, my boy. It is great to see you again. It has been too long." They shook hands, and Freddie handed him a beer. "It is good to be here Uncle Koos. Thank you for having me."

"You must remember Freddie. He was only twelve when you were last here, and you beat the crap out of him on the tennis court. He is looking forward to having his revenge. And you remember our baby, Beryl. She was only ten, and look at her now. She has blossomed into a real beauty don't you think. Just look at all those luscious curves. Do you think her love-handles are big enough? Tell us what you think."

"Ag ma, stop embarrassing me. And look! You have embarrassed Justin as well."

Justin could feel his face turning red.

"Ag, he can handle it. He is a big boy now."

Justin stared at his feet to avoid looking at Beryl's chest.

"You must go riding with Beryl tomorrow. She has a new horse. You do remember how to ride don't you, or have you become a useless city boy?"

"Tannie sad to say, I have to leave early in the morning."

"Nonsense. You cannot just drop in for a night and leave us again. I insist that you stay."

"I am sorry. I have a meeting in Cape Town tomorrow afternoon. I would have come earlier, but a friend of mine got married yesterday, and I had to stay for that."

"Well what about on your way back? I will forgive your rudeness if you promise to stay longer on your return trip. What do you say?"

"Yes. With pleasure. I promise."

"Well that's settled now. Don't you forget."

"By the way, I will need to leave at about six tomorrow morning. I can grab some breakfast in Richmond."

"Nonsense. You will have breakfast with us. Your Uncle Koos meets with his staff early every morning, so breakfast at five is normal for us—well for some of us that is. You had better say good bye to Beryl tonight."

"What about David and Robert? Where are they?"

"You have just missed them. They are working for an agricultural supply company in Port Elisabeth. They were really sorry not to see you again. Freddie here will be starting at Rhodes next week. Anyway, enough chatter. Come on gang, its time for dinner."

After dinner Justin was helping Tannie Marie with the washing of the dinner dishes. It was the first time since his arrival that he had time alone with her. She made the most of it.

"So how is your love life coming along?"

"Believe it or not Tannie, but I do have a girl friend now."

"I will believe it when I see her."

"Actually I have a photo of her right here." He took the photo of Colleen out of his pocket and handed it over.

"Gids! That girl is drop dead gorgeous. You must be having me on. You must have cut that photo out of some fashion magazine."

"Not at all. She is for real. Look, that is me standing next to her. I still find it hard to believe myself. I guess it is a kind of beauty and the beast situation."

"Well I wouldn't actually call you a beast. Anyway, what is her name?"

"Colleen. Colleen Jansen."

"Well all I can say is that this one is a keeper. Don't you dare let her slip away from you."

Around mid-afternoon on the next day Justin arrived at the address that he had been given—a house on the edge of the campus. The house seemed deserted, and when he knocked on the door there was no answer. He was about to give up when a figure materialised from across the road. It was a young girl. "Are you Justin Roberts?"

"Yes."

"Good. I have been keeping a look out for you. The meeting has been moved to a new venue. My job is to take you there."

"What is going on?"

"Get back in your car. I will explain on the way."

Once they were back on the road, and following her directions, she spoke again. "It seems the police got wind of this meeting and planned to raid it later on, so it has been shifted to a new secret location. I have been waiting for you in the garden across the road. I had to be sure that you had not been followed before approaching you. Turns out you were clean."

"So where are we going now?"

"The meeting will be held in a student digs in the old part of town, somewhere between the gardens and District Six. Luckily it has a garage where you can hide your car."

With his car safely stowed, Justin entered the house by the back door. The living room was packed with students, some of whom he recognised, but many of whom were strangers. He did recognise Hugh Diamond, president of the local Student Council. Apparently the recognition was mutual, "Good to see you Justin. You are the last to arrive, so we can begin. First some quick introductions. It may sound melodramatic, but some of those here, and especially our African colleagues, would prefer not to give their real names. Actually it could be just as well for all of us. If any of us are detained and questioned, we will not be able to give names however much pressure is exerted. So for the purpose of this meeting, we will simply identify ourselves by the city or town from which we come, along with a number. I will go first, and from now on I will be known as Cape Town One."

Every one else in the room proceeded to introduce themselves in the same manner. Cape Town One then continued, "Before we get to the main business of the meeting, I suggest we take the time to share strategies for the coming year. We all know that it is going to be a difficult one, and that we have not seen the end of police crackdowns. Despite these, we need to find ways of escalating our resistance. By sharing what we plan to do, we might be able to get ideas from one another. Jo'burg One, why don't you go first. I understand that your Council has already met and come up with a variety of actions."

Justin thought that Jo'burg Substitute might be a better designation, but he kept that to himself. He outlined some of what they had planned, and then campus by campus others did the same. Justin made a mental note of some of these for possible adoption. The Cape Town students had decided to fly kites on the beaches with banners reading slogans such as 'No detention without trial' and 'End police torture'. Durban students planned to use some of the Gandhian tactics of passive resistance such as lying down in front of police vehicles.

Following this first session, there was a break for dinner, which consisted of take out pizza. Justin was able to mingle and chat with a number of the participants. By and large they were a scruffy looking bunch—hardly the common stereotype of revolutionaries. Most were wearing faded jeans and shirts which had long past their sell by date.

While the stragglers were still finishing off their meal, Cape Town One reconvened the meeting. "The main reason that we are here is to decide on a course of action now that the National Organisation is for all purposes defunct. I would suggest that there are essentially three options. One would be simply to replace the members that have been detained or fled with new members. The second option would be to start a new, but similar, organisation, but with a new name, constitution, and of course leaders. The third option would be to start a new but informal organisation, one which would essentially operate underground. There are, of course, pros and cons, to each of these options. I suggest that we debate each of these options tonight, and then sleep on it. When we meet again tomorrow, we can decide on how to move ahead. So let's start with the first option."

Justin was not sure how much his voice should count seeing as that he was basically a substitute. However he did realise that it was important to listen carefully so that he could present a coherent summary to Jenny and Ian. Opinions, both short and long, were expressed by most present. When all was said and done, Justin was able to summarise for himself most of what had been said in a couple of sentences.

The pros for the first option were that the structures were already in place. However the organisation's funds had already been frozen, which nullified the advantage. Also on the con side was that any newly appointed leaders would almost certainly be detained immediately.

The issues relating to the second option were more varied and complex. It was deemed to be important that the students of the universities represented at the meeting continued to have a national voice. However, in order to have the ability to open a bank account, any new organisation would first have to be registered. Concerns were raised that any such attempt would be blocked by the government. The old organisation had been banned based on the findings of the Slabbert Commission. Therefore it might just be possible that there would be no grounds to ban a new one. However it was equally possible that any new organisation could be declared as the re-emergence of the old one, and hence declared illegal. It was also clear that the office bearers of any new organisation would have to be publicly named, and hence they would be vulnerable to harassment and worse.

The third option also elicited much heated discussion. A clandestine organisation could still provide students with a national voice, but it would not carry the same weight as a formally constituted body. Its leaders would have the protection of anonymity, but at the same time logistics would be a nightmare. Without a bank account, there would be no funding for projects, meetings, and travel.

It was after mid-night when Cape Town One finally said, "I think we have exhausted all that can be said about the three options. Let's sleep on it and decide how to proceed tomorrow morning. Everyone, just find a place to doss down. We did manage to bring some blankets and pillows, but for the most part you will just have to sleep on the floor. A few lucky ones might be able to find a bed or sofa. Justin found space in one of the bedrooms. Two girls had already claimed the only bed. Those on the floor were for the most part boys of all races, African, white, and coloured. It was the first time that Justin had slept in room with others of another race, but it did not seem as strange as he had at first anticipated. In fact it seemed perfectly normal. What seemed less than normal, as Justin reflected on the day's events, was the meeting itself and the surreal atmosphere in which it occurred. Were they really under such a threat that they needed to meet in secret and to adopt ridiculous names? Surely they were all well known to the police whatever they chose to call themselves. Perhaps they were all simply actors engaging in a version of the theatre of the absurd.

The next morning, breakfast, if that is what it could be called, only served to make Justin nostalgic for the slop that Neville sometimes dished up. At least the coffee was drinkable. However there was no time to complain, as Cape Town One clearly wanted to get the proceedings under way. Most were still sipping their coffee when he announced, "Time to get going. We need to be out of here by the end of the day."

Everyone made themselves comfortable. "Last night we explored at some length the three possible options that I outlined. This morning we need to settle on one of them, and then make some concrete plans on how to make that option succeed." It soon became clear that only options two and three were considered viable, and as the debate proceeded it was the latter that appeared to be favoured the most. It was at this juncture that the girl who had met Justin burst into the room. It seemed she was the appointed lookout. "Someone is approaching the front door. I do not think that it is the police, but on the other hand it is not anyone that I recognise." Cape Town One shot to the window and peered out. "Relax everyone, it is a friend." He went to open the door, and to Justin's surprise, it was David Cohen who strode in. He was about to call out a greeting when he remembered the no name rule.

"This is Arthur, which of course is not his real name. Things are going well here. We are about to reach a consensus. But what brings you here?"

"Bad and then even worse news, I am afraid. The bad news is that we have just found out that the Special Branch managed to place a spy right in the Student Council in Jo'burg."

"What did he do? Did he advocate for the government policies?"

"Just the opposite in fact. He came off as a dedicated revolutionary. He tried to goad council members into undertaking acts of violence. He was likely taping the meeting when he did so. He also conned most council members into taking a test to find out how they would react to detention and torture, and so now the police know each member's weak spots."

"Why go to the trouble of taping some of us agreeing to commit sabotage or other acts of violence, when all they need to do is to detain us indefinitely? It does not make sense."

"The government does like to present a veneer of respectability. If they can put on a show trial from time to time, it helps to justify all the detentions where there is no recourse to the law."

"Yes. That does make sense."

"The reason that I am telling you this is that it is more than likely that other councils around the country have also been infiltrated. Be on your guard. Be aware of anyone who tries to come across as the most radical of all, and of someone who seems to have appeared from nowhere."

"Thanks for the warning."

"The other news is even worse. From what our sources tell us, in the next few months it is likely that some members of most student councils around the country will be rounded up. In fact most of you here in this room can expect to be detained sometime in the future. I am not telling you this to frighten you, or to suggest that you need to get out. But it is something that you need to consider carefully as you make your plans. That is about all that I can tell you. Be strong and keep the faith."

"Thank you for taking time to come and speak with us. All the best to you as well."

On his way out, David nodded to Justin as if to say, 'Come out with me for a minute'.

Once outside he asked, "When are you going home?"

I guess I will leave tomorrow morning. We expect to finish here this afternoon sometime. Most will be leaving then, but I can spend another night here if I so wish."

"Good. I have a favour to ask. I need to find a ride back to Johannesburg for a colleague. It is not safe for him to take the train. Can he hitch a ride with you."

"Sure thing."

"Okay. Listen carefully. Park your car at the top end of Government Avenue. Stroll up and down the avenue, all the way to the end and back. Keep doing so until we make contact."

"Will do. See you tomorrow. I should be getting back to the meeting. Wait. Before you go, what you were saying about a police spy. Were you taking about Jacob Tremor?"

"I am afraid so, yes."

"So he was a spy all that time."

"So it would seem."

"So how did you find out?"

"There is no mystery to it. The police themselves made the announcement. It seems they need him as a key witness in some high profile trial."

"So why would they simply blow his cover?"

"Good question. My guess is that he had outlived his usefulness. If the rumours are true that there is going to be a major crackdown on student councils all around the country, then there is nothing more that he could do undercover anyway."

"Yes, that does make sense. I had better be going. See you tomorrow."

By the time Justin returned to the meeting, the consensus was rapidly honing in on the third option, a clandestine organisation. The news that David had imparted had clearly made an impact. A few minutes after his return, the third option was officially approved by a show of hands. It was seen as the best possible interim option. Depending on how the situation developed, it might be possible in due course to resurrect a formal national student organisation. But until such time a clandestine group could at least hold the fort. Cape Town One resumed, "Now that we have come to a decision, I suggest that we break up into three groups. The first committee will try to get to grips with what the organisation will try to achieve this coming year. The second committee will come up with ideas on how the organisation will communicate. The third committee will discuss security procedures. Each group should come up with a set of recommendations, which will be presented to all of us. Let's spent the rest of the morning in committee, and then reconvene as a whole just after lunch."

After a somewhat meagre lunch, the committees began their report backs followed by discussion. The committee on what to achieve suggested that one main function of the new organisation should be to support the efforts of the student councils on each campus. This would entail providing support for their various undertakings, but also to groom replacements for if and when various members were either detained, banned, or fled the country. Over and above such support, members of the new organisation should also take independent actions, such as the distribution of leaflets calling for the boycott of companies that supported the government or in support of calls by labour unions for general strikes. The group on each campus should decide on these actions on their own, independently of the national body. The main point of contention in the discussion was on whether to embrace violence, such as the planting of parcel bombs or the sabotaging of government installations. To the disappointment, and perhaps disgust, of the more radical members, the use of violence was firmly ruled out.

Before the second committee reported back, Cape Town One observed, "We keep referring to ourselves as the 'new organisation' or 'national body'. Any ideas on a new name?" None of the suggestions rang a bell until Justin suggested, "How about something with Phoenix in it." The suggestion met with applause, and additional names were offered.

"Phoenix brotherhood."

"Phoenix knights."

The girls present quickly shot both down, one as sexist and the other as chauvinist. Finally 'Phoenix Brigade' received unanimous support.

The committee that dealt with security procedures was next to present their recommendations, most of which were accepted. It was agreed every effort should be made to recruit new members who had no record of exposure to the police. It was pointed out by one of the girls that females should not be overlooked, and that they in fact could be ideal recruits. "Remember that during World War II, some of the most successful British agents to operate in occupied France were women. The Nazis often laboured under the assumption that all women were good for was to please men, and hence overlooked the female agents." It was also agreed that no names, only numbers and location, would be used. "We also need to keep membership fluid and secret. For example, as soon as possible, since I already have a high profile, I will designate someone new as Cape Town One for the new Phoenix Brigade. Only I will know who this new person is."

Communications proved to be the most intractable problem. Phones could be tapped and letters intercepted. The safest method was deemed to consist of a network of couriers. Trusted members of the Phoenix Brigade could attached themselves to sports teams that travelled around the country as they participated in inter-varsity sports events. An alternative, but less safe, method might be to embed correspondence in official student council communications between one campus and another.

Despite the swords hanging over their futures, the delegates were pleased with what they had been able to achieve within the short space of just over a day. Cape Town One thanked everyone for their participation, and wished them a safe journey home and a jail-free future.

Justin now regretted his undertaking to meet with David in the morning. If he left now, he would be able to make it to Mooivlei by two or three in the morning. On the other hand, that would not be a propitious time to arrive. Koos and Marie, like most farmers, lived by the dictum, early to bed and early to rise. He resigned himself to spending the night in Cape Town. Perhaps he could find a decent restaurant somewhere and then take in a movie. His dilemma was solved when Cape Town Four came up and asked, "You look a bit lost. Are you planning to spend the night?"

"Yes, it is too late to leave now, so I will be off in the morning." He felt it best not to mention his pledge to David.

"Me and some of my skollie friends are planning to hit the town. You are welcome to join us."

"That would be great. I am at a loose end, and I do not know my way around Cape Town."

"Bak gat! Let's go if you are ready. By the way, my real name is Kenny. No need to keep calling me Cape Town Four."

"Mine is Justin."

The first port of call was a rather dingy looking bar. Besides the counter, there were about ten rickety tables covered with plastic clothes that had seen better days. The chairs were all unmatched, and pushed around from one table to the next as groups formed and dispersed. Some of Kenny's friends were already there, and so they pushed a couple of tables together and made themselves comfortable. Most of the clientèle were coloureds, but there were also a few African faces to be seen. Justin would have been the only white, except that at that moment two white guys strode in through the door. They were obviously regulars as they were greeted with a chorus of "Kom sit Boetie", "Hoekom so laat?" and so on.

"What is your poison?" asked Kenny.

"Make it a Castle."

Justin looked around trying to hide his amazement. All public places were by law strictly segregated, especially those that served alcohol. Yet here were members of all races drinking together, and no one present, except himself, seemed to think it unusual.

When Kenny returned with his drink, he asked, "How is it possible that there is a multi-racial crowd here? Isn't it illegal?"

"Of course it is. But here in Cape Town, things are a little more relaxed. The police simply turn a blind eye to places like this. Does it make you uncomfortable?"

"No not at all. I think it is great. It is just that I have not been in this kind of situation before. This is how South Africa should be."

"Ja. It is beyond me why the government should make a fuss about friends drinking a few beers together."

It turned out that most of Kenny's friends were also students, but not really involved in politics. They were all keen to hear more about student life in Johannesburg. Justin filled them in as best he could, but downplayed his political involvement. It was best to be cautious when speaking with strangers. What seemed to interest them most were his stories about flying. "Are coloureds allowed to become pilots?", one of them asked. It was something that Justin had never considered. "You know, I am not sure. Come to think of it, I have never come across any but white pilots." It might have been an awkward moment—the spectre of apartheid was always present. However, the conversation moved on seamlessly to other topics. Drinking with coloureds was a new experience for Justin, and something he savoured. They were a fun group and often unintentionally funny—it was just the way that they expressed themselves in an odd mixture of English and Afrikaans. Phrases that they uttered quite normally seem to verge on the hilarious to Justin. He was disappointed when Kenny announced, "Well time to move on. We had better find a place to get dinner."

It was just the two of them now as they walked towards the Malay quarter. Although it was now almost eight in the evening it was still light. Justin remembered how others had spoken of the long Cape Town evenings. "While you are here you need to sample some traditional sea food."

"Where are we going?"

"There is a great little Malay restaurant just around the corner. I thought we could grab a bite to eat there."

The restaurant turned out to be all Kenny had claimed. It was small but immaculate. The hostess, a pretty, young Malay girl, showed Kenny and Justin to a table. It was obvious that Kenny was well known and a welcome customer. He ordered for both of them, and when dinner was served it was like nothing Justin had ever tasted before. It was an exotically spiced seafood curry—not too hot—served on rice, with mango and apricots. "What all is in this seafood?"

"It changes from day to day, but from what I can tell tonight the main ingredients are kingklip, hake, and prawns."

For dessert they were served Cape Malay Potato Pudding with dried stewed fruit. Justin could not conceive potatoes as a dessert, but the sweetened condensed milk certainly transformed the potatoes into a brand new culinary experience. It was only when they were sipping coffee that the conversation turned serious. "It seems that you know that Arthur guy who came to speak to us. Do you trust what he told us?"

Justin was at first hesitant, but then decided to level with Kenny. Surely one cannot go through life distrusting everyone. "Yes, I know him well. We are house mates. Why do you ask?"

"You may not know this. I was picked up at the same time as Richard Levine. We actually worked together on some projects. We likely both received much the same treatment, but he cracked and I somehow didn't. But I am not sure that I could go through it all again. That is why I was so disturbed by what Arthur had to say."

"Well, that bit about the Special Branch placing spies on student councils is absolutely true. There was one on our Council, and I was taken in along with all the others. I am not sure where Arthur gets his information, but I have no reason not to trust him. He has always been right in his predictions in the past."

"So it is quite possible that a major crack down on student organisations is in the works?"

"If he says so, it is quite likely." Kenny just shook his head.

"If you don't mind me asking, how did you survive solitary confinement?" Justin went on to explain his attempt to prepare himself.

"What you did is certainly the way to go. The main struggle is to keep from going insane—from cracking up. You have no idea how difficult it is to sit in a cell by yourself day after day with no human contact. Unless you can keep your mind occupied you are sunk. So the disciplined way you went about your mental activities is exactly the right approach. But being in a real cell will be very different from being outdoors in a pretend cell."

"Do you think you will be able to withstand it again?"

"Knowing what it is really like—no I don't think I could do it again."

"So what will you do?"

"I guess my only choices are to go underground or to leave the country. But these are both drastic steps from which there is no turning back. That is why I want to be sure that your Arthur's information is correct."

It was on that sober note that Justin thanked Kenny for his hospitality and they went their separate ways.

District Six had been much in the news of late and for all the wrong reasons. Indeed it had been part of the conversation the previous evening between Kenny and his friends. It was one of those anomalies so hated by the apartheid government—a place where non-whites still owned land in the so-called white-designated areas. For this reason it had to be erased from the map of Cape Town. It had once been a vibrant, multi-racial community until recently, when the government began forcing its inhabitants to move out to new, segregated townships on the Cape Flats. There had been much opposition to the removals, but in the end the government prevailed. The process of removing people was about three quarters complete by the time of Justin's meeting. The digs where he was to spend the night was not far from District Six, and so Justin decided to get up early enough to experience what was left of the area, before his meeting with David. So he rose early and made his way to the remains of the once colourful district. It did have a run down appearance, which provided cover for the government's actions. The whole operation was billed as slum clearance. It was clear that many of the buildings had already been torn down, but some of those that remained were surely architectural, if not historical, gems. He wandered up and down the streets. Perhaps a quarter of the original population still remained, waiting for the hammer to fall. Shops were in the process of being opened and people going about their daily business. House wives in colourful dresses were out and about looking for the freshest vegetables or newly baked bread. From what Justin could tell, they were a mixture of Coloureds, Indians, and Malays. Turning a corner he found a man sitting in the gutter. Did he need help, or was he simply wearing off a hangover? Before he could decide, a well dressed man came striding down the street. The man in the gutter greeted him, "Dag se ou Manie. En waar gaan djy so opgedress?"

"Nee man, ek gaan kerk toe."

"Ja, maar hoekom so fancy. Djy is moes 'n gammet, nes soos ek."

"Ja dis waar, but a man must try to keep up appearances."

It was a colourful, but friendly, exchange, which perhaps epitomised the easy going nature of the District. Justin was glad to have caught a glimpse of it before it was gone forever.

It was time to meet David and the person who would be travelling with him. Justin parked his car as planned and walked down Government Avenue. It was one of those bright and breezy Cape Town mornings. The avenue, which was in reality a pedestrian-only paved walk way, was lined with old oak trees. Once he had walked past the South African Museum, he was in the gardens proper. Despite its being the dry season, the lawns were emerald green, and the flower beds a profusion of colour. Squirrels ran hither and thither, busily collecting up the fallen acorns. As he approached the end of the avenue, the Houses of Parliament were on his right hand side. He peered curiously at the building, but no members were in sight. He pondered the irony that some of the country's ugliest laws had been crafted in such an idyllic setting. Having reached Adderley Street, he reversed his course and started to stroll up the avenue. Now the full magnificence of the avenue was on show. Looming through the trees was the grand vista of Table Mountain. The seasonal south-easter, known as the Cape doctor, was blowing and hence the mountain was bedecked with its famous table cloth. The gardens with their back drop of Table Mountain were surely one of the great vistas of the world. By the time he reached the top end of the avenue, there was still no sign of David, and he began to worry that something might have happened to him. There was nothing to do but to walk the avenue for a second time. He got to the Adderley Street end, and still no sign of David, so he turned to walk back again. Just as he was approaching the end for the second time, David materialised out of nowhere.

"Good. You have not been followed."

"I was getting worried that something might have happened to you."

"No, all is well. Here is your passenger for the trip." A second person had just materialised. Justin did a double take. "Good grief, is this Peter, Peter Sisulu?"

"It is, but now I go by the name Sipho Dlamini."

"Once I had dropped you off near Joubert Park, I did not expect ever to see you again."

"Well here I am, just like a bad penny."

"By the way David and Peter ..."

"It is Sipho. Please remember that."

"Okay, sorry. I did not have time to tell you before that I will be stopping off on the way back to spend a day or two with some distant relatives. I hope that will not be a problem for you."

"Is there any way that you can skip the visit?"

"Not if I want to keep living. I promised my Tannie Marie to spend some time on the way back. She will not take it lying down if I back out. Will that be okay with you?"

"It is unfortunate, but I guess we do not have an option. If possible keep the visit as short as possible. Now show us to your car so that you can get under way. I don't want to be hanging around here for too long."

Minutes later Justin and Sipho were in the car and on their way.

Cape Town has an excellent network of freeways, which to strangers can be somewhat daunting. Justin needed to focus on finding his way to the N1 north, leaving little time for conversation. Just one missed turn could result in driving miles in the wrong direction. It was only once they were on the N1 and clear of Cape Town traffic that Justin relaxed enough to talk.

"Last time I saw you, you were headed for Tanzania. What happened?"

"That is also what I thought. However there was a change in plans, and I was sent to a training camp in Angola instead. At least I think it was in Angola. It was all very secret."

"What kind of camp?"

"Mostly we were taught military type manoeuvres. Our instructors were mostly Russians and Cubans."

"What was is like?"

"Exhausting mostly, and scary at times. Certainly not a holiday camp. Plus most of the Russians were as racist as your average white guy here. We got on better with the Cubans who seemed to dislike the Russians as much as we did."

"So what brings you back?"

"Have you heard of an organisation called *umkhonto isibashu*?"

"Can't say I have."

"Well then, what you don't know won't hurt you. Best to say no more."

Justin got the hint, and for the next hour of so they spoke mostly about mutual acquaintances in Soweto. Beyond Paarl the scenery began to change as they headed up into the mountains via du Toits Kloof pass. The mountains in this part of the Cape are distinctive for their rock formations and shapes, not to mention the dark brown, but clear running streams. Justin stopped at the far end of the bridge spanning the first of these.

"Let's take a short break and stretch our legs."

They walked back across the bridge and peered down into the swirling waters below them.

"It looks like a stream full of beer, or perhaps whiskey," commented Sipho.

"Exactly right. I think it is called the Elands River. One of the delegates at the meeting was talking about it. It is a favourite site for kloofing."

"What is that?"

"Well you climb down into the river. Then you simply work your way upstream or downstream as best you can. When you come to one of those deep pools you have to swim across it. At other times you wade, or simply jump from rock to rock. The main thing is that you have to stay in the river and not walk along the bank."

"Have you ever done it?"

"No. But I would love to come back and try it some time. Apparently there are many rivers in this part of the world that are great for kloofing."

They returned to the car and shared a couple of rolls that Justin had slipped into his pocket after breakfast. They continued to follow the N1 as it wound its way through the Cape mountains. The road then entered the sumptuous Hex River valley. Down below the road Justin spotted a train. "Look, there is the Blue Train on its way to

Cape Town. It is said to be a luxury hotel on wheels. I would love to ride on it someday."

Sipho did not respond. The train was not for Africans.

The road began to climb again and as the last of the mountains slipped away, they entered the beginning of the Karoo, flat and dry, dotted with weird shaped koppies. As they pulled into the town of Beaufort West, Justin suggested, "Let's stop here for a quick bite of lunch."

"Fine with me."

Justin pulled up in front of the first café that they came across. It looked as if it had seen better days, but it would have to do as it might well be the only one. They both entered and Justin selected a couple of meat pies for both of them off the shelf. Before he could take them to the counter the voice of the woman behind the till boomed out, "Tell your boy to go around to the back door. My meid will give him some bread to eat."

Justin was about to explode with an angry retort when Sipho got in first, "Jammer my baas. I will wait for you in the car." With that he quickly left the café. Justin glared at the woman as he paid for the pies. However she still had more to grumble about. "These kaffirs are getting cheekier by the day." Justin bit his tongue and left as quickly as he could.

Back in the car and on the road again, Justin complained, "How could you debase yourself like that?"

"What were the options. We make a scene. The police get called in. I do not have a pass, so they arrest me. Then they find out who I really am, and I am a dead man. I would much rather put up with her insults. You were about to act like a naive white liberal trying to make himself look good."

"You are right. I am sorry. I was not really thinking. Back in Cape Town all of us, all different races, could go into a bar or restaurant together. I had kind of forgotten that we were back in the real South Africa."

"It was my fault too. I followed you in. I have only been back for a couple of days. Every where else that I have been recently there would not have been any trouble. I too was not thinking straight—forgetting where I am now."

They drove in silence for a while, but something was obviously troubling Sipho. "This family where we will be staying—do they know that I am coming?"

"No. I didn't have time to tell them."

"So you will be showing up with a friend, who just turns out to be black. I suppose I will be told to go around to the back door, or to the stable. Is this another example of your white liberal naivety?"

"It will not be like that. They will welcome you as a friend."

"You do realise that I am black don't you."

"Of course. I am telling you all will be okay."

They drove on in an uneasy silence for a while.

"Perhaps you should let me off at the next town and I will make my own way to Jo'burg."

"So what will you do?"

"I could take a train."

"You and David both said that the train would be too dangerous. Stations are being watched."

"I could hitch hike."

"Not very safe or reliable. You have no idea of who might pick you up."

"I could walk."

"That is ridiculous. Look stay with me. If you are not welcome, we will leave immediately. Deal?"

"Okay. Deal."

The tension between them gradually dissipated as they made their way north through the seemingly endless Karoo.

Once they had turned off the N1 and were driving along the unpaved roads taking them to Mooivlei, Sipho grew apprehensive again. "I have never stayed in a white family's house before. I have no idea how to behave. Do you have any advice?"

"It is quite simple really. Don't eat with your hands. Don't spit in the soup. Don't pee on the living room floor."

Sipho glared at Justin for a moment and then broke out into uncontrolled laughter. "I guess I deserved that," he spluttered. Once he got control of himself again he added, "But seriously, is there anything that I should know?"

"Just be yourself and act normal. I do have one piece of advice. Try not to whimper in pain when Tannie Marie hugs you."

"Now I know you are pulling my leg again. Most white men will not even shake my hand, and now you want to believe that a white woman will hug me. How gullible do you take me for?"

"Well don't say later that you were not warned."

Sipho still could not determine whether Justin was serious or not. Only time would tell.

A few minutes later they pulled up in front of the farm house. Tannie Marie rushed down the front steps to greet them. Before he could say anything, she gave Justin a big hug. Once he managed to extricate himself he made the introductions. "Tannie, this a friend of mine, Sipho Dlamini. He happened to be in Cape Town as well, and needed a ride back to Johannesburg. I hope you don't mind my bringing him."

"Of course not. You know we always have room for one more. Any friend of yours is welcome here." She turned to Sipho and gave him a bone-crushing hug. Justin noticed that he did wince, but luckily did not cry out. He gave Sipho a big wink.

"You boys must be tired. Come in and make yourselves at home. Justin, you know the way to your room. Sipho can have the other bed. Drop off your stuff and then come to the living room and I will get you something to drink. Koos is still out on the farm somewhere. I don't know where the kids are, but they should put in an appearance before too long." With that she bundled them into the house and disappeared into the kitchen.

Once in the room, Sipho asked, "So we are going to sleep in the same room?"

"Yes, unless you would rather sleep in the car or out on the veld somewhere."

"This is not what I expected. Pinch me in case I am dreaming."

"Don't be so melodramatic. Any way let's go and see what goodies Tannie has on offer."

They had no sooner settled themselves in the living room when Tannie Marie arrived bearing a tray with tea and cake. They were still into their first cup when Koos arrived, followed shortly by Fred and Beryl. Tannie Marie did the introductions and everyone tucked in. It was Beryl who got the conversation going, "So how do you two know each other?"

Justin explained about the Soweto tutoring scheme, with Sipho filling in many of the details. They avoided any mention of the brushes that they had had with the law. However their descriptions opened up a whole new reality, especially for Fred and Beryl.

It was finally Koos who said, "Goodness look at the time. I am sure you boys would like something stronger to drink. Let's go out on the patio where we can watch the sunset. Tannie Marie and Beryl retired to the kitchen as the men folk poured themselves a beer and headed outdoors. By now Sipho was feeling completely at home, and pressed Koos for details on the operation of the farm. Given the reputation that some farmers had for mistreating their workers, Sipho was especially interested in labour issues. Justin was worried from time to time that Sipho's questions were perhaps too pointed, but Koos took no offence, and in fact seemed to relish in the opportunity to talk about how he and his workers interacted. Just as they were being called to dinner he added, "But this is all talk. Come and see for yourself. We start off every morning by getting together to share concerns or joys, and to plan for the day. If you don't mind getting up early you are welcome to join us."

Dinner consisted of roast lamb, potatoes, and peas. The conversation throughout was lively and continued well after desert. Finally Koos said, "This has been a most interesting evening, but for us farmers it's early to bed and early to rise. You young folks can stay up if you like, but for us oldies it's off to bed."

Justin and Sipho decided to turn in as well, as did the rest of the household.

Tannie Marie woke them up early, just as the sun was about to rise, with a cup of coffee. "If you want to join the meeting you had better get going."

They dressed quickly and joined Koos in the kitchen, and from there on to the meeting. On the way Koos asked, "Do either of you speak Afrikaans or Sotho? Those will be the main languages spoken at the meeting." Sipho admitted to being fluent in Sotho, but only with a nodding acquaintance with Afrikaans. Justin could only speak the latter.

The morning meetings were held in one of the barns. The workers had already arranged themselves on various hay bales which served as seats. From what Justin could tell, they were about an equal mixture of Cape Coloureds and Africans. Koos introduced them to a man call Johannes who was the foreman. It was Johannes who got the meeting under way. "Let us begin with prayer," he said in Afrikaans. Everyone rose to their feet as one of the other men began to pray, this time in Sotho. At the end of the prayer, a second man sang the first line of a hymn. On the second line all joined in in perfect harmony. It had been a while since Justin had last been to church, but he was deeply moved by this soaring rendition of a familiar hymn.

At the end of the hymn, all sat again and Koos asked, "Does anyone have news to share, good or bad? My good news is that we are blessed with two young visitors." He went on to introduce Justin and Sipho. When he had finished, one of the men shared that his wife was well on her way to recovery and thanked everyone who had helped out during her illness. Koos then outlined what needed to be done over the coming days, workers offered suggestions how best to tackle the various tasks, and finally decisions were made on who would do what.

At the end of the meeting Sipho asked Koos if he would mind if he spoke to some of the workers. "By all means, go ahead and speak to anyone you wish."

Sipho approached one of the African workers and engaged him in conversation. Once preliminaries had been dealt with, he asked in Sotho, "Does the boss make you pray and sing hymns?"

"Who are you talking about?" Sipho nodded towards Koos. "Oh him! We just call him Koos, not boss. No, when we first started these meetings it was all business. Then we told him that we would like to begin with prayer and he agreed. So I guess you might say that we made him do it, not the other way around."

Sipho would have liked to ask more questions, but clearly everyone was leaving to start working. Instead he put his questions to Koos as they walked back to the house for breakfast. "If you don't mind my asking, how are decisions made here on the farm?"

"Not at all. It is a good question. We have an executive committee comprising two permanent members, myself and Johannes the foreman, and then three members elected by the workers to serve for one year at a time. However all decisions made by the executive have to be approved by all at one of our morning meetings."

"Can the workers then vote against an executive decision?"

"Yes, in theory anyway. However since the worker members are a majority on the executive, it rarely happens. I can only think of one time about six years ago when this happened, and the executive then had to reconsider."

"Does the executive decide on all matters, or are there things on which you alone decide—say for example on salaries?"

"All decisions are made by the executive. You may be interested to know that everyone, myself included, receives the same basic salary. It is not that much, but it is a liveable wage. Besides no one here pays rent on our dwellings. However that is not the end of the story. As you have probably gathered, sheep are our main source of income. Any one who works on this farm may buy shares in our flock. If you contribute one sheep, or the monetary equivalent, you get one share. Our flock numbers around one thousand heads, and I own about four hundred shares. Johannes, who has been here for ever owns about two hundred. The remaining four hundred are owned by the workers in varying amounts. Whatever profit we make, once all expenses, including salaries, are met, is shared out according to share ownership. Some years we only manage to break even and then no one profits. But most years we do manage to run at a profit."

"I am impressed. I have never heard of a farm run this way."

"Unfortunately there are very few. However it makes sense to me. Everyone has a stake in the running of the farm and has a sense of ownership."

By this time they had reached the house where breakfast was waiting for them. They tucked into porridge topped with fresh cream from the farm's cows, bacon and eggs, and finally 'kudu dust' on toast. "What is this kudu dust?" asked Sipho.

Tannie Marie laughed, "It is just dry, grated biltong. But there is quite a funny story that goes with the name. We had some Englishmen staying here once and they refused to try eating biltong. However, at breakfast time they could not get enough kudu dust. Eventually one of them asked how we made it. Once they found out it was biltong, they refused to eat any more. Silly rooineks!"

After breakfast Koos suggested to Justin and Sipho, "Why not spend the morning with me. As you know from the meeting, we will be dipping sheep this morning. If you have never seen sheep dogs at work, you are in for a treat. Then if there is still time, I would like to show you around the farm."

Although Justin had seen the dogs in action before, it was still a thrilling sight. For Sipho, it was an amazing new experience. The few sheep that were not to be dipped, first had to be cut out of the herd. The one dog cut an indicated sheep from the herd and shepherded it to a separate pen, while the other dog kept the herd intact. All instructions were achieved my means of a series of whistles from Koos. Then both dogs herded the remaining sheep towards the dipping tank. To Sipho, the agility and intelligence of the two dogs was beyond amazing.

Once the dogs had finished their work, there was still time before lunch. "Come with me and see the rest of the farm." Koos first showed them the school, which went up to Standard Five. The teacher was the wife of one of the workers, and there were ten children with ages ranging from seven to eleven. The school itself comprised a classroom and a small store room cum office. The classroom was bright and welcoming, bedecked with youthful creations. Most of the children were busy at their desks while the teacher was working with the two youngest ones.

"It is quite a challenge working with such a wide age range, but also very rewarding. What really makes it all possible is how the older kids help the younger ones with their learning. It makes the classroom seem like one big family."

"What is the language of instruction?" asked Justin.

"I guess we do not have one. Every child here, even the youngest, is fluent in three languages, English, Sotho, and Afrikaans. We use them all. Excuse me now. I need to get back to these two kids."

They stayed and observed for a while until Koos said, "Let's move on to other things."

Once outside, Sipho asked, "Did you send your kids here?"

"No, but I wish we could have. The school has only been going for about five years. We had to send ours to a school in Graaff-Reinet, where they had to board with friends. It was very hard on Marie to have them leave home as young as seven. I wish we could have sent them to a school here on the farm. Having to send our kids away for schooling was one of the motivations for starting a school here."

"Even although there are no white kids, isn't it illegal to have Coloureds and Africans in the same school?"

"Yes it is, but fortunately the local inspector turns a blind eye."

"Would he have also turned a blind eye if there were also white children in the school?"

"An interesting question, but I guess we will never know the answer. Any way, this building next to the school is the clinic, although that is rather a fancy name for it. One of the worker's wives had some training as a nurse, and she comes in only when called to do so. We stock a few essential items to treat minor injuries or sicknesses. Anything more serious has to be treated in Richmond, or even Graaff-Reinet if it is more complicated."

The clinic was a simple, but functional room. There was a bed in the one far corner and an examination table in the other. A closet in which all the supplies were kept, was located near the table. A desk and filing cabinet were on one side of the door and a couple of easy chairs on the other. It was clearly designed to serve the purpose for which it had been established.

Finally Koos drove them around the farm proper. He was always in his element when talking about the efforts being made to restore the pastures to what they had been before they had been overgrazed by a previous owner. On some parts of the property, serious erosion had occurred, resulting in some deep dongas. But surely, year by year, the land was healing. He could talk for hours about the various ways in which restoration was taking place. To finally illustrate his point, he drove them to the boundary between his and the neighbour's farm. Even Sipho, who had never been exposed to agriculture, could see the difference between the two farms. On the one side of the fence, the pasture was thick and sturdy, and on the other meagre and poor. "Other farmers scorned my efforts at first, but now many of them are coming here to learn. Here along this fence line is a graphic example of what once was and what is now possible."

During lunch new plans for the afternoon were hatched. "On your way down, you promised to come riding with me and my new horse," Beryl told Justin. He could not recall having made any such promise, but he did want to go riding with Beryl.

"Sure. I would love to as soon as we have finished up here."

"What about you Sipho? Have you ever ridden a horse before?"

"No. Never. I grew up in a township."

"Would you like to try?"

"Why not."

A long discussion ensued as to which horse would be the best one for Sipho to ride. In the end it was Christmas who got the nod. "You actually have a horse called Christmas?" asked Sipho who now had a personal stake in the outcome.

"Actually his real name is Starlight. We just call him Christmas," explained Beryl.

"How come?"

"It started one day when we were all out riding in a group. When we got home, Starlight was not with the rest of us. Someone asked, 'Where is Starlight?' and the answer was 'He is coming.' Someone else then said, 'So is Christmas.' Since then he has always been known as Christmas. You may gather from this story that Christmas is not a fast horse. A slow walk is what he likes best, but he can be enticed into a slow trot. However he is a good natured beast and ideal for a beginner."

"He sounds like just the right kind of horse for me, but I think that I will call him Starlight. One should not insult a beast who is able to do one harm."

"Once you both are done with riding, there is something else that you might enjoy," said Fred. "Mooivlei boasts a soccer team—quite a good one if I do say so. We have a big match coming up this Saturday, and we will be practising this afternoon. You are both more than welcome to join us."

"I would be delighted. How about you Sipho?"

"Yes, count me in if I survive my horse ride."

And so it was decided.

As it turned out, Fred offered to stay with Sipho and help him ride Starlight. Once Sipho was set in the saddle, Starlight and Caesar, Fred's horse, walked sedately down the road leading away from the sables. "This is not as hard as I expected."

"You are doing just great. Just try to relax more. Let your body adapt to the movement of your horse."

Sipho complied. "I am really beginning to enjoy this."

"Good the next step will be a little harder. We will get the horses to trot. You have to lift yourself off the saddle with each step of the horse otherwise you will simply bounce around and end up with a sore bum. Watch how I do it."

After the demonstration Fred urged Sipho to try the trot. "How do I get the horse to change gears?"

"Sorry I forgot to tell you. Dig your heels into the horse's flank." Starlight did indeed break into a reluctant trot. After a few painful bounces, Sipho mastered the art of trot, lifting himself up and down to match the rhythm of the horse's movement. From there Fred went on to show Sipho how to canter.

Meanwhile Justin followed Beryl to meet her new horse and then to go riding with her. Prince was a handsome chestnut who had obviously been carefully groomed. His coat was shiny and his mane meticulously brushed and braided. He was obviously fond of Beryl, and nuzzled her chest as she fed him a carrot. Once saddled, they set off at a canter for the open pastures, where Beryl gave Prince full rein. Justin did his best to follow the pair of them, now in full gallop. However there was no way he could keep up. Even if his horse was as fast as Prince, he was nowhere as good a horseman as Beryl. By the time they reached the end of the pastures, Beryl was a good half a kilometre in front of him. "Well look who finally arrived! Let's rest up the horses and then we can head back home."

Beryl wanted to make the most of the rest time. "Ma tells me that you actually have a girl friend."

"Yes, that is true."

"Will you show me her photo when we get back home?"

"I have it with me right now."

"You mean you carry it around with you all the time."

"Yes."

"Jeez, Just. You must really have it bad."

"Actually, I think I have it good."

"Can I see it?"

Justin took out the photo from his shirt pocket and handed it to Beryl, who studied it carefully.

"Jislaaik. I have never seen anyone so beautiful. How come she fell for you?"

"Why? Is there something wrong with me?"

"No. Of course not. But what I mean is ... well she is absolutely gorgeous. I am not trying to imply ... It is just that you ..."

Justin took pity on her. "Perhaps we should be getting back." Thankfully, she returned the photo.

"I will race you back home."

"I thought you believed in fair play."

"I do. I will give you a one minute lead."

Beryl was as good as her word, but she still beat Justin back to the stables, where Fred and Sipho were busy unsaddling their horses.

Justin, Fred and Sipho had just enough time to enjoy afternoon tea with Tannie Marie before changing clothes and heading for the soccer field. The team was already at practice as they arrived. Sipho may have been a novice when it came to horse riding, but he was clearly a star on the soccer field. After a short practice game, the team's captain asked him, "Well what do you think of our team?"

"I love the enthusiasm, but perhaps it would be better if you tried to hone your ball skills."

"Would you be prepared to give us a few tips and drills."

"Of course, with pleasure."

"Sipho worked with the players for a while, followed by another practice game. There was a marked improvement in their performance.

"After the practice the captain asked Sipho, "Is there any chance you could play for us this coming Saturday? We will be facing our arch rivals."

Justin butted in, "If you play him, you will have to take me as well. We are a unit."

One of the other players joked, "Ai kona! One white guy in our team is already enough of a handicap. We could not survive two. No offence meant."

"And none taken." Everyone joined in the laughter.

Sipho asked Fred in surprise, "Do you mean to say you play for this team?"

"Yes, when I am home. They say it is the reason the team loses so often." More chuckles.

"Don't you find it strange being the only white guy on the field?"

"Not really. It does help that I speak Sotho. I no longer notice it. But it often takes our opposing teams some time to get used to the idea."

The captain persisted, "So will you be able to play with us this Saturday?"

"I am sorry. I really need to get back to Johannesburg."

"Is that where you learned to play soccer? You really do have some wonderful skills."

"Yes, I used to play in the Soweto league. I was known as Twinkle toes Si...." He stopped abruptly. He had nearly blurted out his old name, Sisulu. It would still take some time before he was completely at home with his new identity. "I mean Twinkle Shoes. I will be sorry to miss your game, but Fred please let us know how you get on. Best of luck to you all."

"Of course. With what you have taught us, we might have a real chance at winning."

They left early the next morning. For most of the trip back, Sipho kept reminiscing about his stay at Mooivlei. "As you know I had never before stayed with a white family, but in all my wildest dreams I could never have imagined this." He would then recount every possible episode he could remember. At one stage, for example, he observed, "From what I have heard, most whites will not even eat off a plate that has been used by an African. Servants say that they are under strict orders never to eat off the bosses plates. Yet yesterday we not only ate off the same plates, but sat at the same table. Unbelievable." Justin, for the most part, just listened while his friend rambled on. He was tempted to say something like, 'It is not such a big deal', but he had to admit to himself that very few white families would have welcomed Sipho into their midst.

Sipho was also interested in Justin's plans for the coming year, but said very little about his own. At one stage he did say something to the effect that if there were more places like Moovlei he might have to rethink his plans for the future. Justin did not press him on his plans. Instinctively he realised that it was best not to know. What he did know was that places like Mooivlei were few and far between.

Tannie Marie had packed them a sumptuous lunch, which they ate at a roadside picnic area, thus avoiding the débâcle at Beaufort West. As they were approaching Johannesburg, Justin asked, "Where do I need to take you?"

"Just drop me off by the Baragwanath Road. I will make my own way from there."

"I would be happy to drive you into Soweto."

"Thanks, but that would not be a good idea."

"Talking about Soweto, if we start up the tutoring programme again, will you be helping out as before?"

"Will you be starting it up again?"

"I am not sure. There is talk of boycotting the schools. Students are saying things such as 'Freedom first, then education'. We would not want to be seen as undermining any potential boycott. We will need to feel our way carefully."

"Even if you do start the programme again, count me out. I now have other priorities. Also, please do not mention to anyone that I am back in the country."

On reaching the Baragwanath Road exit, Justin pulled over. Before getting out, Sipho surprised Justin with a hug. "Thank you for everything. These past two days have been an eye opener for me."

"If there is anything that I can do to help you, just let me know. You know where I stay."

With that the two friends went their separate ways.

Although Justin had been away for less than a week, even one day without Colleen seemed like an eternity. Having dropped Sipho off he made straight for her flat, and by good fortune arrived in time for dinner. He and Colleen wasted no time in catching one another up with all the latest news. As they were relaxing on the sofa afterwards, each with a glass of wine, Colleen tried to sum up her feelings. "It is like riding a roller coaster. Sometimes I am up and sometimes down. All this past week I have been down—worried about you, imagining that you might be detained and tortured. It was hard to sleep at night. All I could think of was that now is the time for us to get out of the country before the situation gets even worse. The government seems to hold all the cards and the future seems so bleak and hopeless. But then my mood changes, and I can see so many hopeful signs. Think of Ian and Jenny's wedding, where people of different races mixed and interacted so naturally. Remember how we felt the same way after Lucky's funeral. Then there is what you told me about your time in Cape Town—how students of all races plotted the future together. And how you went to a pub and restaurant with Kenny. Think of your time with Sipho coming back and how he reacted to his stay at Mooivlei, talking of which when will you take me there? I would love to meet Tannie Marie and her family."

"You are right. We should go there soon. Tannie Marie would love to meet you. She still needs some convincing that someone as gorgeous as you would go out with the likes of me."

"Now Justin Roberts, stop fishing for compliments! But seriously, can you feel as I do? At times I feel that there really is hope for the future of this country, and that we could be part of it. Sometimes I feel so hopeful and then at other times filled with despair."

"You have summed up my feelings perfectly. But for now we have each other, so let's live one day at a time."

FOURTEEN

THE PHRASE 'PHONY WAR' WAS COINED TO DESCRIBE THE PERIOD immediately following Britain's declaration of war on Germany in September 1939. Although war had been declared, no visible military action followed—no air raids, no battles between troops, no naval battles. Nevertheless Britain was at war, and sooner or later its consequences would be obvious. However during this period no one knew what these consequences would be and when they might be experienced. Although on the surface life continued as normal, there was no doubt in anyone's mind that difficult times were on the horizon.

The couple of months after Justin's return from Cape Town had all the characteristics of Britain's phony war period. He and his colleagues on the Student Council kept waiting for the crackdown on student activists predicted by David to start, but as one week merged into the next, nothing happened. It was both uncanny and unsettling, like living in a state of limbo. In the first week after his return, he had reported back to Jenny and Ian, and between them they had organised a local branch of the Phoenix Brigade. They had decided at the outset that none of the current Student Council would be part of the Brigade. They were all too well known by the police, thanks in part to the information provided by Jacob Tremor. With the help of David, persons who had not yet come to the attention of the police were recruited. Once constituted, only Jenny knew the identity of Jo'burg One, and even she did not know the names of the other members.

The protest activities went ahead as planned. The weekly lecture series proved to be a huge success. The attendance grew from one week to the next and prominent speakers from opposition circles were often featured. In fact, the invitation to be a speaker was fast becoming a sought after honour.

A huge sign had been erected near the main gate on which a daily tally was kept of the number of persons in detention and the number of detainees who had died. Newspapers such as the Daily Mail and Sunday Times included photos of the sign once a week.

The weekly vigil near the main gate was also attracting more and more supporters. With the increase in numbers, the protesters now lined both sides of the street in front of the university gates. Some brought their own home made placards, while others carried those supplied by the Student Council. It was an ongoing concern to keep the home made ones from being too inflammatory or provocative. Justin and Colleen took part in these vigils almost every week. The protesters received a mixed reaction from passing motorists. Some gave them the thumbs up, some hurled insults at them, but the majority simply ignored them. It was a sad reflection, Justin mused, on a city where most citizens were English speaking, that so many refused to even acknowledge the draconian measures being taken by the government.

Thankfully there was little violence at these vigils, but one incident did stand out in Justin's mind. He and Colleen were standing on the university side of the street when a protester on the other side was attacked. A burly thug put him in a head lock and dragged off to the fountain in the small park across the road from the university. Justin knew he should go to the protester's aid, but the traffic was heavy. The protesters on the other side of the road seemed to be too shocked to act. Suddenly a diminutive, but wrathful, blond appeared from nowhere and hurled herself onto the back of the thug, beating his head with her fists. Surprised, the thug dropped the protester into the water and turned to confront his attacker. All present held their collective breathes. What would happen next? The thug simply lifted the girl off his back with one hand, lowered her gently to the ground, and to the astonishment of all, kissed her and then walked off. The wet protester then climbed out of the fountain to the cheers from all. The girl had disappeared, but she had defused the situation and saved the day.

And all of these protest activities were happening without any interference from the police.

The one new activity had also gone off without a hitch. At the end of one of the vigils it was decided that those participating would march from the campus to the police headquarters carrying placards. Since all protest marches were banned under the emergency regulations, the march was an open provocation. Jenny and Ian lead some two hundred protesters out of the main gate and along the pavement towards the police headquarters. It was only when they were about half a kilometre from their destination that they were finally halted by a squad of heavily armed police in riot gear. An amplified voice intoned, "You are all part of an illegal demonstration and will be arrested and charged unless you disband immediately." Jenny decided that they had made their point, thanked the protesters, and suggested that they return to campus, or the local pub, in small groups. No further action was taken by the police.

Ironically the only night that Justin did spend in jail had nothing to do with the student protests. A week or so earlier, a well-known clergyman and anti-apartheid campaigner had been detained. Consequently a group of religious leaders had decided to organise a protest march, even although such an action was illegal. The speaker of the weekly lecture happened to be one of the organisers of this march, and Justin happened to be the chair of the meeting. At the end of the lecture the speaker had invited all present to join the march. As they were exiting the stage the speaker asked Justin whether he would join, and Justin could not think of any way to decline. So it was that the next day he found himself marching with a group of about forty clergymen and a handful of students. When the order was given to disband, the leader of the march, the archbishop of Johannesburg, refused unless their colleague was released immediately. Everyone was subsequently arrested and hauled off to large holding cells, where they spent the night. For some reason the group was not separated by race, and so black and white all shared the same cells and food. The mood was festive. Somehow the locks to the cell doors were broken and the inmates joined together and organised a football match using rolled up newspapers and cardboard for the ball. The wardens begged them to return to the cells, where they spent the night singing hymns and praying.

In court the next day, all who had been arrested refused to plead guilty, and in fact said that should the same situation arise, they would do it again. The State was clearly worried as to what to do with about forty ministers and priests. Charging and imprisoning students was one thing, but do that to religious leaders was another. It was an embarrassment. In the end the protesters were told that someone had paid their fines and all could go free. It was almost certain that no fines had been paid, and that it was probably the best way that the government could save face.

For Justin it had been an incredibly uplifting experience, and one which he would always remember. He remarked to Colleen afterwards that one could not find a better cell mate than the archbishop, who incidentally later in life received the Nobel Peace Prize.

It was not only the student leadership, but the country as a whole that was experiencing a phony war like period. The political map of Africa was changing rapidly. Salazar, who had ruled Portugal as a dictator for over thirty five years, was dead, and the country was in the throes of becoming a democracy. One thing was clear that Portugal had no designs on retaining its grip on its two African colonies, Angola and Mozambique. Consequently liberation movements in these two countries were battling each other to determine who would rule after independence. The South African government was doing its best to stoke up the divisions and support the movement it feared least. Newspapers were filled with articles and photos of Portuguese settlers fleeing these two countries, taking as many of their belongings as possible strapped to the roofs of their vehicles. The roads leading south from Angola and west from Mozambique were clogged with convoys of these cars and bakkies. Meanwhile in Rhodesia, the situation was going from bad to worse from a white point of view. In 1965 the white minority government had proclaimed a Unilateral Declaration of Independence, and consequently African political parties had launched a war of liberation. It was becoming increasingly clear that this bush war could not be won by the white government, and that sooner or later Rhodesia would be governed by one or more of the liberation organisations. The three countries, Rhodesia, Angola and Mozambique had provided a useful buffer on South Africa's northern borders. Its own liberation movements had to cross these countries in order to infiltrate South Africa. With the prospect of these three countries in the hands of governments sympathetic to South Africa's liberation movements, the country faced a whole new set of challenges. The future had suddenly become a whole lot less certain, except for one thing—it could not be the same as the past. The images of the fleeing Portuguese were both disturbing and sobering.

The sense of waiting for something to happen even affected the Soweto tutoring programme. Many of the schools in Soweto were either closed or barely operating due to a student strike. Professor Armstrong, Ian and Justin went out to Soweto to consult with the student coordinating committee. The streets in the township were eerily quiet and devoid of people.

Once all had gathered, the professor began proceedings, "The last thing that we would want to do is to be seen as undermining the student strike, but we are willing to continue the programme if that is what you want."

A number of diverse positions were then put forward.

"There is no danger of your undermining our strike. We are protesting against Bantu Education only and not against learning."

"On the other hand, our slogan is 'No education until freedom.' How would it look if we were to be receiving some education while others receive nothing?"

"As I see it, it is a logistical question rather than a political one."

"What do you mean?" asked Ian.

"Every weekend dozens of funerals are held. Most of us need to attend these funerals rather than take part in a tutoring programme. In any case the hall where we met last year is now fully given over to funerals."

"Are these funerals due to AIDS?"

"Some of them, but mostly they are the funerals of protesting students. All protests are banned, but the police do allow us to bury our dead. However often at the conclusion of a funeral, a spontaneous protest erupts, the police move in, and more students are shot dead."

"And that means that there will be more funerals on the next weekend. And so the vicious cycle continues."

The discussion continued in this vein for some time, but in the end it was decided to put the programme on hold pending future developments. It seemed to Justin that his whole world now consisted of waiting in limbo to see how things might turn out.

Or almost his whole world. His relationship with Colleen continued to grow and deepen, and without the Soweto project eating into weekends, they were able to spend more time together. They decided to make the most of the glorious summer weather and to spend a whole weekend in the Magaliesberg. On Friday after classes, they loaded some camping gear into Justin's car and set off. Rather than spend the weekend at the Dome pools they chose the less well-known Eel Pool, where the chances were good that they would have the place to themselves. They arrived hot and sweaty after an hour's hike, stripped off their clothes, and plunged into the cool water. Refreshed, Justin set off to collect some fire wood, while Colleen unrolled their sleeping gear next to the pool and prepared their dinner. Once the fire was well set, Justin braaied some boerewors while they savoured some red wine.

Their hunger satisfied, they sat around fire as the first stars appeared in the evening sky. Justin had his arms around Colleen's waist as they watched the mesmerising flickering of the flames. "You know, there is no-one in the world with whom I would rather spend the rest of my life than with you."

"Do you really mean that?"

"Yes, I really do." Was this actually a marriage proposal at last?

"That is exactly how I feel as well."

A new page in their relationship was being written—they both knew it and were glad of it. They sat in silence for a while with their arms around one another, neither wishing to break the magic of the moment. It was some time before either of them spoke.

"My parents really do like you, even my father in his rather gruff way. I wonder what your parents would make of me."

"Perhaps it is time to find out. Let's go down to the farm together next weekend."

"I agree. Let's do it."

That night they went to sleep with their arms around one another. They woke up the next morning to find a family of baboons sitting one the cliffs above the pools staring at them. Was it the smell of food that had attracted them, or just the entertainment provided by two hairless apes?

The weekend slipped by far too quickly. Mostly they swam, sunbathed, and made love. They also took a break from these activities by hiking over to Castle Gorge and back. On the Sunday afternoon they reluctantly packed up and set off for home. Justin often wished that that weekend could have lasted for ever.

Besides spending time with Colleen, Justin found time to practice and hone his flying skills. On Tuesdays and Thursdays his first class of the morning only began at 10:00. By rising at five in the morning, he was able to put in an hour's practice and still have time to change and make it to his first lecture. The arrangement with his instructor was working out well. Provided he let them know, the key to the aircraft would be waiting for him in the lock box, and he could make his early morning flights. He was confident that in a month or so he would be ready for the test that would make him a qualified private pilot.

The atmosphere at the first Student Council meeting following Justin's return from Cape Town was strained. It did not help that there was an empty seat where Jacob Tremor had once sat, or that Jenny had announced that they would have to hold a special by-election. "How could he have fooled us all for so long?"

"Well, I for one never liked or trusted him," declared Amy Adams. "We should have known he was a fake when he told us we needed to remove the phone handle from the cradle to prevent eavesdropping. It made no sense scientifically."

"I don't think any of us liked him, but we certainly never suspected him. He was always the first to volunteer for anything mildly subversive."

"Exactly, he was always setting a trap for us—easy to see now with 20/20 hindsight."

"Well let's be more careful in the future. We will need to post notices for nominations for the by-election."

"Let's send a copy to the Special Branch. Let them choose their candidate."

At least they could still laugh about what in reality was a painful episode.

Justin had spent time in the library after classes, and was now hurrying home so as not to miss dinner. Andy Kaplan was the cook for the week, and while his cooking might not exactly be classed as gourmet, it was certainly several cuts above what anyone else dished up. He was about to turn into the driveway when a figure materialised out of the hedge. It was Sipho.

"Jeez Sipho, you scared the hell out of me."

"Sorry about that. I wonder if you would help me out with a favour."

"Of course. As I told you before, I am always ready to help. What do you need?"

"I was hoping you would be able to drive me down to Sharpeville."

"Sure thing. How about you join us for dinner and then I will run you down."

"Thanks, but no thanks. You forget I have already had one of your dinners."

"That was when Neville was cooking. Tonight Andy is the chef. It will be delicious."

"Thanks again, but no. Your friends will recognise me as Peter, so it is best if I do not join you."

"Okay, I understand. Well let's be off. My car is just around the back." Justin regretfully imagined the dinner he would be missing. The first part of the journey was slow as they were embroiled in the end of the rush hour traffic. Once clear of the city, they were able to make better time. When they reached Sharpeville, Sipho directed Justin to where he was to meet a comrade. "Just drop me off here. I will be less than ten minutes. I just have to deliver a message. Best you do not park here though. Just drive around slowly and be back in ten minutes."

Left to his own devices, Justin felt uneasy. The ghosts of the past were ever present. Sharpville was engraved into the history of South Africa. It had been the site of one of the early protests against the hated 'pass laws'. What had started as a peaceful protest—the burning of pass books—had turned into a massacre when the police fired on the peaceful protesters. Many had been shot in the back as they tried to flee the scene. The death toll was in the hundreds. Despite its fame—or was it notoriety—Justin had never been to Sharpville before. But it was more than history that contributed to Justin's unease. He did not know exactly what Sipho was up to and was not sure that he wanted to be involved. It was more than likely that Sipho was now part of a group that had turned to violent action against apartheid. What Sipho was doing was most certainly illegal, but so then were the protests that the Student Council organised. The only difference was that one was peaceful and the other violent. No doubt, Sipho had turned his back on peaceful means as ineffective, and perhaps he was right. What had they on Student Council really achieved? It seemed that the white population was now more solidly behind the government than ever before. At times all their protests and other activities seemed futile in the face of an entrenched regime supported by a fearful white population. Sharpville was the symbol

THE RIVERS OF JOY AND SORROW

of the futility of peaceful protest when faced by opponents prepared to resort to violence. However Justin could not envisage himself ever embracing a violence option, even if it was the only effective one. On the other hand, his assistance to Sipho was in of itself non-violent. He was simply a driver.

Justin drove around the township as instructed, and ten minutes later Sipho was back in the car and they were on their way home. "Just drop me off at the Baragwanath Road as before."

"Sure thing. Any time you need help, just let me know."

By the time Justin got home, there was no dinner to be had. Left overs were a rarity when Andy cooked.

Colleen was unusually pensive on the way down to the farm. They would be arriving just in time for dinner, which was as always at midday on the farm. "What do you think your parents will make of me?"

"Are you kidding? They will simply lap you up—probably tell you that you are too good for me."

"Are you sure that you are not just saying that?"

"Quite sure. Just relax and be yourself."

"Okay, if you say so."

Justin turned off the main road onto the dirt track that would take them to the farm—that place where he had spent his childhood. It was lined with blue gum trees and beyond them fields upon fields of mealies. So far all seemed to point towards another good crop. However just one hail storm could wipe all of it out in just a moment. Months of work gone in the blink of an eye.

Justin's mother came out to meet them as they pulled up by the front door. "Mom, I'd like you to meet Colleen. Colleen, my mother."

"Glad to meet you Colleen, and welcome. Justin, I have a surprise for you. Look who is home for the weekend." With that his brother Steven and sister Moira spilled out of the front door.

"What are you two doing here? Shouldn't you both be at school?" To Colleen he explained, "My brother and sister are both at boarding school."

"Mom got us a special weekend pass for a special family occasion."

"And what is the occasion?"

"You of course. The first time our big brother has ever brought a girl home." Colleen could not stop blushing. What had she let herself in for? However it was around the dinner table that Justin's father put her at ease. He was attentive and warm, but not so much that it might be construed as flirting. Colleen found herself warming to him and grateful for the way he made her feel both at home and at ease.

After dinner the three Roberts kids and Colleen retired to the pool where they swam and chatted, mostly about school and sport. After a while Justin suggested to Colleen that she might want to see more of the farm itself. They drove around the farm as he pointed out the various 'camps' in which the crops were growing, mostly mealies and sunflowers. They then went to the milk shed as the cows were entering for the afternoon milking session. What fascinated Colleen most was that each cow knew exactly which stall was hers. She herself could not tell the difference between one stall and the next. The milking was done by hand and she was offered the chance to give it a try. It was not as easy as the workers made it seem. Finally Justin took her to a series of sheds.

"There is something special here that I would like to show you." He pushed open the door, and there sat a dilapidated looking old fashioned car. "It is a 1928 model-A Ford coupé," explained Justin.

"So what is so special about it? Does it even run?"

"It used to belong to my grandfather, but once he passed away it just stood in this shed rusting. Then a couple of summers ago, while I was still in school, a friend of mine and I decided to fix it up. Stephen also helped a bit. We finally got it going again, but we never did fix the brakes. So we drove it all around the farm with no brakes. We sort of learned how to stop it, or at least slow it down using the gears. Sometimes when we approached a gate too fast we would drive in tight circles until we could finally bring it to a halt. I learned a lot about driving that summer, plus we had a lot of fun."

"Would you let me drive it?"

"Of course, but not this time. It will probably take a couple of days work to get it going again. I was hoping Steven would keep it running, but he does not seem interested."

That evening after dinner the family sat around the table and played cards. "It has become something of a family tradition," explained Mrs. Roberts. "We have only had electricity here for the past five years. Before that we only had lamps and candles for lighting, and of course no stereo or TV sets. So playing cards was our main source of entertainment. Isn't there a saying, 'a family that plays rummy together stays together' or something like that?"

"It is not quite the way I heard that saying, but it sounds okay to me," added Justin.

"Talking of family tradition," added Mr. Roberts, "we usually play tennis on Sunday mornings. I hope that you will play with us Colleen."

"I used to play a little in high school, but have not played since then. In any case, I did not bring any gear."

"No problem," said Moira. "Since we are about the same size, I can lend you anything that you need. Plus Justin has several racquets that he keeps here."

"Well if you are sure, I guess I could see if I still remember how to play."

"Good for you. That's the spirit."

The next morning the whole family made its way to the 'tennis club', which in reality comprised two courts on the neighbour's farm. The players, about sixteen all told, comprised farming families in the immediate vicinity. Mr. Roberts invited Colleen to be his partner for the first game. "Don't worry about the score—we just play for fun anyway." Once on the court, he said, "You serve first."

"Are you sure?"

"Yes. Go ahead."

Colleen's first two serves were both aces. On the third serve her opponent managed to get a racquet on the ball, but only for it to hit the net. The fourth serve resulted in a soft return to Colleen's back hand, which she whipped onto the baseline between their two opponents. The first game was won at love. The final score for the match was 6-0.

"Well partner, you certainly showed some form there. My role was mostly that of a spectator. Did you say last night that you played tennis at high school?"

"Yes, I was on the girls' team."

"I'm guessing that the team did quite well?"

"Actually we were the Lowveld champions."

For the rest of the morning all the other players vied with one another to have Colleen as partner.

Justin and Colleen stayed on for dinner before driving back home. It had been a traditional Sunday dinner of roast beef and potatoes with fresh farm grown vegetables. In addition, his mother had made his favourite dessert, a caramel/cream mix on top of tennis biscuits.

"Well you certainly were a great hit with my family. Congratulations."

"I guess it was the tennis that did it."

"No they liked you a lot before, but I admit the tennis did sort of cement things."

They drove on in silence for a while. "What next?"

"What do you mean?", asked Colleen.

"I was wondering if we should announce that we will be getting engaged."

"Isn't that putting the cart before the horse. You haven't actually asked me to marry you yet."

"I know, but I would have to wait until next month."

"Whatever are you talking about?"

"This is February of a leap year, when girls are supposed to make the proposal. So I will have to wait until March."

"You are such an idiot, but a nice one."

"I'm glad you think so. But if I do ask you next month, would you say yes?"

"I will give you my answer then."

"But seriously, should we let others know that we are engaged, or should I say about to get engaged?"

"Let's not say anything until we have told my parents. I would not like them to hear the news from anyone else. They are old-fashioned in that way, especially my father. He would expect you to make a formal request for my hand."

"Yes, you are right. Let's go down over the Easter break. I will ask him then, but I want all of you, not just your hand."

Later on Colleen asked, "What are your plans for the next week or so?"

"To see as much of you as possible. But why do you ask?"

"I was wondering if you wanted to continue our study of the Ring. We have finished with Das Rheingold. Die Walkure is next in the sequence. But don't feel you have to. We will only go on if you really want to."

"I would like to go on. There is something about that music that resonates with me. But there is also a lot that I still don't understand. So I am all for continuing. Let's do it."

The next couple of weeks passed by smoothly and without incident for Justin. He attended lectures, protests, and meetings as planned. Sipho provided the only unexpected occurrences. He showed up twice, each time asking if Justin would be able to drive him places. Justin agreed, and took him once to Hammanskraal and once to Mamelodi. He spent his spare time with Colleen and as decided started their exploration of Die Walkure.

It was the Saturday two weeks after their weekend on the farm that Sipho made yet another of his unexpected appearances. It was Justin's turn to clean the house, and he was just finishing this chore when Sipho showed up. "I have a huge favour to ask. I need to pick some things up, but the kombi that I had found for the job broke down. Unless I am at the appointed rendezvous by this afternoon, I will miss my contact altogether. I know it is a big ask, and at short notice, so if you cannot help I certainly understand."

"Where are you supposed to meet your contact?"

"Oh yes, I forgot to mention that. It is near Komatipoort on the Mozambique border."

"And what time is your appointment?"

"Four this afternoon."

"Okay. I have nothing important on for the rest of today. If we leave now we should just be able to make it."

On the drive down Justin, using as much subtlety as he could muster, tried to find out more about Sipho's mysterious mission. Sipho, on the other hand, was gently evasive. He replied to Justin's probing with general remarks about how they were working together to make a better country. Often he would refer back to the time that they had spent together on Mooivlei and use that experience for how he envisaged South Africa might become one day.

Once they reached the turn off to the town of Komatipoort, Sipho said, "Go more slowly from here on. I have never been to this place before. Next we should come to the turn off to Swaziland, but just keep going." After they had passed this turn off he added, "We should come to a motel next, and about half a kilometre past the motel you need to turn to the right." They passed the motel and kept going slowly, but Justin could not see any road off to the right. Finally Sipho said, "Stop. Here it is. Turn right"

"I cannot see any road."

"You see that track. Drive down it."

"Okay. But it does not seem to lead anywhere."

"Just follow it. I think we are on the right track. If so, there should be a windmill and water tank in about three hundred metres." Sure enough the windmill was just where it was supposed to be. Beyond the windmill the track entered into a thickly wooded area. "We should come to a T-junction in half a kilometre, where we must turn right. Drive for another kilometre and then pull off the track to the left by a large baobab tree and park there." Justin found the tree and pulled up next to it. "Now what?"

"Just wait here with the car. The border is just through these bushes. I will meet my contact at the border fence." Sipho disappeared into the bushes, but returned some five minutes later followed by two other men. Each of them were carrying some heavy boxes.

"Let's load these into the boot. We need to go back for some more." It was not long before the trio re-appeared with another load of boxes. Justin tried to fit as many as possible into the boot, but had to put some on the back seat as well.

With a curt "Thanks guys" the two mysterious strangers melted back into the bushes, and Justin and Sipho were on their way home. Once they were back on the main road, Justin felt there were some issues that he needed to get off his chest. "I am not sure whether I am comfortable being part of whatever it is that you are involved in. Are go going to tell me what is in these boxes?"

"I am sorry that I have made you uncomfortable. Also you have earned the right to know what is in the boxes. But before I tell you, you must decide if you really want to know. Ask yourself if you are better off knowing or not knowing. If I tell you, it makes you complicit. If I don't, and things go wrong, you can claim you are merely an unwitting pawn. So what do you want?"

"I suppose I could make an educated guess about the contents, but you are right. I would rather not know. Are you sure you know what you are doing?"

"You and I think alike. We are like brothers now. We both want the same things for our country, but we differ on how to get there. Yours is perhaps the better way—the way Gandhi would have approved of. Non-violence. But we are dealing with the apartheid government, and for sixty years non-violence has not worked. Our non-violence has always been met with violence. The time has come to try other methods. I wish it were not so."

"I do understand. Tell me, is this the organisation that you mentioned to me before, umkhonto isibashu?"

"Yes it is."

"I wish you well, but I cannot be part of whatever it is that you are planning. Best you do not tell me any more."

Whether it was because he was worn out, or because it was best to leave the conversation at the point it had reached, Sipho leaned back and was asleep within minutes. Once they had past Nelspruit, darkness had set in, and Justin drove on through the night his mind in turmoil. Could it be that Sipho was right—that violence was the only way? After all, what had all their protests and speeches achieved? It was only as they were approaching Johannesburg that he woke Sipho up. "Tell me where I need to take you."

"Make for the Four-ways crossroads and I will direct you from there."

Once the crossroads were reached, Sipho gave a series of directions which eventually brought them out on what appeared to be a typical small holding, of which there were many in this area. There were even signs of small scale farming. Sipho directed him to pull up in front of a shed from which a number of figures quickly materialised, and within seconds all the boxes had vanished.

"Thank you again for your help. And please forget all about this trip. Especially forget about this place. It is our headquarters and no-one who is not already here knows where it is."

"Stay well my friend. And stay safe."

It was well after midnight before Justin finally got to bed.

The trip to the border had exhausted Justin both physically and emotionally. It took him some time to drop off to sleep and only woke up late on Sunday morning. After a quick lunch, he walked over to Colleen's flat hoping to find her in. He was in luck.

"If you are free, let's do something together."

"Sounds a good idea to me. Any ideas?"

"Anything outdoors. It would be nice to hike in the Magaliesberg, but it is too late for that. How about something outdoors that we have never done before."

"That is quite a challenge. Okay, I have it. Let's go and row a boat on the Zoo Lake."

"Great idea."

"Then let's come back here, have supper and listen to to the end of Die Walkure."

The Zoo Lake, it turned out, was a popular venue that afternoon. Many of the row boats had already been hired out. Justin chose one of those still available and they rowed their way around the lake, each taking one of the oars. The lawn beyond the far end of the lake was packed with Africans, mostly clustered in groups of worshippers. The Zoo Lake was one of the few places in the Northern suburbs where Africans were allowed to congregate to worship, or even simply relax. Most of them would be servants from the affluent houses in the area. Relaxing in the sun in the boat with Colleen helped restore Justin's peace of mind. He debated telling her about his trip with Sipho, but in the end deemed it wiser not to.

Colleen made them an omelette for supper, and then they settled down on the couch to listen to the final scene of Die Walkure.

"Give me a quick run down of the plot before we begin the music."

"First Brunnhilde tries to justify her reason for disobeying her father, Wotan, but he is unmoved and determined to punish her. She will be stripped of her godlike immortality and put to sleep on a rock overlooking the River Rhine until wakened and claimed by some man. The only concession that she is able to wring out of Wotan is that her rock be surrounded by flames, so that she can only be claimed by a fearless hero. Wotan carries out his threat, but at the same time agonises over the loss of his favourite daughter."

Colleen turned on the tape. The scene begins with the haunting music depicting Brunnhilde's justification, beginning somewhat hesitantly but finally swelling out triumphantly in the major key. At first Colleen explained how some of the leitmotivs were developing, but as the scene unfolded became quiet and allowed the music to speak for itself. The scene, and indeed the whole opera, ends with the music of the magic fire and sleep, both peaceful and resigned.

"I would like to listen to the last part again, but please hold me tight." Tears were streaming down her face. They listened for a second time.

"That music is so beautiful, but also so sad. It is like nothing I have ever heard before. And it is not just the music. It is the dreadful sense of loss. Wotan abandons his favourite daughter. Brunnhilde loses everything from the love of her father to her very existence. The music, and the sense of loss that it evokes, haunt me beyond what I can even put into words. I wonder how I could hope to cope with that kind of loss."

Tears were still spilling down her face. "Please stay with me tonight. I need you to hold me tightly all night. I need you to tell me that you will never abandon me."

"Colleen you are more precious to me than words can describe. There is nothing in this world that could make me abandon you."

They were a subdued couple the next morning, sharing breakfast. It was the first time Justin had stayed over night, but it was the power of the music that still affected them most.

He had been happy to note that the photo of the two of them was on her bedside table.

"I think I will skip lectures today. I don't think I can face others and act normally. Not yet anyway."

"I need to go, but I will come back as soon as I can. No later than mid-afternoon." With that they kissed and Justin left.

As soon as he could, Justin hurried back to Colleen's flat. He had decided to go straight there rather than first going to his place to pick up some clean clothes. He was a couple of blocks away, and passing the doorway of a pub, when an arm shot out and grabbed him by the elbow. He was about to fight back when he realised his assailant was Ian.

"Don't go any further. The Special Branch are in Colleen's flat. They are holding her and waiting for you."

FIFTEEN

"WHAT DID YOU JUST SAY?"

"I said that the Special Branch are in Colleen's flat and that they are waiting there for you."

"How do you know?"

"Neville went to their flat to visit Julie, and saw them. Also it seems that they are looking for you all over the place. Your house is being staked out."

At this point David appeared from around the corner. "Thank goodness you found him before they did."

"I must go to Colleen immediately."

"Don't be a fool. That is exactly what they want."

"I don't care. I am going."

"No, you are not."

"You can't stop me. Let go of me." With that Justin hit Ian in the solar plexus. As Ian bent over in pain, David pinned Justin from behind.

"Come inside the pub quietly. The last thing that we want is to cause a scene and have the police show up. Will you do that if I let you go?" Justin nodded, and the three of them entered the pub and found a table in the far corner.

"Sorry that I hit you."

"That's okay."

Ian said to David, "Get us some beers so that we do not stand out." David went to the counter.

"You cannot hold me here forever, and as soon as I can I will go to Colleen."

"You are right, we cannot hold you, but first at least let us discuss the situation. Why do the Branch suddenly want you so badly?"

David returned with the beers. "I think you know the answer to that. Did you drive someone down to Komatipoort on Saturday?"

"Yes."

"And then you delivered some boxes to the secret headquarters of umkhonto isibashu."

"I guess."

"Jeez. Do you realise that you are one of the few people who know where the headquarters are? Even I don't know that. No wonder the Special Branch are after you. Right now you must be the most wanted man in the country. There must be an informant down at the border who got your licence plate number."

"What is this umkhonto isibashu?" asked Ian.

"Just pretend that you have never heard of it. What you don't know won't hurt you."

"Well I am going to Colleen right now. I am not going to let her take the wrap for anything I might have done."

"I know we cannot stop you, but at least think this through with us. Once they have you they will get that information out of you one way or another."

"No. I am fairly sure that I can hold up to anything that they might try. I will not reveal the location of the headquarters."

"Okay. So they try a little torture on you—maybe even some sensory deprivation—but they already suspect that that will not work, thanks to the information that they got from Jacob. So what comes next?"

"You tell me."

"You are in this soundproof interrogation room and so far nothing has induced you to speak. Next they bring in Colleen. Why do you think they are holding her as we speak. Perhaps they strip her naked in front of you. Next they start to molest her—perhaps even rape her. Will you still remain silent while she screams out to you to help her?"

Justin turned pale. "No, that would break me. In the final analysis she means much more to me than umkhonto isibashu. So I will still go to her from here even if it means betraying umkhonto isibashu."

"I understand. But consider what happens next. Having abused and tortured both of you, what happens next? Do you really think that they can simply let you go? Colleen's father has some influence. She is not just another torture victim, like some of the Africans that we know. There would be hell to pay. So the two of you will simply have to disappear. Maybe they will kill you both or maybe just lock you up some place and throw away the key. Whatever they do to you, they will most likely announce that they let you go and that you were then abducted by terrorists."

"So I really have no good choices?"

"Perhaps there is one," said Ian, speaking for the first time. "If you get out of the country fast, and they know that you are beyond their clutches, they will have no more use for Colleen, and they can simply let her go unscathed."

"You seem to forget that my passport has been confiscated."

"Your passport would be of no help anyway. You can be sure all points of exit are being closely monitored. David, don't you know people who could smuggle Justin over the border?"

"I do, but it takes days if not weeks to set up such a chain. And we simply do not have the time. We need to get him out in less than twenty four hours. The ongoing search is massive. Plus it is more than likely that all border patrols have been stepped up making it even more difficult to set up a safe exit route."

They sat in silence for a while.

Suddenly Ian said, "I have a thought. Could you not fly yourself out in one of those small planes?"

"I suppose I could. But it would not be legal." The absurdity of the final sentence struck them all simultaneously, and for the first time since entering the pub they laughed. "I would want to take Colleen with me."

"Do you really think we could spirit her away from under the watchful eyes of the Branch?"

"No, I suppose not. It was just wishful thinking."

"I tell you what we could do. As soon as she is released, we could put her on a plane and fly her to wherever you end up. I am sure that she would agree to that."

"Would you really do that? Promise?"

"Yes, I promise."

"Thanks. But I still do not feel right about leaving her. It was just last night that I told her I would never abandon her."

"Look at it this way. If you really love her, do it for her sake."

"So I guess that I have no choice."

"You do have choices, but if you want to prevent harm to Colleen, there is realistically only one thing that you can do. Get out fast."

"Okay. You are right. So what do we do next?"

It was David who now took charge. "First, all of us take a deep breath and calm down. We need to think through the next steps carefully and rationally. Keep sipping your beer. We do not want to attract attention."

After a few swallows, David continued, "Justin, how easy will it be for you to reserve a plane?"

"It should not be difficult. For the past couple of weeks I have been practising before lectures. To make that possible I have come to an arrangement with the club. I let them know in advance that I need a plane early, and one is left out on the apron with the key in a lock box to which I have the combination."

"So on these occasions, are you the only one on the field?"

"Yes, almost always."

"Great. That solves one problem. What kind of range do these planes of yours have?"

"As far as needed. I would be able to reach Botswana, Swaziland, or Mozambique. So there is no problem as far as range is concerned."

"Botswana would be your best bet."

"But there are problems with flying to Botswana. As a student pilot I am prohibited from flying to international destinations. And even if I did have my license, I would be required to file a flight plan and to go through customs. So if I simply landed at the airport in Gaborone, I would be arrested and likely deported."

"Yes, it would be out of the question for you to land at Gaborone. However I know of an abandoned airstrip north of Gaborone and just over the border. We have used it on occasions. I could show you where it is on the map."

"That raises another problem. I would not feel comfortable flying without my charts, especially if I am to find this airstrip of yours."

"Then we will need to get your flying kit. So let us start planning. First you need to reserve a plane. You can make a call from the phone booth down the road. Second, we need to get your flying kit. None of the three of us can go near your house since it is under surveillance. Any ideas?"

Ian spoke up, "Perhaps we could get someone like Andy or Julie to go and fetch it—someone who is not under suspicion."

"Leave Julie out of this. Where would we find Andy?"

"At this time of day he should be at the Civic Theatre rehearsing. Perhaps we could ask him to slip down to the house and get the kit."

"Good plan. Now we need to think about where Justin can spend the night. It would have to be a place that is not known to the police. Any ideas."

No one had any.

Finally Justin asked David, "Do you know the identities of any of the local Phoenix Brigade members? They seem to have remained under the radar to date."

"Excellent suggestion. Yes, I think that might solve this problem."

"So what next?" asked Justin.

"Here is what we will do. First, you need to reserve a plane. I will walk towards the phone booth, and you two follow me at a distance of about one hundred metres. I will keep a look out for any police activity. If I do see something suspicious, I will bend down to tie my shoe lace. At that point, play it cool. Don't run or make any sudden moves. If there is a handy shop, slip into it. Leave by another entrance if there is one. Otherwise gently turn around and go the other way. Does this make sense?"

Both Justin and Ian nodded.

"After you have made the call, I will lead you to the Civic Theatre using the same protocol. I will leave you there and try to and find a place for you spend the night. Meanwhile you must persuade Andy to fetch your flying kit."

"Maybe he could also pick up some clean clothes for me."

"Definitely not. Anyone leaving the house carrying a suit case will be followed. In fact tell him to make it look as if he has gone home to pick up a costume for his part in the play—perhaps a dressing gown or something like that. Also ask him to find a safe place for you to hang out in the theatre until I get back again. There must be any number of rooms that you could use to hide in. Okay, let's go."

All went according to plan. They reached the phone booth without incident. Justin reserved a plane for the following morning, and they then proceeded to the Civic Theatre. Fortunately the scene that was being rehearsed did not involve Andy, who readily agree to fetch the kit. As he was leaving, Justin pulled him aside. "There is a photo of Colleen on my bedside table. Please slip it into my flying kit. Perhaps you could also slip a couple of pairs of socks and underpants into your pockets."

While Andy was gone, Justin and Ian hung out in one of the unused storage rooms. Andy returned an hour later, bringing not only the flying kit, but also the photo, a couple of pairs of socks, and underpants, which he had secreted in his pockets. Ostentatiously draped over his shoulder was a dressing gown which he hoped would explain his trip to any possible watchers. It was over two hours before David reappeared.

The two plus hours spent with Ian in the store room were the most surreal of Justin's experience. It seemed to him that he was suspended in a vacuum between two lives. The life in which he had lived was rapidly coming to an end, but any future life, if indeed there was any hope of one, was completely unknown. Normally he and Ian would have chatted about topics such as student affairs, protest activities, news of the world, and weekend outings. But these all belonged to a life which had now been taken from him. Ian tried his best to make conversation about Justin's future, but it was tough going.

"Where do you hope to end up?" Justin simply shrugged.

"Do you have any family or friends in the UK?"

"No. No one."

"Do you know any one overseas?"

"I did meet some people in New York, but I can hardly count them as friends."

"If you have a choice, where would you like to go?"

"Maybe America or Canada. Although from what I know it is almost impossible to get into the USA. Canada may be more willing to take me."

"What about the UK?"

"I suppose it is an option, but it strikes me as a somewhat soggy and dreary place."

Ian tried to change tack. "Is there anything you would like me to do for you here?"

"You mean other than keep your promise to get Colleen to me as soon as possible?"

"Yes." The realisation suddenly struck Justin that there might be all kinds of lose ends that needed tying up. How many of these should he burden Ian with? Should he ask Ian to let his parents know? They would find out soon enough on the national news, but better to hear it from a friend.

"Please call my parents and let them know."

"Okay. Anything else? What about your lecturers?"

"No need. They will all find out soon enough. But there are all my things at the house. You can have, or else give away, all my books and clothes. Sell my car and use the money to help with Colleen's expenses such as a ticket to wherever I am."

"I can do that."

"I guess you and Jenny can pick up my responsibilities on the Council."

"Yes of course. Don't you worry yourself about Council affairs. Jenny and I will manage."

"There is one other thing now that I think about it. What about the plane? Do I just leave it in Botswana? It would be best to try and get it back somehow."

"Good point. I had never considered that. Perhaps we could get Neville to fly down and fetch it."

"He would need to get help from someone else at the club."

"I am sure club members would rather get their plane back quietly than to be embroiled in some international incident involving the escape of a dangerous criminal. With luck, Neville might even get the plane back out before anyone realises that it had been there. I will speak to Neville. I suspect it will appeal to his sense of adventure."

David finally arrived with the news that he had found a place for Justin to spend the night. "As you suggested, it belongs to one of the Phoenix Brigade members. She has agreed to let us spend the night in the unused servant's room. I will stay with you as well, and then drive you to the airport early tomorrow morning. Speaking of which, do you have the aeronautical map of your destination?"

"Yes, it is right here. Andy was able to get it."

"Get it out so that I can show you where to land."

David studied the map for a while. "It is not marked on the map, but it should be right here. Once the new international airport was opened, it was decommissioned. The area around it has been developed as an industrial park. However the runway, although dirt, is still there. It should not be too difficult to find."

"What should I do when I get there?"

"I have alerted some of our people that you might be on your way, but you cannot stay with them. Your best bet is to make a beeline for the British embassy, and to immediately ask for asylum. Once granted our people may be able to assist you with logistical matters. Above all, do not approach the Botswana police. Since you will be entering their country illegally, they are not likely to help you. Just the opposite in fact."

Ian explained to David the idea that they had come up with for retrieving the plane.

"An excellent idea. But do not approach Neville until Justin is well on his way. Assuming Justin is in the air by around five, maybe wait until six before waking him up and asking for his help. The fewer people that know about Justin's plans the better."

David drove Justin to the place where they would spend the night. It was an older home in Orange Grove, only a few blocks off Louis Botha Avenue. He parked in the lane behind the house and showed Justin to the room where they would spend the night. There was only one bed, and David urged Justin to take it. "You need to be fresh and ready to fly in the morning, so get a good night's sleep. In any case, I want to keep watch just in case we were followed here."

Despite David's urging, Justin did not sleep well. Any time he dozed off he was plagued with nightmares. In one of these he could not get the plane to start, and before long he was surrounded by police. In another he got lost and ended up where he had begun. In yet another he was shot down by Mirage jets of the South African Air Force. He was relieved when David shook him by the shoulder and announced that it was time to go. It was still dark outside.

Traffic was light—almost non-existent—on Louis Botha, and in no time they were at the turn off to Grand Central Airport. David dropped him at the gate to the apron where his plane was waiting for him as requested. There were no other cars in sight. "I will not hang around. A car standing here is too conspicuous. All the very best for your flight and for wherever you end up. I do hope we meet again in better circumstances." With that David drove off just as the sun began to rise.

Justin fetched the keys to the plane and began the pre-flight procedures. He was about halfway through when he realised that his mind was so occupied with other thoughts that he was just going through the motions without paying any attention to what he was doing. For all he knew, the oil level might have been on zero, or the fuel tanks empty, for all the attention that he was paying. He admonished himself to get a grip on things and started the pre-flight over again. Once completed he started the engine and went though the warm up checks. How should he handle the radio? It was too early for anyone to be in the tower, but perhaps radio transmissions were automatically recorded. He decided to follow the standard procedure just in case. He announced his intent to taxi to the holding point of runway 35, and having completed the final checks, he announced his intention to fly to the general flying practice area. Now came the crossing of the Rubicon. There was no turning back. He gripped the yoke tightly to stop his hand from shaking, pushed the throttle to full power, and began the roll down the runway. The still morning air made for a smooth take off, and in no time he was airborne and looking down at the houses below.

Should he contact Johannesburg Approach? Best not to. In any case they would have their hands full at this time of day when many of the international flights from Europe would be arriving. No, best that from this point on, no one should know that he was in the air. How low did he need to fly so as not to be picked up by radar at Jan Smuts? It is a question that he has never thought to ask—never had the need to ask. He decided to fly at one thousand feet above ground level, the lowest legal altitude above a built up area. He was over halfway to his first check point, Hartbeespoort Dam, when he suddenly realised that the plane was still configured for climb and not cruise. The flaps were still at ten degrees, the power on full, and the mixture full rich. He quickly corrected his oversight and admonished himself, fly the plane, fly the plane, pay attention.

He would need to fly in a westerly direction, following the Magaliesberg range, once he reached the Dam. On which side of

the Magaliesberg should he fly? Surely the defence force radar would
be scanning the northern skies. He decided to stay to the south the
Magaliesberg range, and below the line of the ridge. Surely radar
would not pick him up at this altitude. If he was picked up, what
would happen? Would Mirage jets be scrambled to intercept him? If
so, where were they based, and how long would it take for them to
reach him? Would they simply shoot him down or force him to land?
What should he do—try to out run them? The thought of his Cessna
trying to outrun a Mirage jet made him laugh out aloud, but it was
close to a hysterical laugh. Get a grip on yourself. Stop worrying and
concentrate on flying the plane.

The thought of trying to outrun run a Mirage brought back a
memory. It was an incident during his first year when he had stayed
in a residence. His residence traditionally entered a float in the annual
rag procession. Running short of materials with which to build the
float, someone had the bright idea to fetch some floor boards from one
of the condemned houses nearby—not far from the house Justin and
his friends had moved into the following year. It was fondly known
as the Dingleberry house was was mostly used by students for illicit
drinking and sex. It was already in an advanced state of disrepair.
The only transport available for the venture was a clapped out Morris
Minor belonging to one Billy Branson. Billy's prize possession, other
than the car itself, was a speeding ticket showing that he had clocked
eighty clicks in a sixty click zone. Most believed the ticket to be
a forgery since eighty clicks seemed well beyond the clapped out
Morris's capability. Some five 'res boys' piled into the Morris to
fetch the materials that they needed from the Dingleberry house.
The purloining of floor boards was well under way when the Flying
Squad arrived in one of their new Studebakers, manned by a sergeant
and constable. They were all to be taken to the Braamfontein police
station for booking, but there were too many of them to fit into the
Studebaker. "The rest of you get into that Morris and I will follow
you to the police station. Now don't you try to out run me, heh,"
ordered the sergeant. The story had been told and retold many times

over the following weeks until it became the stuff of which legends are made. Justin laughed at the memory, this time less hysterically. Concentrate on flying the plane.

He continued to follow the Magaliesberg past Rustenburg, and then changed direction to head for Gaborone. As the countryside began to flatten out, he descended so as to maintain an altitude of one thousand feet above ground level. Without the protection of the Magaliesberg range off his right wing, he felt far more vulnerable. Is this where the Mirage jets would find him and shoot him down? He scanned the skies anxiously, but nothing was in sight. On the other hand, was it not the case that he could be shot down by a missile even before the jets were in sight? There was nothing to do but to keep flying and hope for the best. Surely the air force's radar scanned the skies for incoming threats rather than small planes fleeing the country?

Right on time he spotted the Kopfontein border post, the main gateway to Gaborone from South Africa, and flew past it on the South African side. Once clear of the border post, he turned to the left thus entering Botswana air space. The remaining task was to find the deserted airstrip and land. He should shortly see a relatively large school, and to his enormous relief, there it was. David had instructed him to keep flying west from the school for about another five kilometres, which should put him at his destination. Look for some industrial type buildings, had been his instruction. He missed it at first, but on his second circuit he spotted what must be the old runway, descended, and flew its length checking for any obstacles. Despite some weeds, it seemed a perfectly safe place to land, and since there was no windsock, he judged the direction of the wind from the smoke from local chimneys. Basically there was no breeze meaning he could land in either direction. Having decided on landing in a northerly direction, he went through the landing procedures, turned from down wind, to base leg, to final approach, and made one of his best landings ever.

He was about to shut down the plane where it had come to rest at the end of the runway when it suddenly occurred to him that if

Neville did come to fetch it that he would need the runway on which to land. Consequently he turned the plane into the weeds on the edge of the runway before shutting it down. So far the arrival of the plane had not attracted any attention, but at about six thirty in the morning it seemed that no one was around. It was after all an industrial rather than a residential area. There was no one to report his arrival to the police.

According to his map, the airstrip was about one kilometre east of the main Gaborone-Francistown highway. From there it would be another fifteen or so kilometres into the town itself—too far to walk. He would not be needing his flight kit any more, but he did tuck the photo of Colleen into his shirt and the extra underwear and socks into his trouser pockets, after which he headed down the road to the main main highway, where he decided to hitch a ride into town. There was quite a bit of truck traffic at this time of day, but none of them stopped for him. Maybe it was against the rules to stop for hitch-hikers. However it was not too long before a bakkie with two goats in the back stopped to pick him up. Justin was glad that the driver invited him into the cab rather than sending him to the back with the goats.

"What is a white boy like you doing on the road at this time in the morning?"

Justin had to think quickly. "I managed to get an overnight ride on a truck from Francistown, but it only went as far as where you picked me up. So now I am trying to get all the way into Gaborone."

"So what are you doing in Botswana?"

"Basically sight seeing. I spent a couple of months up in the Okavango, but now I am on my way back home."

"And where is that?"

"My home is in England. I will be starting university later this year."

"So you are one of those clever boys. My son would like to go to university, but we may not be able to afford it." He spent the rest of the journey talking about his family and the plight of small time farmers. As they approached the city centre he asked, "Where do you wish to be dropped off?"

"Anywhere near the British Embassy will be fine. And thank you very much for giving me a ride."

As it turned out, the embassy did not open until nine, meaning he had nearly two hours to kill. His main concern was to avoid being arrested, although quelling his hunger was a close second. Surely everyone who saw him could see that he was a criminal who had entered the country illegally. Was it not stamped on his forehead? However no one seemed to pay him the slightest attention. He walked around the streets until he found a likely spot to get some coffee and a bite to eat. He searched his wallet, but of course all he had were South African Rand. However as it turned out the café owner was more than willing to accept rands as payment (with a commission) and Justin was able to buy boerewors and pap to eat, washed down with some coffee. It was not a typical breakfast, but when you are that hungry, who cares.

Justin returned to the embassy just as it was opening, but already there was a queue for consular services. There were information boards showing where to line up for visas and passports, but nothing about asylum applications. In the end he joined the general inquiries queue. He did not mind the wait as it gave Neville more time to remove the plane from Botswana before his escape became known. Finally when it was his turn he simply stated that he was here to seek asylum. The clerk behind the counter seemed somewhat taken aback. Clearly this was not an every day occurrence, and he had to go and ask for directions. When he returned he simply said, "Follow me." Justin was taken to a rather austere room with little more than a table and a few chairs. It did not even have a window. After waiting there alone for about ten minutes, a man who introduced himself as the consul entered the room.

"Am I correct in assuming that you are seeking political asylum?"

"That is correct, sir."

"We have never found reasonable cause to offer anyone from Botswana political asylum."

"Actually I am from South Africa, sir."

"Then why did you not apply in that country?"

"Actually I had to leave in rather a hurry. The security police were trying to arrest me."

"So when and how did you arrive in Botswana?"

"It was early this morning. Unless I have to I would rather not say how in order to protect those who helped me."

"For now that is enough. I take it you did not enter legally."

"Correct. In any case my passport was confiscated last year."

"I see. Just a few more questions. Do you know anyone in the UK who could sponsor you—any family or relatives?"

"Not a soul."

"And here in Botswana?

"No one here either."

"I will need to discuss your case with the ambassador. In the meanwhile you will remain here in custody. I will take you to a more comfortable room, but you are not to leave it. If you need anything to eat or drink, or if you need to use the bathroom, just ring the bell."

Justin was led along a series of corridors to a plush room which had all the trappings of an up-scale doctor's waiting room. At least there was a good selection of magazines with which to occupy his mind. He picked out one, a British travel magazine, but lack of sleep finally caught up with him, and he dozed off before completing the first article. He did not know how long he had slept when he was woken by two men entering the room.

"It seems you do have friends here after all," said the consul. Justin stared at him blankly. "Allow me to introduce you to Mr. Adler. He is a lawyer for the Anti-apartheid Movement. He has been authorised not only sponsor your stay in the UK, but to pay for your trip there."

Justin looked dumbfounded. "How did you know that I was here?"

"We were tipped off last night that you might be arriving. I phoned the consulate this morning, and sure enough here you are. It is my job to get you to the UK as soon as possible."

"That is very generous of you. Would it be possible for me to stay here in Botswana until my girlfriend can join me?"

"I am afraid not. First of all you are not here legally. If the South African authorities put pressure on Botswana to return you, they would most likely comply. But more than that, from what I was told you are desperately wanted by the Special Branch. It would not be beyond them to mount a cross-border raid and simply nab you if they knew where you were staying. They have done that before. They have also sent assassination squads in the past, but from what I gather you are wanted alive."

"I see. So what comes next?"

"We will get you out of Botswana as soon as possible, this afternoon or evening if we can. Obviously you cannot fly to London from Jan Smuts, so it will have to be from Nairobi. We are looking at ways to get you from here to Nairobi."

"If I could add to that," continued the consul, "your application for asylum has been approved on a temporary basis and will be finalised in London once you get there."

"It should not be a problem since the Anti-apartheid Movement will provide you with a stipend until you can get back on your feet."

"Can you let my friends in South Africa know that I have arrived safely?"

"That has already been done. However it will not be made public until you are safely out of Botswana."

At this point a third man entered the room and whispered something to the consul. After he had left the consul said, "We have an embassy plane leaving for Nairobi tonight. I have managed to have you put on that flight. Then you can take the first plane from there to London."

"Thank you both for all you have done."

"Perhaps it is us who should thank you. I don't know what you have done, but if the South African police are so desperate to get their hands on you, it must been some thing major to further the cause of a free and non-racial South Africa."

"Thank you, but I am no hero," Justin mumbled. What he really wanted to say was that he was a coward, a rat, who was willing to abandon the one he most dearly loved.

SIXTEEN

JUSTIN'S FIRST MONTH IN LONDON FELT LIKE AN UNREAL DREAM—A series of seemingly unconnected, confused, and jumbled events. He had been apprehended in the arrivals hall after his British Air flight from Nairobi had landed. From there he had been led to a cubicle, where he was welcomed by a member of the Anti-apartheid Movement, as well as an immigration official. He was processed quickly and given temporary asylum documents, after which he was driven to the headquarters of the Anti-apartheid Movement in Bloomsbury. Here he was allocated a room reserved for visiting dignitaries and then taken to lunch with some of the leaders of the Movement.

Lunch for Justin unfolded as a blur. He had not had a proper sleep for the past three nights, and it was catching up with him. At least his host realised that he was finding it difficult to remain awake and suggested that he get some sleep. "You will need to be rested and wide awake for the press conference that we have scheduled for tomorrow morning." Justin perked up at this announcement. It would be his opportunity to make his whereabouts known to the South African authorities, who would then have no cause to continue their detention of Colleen. More importantly, it would provide Colleen with a way of contacting him when she arrived in London. He could already picture himself going out to Heathrow to welcome her to the UK. No doubt the Anti-apartheid Movement had other motives for the press conference, but these would not be problematic for him. After all, the Movement had made his flight and asylum application possible, besides which they all wanted the same thing. Following lunch, Justin gratefully fell into bed and did not wake up again until the following morning. Not even sure of his whereabouts, he tried to decide what to do next. His dilemma was solved when an earnest young woman knocked on his door and offered to show him where he could get breakfast. After breakfast he was taken to meet with a member of the Anti-apartheid Movement, one who had seemingly been assigned as his mentor and handler, and who simply introduced himself as Alan.

After a few polite inquiries as to how Justin had slept and whether breakfast had been satisfactory, Alan got down to business. "Can you give me any more details about your escape from South Africa to Botswana?"

"I could, but it would involve compromising those who helped me. Is it really important?"

"Yes, I do understand your position. However please understand ours. There have been various attempts by the security police of your country to infiltrate our Movement, and so we have to be cautious. We do need to satisfy ourselves that you are a genuine refugee and one of us. I am sorry to have to ask you these questions, but perhaps you can see why they are important to us."

"Yes, I do understand. After all, our Student Council was infiltrated by the police." Justin proceeded to give a short description of his escape.

"Thank you. We can now easily verify your story. If, as you claim, David Cohen was responsible for your escape, then you are in the clear. We know and respect him. However, there is no need for you to divulge the details of your escape at the press conference. In fact, I advise you not to."

"Thanks for the advice. When is the press conference by the way?"

"It was been scheduled for two this afternoon."

At this point the girl who had taken Justin to breakfast entered the room with morning tea. Once they had been served, Alan continued.

"Let me outline what we can offer you over the coming weeks. I have permission to offer you a position as a consultant for the period of one month starting today. The stipend attached to this position is nothing to write home about, but it will cover your living expenses. In addition you may continue to stay in our VIP room until such time as we need it again, which might be in about two weeks time. If you still need a place to stay after that you might want to have a word with Amanda."

"Who is she?"

"She is the girl who brought you here this morning."

"Of course. My mind does not seem to have caught up with my body yet."

"She rents an old house in Islington. She occupies one room and rents the others out, often to persons associated with our Movement. As a result there is a lot of coming and going, and quite often there is a room to spare. Besides, she has a soft heart and likes to see herself as rescuing victims of lost causes. Not that you are a lost cause."

Justin ignored Alan's attempt to recover and asked, "What is expected of me as a consultant?"

"Not much. We receive quite a lot of information from South Africa, but we are not always sure what to make of it. We would appreciate your take on some to the reports that we receive. Then we would also like you to meet personally with some of the people that we are trying to influence, such as members of parliament and businessmen. Hearing from someone who has actually experienced apartheid first hand often cuts more ice with them than simply hearing from those of us who can only talk about it second hand. But we will not take much of your time. For the most part you can work out how to get back on your feet. By the way, have you given any thought as to what you might do with yourself in the future?"

"I cannot really say that I have. Only three days ago, I was back in South Africa with no intention whatsoever of fleeing. I can barely comprehend that I am here in London. It all seems so unreal. My girlfriend and I did talk once or twice about possibly leaving the country sometime in the future and going to Canada or the USA, but we were never really serious about it. Anyway, until my girlfriend arrives in the UK, I will stay here. Then we can decide on our future together."

"That sounds like a viable plan for now. By the way, why did you leave so suddenly?"

Justin paused to consider his answer to this question. How much should he divulge? "Let me just say that some information that the security police consider vital sort of fell into my lap unexpectedly. It seems that they will stop at nothing to extract that information from me. That is why David Cohen and others basically forced me to flee."

It was at this point that a new person entered the room. "There is some news that you both might want to digest before going to the press conference. We are getting reports from South Africa that arrests on a massive scale are occurring throughout the country. There are bound to be questions about it at the press conference. You might want to have some of this information at your finger tips." Looking at Justin, she continued, "You do not seem that surprised."

"No. We have been expecting it for some time. We have even taken some steps to survive the rounding up of our leaders. But before the press conference I would like to try to find out how extensive the round up has been. It is likely that I know many of those who have been detained." Privately he wondered whether David, Ian, and Jenny were amongst those detained. More than likely. What about Colleen? And what about Sipho and those at the headquarters of umkhonto isibashu? Had his flight been in vain? Might it not have been better to have been detained along with all the others than to be alone and isolated here in London? Was he no more than a rat who had deserted the sinking ship?

Alan seemed to sense Justin's distress. "If you would rather, we could postpone the press conference in the light of the ongoing events."

"No. I would rather get it over with."

The press conference unfolded along the expected lines. Alan introduced Justin, who then gave a brief description of some of the protest activities in which he had participated. The session was then opened for questions. While many were about the ongoing crack down and about Justin's activities, a couple of them gave Justin pause to consider.

"The protest activities that you have just described do not seem particularly seditious. Why do the police want you so badly?"

"Any protest is considered by the government to be seditious, and hence needs to be put down. But yes, there are a couple of actions with which I was involved and which I cannot and will not elaborate on here."

"How did you manage to escape to Botswana?"

"I cannot reveal the details of my escape as it would endanger those who helped me. Suffice to say that it was the first time that this means of escape had been employed, and perhaps it might be used again. So no comment."

After the news conference some of the journalists stayed on and tried to press Justin for more details, which he politely, but firmly, refused to supply. Alan afterwards proclaimed the conference to have been a great success.

The next morning Amanda burst into Justin's room, even although he was still in bed. She was holding a pile of newspapers. "You are featured in every one of these papers—on the front page in at least half of them. Just look at this headline. It is my favourite. 'Anti-apartheid hero makes a daring escape.'"

Justin shook his head. "I am no hero. I fled like a coward leaving behind my friends and girlfriend to face the music. They are the real heroes."

"So you have a girlfriend." Amanda seemed somewhat disappointed. "Can you tell me about her. What is her name?"

"Perhaps another time. I still need to get dressed."

Amanda took the hint and started to leave. "By the way, drop in to see Alan as soon as you can."

"Thanks for coming in. It seems your press conference has stirred up quite a bit of interest. I have taken the liberty of arranging a number of interviews for you. There some Labour MPs who would like to meet with you, and I have scheduled them for ten o'clock tomorrow morning. Then there are some sports administrators, who would like your take on the proposed boycotts of various sports in South Africa. I have scheduled them for eleven o'clock."

It also turned out that Alan had received multiple reports concerning the ongoing crack down and wanted Justin to fill him in on details, such as when a location was mentioned. Justin scanned the reports eagerly for the mention of any names, but there were none. As usual, the police were refusing to divulge the names and whereabouts of those detained. Having answered Alan's questions and cleared up some misconceptions, Justin had time to consider some of his own concerns. He desperately needed to find out whether Colleen was on her way to the UK. Perhaps he could phone someone, but who? Ian and Jenny had applied for a phone, but their chances of getting one were practically zero. None of his other colleagues had even bothered to apply for one. And then it struck him. Perhaps he could phone the Student Council office.

"Alan, would it be okay for me to phone the university to see if I can get some more up-to-date information?"

"By all means go ahead. The more information that we can get the better." Justin dialled the overseas operator and placed a call to the student office. He was informed that it would be put through in two hours time.

As promised the operator returned the call exactly two hours later. "When I tried to ring the number that you gave me, all I got was a recorded message informing me that the number had been discontinued. Is there any other number that you would like me to try?"

"Thank you for trying. There is no other number."

While on the phone, Justin contemplated calling his parents to let them know about his whereabouts and to assure them that he was well and unharmed. However, they still only had a party line, and he could not stand the thought of all the neighbours listening in and then spreading gossip around the district. Instead he sat down to write them a letter. While he was at it, he decided to write to as many of his colleagues as possible, asking about Colleen's proposed trip to join him. It would take at least a week for these letters to arrive, and another week for the replies to reach him. At least it felt good to be doing something positive rather than simply sitting around fretting.

Justin's interview with the sports administrators led to further publicity. During his time with them he had cautiously endorsed the idea of expanding the sports boycott of South Africa, and had given his reasons for doing so. These remarks again made headline news in a number of newspapers. After the interview, Alan asked Justin to come to his office.

"Well done on both interviews. The MPs were certainly impressed with the first hand information that you were able to give them, and your answers to the questions of the sports administrators will almost certainly increase the pressure for a blanket boycott."

"Thank you. I did my best."

"I have some more meetings scheduled for you. A representative from Amnesty International would like to meet with you. He was especially interested in the fact that you have met with and interviewed victims of torture. I have scheduled that meeting for tomorrow morning. Then the BBC would like to do a TV interview with you. We will need to go to their studios for that. I have agreed to the day after tomorrow. Meanwhile there are a few more reports on the ongoing crackdown that you might like to see, and about which I have a couple of questions."

The first week bled into the second. It was mostly more of the same—meeting with interested persons and organisations, and reading and interpreting reports. It was becoming increasingly difficult, if not plain farcical, for him to maintain the façade of a hero, while in his own mind he was no more than a coward. Justin made a habit of checking the mail room twice a day for letters. At first there was nothing, but by the beginning of the second week he was inundated with letters. Most were simply from well-wishers in the UK, but there were a few from various universities, offering him a place to continue with his studies. At first he considered responding with a thank you note to all the former, but within days such a task would have been overwhelming. He kept a file on the latter as he knew that before long he would need to make a decision about his future. However the letters that he most eagerly sought—those from South Africa—did not materialise.

By the end of the second week he was becoming desperate for news about Colleen. In the end he shelved his reluctance and placed an international call to the Jansen household. Again he had to wait for about two hours. When the operator called him back she informed him that the party at that number had declined to accept his call. Misgivings crowded his mind. Had he been too quick to accede to David's and Ian's urging and flee the country? Could he not have cut some kind of deal with the Special Branch—the information that they sought in return for an exit permit for Colleen and himself? But then why would the Branch bother with a deal when they could surely break him? And even if a deal was made, what were the chances that the Branch would actually stick to their side of the bargain? It was all so confusing.

At the end of the second week, Alan explained to him gently that he would be needing the VIP room during the following week, and that Justin would have to move out. "Why not ask Amanda to fix you up with a place to stay. I am sure that she would like to help you." Justin suspected there might be complications if he turned to Amanda for help, but on the other hand he had no idea how to even go about looking for a room to stay in a city as bewildering as London. As it turned out, Amanda was more than willing to help out. "Why not simply move in with me. My room is plenty big."

"I appreciate the offer, but at this stage I would prefer a room of my own."

"Well, there is a room in our place that is unoccupied until the end of next month. I have promised it to Fiona if she does actually return. However, she seems to have taken up in an ashram somewhere in India, and I doubt if whether we will see her again. It's a pity. She was one of our best protest organisers. Anyway you are welcome to her room until the end of next month and longer if she does not return."

"Thanks. I will move in over the weekend."

"Will you need any help with your things?"

Justin laughed. "I escaped in the clothes that I was wearing. At least that makes moving less of a hassle."

Justin was not sure what to expect, but it was certainly not what confronted him when he arrived at Amanda's apartment building. The house that he had lived in previously was by no means luxurious, but compared to his new digs, it was infinitely more preferable. It was a far cry from what he had expected of London. It was an old, four story structure. The ground floor was occupied by a dry cleaning outfit. A narrow staircase led to to the first floor on which there were two rooms, both rented to friends of Amanda. The second floor was given over to a common area, comprising of a kitchen and what might have passed as a dining area except that there was no table. There were two rooms on the top floor, one of which was Amanda's and the other Fiona's—now Justin's for the time being. The house had originally been built without a bathroom. That deficit had been rectified by building a room which was accessed from a turn in the landing of the staircase. It clung to the side of the building something like a swallow's nest on a barn. One could peer through the cracks in the floor to a courtyard below. It comprised a shower, basin, and toilet.

Amanda must have sensed Justin's shock. "Never mind. Everyone in London lives in squalor." If her explanation had been meant to reassure him, it did not succeed in its intent. It did underscore the urgency to chart his future moves.

In the week after moving into Fiona's room, Justin paid a visit to the Canadian consulate. It proved to be somewhat discouraging.

After waiting for nearly an hour, he was finally shown into a room where he could speak to someone. Having introduced himself, Justin immediately made his pitch. "I was wondering if it might be possible to apply for asylum in Canada?"

"That is a very unique request. No one has ever asked for asylum from the UK before. I cannot imagine what the basis might be for such a request. It is not as if there is any political prosecution here that we know of."

"No, I am seeking asylum from South Africa."

"But if you are now in the UK, have you not already received asylum here?"

"Yes, that is the case."

"Well you cannot very well request asylum from a country where you have already received asylum. Since you have already received asylum here, there is no basis for another request."

"So what you are saying is that there is no way that I can apply for asylum in Canada."

"Exactly. If you had gone to our embassy in Pretoria and requested asylum, it would have been a different matter altogether. But now it is too late."

"Yes, I understand. What is the possibility of applying to immigrate to Canada?"

"Do you have a sponsor in Canada?"

"No. I do not know a soul there."

"That makes it much more difficult. Do you have any qualifications? Would you be able to support yourself?"

"At this point I am working on my bachelors degree—or was until I had to flee."

"So you have no qualifications."

"No, I guess not."

"Well you can always go ahead and apply to immigrate to Canada, but I must be honest with you. Your chances are not very good. I suggest that you complete your degree here in the UK and then, if you are still interested, make your application."

Justin thanked the man and left.

His visit to the United States consulate was even more discouraging. Unlike Canada, the USA also had some kind of quota system, according to which Justin figured that he might well be in his seventies before his turn came up.

With less than a week to go of his consultancy with the Anti-apartheid Movement, Justin began to think seriously about his next move. He had received a number of offers from various universities to further his studies. A few even offered a small stipend. However, he did not think that any of them would provide enough money to support both Colleen and himself. In any case, he did not know enough about the universities concerned, or even what constituted a living wage in the UK. He decided to show the offers that he had received to Alan and solicit his advice. The move proved most fortuitous.

"A good friend of mine, and incidentally one of our most loyal supporters, is a Dean at a university in Surrey. I see that one of your offers is from his institution. I will call him and see if he can offer you something better."

Sure enough, a few days later Justin was offered the position as a tutor—an offer that he immediately accepted.

It was also during this week that finally a letter from South Africa arrived. It was from Neville. Justin read, and reread, it a number of times. The news did not get better with the rereading of it.

Hi Justin,

Just to let you know I did received your letter. Unfortunately I do not have many answers for you.

Many of our friends were detained a day or two after you had left. These include Jenny, Ian, David, and Tony. Prof. Armstrong did his best to find out where they are and how they are coping, but he was not successful. As I write this letter there is a rumour that he too has been picked up.

You asked about Colleen. Three days after you left, the police released her to her father's custody. That same day he put both her and Julie on a plane to some unknown (to me) destination. I do remember Julie once telling me that they had a second cousin, or perhaps an aunt, in Australia or New Zealand, or some place like that. Sorry I can't be more specific. So they might have been sent there.

The only good news that I have for you is that I was able to retrieve your plane from Botswana, and no one is any the wiser that you 'borrowed' it. Nifty move by the way. The other good news is that I might be selected to play hockey for Transvaal this coming season.

Your friend,
Neville

Justin was devastated. He had always been sure that Colleen would be on her way to London sooner or later, but now he knew that she had been spirited off to some unknown destination. Did she even know how to contact him? Would she be allowed to contact him? Did she even want to contact him after he had abandoned her? Would he ever see her again?

There seemed little point in going to Surrey now. On the other hand, what choice did he have? He could not support himself if he stayed in London, not that that prospect held out any attraction. There was nothing for it but to continue with his plan to move to Surrey and see how things eventually worked out.

That fateful Monday morning had begun blissfully for Colleen. She and Justin had had breakfast together, subdued by the memory of haunting music that accompanies the abandonment of Brunnhilde in Die Walkure, but still glowing from a night of love making. It was the first time Justin had stayed over night.

"I think I will skip lectures today. I don't think I can face others and act normally. Not yet anyway," announced Colleen.

"I need to go, but I will come back as soon as I can. Not later than mid-afternoon." With that they kissed and Justin left. It was only later in the morning that Julie emerged from her room remarking, "Well you and Justin certainly made up for lost time."

Later in the morning, while Colleen was doing her laundry, there was a loud knocking on the door. It was Julie who opened the door, and three men pushed their way in before a startled Julie could react. She gave a stifled scream and Colleen came running to her help. She immediately recognised one of the men as Col. Snyman.

"Has something happened to Justin?" she asked in terror.

"You tell me! Is he here?"

"No."

"Search the flat," he ordered the other two men.

The sounds of their bedrooms being searched incensed Julie, who burst out, "Just who do you think you are bursting in like this?"

"Did your father never teach you that children should be seen but not heard?"

Julie was about to explode, but was silenced by a stern look from Colleen, who shook her head and put a finger to her lips. Colleen knew full well that the Special Branch were a law unto themselves and could do whatever they liked.

The two policemen returned to the living room reporting that no one else could be found in the flat. "In that case you can all depart and leave us alone in peace," said Colleen hopefully.

"I think not. We will stay here until your boyfriend arrives. When do you expect him?"

Justin had said he would return around mid-afternoon, but Colleen replied, "I have no idea."

"In that case we will wait here until he does show up."

The two girls looked at one another in dismay. It was Julie who spoke first. "Since you have no use for me, I think I will go now. I have some lectures that I need to attend."

"Not a chance. You will both stay here with my two men until I say so. I cannot risk you alerting Justin Roberts somehow. He is a wanted man."

Nothing was said for a while. Suddenly there was the sound of footsteps outside the door. "He is here whispered one of the men."

Col. Snyman flung the door open and pounced on a surprised Neville. "Oh! It's only you. Get the hell away from here if you know what is good for you." Neville needed no second bidding.

He then addressed his two men, "One of you stay here with the girls and the other cover the lobby door from across the street. Make sure that these girls do not try to warn Roberts if he does approach. If he has still not shown up by evening, I will send a relief team."

With that Col. Snyman left, slamming the door behind him.

Colleen could feel tears coming, but she was damned if she would cry in front of these loathsome men. She went to her bedroom, closed the door, and lay down on her bed. But the door to her room was immediately flung open. "You will remain in my sight at all times, and stay away from the window."

Colleen turned her back on her tormentor.

Morning dragged on into afternoon and there was still no sign of Justin, much to Colleen's relief. But where was he, and why were the police so anxious to get a hold of him? At one stage the man who was stationed outside entered the flat and asked if he could use the bathroom.

Colleen said no, but he used it anyway.

As it was getting dark, Col. Snyman returned with two new men. The policeman who had been watching the girls asked, "Is there still not sign of Roberts?"

"No. We cannot find the bliksem anywhere."

Colleen tried to smirk, but it only came out as a rather sad and worried smile.

As it turned out the orders of the two relief men were to both stay in the flat overnight. Colleen and Julie rustled up a dinner, but neither of them were inclined to eat it. They pointedly did not offer any food to their guardians, but this gesture seemed to slip by unnoticed. Later the two girls were forced to sleep with their bedroom doors open. Sleep eluded Colleen for most of the night.

The next day passed by uneventfully. The night watchmen were replaced soon after daybreak, and they in turn were replaced by another set of night watchmen that evening. Colleen and Julie ignored their minders to the best of their ability, and the policemen were quite content to do the same. The girls tried to busy themselves with household chores and by studying, but it was mostly just for show—a pretence that they did not care that they were being held captives. Worst of all was that there was no news at all about Justin. Had he been captured, or was he still at large?

It was on the afternoon of the third day that Col. Snyman made his appearance again. He was obviously in a foul mood. "Well it seems that your precious boyfriend has buggered off to England, leaving you behind to face the music. That's what you get when you shack up with a dirty, commie coward."

"I don't believe you!" retorted Colleen, to cover up her shock and relief. So it seemed he was safe, but how could he simply abandon her? Feelings of relief and anger surged through her body and she started shaking.

"I couldn't care what you believe. It is nothing to me."

"So what will happen to us now?" asked Julie.

"You will stay here for at least another night until I decide what to do with you. If you, Colleen, had anything to do with his escape, you are in deep trouble. If fact you might as well tell me right now what you know."

Colleen shook her head saying, "I know nothing."

"Well after sometime in detention you might suddenly remember something." As he left he instructed the two policemen, "Watch them very carefully tonight. They may try something stupid."

The next morning Col. Snyman arrived and told the two night watchmen that they could leave. He said nothing at all to the girls, and simply made himself at home in the living room. An unreal silence settled over the room. No one spoke a word. Colleen was relieved when her father burst through the door of their flat. However, she was immediately put on her guard when her father shook Snyman's hand rather than berating him for the treatment of his daughters. The two men went outside to talk, and when they returned her father said abruptly, "You two are coming with me. Pack a suitcase each." It seemed that some back room deal had already been agreed upon. The two girls packed as quickly as they could, not wanting to spend another minute in Snyman's presence. Colleen made sure to pack the photo of Justin and herself.

"Where are you taking us? Home?"

"I will tell you once we are in my car." But even once they were in the car, Mr. Jansen remained silent. It seemed he was seething with anger. They were heading east out of town, the direction in which Sabie lay. However, instead of continuing in an eastbound direction, Mr. Jansen took the exit for Jan Smuts airport. It was only then that he spoke.

"I am sending you to stay with a distant relative of mine in Australia."

"Why not just take us home?"

He turned on Colleen. "If you stay in South Africa, it will be in detention. This is the best deal I could cut with Snyman. And, I might add, it took a lot of persuasion and threats to get him to release you at all. So be thankful for small mercies."

"So why do I have to go to Australia?" asked Julie.

"One to keep your sister company. But more importantly to keep you out of trouble. I do not trust either of you now that you are in with a bad crowd."

At Jan Smuts airport, Mr Jansen dropped off his daughters at the terminal entrance, where a policeman met them and escorted them through the check-in process. Finally, Colleen and Julie were put on an South African Airways plane bound for Australia under the watchful eye of the policeman.

Both girls were exhausted, as neither of them had had much sleep during the previous three nights. They fell asleep almost immediately after take off, and slept through most of the flight. Colleen and Julie exited the plane when it landed in Perth, and after a two hour layover they continued their journey to Alice Springs. Here they were met by a Wilma de Kock, who immediately took them back out onto the apron where a plane, which Colleen recognised as a Cessna 182, was waiting for them. The two girls was shown into the back seat, while Wilma took the right hand seat next to the pilot. Colleen watched in dismay as a seemingly endless, flat, monotonous, brown desert, set about with small hardy shrubs, unfolded mile after mile. Her father could not have picked a more remote prison. It took another two hours before they reached their final destination—a dirt strip on some typically remote outback sheep station. An empty car was standing in the shade of a scruffy tree. Before they reached the car, the Cessna had already taken off again. They were driven down a rutted track to the nearby farm house. It was surrounded on three sides by an open verandah. The corrugated iron roof was in severe need of a new coat of paint. Behind the house a lonely windmill was lazily pumping water into an above ground circular tank. A row of blue gum trees provided the only shade.

It was only after she had served coffee all around that Wilma finally spoke. She was a small and wiry woman with short greyish hair and a weather-beaten face. Colleen estimated her to be in her sixties, although she was probably younger than she looked, the harsh desert climate having taken its toll.

"You are probably wondering who I am and why you are here. I have already told you my name. I am the daughter of the first, or it might be second, cousin of your father's father. So you can work out our relationship for yourselves—I have no idea. We were quite close as kids, but then my family moved to Australia. We never saw one another again, but over the years we did keep in touch via Christmas cards. So I could not have been more surprised when he actually phoned here and asked me to put the two of you up. I gather that you are in some kind of trouble with the police."

Colleen tried to interrupt to explain the situation, but Wilma got in first. "No. I do not even want to know. It is your father's wish that you stay here with me for the time being."

Colleen was in a truculent mood. "If you think that you can keep me here as a prisoner, you are mistaken."

"You are free to leave any time. However, your father is paying for your board and lodging, and so I have no incentive to help you go. Heavens knows we need the money. But there a few facts that you might want to bear in mind. It is fifty kilometres from here to the nearest town, Wallagera. You could walk it I suppose, but it would take two to three days. Even the most hardy of my sheep crew would not survive three days in this desert. I suppose you might think of stealing my car, but there is only one road around here and it goes straight to town, where you would be picked up by the local policeman. It would make his day to arrest a pretty young girl. He has basically nothing to do around here."

Colleen was smart enough to realise that she was defeated. Even if she evaded the town's one cop and perhaps made it back to Alice Springs, she did not have a cent on her, and nowhere to go. She was so angry she began to shake, and retired to her room. She was not even sure with whom she was most angry—just that she felt an uncontrollable rage. She was mad as hell at Snyman in particular and the Special Branch in general. They were all monsters. She was angry at her father. How could he make such a cruel deal with her tormentors? How could he support such an unjust system? She was angry with Justin. How could he up an abandon her, especially after he had so recently declared he would never do so? How could she have fallen for such a creep? Gradually her rage gave way to despair, and she lay on her bed sobbing.

Meanwhile Julie had stayed in the room with Wilma and had tried to smooth things over.

"How on earth did you end up here? It must be a fascinating story."

"It is, but I will tell you some other time. You girls must be tired after you long flights. Don't worry about your sister. I am sure she will come around in time. Let me show you to your room. I am sure that you can do with a shower."

By the next day Colleen had resigned herself to the fact that she was stuck on the ranch for the foreseeable future, and so she might as well make the best of the situation. She and Julie helped out on the ranch to the best of their ability. The only way in which the monotony of theirs lives was relieved was the monthly weekend spent in Wallagera. It was a dusty little town on the banks of a dry river. Even the old timers could not remember when it had last flowed with water. Folks from miles around congregated to play, dance, and meet old acquaintances. Some drove for distances of up to a hundred kilometres, while others arrived in small planes. Colleen was a sought after partner on the tennis court, while Julie reigned supreme on the dance floor. A girl of her beauty had not graced the district in years, if ever. Colleen also enjoyed the dances, but somehow she managed to convey the sense that she was not available. She continued to brood about Justin. On some days she was so mad at him she could have spat in his face had he made a sudden appearance. But mostly she yearned to see him anyway. She somehow felt sure that the Justin she knew and loved would not simply abandon her and that there must be more to his disappearance than she knew. After all, she only had Snyman's word that Justin had abandoned her, and how much could she trust that. Did her release mean that Justin had been caught rather than fled the country? But whatever the case, the hurt lingered on.

Wilma was not one to indulge in the luxury of newspapers, and so the girls were effectively cut off from the rest of the world. Events from far away England or South Africa did not make their way to this remote patch of land in the outback of Australia. The only outside news ever to penetrate this isolated community was the price of wool. Thus it was that Colleen missed all the news of Justin's doings in England.

Justin's first week in Surrey was in most respects very similar to his first week in London. He was met personally at the station by the Dean and Joy Mackenzie, who was introduced as the president of the student body. Although he had bought a few clothes in London—a necessity given the city's weather—he still had few enough possessions, requiring no more than a single piece of hand luggage. He was taken immediately from the station to the town's best restaurant for lunch. After a few minutes of pleasantries, Justin decided it was time to get down to business.

"First of all, let me say how grateful I am for providing me with this opportunity."

"Not at all. It is we who are privileged to have a brave person like you at our institution."

"The students are very excited to have you in our midst," added Joy.

"Thank you for this warm welcome. But could you fill me in on what the position that you have offered me entails. I am rather in the dark."

"Certainly. As I understand it, before fleeing you were majoring in mathematics and English. Our students will be sitting for their finals in a month or two. I would like you to be available, at times you can specify, to any student who would like some additional help or coaching in either of those two subjects. In addition, in your own time, you are free to conduct extra lessons in either of these subjects to high school students in town who will shortly be taking their A-level examinations."

"Thank you. That certainly sounds doable."

"Then during the summer, I hope to be able to fix you up as a temporary junior lecturer. We have started to offer bridging courses in mathematics and English to incoming freshmen."

"Thank you. I appreciate your efforts on my behalf."

"Then of course we need to consider your own studies. I assume that you still wish to pursue an undergraduate degree. We are too far into this semester for you to begin your studies now. However, that does give me time to make sure we can credit you with the courses that you completed at your previous university. You should be able to complete your majors come the new university year beginning in September."

"Yes, I would like to do that."

"Joy here has offered to show you around the campus this afternoon. We have fixed you up with temporary accommodation in one of the colleges. This evening there will be a reception, hosted by the vice-chancellor himself, to welcome you into our community."

It seemed that the who's-who of the university community was at the reception to welcome Justin. Apparently celebrities were few and far between in this quiet corner of Surrey, and so the most had to be made of Justin's arrival. The reception was held in the dining hall of the administration building, and featured a lavish buffet and bar. Once the requisite time for eating and drinking had elapsed, the vice-chancellor called for everyone's attention and made a brief welcome speech. He was followed by the Dean who proceed to heap praise upon Justin, using phases such as 'a fearless fighter against oppression', 'nobly sacrificed himself to oppose apartheid' and 'a hero who stood steadfastly for racial justice'. The person described by the Dean was unrecognisable to Justin. He was tempted, when his turn came to reply to the toast, to refute all that had been said. He was on the verge of saying something like 'none of what you have heard is true. I inadvertently came across some damning information and when the police sought me, I ran like a rabbit'. In the end, he took the easy way out by donning the mantle of a modest hero and thanked all present for the warm welcome that he had received, and went on to say that his exploits in South Africa had been rather exaggerated—that he was just one of many opposing apartheid.

The next morning he reported to the Dean's office to begin his new career. The Dean was not present—he was in a meeting—but the department secretary, a Miss Davenport, had been tasked with showing him to his new office. She grabbed a copy of the morning edition of the local newspaper, and with a curt 'follow me' strode down the corridor. She unlocked his office door, informing him that the last person to have occupied this office was a senior lecturer. She then thrust the newspaper into his hands, "I am sure you will want to read about the daring hero who has chosen to grace us with his presence." Justin should have been offended, but in some ways he was relieved. There was at least one person on campus who had not been taken in by the myth of his heroism.

The office was indeed a pleasant one. It had the requisite desk and chair, and was even equipped with a phone. Two walls were lined with bookcases, now mostly devoid of books. In the one corner was a coffee table complete with two comfortable looking chairs. There was a window that looked out over the campus and on to the river beyond. All things told, it was the most pleasant working space that Justin had ever enjoyed. He made use of access to a phone, and immediately called Amanda and asked that all his mail sent to the Anti-apartheid Movement be forwarded to his new address. Perhaps, even if the odds were long, there might be a letter from Colleen.

His first couple of weeks on campus flew by with little time to catch his breath. Almost every student club and society on campus invited him to attend one of their meetings, and to address their members. He was warmly and uncritically received at most of these meeting. At only one—the Young Communists—was there a hint of discord. Was it possible for a bourgeois white South African to be a true revolutionary? Justin had disarmed them by agreeing and pointing out that he had never claimed to be in the vanguard of the revolution. He was simply an ordinary student doing his bit—not a hero.

His tutoring schedule for each week was completely filled up within hours of being posted. However, it transpired that most who came for 'help' were really there to meet and become acquainted with the hero who had descended into their midst. They really just wanted to chat and to find out more about his experiences in South Africa. There were a few who came for genuine help with a mathematics problem, and Justin did his best to help them, becoming aware at the same time that his own mathematical understanding was rather limited. During his free hours he did take on some private A-level students, and so earned a bit of extra cash.

Letters forwarded by the Anti-apartheid Movement did start rolling in, but it was all fan mail. Finally a letter from South Africa did arrive. He tore it open immediately, but it was from his mother. It was full of reproach and anxiety, but nevertheless it lifted his spirits to hear from home. The news from the farm was good, if mundane.

As spring gave way to summer, Justin's life adjusted accordingly. By this point his celebrity status had waned considerably. He had to leave the college digs at the end of the semester. However, it was not difficult to find somewhere to stay in town since many of the students had other plans for the summer. He found a room in an apartment not far from the campus shared by three post-graduate students, two females and one male. It was a vast improvement on his digs in London as it was in pleasant park-like surroundings. His flatmates were congenial, but not intrusive, mostly keeping themselves to themselves. Perhaps it was due to the two girls that the common areas, a kitchen and a living room, were neat and clean. Altogether it proved to be a pleasant arrangement.

He was given two bridging courses to teach, one on algebra and the other on English writing, neither of which kept him fully occupied. He filled in much of his spare time exploring the pleasant Surrey countryside on his newly acquired bike. Still no letters from South Africa arrived except for the occasional missive from his mother.

Towards the end of summer, Justin discovered a new diversion, the Whipsnade Zoo just north west of London. Occasionally on days when he did not have to teach, he would take the train to the zoo to while away his time. He would spend hours on end by the enclosures with the African animals, fantasizing that he and they were in the Kruger National Park. The photo of Colleen always accompanied him on these visits. Did the lions, cheetah, rhino, zebra, and giraffe miss the wide open spaces of the African savannah? What did they think of their forced exile here on this soggy island? Why were they even here? Who had the right to remove them from their native country? Why was he here? Why was Colleen not here? On more than one occasion a zoo-keeper, or a kindly visitor, would stop and ask him if he was okay, and he would respond with a silent nod of the head. He did not trust himself to speak. How could he explain to anyone why he was sitting here so close to tears? How could anyone understand?

On other occasions, Justin would go down and sit on the banks of the river that flowed through town. It was not a boisterous river that had carved a mighty canyon for itself. There were no rocks on which to sit on these banks, only well kept benches. It did not burst from a canyon to make its way across the plains, where it nourished Africa's famous wildlife. Rather it was a placid river that gently made its way through town, and then through the pleasant countryside to meekly lose itself in the distant sea. Nevertheless, watching it flow gently by him did bring some measure of comfort. It was not the river of his dreams, but a river none the less. Perhaps a river of comfort, rather than of joy or sorrow.

At the start of the new academic year, Justin dutifully enrolled in those courses which might see him graduate at the end of the year. In addition, he was reappointed as a tutor and kept his office. However there was still no word from or about Colleen. It was becoming increasingly difficult to remain optimistic.

As the term progressed, it became obvious that there was a large gap, especially in mathematics, between what he had already studied and what was now expected of him. Besides this knowledge gap, there was also his lack of will. He simply did not see the point of continuing with his studies, or for that matter his life in England. As the weeks became months, he seemed to be falling further and further behind.

His tutoring also began to falter. He began the semester with a number of students, mostly first years, who signed up for his tutoring sessions. However, they began to drop off one by one. The students complained that they found Justin aloof and not very helpful. Justin, for his part, found the students shallow and spoiled—uninterested in applying themselves. He compared them unfavourably with the students that he had worked with in Soweto, who were both motivated and keen. Things came to a head when a second generation Pakistani student, new to the campus and unaware of Justin's history, lodged a complaint against the university for employing a racist, white South

African. It was not so much aimed at Justin personally, but simply part
of the ongoing academic boycott of South Africa. The complaint was
quickly squashed, but the wound to Justin's self-worth, already at a
low ebb, lingered on. Even as the mid-year examinations approached,
Justin's tutoring load did not pick up—in fact it dwindled to near zero.

As Justin unconsciously began to withdraw from the university
community, he immersed himself in the world of opera. It was the
world to which Colleen had introduced him, and the space in which
he still felt that he could somehow be at one with with her. He
worked his way through Wagner, and then others beginning with
Verdi, Puccini, Rossini, and Donizetti. It was by chance that one
evening he came across Thais by Massenet, and something about it
immediately resonated with him. It is the story of a monk, Athanael,
who sets out to win a beautiful courtesan Thais, for Christ. But as she
enters a nunnery, he falls hopelessly and desperately in love with her.
At the end of the opera, Athanael agonisingly tries to hold on to the
dying Thais, the women he loves above all else, even his calling as
monk, but who can never be his. She was always destined to be lost to
him forever. Athanael's agony is played out to the hauntingly sad, but
beautiful strains of the music of the Meditation. As the music played,
in Justin's mind Thais evolved into Colleen, and Athanael's agony
became his own, with the certain knowledge that the one woman he
would ever love was irredeemably lost to him, and that even so he
could never stop loving her. For a while, Justin played it every night,
and it never failed to bring tears to his eyes.

Shortly before the Christmas break the Dean called Justin in for a
meeting. He reviewed, as sympathetically as possible, Justin's lack of
progress in his studies and his lack of success as a tutor. "I know that
this must be a difficult time for you, so if there is anything that I can
do to help, please do not hesitate to ask."

"I appreciate your concern, sir, and your offer. I cannot think of
anything offhand. I will just have to try harder."

"There is one other thing that I wanted to see you about. We
have been fortunate in hiring a new faculty member, and I am afraid

she will have to be allocated your present office. It was a temporary arrangement in any case. We have found a new office for you, but it is rather on the small size. Miss Davenport will show it to you when we are through here."

Justin followed Miss Davenport down the corridor. She seemed unusually cheerful as she unlocked a door and threw it open. Justin peered in at what in the past had most likely been a storage room. It had no window, and was no larger than six square metres. Besides the desk and one chair, the only other furniture was a dilapidated book shelf. It had no phone. Justin's face must have registered some kind of dismay, and it was the only time he had ever seen Miss Davenport smile, or was it a smirk.

All three of his flat mates, at different times, invited him to spend the Christmas break with them at their respective homes. It struck him then that he only knew them by their first names. He did not even know their surnames or where their homes were. Each time he had politely declined, perhaps to their relief. Had the Dean put them up to it? Justin could not bear the thought of being in the cheerful company of strangers over Christmas. He needed to spend some time at Whipsnade Zoo with his fellow exiles and the photo of Colleen.

A month or so after Christmas, an item in a newspaper caught Justin's attention. He now spent much of his time in the library rather than in his depressing, pokey 'office'. Neither his studies nor his tutoring were going well. The Royal Opera Company was mounting a production of Die Walkure. It brought back the memory of that final evening that he had spent with Colleen, and how just listening to the opera had left her in tears, and fearful of being abandoned. He decided then and there that he would have to see it, if for no other reason than to feel close to Colleen once more—perhaps to relive those final moments that they had spent together.

Two weeks later he was back in London at the headquarters of the Anti-apartheid Movement. He had arranged with Amanda to spend the night at her place, and so he was checking in with her. They had a quick dinner together before he made his way to the Royal Opera House in Covent Garden. In all respects, it was a stirring production of Die Walkure. Much of what he had learned about the plot and the leitmotifs from Colleen came back. The final act was his undoing. The tears started when Brunnhilde pleaded with Wotan not to abandon her, accompanied by the haunting melody of Brunnhilde's justification. It only became worse as the scene progressed to their final and inevitable parting, when Wotan lays her to rest on the rock overlooking the River Rhine, and abandons her to an unknown fate. The sad but incredibly beautiful music of the magic sleep and fire, which end the opera, was the final straw. Justin was relieved to see the most of the audience was also in tears. However, as the audience filed out, he remained rooted in his seat with his head in in hands. He could not move. He pressed his hand against the shirt pocket containing the photo of Colleen, as if to force the merger of their two separate beings—to end their painful separation. Finally one of the ushers came over and said, "Never mind luv, it is only an opera, it is not real."

"But it is real to me," was the muffled reply. "I abandoned her."

"I am sorry luv, but we need to close up."

Justin nodded and left. He could not stand the thought of breaking the mood by taking the Underground to Islington, and so he ended up walking the whole way though the deserted streets of London. Amanda was worried when he did not appear when expected, and so had waited up for him. She immediately sensed his emotional despair and did not pry. She simply held him tightly for the remainder of the night while he continued to sob quietly before eventually falling into a fitful sleep.

It was about a month after Justin's trip to London to see Die Walkure that Themba intruded into his life with the outlandish request to travel to South Africa to warn Sipho. Although he had been given the night to think it over, even before he left the Kings Arms he knew what his answer would be. It was obvious by now that his time as tutor and student at the university was coming to an ignominious end, and that he had few other prospects available. At best he might be able to secure a job washing dishes at a local Wimpys. So what did he have to lose by agreeing to undertake this mission to South Africa? Nevertheless, he did continue to weigh his options during the night. At worst he might be arrested by the Special Branch, but would that be so bad? At least he would be back in South Africa, even if in a jail, where he was someone—where he had a history and an identity, where he could at least point to some actions in which he could take some pride. Also by spending time in jail, he could perhaps atone in some small measure for his abandonment of Colleen.

He resolved to meet Themba at the coffee shop in the station on the following morning and agree to his request.

SEVENTEEN

When Justin arrived, Themba was waiting for him in the station coffee shop. He had already ordered two cups of coffee. As before, Themba got right to the point with no exchange of pleasantries, "Well, what have you decided?"

"I will do as you have asked."

"I am glad to hear that. It is the right decision."

"So what comes next?"

"Go back to your university and tell them that you need to take a couple of weeks leave. Resign if you have to. But whatever you do, do not tell anyone where you are going. Make up some excuse. Then meet me here at the station in front to the ticket office at noon."

"So soon?"

"Yes. The situation is urgent. Sipho could be betrayed at any moment. You need to meet with him as soon as possible."

"What happens next?"

"The big challenge will be to get you a British passport under an assumed name in the minimum amount of time. While we are waiting for it, we will give you some training on what to do once you get to South Africa, and make sure that you have a credible understanding of your new identity."

"Do I need to bring anything with me?"

"Bring nothing at all. I assume that some of your clothes still have South African labels, so leave everything behind. We will outfit you for your trip."

As Justin rode his bike back to the campus, he mulled over what excuse to give for his upcoming absence. The old chestnut, 'family emergency', would not wash. He did not have any family in the UK and clearly there was no way he would be able to be with his family in South Africa. In the end he decided that his best option would be for an unspecified medical emergency. If at some stage he was pushed for details, he could come up with something like a perforated ulcer (he was certainly a candidate for ulcers), a burst appendix, or a ruptured hernia. He would be going to London for treatment. It was unlikely that anyone would take the trouble to find out where in London.

Once back in his office he proceeded to write a number of notes— to the Dean, to his lecturers, to the one student who still came to him for tutoring, and to his flat mates. He had decided to send these notes via campus mail rather than to meet any of the persons concerned face-to-face. These tasks completed, he headed back to the station where he and Themba took a train to a destination known only to the latter. After a few stops Themba announced, "We will be getting off here."

"Where are we?"

"Reading. I am taking you to a safe venue for the briefing for your mission. Now listen carefully. A car will be waiting for us just outside the station. It is of utmost importance that you are not seen with me during our drive. As soon as you get into the car, lie down on the floor of the back seat and stay there for the duration of the drive. It will be less than half an hour."

Justin did as he was told and after not too long the car came to a halt in what appeared to be an underground garage. He was led to a lift which took him directly to the third floor of whatever building that they were in.

"This looks like a hotel. I figured that you would be taking me to a safe house."

"We only use safe houses for the preparation of long term agents, whose training can take months. You will only be here for three days before being put on a flight to Johannesburg."

Justin surveyed the room that was to be his home for the next three days. It was a standard hotel room with two double beds, a clothes cupboard, a couple of chairs, a TV set, and a bathroom. The curtains were closed, and would remain so for the duration of his stay. Themba opened the mini-bar and took out two beers. "I assume you will not say no to a drink."

"Thanks. It will go down very well."

"Take a seat and let me go over the plans for the next three days."

They both sat down. "We have created a new identity for you. Your new name will be James Roscoe. Most of the time over the next three days will provide an opportunity for you to know all there is about James. Incidentally, there is a real James Roscoe, who is a student at a university here in Reading. It is highly unlikely that anyone will check out your new identity, but if they do they will find a real person. Your first task will be to memorise all that is written about James in this dossier. You will need to know the names of all his family members, including his girlfriend, where he lives, what he does for fun, and the state of of university career. We will be visiting his campus tomorrow so that you get a real feel for his surroundings."

At this point there was a knock on the door and a man with a camera was admitted. "My main task will be to prepare your passport. We need to take your photo for the passport." Justin was lined up against the wall and a number of photos were taken.

Justin spent the rest of the day studying the dossier on James Roscoe, while Themba spent the time watching football on the TV set. Dinner was taken in the room, as was the case for almost all the meals that followed.

After breakfast the next morning, Themba announced that the bulk of the coming day would be spent on assuming James' identity, and in particular his life as a student in Reading. He gave Justin a map of the campus to peruse and a catalogue to study. "Later this morning I will take you to the campus, where you will spend some time in the company of one of our comrades."

Come mid-morning they left the building in the same way as they had arrived, through the underground parking lot. Once again Justin was required, to his chagrin, to lie down out of sight on the back seat floor.

After a while the car came to a halt and Themba said, "Okay, you can get out now. The name of that guy sitting on the bench is Piet. You and he will explore the campus together."

"Why not you and I?"

"A black and white guy together would be more conspicuous. Besides I am a little too old to pass as a student."

As Justin exited the car he realised immediately where he was—just on the edge of the campus near the library. Piet came forward to greet him and together they made their way onto the campus itself. "Since we are already here, let's explore the library first," suggested Piet. He was a young man, blond and with blue eyes—a poster boy for a Springbok flyhalf. For the next hour they browsed through the various sections of the library, even taking the time to peruse some of the current newspapers. From there they made their way to the cafeteria for lunch. While they were eating, Justin tried to pump Piet for more information about himself, but without much success. He would dearly have loved to know why a young Afrikaner was working with Themba, but it was not to be. All that he was able to glean was that Piet came from Pretoria, that he was now studying somewhere in the UK, and that he did the occasional favour for Themba from time to time, but did not say in what capacity. Other than that Piet seemed very reticent about revealing anything more about himself. After lunch they attended a lecture in one of the large lecture halls and then took a stroll around the sports facilities.

Once back in the hotel, Justin was not in a happy frame of mind. "Isn't all of this preparation just so much overkill? Why do I have to jump through all these hoops? It is not as if I will be interacting with anyone other than Sipho, so why this elaborate cover?"

"It is overkill that saves missions and even lives. If all goes well, it will have been a waste of time. But think of all the possible contingencies."

"Such as?"

"Say you are stopped at a road block—and they do exist. The policeman will want to know where you are going and what you are doing in the country."

"But not about my university courses."

"Or say that you are in an accident and wind up in hospital. The doctors will certainly want to know all about you—especially your medical history. And then while you are lying in bed, the nurses will be in and out of the room and eager to chat with you. If you have nothing to say about yourself, they might surely get suspicious."

"I guess you are right. Perhaps I am just a little on edge. So what now?"

"Now I am going to find out how much of your cover story you have internalised. Lie down and pretend that you are in a hospital bed." Themba proceeded to question Justin about every single detail of his assumed cover. Once satisfied, he suggested that Justin relax and spend the rest of the evening watching TV.

The next morning Themba announced, "This evening your new passport will be delivered. When I say new, that is not quite accurate. It will show that it was issued five years ago and so we have had to age it some. It will also show that in the past five years that you have made two overseas trips, one to Italy and one to the Netherlands. Have you ever visited either of these countries?"

Justin shook his head.

"So you need to spend your time today inventing a holiday trip to each of these countries. I would like you to write up a description of each trip in the form of a diary."

"Surely even if I end up in hospital, no one is going to ask me about previous holidays."

"True. But there is more to these exercises that I am putting you through than simply not blowing your cover."

"How so?"

"Have you done any acting?"

"No. But I had a flatmate who was very keen on theatre."

"Well he would be able to tell you that as an actor, when you take on a role you have to convince yourself that you are indeed that person. You have to be that person at all times, not only when you are on stage, but in everyday life as well. So part of what we are doing here is turning you into James Roscoe. You need to think like James and be like James at all times from now on. Believe me, your training is still very superficial. If we were inserting you as a long term agent, you would have had to spend months becoming your new self."

"Yes, I do understand your point."

"Good. Here are some travel guides for both Italy and the Netherlands. Have fun designing two virtual holiday trips. You may go anywhere you like and do anything that you like in both countries, except of course getting yourself arrested. We have not gone to the trouble of creating a police record for one James Roscoe."

Justin suspected that the latter remark was made in jest, but he was not completely sure. As it turned out, he had a lot of fun devising a holiday in each of these countries, and describing what he did on a day-to-day basis. It made him want to visit them perhaps sometime after this mission was over. He enjoyed the task, and the day slipped by very quickly. When he had finished, he handed the two diaries to Themba. "You write very lucidly. It almost feels as if I have been to these countries too. Well done."

Before long it was dinner time again. After dinner Themba said, "Well tomorrow is the big day. Get a good nights rest."

Despite Themba's injunction, sleep did not come easily to Justin. The reality of what he was undertaking was beginning to sink in. Every time he nodded off, he would be plunged into a nightmare. In the one he was locked up alone in a windowless prison cell. In another he was in a pool of water being interrogated by the Special Branch. In yet another he was fleeing across a field, but never getting anywhere. It was a relief when it was finally morning.

After breakfast Themba announced, "We will now get down to the final planning. Here is the suitcase that you will take with you. It looks suitably used. On the bed is a pile of clothing, mostly used. You need to try on each item in turn to make sure it fits. If you were found to have a shirt, for instance, that did not fit, it would be a give away. Also take off the shirt that you are wearing and let me take a look at it."

Justin complied.

"As I thought. It is a brand only available in South Africa."

"Yes. It is the one I was wearing when I escaped."

"Let me check the rest of your clothing—underpants, socks, the lot."

Justin spent the next hour sorting through the clothes and deciding what he would take with him and what he would wear on the flight. He packed the clothes into a suitcase, keeping a few items out for an over night bag.

"Why is there a camera here?"

"You are going as a tourist, remember. Of course you would take a camera. Thinking now as James, where would you keep it? In the suitcase or in your over night bag."

Justin packed it into the over night bag.

"Good. And while you are at it, here is your passport. It will of course go into the over night bag as well. We are also giving you one thousand rand in cash and a credit card."

"I have never had one of those before. Is it easy to use?"

"Yes. All you have to do is present it at the time of payment. Car hire companies prefer them to cash. Many hotels also have started to use them. I suggest that when you get to Heathrow try using it to get something to eat or drink."

"And finally here is your ticket. You are booked on tonight's British Air flight to Johannesburg leaving at nine o'clock. Your return ticket has an open date. We have reserved a window seat for you."

"First class I hope."

"Dream on. Students travel economy. We would hate to blow your cover," he said with a grin.

Once the packing was complete, one final briefing remained—the most important of all—what to do once he reached South Africa.

"Remember all these instructions as if your life depends on it, because it does. You may not write any of this down. Hire a car in Johannesburg and then head down to the Lowveld. Drive north out of Nelspruit towards Hoedspruit. On the way is a small dorp called Klaserie. On the outskirts is one of those typical Indian trading stores. This one is called Abdullah's Cash Store. It is here that you will make contact with Sipho. The way that you go about it is vitally important, so are you listening carefully?"

"Yes, I am."

"You will go into the store and ask if you can buy a pair of shoes. If it is Abdullah himself at the counter, he will say that they do not sell shoes, but that there might be an old stock of sandals in the back room. If it is an assistant, likely his daughter, she will say the same, and then call Abdullah. You will then got into the back room where Abdullah will show you some tacky sandals. You will then say, 'I was looking for sandals with diamonds.' Remember these words exactly, as they are the code to give you access to Sipho. From this point on you will have to do whatever Abdullah tells you to do. All clear so far?"

"Yes, I can remember all of it. Those code words are very odd."

"Well the code had to be something that no genuine visitor would say. Sipho himself chose them. You might remember that he had a great sense of humour."

"Yes I do remember how funny he could be."

"Abdullah might want to give Sipho your message, but you must insist that only you are authorised to deliver it. I am not sure how long it might take before a meeting with Sipho can be arranged. It might be a couple of days, so find something to do with yourself, like perhaps visiting Kruger National Park. When you do get to meet Sipho, explain my concerns about our organisation being infiltrated by the Special Branch, and that a trap is being laid to capture him. Tell him not to act on any instructions coming from our headquarters here in London. Is all this clear?"

"Yes. Perfectly."

"Good. Once you have delivered the message, for your own safety, leave the country immediately."

After lunch, Themba said, "Well the big moment has arrived. Are you ready?"

"As ready as I will ever be."

"I will drive you to the station, taking the same precautions as before. In other words you will need to lie on the floor of the car again. When we get to the station get out of the car as quickly as possible, take your luggage and go to the bus terminal, where you will board the bus headed to Heathrow. You are now James Roscoe and are on your way for a holiday in South Africa. So let's go."

Before leaving the room Themba said, "Let's say our goodbyes here. There will be no opportunity at the station. All the best of luck."

They shook hands African style.

Boarding the flight went smoothly. If Justin had expected someone to query his new identity, nothing happened. He was not even sure if the girl at the check in counter had noticed how his hands were shaking. Or maybe she was accustomed to nervous travellers.

Once airborne, he kept asking for wine to try and settle his nerves. However after three or four glasses the stewardess must have decided that he had had enough as no more were forthcoming. Once again sleep eluded him as he was beset with worries about his mission.

EIGHTEEN

THE RISING SUN BATHED THE BRITISH AIR 747 IN PALE PINK HUES. THE ground below was still in darkness. Justin watched as the first rays of the sun probed the tops of the peaks on the sleeping earth of Africa below.

The cabin crew was still serving breakfast when the captain announced, "We will begin our descent to Johannesburg in less than half an hour. Make the most of this time before the seat belt lights are turned on." The flight map on the big screen showed that they were over the Limpopo River, the northern border of South Africa. Justin was home again.

As the plane descended, Justin tried to pick out features on the ground below. He himself had flown over much of this territory and was familiar with it. As he suspected, the plane was honing in on the VOR beacon at Hartbeespoort Dam. The familiar sweep of the Magaliesberg mountain range stretched out from below the starboard wing. It made Justin homesick as never before. Would it be possible to sneak in a trip to these mountains, where he had spent so many happy hours, before leaving again? Just one quick trip for old times sake? Get a grip on yourself he admonished. You are not Justin, you are now James. You have never been to South Africa before, so stop being nostalgic. In less than an hour you will be facing your first major test—entering the country on a false passport. So pull yourself together and remember your training.

The plane continued its descent and Justin, or rather James, could make out familiar features on the ground. There was the Wanderers Cricket ground, Hospital Hill, next the railway station and downtown Johannesburg, and then the row of old mine dumps. It could be no other city in the world. A few minutes later the plane landed on the main runway in a northerly direction and then taxied towards the terminal.

Justin was in no hurry to get to the immigration check point. He was feeling disorientated from lack of sleep, and also perhaps a little hung over. But he could not put it off forever. Finally it was his turn to present himself at the immigration counter and present his fake passport.

"Welcome to South Africa, Mr. Roscoe. What is the purpose of your visit?"

Justin was convinced that the words 'fake passport' were written all over his face. He had read once that these immigration officials were trained to detect the kind of nervousness that manifests itself in fraudulent visitors. He tried to act casual.

"I am here for a visit as a tourist."

"Where all do you plan to go?"

"I thought that I would start by visiting the Kruger National Park."

"Good choice. It is one of our main tourist attractions and worth a visit. Do you have other places in mind?"

"I have read that there much to be seen in the area around the Park. Also I have been told that Cape Town is very beautiful. I will just play things by ear."

"How long do you plan to stay?"

"My plans are very fluid. I have an open return ticket."

"May I see it please?"

He studied the ticket, and then returning it and passport said, "Enjoy your stay, Mr. Roscoe. Next please."

Justin retrieved his suitcase from the carousel and prepared for the next dreaded encounter—that with the customs official. However, instead of opening and searching through his suitcase, the official simply waved him through. Justin's luck was holding.

The original plan called for him to hire a car at the airport and drive down to the Lowveld. However at this point he could barely keep his eyes open and realised that he would be a danger to himself and others if he even attempted to drive. He would need to spend the day in town and make the drive on the following day. Consequently he took the bus to the South African Airways city terminal near the station, and from there, on a whim, a taxi to the best hotel in town, the Carlton. Cost be damned. It was not the kind of place frequented by impecunious students. It would way above their price range. One advantage of having an assumed identity is that one can make anything up. He quickly invented a rich uncle who could afford the Carlton. In any case, in the actual situation he would not have to pay for the expenses that he ran up on the credit card.

The Carlton was the domain of businessmen, both local and foreign, and so Justin made for an unusual sight as he approached the reception. He was viewed with suspicion by the staff, but the credit card changed all that in a matter of seconds. Having been shown to his room, Justin lay down on the bed and fell asleep immediately. He did not wake up until late in the afternoon.

On waking Justin was totally confused by his strange surroundings, and it took some time for him to piece together his whereabouts and his reason for being here. At least he felt rested and human once more. He took stock of his surroundings. They were the most luxurious that he had ever experienced. Besides the usual furnishings of a hotel room, there was also a well equipped 'office' corner stocked with paper, ink, some directories, and even a phone. However his first interest was with the bathroom, which proved to be equally luxurious. He soaked himself in the bathtub making full use of the soaps, lotions, and shampoo provided by the hotel.

Feeling refreshed, he pulled back the curtains and surveyed the city from his twenty second floor window. He immediately began to feel conflicted. Out there in the city there might well be some vital pieces of information that he could uncover, but these would only be of interest to Justin, not to James. Dare he break cover and become Justin again for a few hours? Might he not be able to find more about the whereabouts of Colleen, and perhaps to learn the fate of some of his former colleagues. The more he thought about it, the more tempted he was to make the move. But how? Was there anyone whom he could at least phone. He started skimming through the phone directory not expecting to find anyone that he knew, but taking comfort in some familiar names. There were a whole list of Armstrongs, and also Cohens, Kaplans, Jansens, and then suddenly one entry leaped out at him—Ian and Jenny McCall. It had to be them, but how in earth had they managed to get a phone? How long had it been since they were released from detention? Should he try to call them? Would he be putting them and himself at risk if he did so? But in the end he knew he just had to take the chance.

The phone was answered almost immediately. "Hello. This is McCall."

Before Justin could reply he heard some shouting in the background. Something to the effect of 'Don't answer the door' shouted over and over again.

"Just a minute," said Ian on the phone. Then away from the phone Justin could hear him saying, It's okay my love. Just calm down. It's okay. It's okay. It's okay. It's just the phone, not the door bell."

"Sorry about that. Who is this?"

"It's a former colleague of yours."

"I have many former colleagues." Ian's voice was colder now.

"I took you flying a couple of times."

"Jeez. Don't tell me it's ...."

"Yes it is," Justin cut him off.

"Where are you calling from?"

"I am here in town."

"Are you crazy?"

"Perhaps, but could I come around and see you?"

"No. That is out of the question."

"Okay. I am sorry I bothered you. It was stupid of me."

"No. Wait a bit. We could meet somewhere."

"I would appreciate that."

"How about our old pub?"

"No. There is too great a chance of someone recognising me there. Can you come to where I am staying?"

"And where is that?"

"The Carlton."

"No kidding. You are full of surprises. What brings you here?"

"Let's get off the phone. I will fill you in when we meet."

"Right. I will be there in about half an hour. Cheers."

Justin waited in a secluded corner of the lobby for Ian to arrive. He recognised him immediately, but waited to be sure that he had not been followed before stepping forward to greet him. "It's good to see you again." They shook hands.

"Did you not bring Jenny with you?"

"No. It is not possible. However, you seem to have done well for yourself to be staying here. What brings you back?"

"It is a long story. Let's go somewhere more private first. Will you join me for a drink and perhaps stay on for dinner. I bet you have never eaten in the Three Ships restaurant."

"I can stay for a quick drink, but I need to get back home as soon as I can."

"Okay then. Let's go up to the roof top pool. We can watch the sun set from there, and it is likely to be fairly deserted at this time of day."

They settled themselves into two chairs of the pool side bar, where Justin ordered them a glass of cabernet sauvignon each, putting the ridiculously large price tag on his room account.

Ian seemed ill at ease. "Before we say anything more, tell me what you are doing here."

Justin wondered how to navigate his answer. "I could tell you all, and I will if you insist. After all, we go back a long way together.

But you may not want to hear all the details. Let me just say this, I have come to warn an old acquaintance of ours that his life is in danger—that he is being betrayed. I am travelling on a false passport under cover as a British tourist."

"When did you arrive, and how long are you planning to stay?"

"I arrived this morning and will leave again as soon as I can. If I make contact tomorrow I might even be on tomorrow night's flight back to London. However I expect it might take a couple of days at least to make contact."

"You are right. I do not want to hear any more details."

Justin heaved a sigh of relief. "So tell me about yourselves. When were you released?"

"It was about three months ago."

"So what are you and Jenny doing with yourselves now?"

"I suppose one might say we are simply trying to put our lives back together again, and not being very successful at it. Especially not Jenny."

"Is that why you did not bring her to meet me?"

"Yes, but there is more to it than that. I have not been able to get her out of the flat ever since we were released."

"I am so sorry to hear that."

Now that Ian had started pouring out his troubles, it seemed that he could not stop. Perhaps it was a relief to him to share his experiences. "For the first couple of weeks, she lay curled up in a tight ball on our bed. She would not even talk to me. It was all I could do to get her to take some soup occasionally. Neville came over once, but when he knocked on the door she flew into a hysterical fit and I asked him to leave. I tried to get her mother to come and talk to her, but I don't think that Jenny recognised her. She seemed to think that her mother was a warden and became catatonic."

"How are her parents, by the way?"

"They are divorced. I think that the final straw was when her father kicked her out of the house."

"Sorry. I interrupted you. Is she getting any better?"

"Perhaps slowly. See moves around the flat now, and even has something to eat at times. But never very much. She hardly ever speaks, not that we really have anything to talk about. But she is very fragile. The slightest thing can set her off, like a knock on the door or the sound of a police siren outside. I know that I should get her professional help, but any time I broach the subject she reverts to her earlier state—lying curled up on the bed."

"This is such distressing news. I remember her as the most fearless and outspoken of us all. She was always brimming with new plans and ideas. She was so full of life. What on earth did they do to her in detention?"

"I have absolutely no idea. She refuses to talk about it. Perhaps she does not even remember. It might be a blessing if her mind has simply erased all memories of that time. But the few times that I have asked her about it she just starts shaking and then curls up on our bed. So I guess that the memories are still there, perhaps deep in the unconscious."

"I am so sorry. I don't know what to say. How was detention for you?"

"What you might expect. But I survived. I can tell you that it was much worse than we expected." Clearly he did not want to elaborate, and Justin did not press the issue. Instead he changed the topic.

"What news of David?"

"Do you mean to say that you have not heard? It has been in all the newspapers—including, I assume, the ones in the UK."

"I was in isolation during my training for this mission, so I have not seen any news."

"He is dead. He died in detention."

"God, that is terrible. When did this happen?"

"Three or four days ago."

"What happened to him?"

"Of all of us he probably had the most information of interest to the Special Branch. So I imagine he had a really rough time of it. I guess he refused to break right up until the end. They are saying that he died because he went on a hunger strike, which of course is complete nonsense."

Justin did not know what to say or ask. Another brave life lost. What could one say? In the end he asked, "What about Tony?"

"He was released after only a couple of months. As soon as his exit permit came through he left for Canada. I have not heard from him since."

"And Andy?"

"He found a job as an actor in Sydney. He left while I was still in detention."

"What about Neville?"

"He is still around. I think he flies for SA Express. As far as I know he also plays cricket for Transvaal B. I guess he is the last of us still standing. He also has your old car by the way. He has not been back since that one time I asked him to leave."

"So who is staying in our house now?"

"The municipality finally came through and widened the road. The house is gone. It was bulldozed to the ground."

There did not seem much else to be said.

"Look, thanks for the drink. I really need to be going. I do not like to leave Jenny alone for any length of time. If she gets into one of her states she might injure herself. Good luck with your mission. Try not to get caught. Drop me a line when you get back to London."

"Will do. All the best to you as well. I do hope Jenny will eventually get back to her old self."

"Thanks. Let me see myself out. Best not to be seen together." And with that he left.

Justin did not feel like sitting alone in any restaurant, not even the Three Ships. He felt sick to his stomach. He should never have agreed to this crazy scheme. Why did he even think that he might enjoy a trip back to South Africa? Was too late to catch tonight's flight to London? But what would Themba do to him, especially if Sipho was caught? There was nothing he could do for David or Jenny, but at least he could perhaps save Sipho. He had to go through with it. He returned to his room and ordered room service.

When he woke up the next morning, he saw that a copy of the Rand Daily Mail had been pushed under the door. However he wanted to get going and get this whole episode over. He had no time to read. The first thing he did was to phone the car rental agency that operated out of the Carlton complex. "I would like to reserve a car for a few days."

"Certainly sir. We can offer you a brand new Mercedes Benz."

"Thank you, but I would prefer something smaller." And less conspicuous, he wanted to add but did not. "What do you have?"

In the end he settled for a Ford Anglia.

Next he ordered breakfast to be brought to his room. By the time he had showered and dressed, breakfast had still not arrived, and so to kill time he picked up the Rand Daily Mail. The ongoing saga of David Cohen was on the front page.

Suzman demands inquiry

In parliament today, Helen Suzman demanded an independent inquiry into the death of David Cohen while in police custody. In reply the Minister of Police said that such an inquiry was not warranted. The Department had already conducted its own inquiry and found no wrong doing. Cohen had simply decided to go on a hunger strike and had starved himself to death. It was unfortunate but that is how it was.

Justin wondered why Helen Suzman even bothered—why she kept on with her futile efforts year after year. Parliament was redundant when it came to any possibility of change. Besides, relatively few white detainees died compared to other races, but when one of them did it made headline news. By contrast, little notice was taken when yet another African died in detention.

After breakfast Justin checked out of the Carlton, picked up his rental car, and set off to fulfil his mission. Morning traffic was heavy as usual in Johannesburg, but once he made it to the open road he was able to make good time. The road was a familiar one to him. He had travelled it often since his first meeting with Colleen. However this would be the first time he travelled this road with no expectation of seeing Colleen at his destination.

He kept looking in his rear view mirror. Was he being followed, or was he just being paranoid? He kept catching sight of a dark coloured Volkswagen Passat. However, after a few more miles, it was no longer there. A short while later, once again there was a Passat behind him. Was it the same one, or was it a different car? The Passat was after all a popular brand. He accelerated and left the car following him behind. However, after a few miles there was once again a car in his rear view mirror, but it was so far behind that he could not determine the make. He decided that he would need to take action.

The part of the Highveld through which he was now travelling is famous for its rows of blue gum trees. Most farm roads, however insignificant, are lined with them. Just ahead of him one such line of trees intersected the main road. Justin hastily pulled over onto the side road, hoping that the line of trees would provide cover for his car. He exited the car and made his way quickly back to the main road, where he hid behind a tree. He made a note of each passing car writing down both the make and licence plate number. Sure enough, two of the cars that passed him were Passats, but there were also a number of other types of cars. He waited to see if any of the cars would retrace its route having lost sight of its prey, but none did.

He continued his journey. Not far down the road was the Bambi Inn, which provided both petrol and food. It had been one of Colleen's favourite stopping off places, with its fabulous sandwiches, real coffee, and spotlessly clean loo's. But stop thinking about Colleen he admonished himself. You are now James Roscoe, who has never met anyone called Colleen. Justin pulled into the parking lot and surveyed all the other parked cars to see if any on his list were there waiting for him to catch up. But he drew a blank. Justin chided himself for letting this mission prey too much on his nerves. He filled up and proceeded on his way.

Justin made it to Nelspruit in time for a quick lunch and then continued north, passing through White River, Hazyview, and Bushbuck Ridge. Klaserie would be the next town to the north. Just as Themba had told him, Abdullah's Cash Store was on the side of the road on the edge of town. He drove past it slowly checking for Passats or any other suspicious cars, but saw none. Consequently he made a U-turn further up the road and returned to the store. It was dark inside and it took a while for his eyes to adjust. Counters flanked three of the sides of the room, while the fourth wall, the one facing the street, contained the front door and windows. The other three walls were stacked with shelves crammed with the goods on offer, mostly food, utensils, and clothing. Larger items, such a wheelbarrows and gardening tools, littered the floor. The young girl at the counter registered surprise at his entrance. It was not the kind of place frequented by tourists. She must not be much older than twenty and was dressed in a colourful sari.

"I wonder if I might buy a pair of shoes?"

"I am sorry sir, we do not stock them. You could try the OK Bazaars in Hoedspruit." She looked at him, expecting him to leave disappointed. This was not going according to script.

"Perhaps you have sandals?"

The penny dropped. "Oh yes, I am sorry sir. Let me call my father." She disappeared into the back room.

An older man of Indian origin, who Justin took to be Abdullah, appeared. "My daughter tells me you were asking for shoes or sandals."

"Yes. If you do not have shoes, even a pair of sandals would suffice."

"I might have a few pairs of sandals in the stock room. We do not sell many of them. Follow me." To his daughter he said, "Mala, put the 'Back in 10 minutes' sign on the door."

Abdullah rummaged around in the room and eventually did produce a tatty looking pair of sandals. "These are all that I have."

Justin looked at them. "I was looking for sandals with diamonds."

Abdullah put the sandals down. "Okay. What do you want?"

"I have an urgent message for Sipho Dlamini."

"I will give it to him."

"My instructions are to give the message to no one but Sipho himself."

"Who are you anyway?"

"My name is Justin Roberts."

"Sipho will not show up here just because some white boy pitches up and demands to see him. He is much too wily for that. Anyone could come here calling himself Justin whatever other name you gave yourself. Do you have any identification?"

"I have come from the UK to warn him of the danger that he is in. I had to come on a false passport since I too am wanted by the police. So my passport and driver's licenses are in a false name."

Abdullah seemed a little mollified, but not much. "Can you think of any incident that would convince Sipho that you are who you say you are?"

Justin thought for a while. "Tell him that I am the idiot from the café in Beaufort West."

Abdullah gave him a strange look, but nodded. "I will give him your message if I can, but I cannot guarantee that he will be checking in with me in the near future. I also cannot guarantee that even if I do give him the message that he will agree to see you."

"So what should I do?"

"Check back here in three days time. Let's see, today is Tuesday. Come just before noon on Friday. In the mean while get out of here now. I do not want to catch even a glimpse of you before Friday."

Justin thanked him and left.

So much for his wish to be on tonight's late flight back to London. He would need to find a way to occupy himself for the next couple of days. The obvious choice was to spend time in the Kruger

National Park, since he was already on its doorstep. He decided to enter via the Kruger Gate and stay in Skukuza. It would not have been his first choice, since Skukuza was more of a small town rather than a simple rest camp like so many of the others found in the Park. However because of its size, he would be more likely to find accommodation without a prior booking. He did indeed manage to find accommodation in a rondavel. Since it was getting late, and he had already spent much of the day in the car, he decided to forego an evening game drive. Instead he bought some boerewors in the camp's store and had himself a braaivleis for one.

He spent the following day driving around the Park. He was reminded of the times he and Colleen had spent together in these surroundings. Unlike many of the tourists, they did not rush from one lion sighting to the next. Instead they savoured the ordinary aspects of the Park, spending hours at time simply observing one animal. Even when there were no animals, they enjoyed absorbing the rhythms and sounds of the African bush. However on this occasion Justin was not able to sit quietly and patiently in just one spot. His mind was in too much turmoil. He was restless and had to keep moving. Nor did being in the Park give him much pleasure. He tried stopping off along the Sabie River, as Colleen and he had done in the past. But even the river could bring him no joy. He kept turning to Colleen to share a sighting or a comment, but of course she was not there. Seeing the animals in the wild only brought back memories of the sad, exiled creatures he had visited so often in the Whipsnade Zoo. At the end of the day he resolved to leave the Park and rather spend the next day up on the escarpment.

The next morning he left Skukuza, heading up to Graskop and from there on to Pilgrims Rest, where he checked into the hotel. Anything to keep busy, he then started to visit some of the tourist spots for which the area is famous—the Pinnacle, God's Window, Lisbon Falls, Berlin Falls, Forest Falls, and Bourke's Luck Potholes. He had of course visited them all before, but they were all worth second and third visits, their beauty and grandeur unblemished by time. However even before he made the decision, he knew where he would end up—Colleen's Rock. And indeed that was where he spent the latter part of the afternoon lost in memories. Here on the escarpment he was once again Justin, not James. This was his country. It was where he belonged. It was not surprising therefore that he failed to respond to the hotel's receptionist when she called out to him as Mr. Roscoe.

The next morning he left for Klaserie, for the final chapter of his mission. If Sipho showed up, he would give him the message. If not, he would leave anyway. He would simply tell Themba that he had done his best. Whatever the outcome, he would be on tonight's British Air flight to London.

As before, he was the only customer at Abdullah's Cash Store, but Abdullah himself was at the counter and not his daughter. He immediately motioned Justin into the back room. "Sipho has agreed to meet with you. Here is how you are to meet him. Drive leisurely from here to Hoedspruit. Do some quick shopping in Hoedspruit, maybe a quick cup of coffee, and then drive back here. About five kilometres from Klaserie you will see an abandoned bus shelter. There will be a hitch-hiker near the shelter. Pick him up. It will be Sipho."

"So why don't I just pick him up on my way to Hoedspruit?"

"You really are an amateur. Sipho's men will be checking for a trap. If any of the vehicles that are behind you on your way to Hoedspruit, and then follow you back again, Sipho will disappear and not meet with you."

"Yes of course. I get it now."

"You will then drop Sipho off here at my store and then vanish for good. I take it you are not planning to stick around."

"No. I plan to fly back to London tonight."

"Good plan. Now be on your way."

Justin followed the instructions to a tee. As promised there was a lone hitch-hiker not far from the shelter. It was Sipho. He climbed into the car and they shook hands African style. Once under way, Justin said, "It is wonderful to see you again."

"You too, the famous idiot from the café in Beaufort West! So how is life in London?"

"Actually I live in Surrey now. It is a life. I have no complaints."

"I am sorry for getting you into trouble. I did not mean to. I think there was an informer somewhere along the line."

"No need to apologise. What you do is important. So what can you tell me about your current assignment. No need to tell me anything that I should not know."

"There is no harm in telling you. The police know all about it anyway. I am the regional commander for umkhonto isibashu. It is my task to smuggle in arms and soldiers across the Mozambique and Swaziland borders."

"It sounds exciting but dangerous."

"It is, but also not as difficult as it may sound. The borders are very porous and we have established some fairly reliable routes. Some even run through the Park."

"So you get to see the Park without paying an entry fee."

Sipho laughed. "But enough small talk. Tell me why you are here."

Justin explained how he had been contacted by Themba, who believed that the London branch of the Movement had been compromised, and that there was a plot to capture Sipho by sending false instructions.

Sipho looked puzzled. "What did you say his name was?"

"Themba."

"I do not think that there are any Thembas in our Movement in London."

"I do not think that Themba is his real name."

"The other strange aspect to your message is that I never receive instructions from London. I answer only to our headquarters in Johannesburg. So London could not send me false instructions."

"But you are wanted by the police."

"Very much so. I am now called the Black Houdini. But your whole story sounds fishy to me."

By this time they were approaching the outskirts of Klaserie.

Sipho said urgently, "Justin, I do not like this at all. Instead of dropping me off at Abdullah's, let me get out here. I can melt into the location."

As Justin slowed to a halt, a truck pulled into the middle of the road from a side street.

"Quick, do a U-turn and gun it. We should be able to outrun them."

But by now another truck had blocked the road behind them as well. It did not take long for a police car to appear. A policeman got out, approached Justin's car and peered in.

"I am a British tourist and this here is my local guide, Lucky. What is going on here? Why are you stopping us?"

"Cut out the crap Roberts. I know exactly who you are and you know me as well. Col. Snyman in case you have forgotten. And now thanks to you we finally have your friend Sipho. Both of you get out now with your hands on your heads."

Justin looked at Sipho stricken and offered a silent apology.

"Sergeant, take this piece of shit to the police cells in Phalaborwa. I will deal with him tomorrow. My first task is to get our famous Black Houdini to his new home in Pretoria Central Prison, where he will sing like a canary."

NINETEEN

The jail cell in Phalaborwa was like none Justin had experienced, or even expected. In his previous incarceration he had been held in a cell, along with others, which had open grill work. One could see out into the corridor and into neighbouring cells. His current cell comprised four blank walls, the monotony of which was relieved only by a solid iron door. The door did have a peep-hole, which could only be opened from outside, and a flap, again which could only be opened from outside, through which his food could be passed. There was a raised concrete platform, which served as his bed. Besides the bed, the only other items in the cell were a bucket of water and a slops pail. The only lighting in the room came from a weak electric bulb in the ceiling, which was heavily protected by a wire cage. It was never switched off. There was no window.

When Justin had arrived at the police station around mid-afternoon, he had been stripped of his clothes, dressed in an ill-fitting prison outfit, and taken to this cell. No one had spoken a word to him. At some point later, a bowl of thin soup and a dry crust of bread had been pushed through the flap. He estimated that this must be his dinner. With nothing else to do, he lay on his bed and relieved the monotony by going through some of those exercises that he had devised during his week of self-imposed solitary confinement. He began to go through the play Romeo and Juliet. Where he could not remember the exact lines, he recreated them, holding to the original as closely as possible. The time that he had spent in solitary confinement was not wasted after all. He may have dozed off at some point during the night. A bowl of porridge was pushed through the flap, suggesting that it was now morning. A few hours later the door opened, and without speaking an orderly beckoned Justin to follow him. He was shown into a room comprising a table and a single chair. Col. Snyman was sitting in the chair. Clearly Justin was expected to remain standing.

Neither of the two men spoke. It was Justin who finally broke the silence. "So what are you going to do with me?"

"I like it. Consistent to the end. I thought that you might ask about your friend Sipho, but no, you are only concerned about yourself."

Justin remained silent.

"You are behaving just like you did before. When I was holding your girlfriend, you could have come to her rescue but no, you fled like a rat to save your own skin."

Justin willed himself not to be provoked by this taunt. He would not stoop to justifying his previous actions to his tormentor.

"However, I will answer your question. I am going to let you go."

Justin must have looked surprised at this statement, but he remained silent.

"You must be curious to know why I am letting you go. You are worthless to us now that we have your mate Sipho. There is nothing that you know that is of any value to me. To put you on trial would be a waste of my time and resources. I could simply lock you up for good, but why waste money on you."

Justin could no longer keep silent. "Do you mean to say you are going to let me walk out of here a free man?"

"Not exactly. I will be putting you on a police plane, which will take you to Jan Smuts, where you will be put on tonight's flight to London. You can go there and commiserate with your lefty, limey friends."

"What about my car and luggage?" Justin immediately regretted his focus on such mundane and unimportant details.

"You will get your luggage back at Jan Smuts. We will take care of your car. You will be given your clothes once I leave. Get dressed quickly as you will be departing in ten minutes."

Justin was on the point of saying thanks, but kept silent.

"Oh! There is one more thing. I had hoped that Sergeant Sebe would join us here, but in the end he declined the honour."

"I do not know Sergeant Sebe."

"Oh, but you do. He took rather a liking to you, although I cannot for the life of me understand why. I think he may be a little conflicted about the role that he played in your life."

"You must be mistaken. I do not know a Sergeant Sebe."

"I am never mistaken. Of course, you knew him as Themba, not as Sergeant Sebe. He did a great job. Thanks to his time with you, he will be getting a well deserved promotion."

Justin's escort from the jail to the airport was slightly more communicative than had been the wardens, but not by much.

"What about my suitcase, my passport and my wallet. Where are they?"

"Don't worry. You will get every thing back once we get to Jan Smuts."

Pointing to his handcuffs he asked, "Are these really necessary?"

"Colonel's orders. I do what he tells me to."

A little while later in the drive, Justin asked again, "What kind of plane will we flying in from here to Jan Smuts?"

"I have no idea. And as long as it gets us there I couldn't care less."

When the car pulled up onto the apron of Phalaborwa airport, Justin was delighted to see that they would be flying in an old Dakota. It seemed that the police must have acquired it from the South African Air Force. As it turned out, they were the only passengers.

Once they were airborne Justin asked his escort whether he could go up to the cockpit and speak to the pilots.

"And let you high-jack the plane. Not bloody likely." The escort may have been short on communication skills, but he certainly had a well developed imagination. Justin spent the remainder of the trip watching the scenery float by underneath the wing of the plane.

Once the Dakota landed at Jan Smuts, it taxied up in front of the terminal and stopped long enough for the two of them to disembark, before continuing on its way. They entered by what Justin took to be some kind of VIP entrance, and proceeded to walk to a small waiting room. All Justin's belongings were laid out on a table. He checked them out and everything was there—his money, passport, credit card, driver's licence, the lot.

"This is where I hand you over," his escort announced, while at the same time removing the handcuffs. "From here on airport security will take over and make sure that you get onto the plane safely." Did the police really think that he would do a runner and likely choose jail in South Africa over freedom in the UK. A couple of officials arrived in the room.

"We will check you onto your flight here. Nothing like getting the VIP treatment, heh." Justin was given his boarding pass and his suitcase was weighed, checked in, and taken away by the British Air representative. The other man, airport security no doubt, next led Justin along a series of corridors and turns until suddenly there they were, at the gate of his flight. Justin was amongst the first to board—he felt safer on the plane. In the back of his mind he could not help but worry that Col. Snyman might still change his mind. Even so, he could not relax until the plane had taken off and was clear of South African airspace. Only then could he begin to celebrate his unexpected release to freedom. He continued to celebrate until either the cabin crew had decided that he had had enough or until the meagre supply of booze for the economy cabin had been depleted. He was not sure which, and by that time did not care.

Justin realised that he had slept through breakfast, since as he woke up the cabin crew were collecting the last of the breakfast trays. The 747 was already well into its descent, but there was nothing to see but an unbroken cloud cover. Justin watched as the plane continued its descent until at last it was skimming the surface of the cloud cover, penetrating the occasional errant wisp. Before long the plane dipped again and they were now well and truly into the murk. Water droplets condensed on the body of the plane and ran in diagonal rivulets across the windows. The plane turned this way and that in the dense murk, presumably at the instructions of an air traffic controller. Suddenly they burst out from under the cloud cover to reveal the sodden English countryside. They were already on their final approach to Heathrow. After the landing came the endless taxiing through the rain—not the 'sweet April showers' of Chaucer's pilgrims, but a relentless downpour. It was a dreary homecoming.

Justin was in no hurry to disembark. All that he had to look forward to was a confrontation with the Dean, or even worse, with Miss Davenport. Hence he was one of the last of the passengers to arrive at the immigration kiosk. As he presented his passport, he was surprised to hear the official say, "Ah yes Mr. Roscoe. We have been expecting you. Would you please come this way with me." Justin followed the official to the baggage claim carousel, where his suitcase was already making its endless rounds. He reclaimed his suitcase and followed the official to a private room in which two men were waiting for him. Neither of them looked exactly friendly. When requested to do so he placed his suitcase on the table.

"Would you confirm please that this is your suitcase."

"Yes it is mine." Justin sensed that this exchange was being recorded.

"Please open your suitcase." Justin complied. "There is nothing in it but my clothes."

"Kindly unpack your clothes."

Justin started removing his clothes one by one. Once a couple of layers had been removed, numerous plastic bags were revealed. Justin could not believe his eyes. One of the men picked up a bag, opened it and gave the contents a sniff.

"It is heroin all right. Our tip off was spot on."

"There must be a couple of million pounds worth in here," observed the other.

"Those must have been planted," protested Justin hotly. "I had nothing to do with them. I can explain exactly who put them there."

"Son, our job is simply to arrest you and secure the evidence. Save your explanations for a judge and jury."

Two days later Justin found himself in the prison's interview room
to meet with his court-appointed solicitor, a Mr. Ramsay. Following
introductions, Mr. Ramsay began proceedings. "From what I have
been told there are two charges against you, importing an illegal
substance and possession of a false passport. Have you given any
thought as to how you plan to plea?"

"Yes. Not guilty."

Ramsay looked a little surprised. "Do you deny that you travelled
on a false passport and that heroin was found in your possession?"

"No. Those are both facts that I cannot deny. However I was set
up from start to finish."

"Perhaps you should tell me your side of the story."

Justin proceeded to explain how he had been set up, starting with
Themba's appearance in his life to being put on the British Air flight
without having had access to his suitcase. Ramsay did not seem overly
convinced.

"You do believe me don't you?"

"No defence lawyer ever wishes to know if his client is guilty or
not. My job is to provide you with good advice and the best defence
possible. To believe that you are guilty or on the other hand not
guilty would only interfere with my task. So I try not to make any
judgement."

"Okay, I do understand."

"My first step will be to apply for bail. Then if you do plead not
guilty and we do go to trial, I will need to find you a barrister to
represent you in court. Meanwhile is there anything else I can do for
you? Are you being decently treated?"

"Yes I am, thank you."

Justin compared his current accommodation with that in
Phalaborwa. It was like chalk and cheese. The food was reasonably
good for a prison anyway, and his cell was comfortable. He even had
access to a TV set. He had no complaints.

"I will see you again in a couple of days," said Ramsay, taking
his leave.

True to his word, Ramsay did appear again two days later.

"I have a couple of bits of news for you. First, bail has been denied. Since you already had one false passport, it seemed quite likely that you might have several more. Hence you were deemed to be a flight risk."

Justin was not overly upset. At this point there was no question of his returning to the university, and so in reality he had nowhere to go. He was not sure where he would have gone had bail been granted. As far as he was concerned, prison was likely his best option.

"Second, I have looked into previous cases of drug smuggling. If you were to plead guilty, in my estimate, you might get off as a first time offender with about ten years or less. However, if you plead not guilty and it goes to court, depending on the judge, you might end up with around twenty years."

"Only if I am found guilty."

"Quite right. However at this point I do not hold out much hope for a not guilty finding. Have you thought any more about how you plan to plea?"

"There is no way I will plead guilty when I know I am innocent. If nothing else I want my side of the story to be heard."

"I understand your motive. But are an extra ten years in prison worth having your say in court? Think about it. I will contact you again. If you are still set on proving your innocence in court, I will set up a meeting with a barrister and we can see how to go about your defence."

"Make sure that the barrister understands that I would rather spend a life time in jail than to plead guilty. After all I have nothing to live for, so jail does not perturb me."

Rankin found Justin's last remark disturbing, so much so that he requested that Justin be put on a twenty four hour suicide watch.

The meeting took place one week later. The barrister, a Mr. McDonald, listened carefully to Justin's story. He did not seem much encouraged by what he heard.

"I am trying to envisage how your defence could be constructed. But first let's consider the case for the prosecution. They can prove that you entered the country on a false passport with a suitcase full of heroin. We would not even try to dispute that. They also now have affidavits from drug sellers in South Africa, arrested by the local police, who admit to having sold heroin to you. Finally your credit card shows that you used it to pay these sellers."

"I would not have been so stupid as to use a credit card."

"Perhaps not, but the prosecution would turn that into an admission that you now realise that you should have used cash. Their case against you seems all but water tight. So the basis of your defence comes down to your claim that you were set up by the South African police from the start. We will need witnesses, but I am damned if I can see where we will find them. Let's consider your story from the beginning. Themba is the man I would really like to put in the witness box, but if what you say is true, there is no way that we will get him on the stand. Our best hope is to find a witness who saw the two of you together. At least that would prove that he exists. Can you think of anyone? Where all did you meet with him?"

"He was always very careful not to be seen with me. The first time he contacted me, I suggested that we meet at the Black Swan, a pub just off the campus, but he wanted a place where there was no chance of our being recognised. We met at the Kings Arms near the station. The next day we met in the station itself."

"So we have no chance of finding a witness to your meetings."

"I guess not."

"Now you told me that the briefings for your mission to South Africa took place in hotel. Surely we could find a witness from amongst the hotel staff."

"That may also be a problem."

"Why? What is the name of this hotel? Where is it located?"

"Believe it or not, but I have no idea. All I can say is that it is not more than half an hour's drive from Reading Station."

"How is it possible that you have no idea?"

Justin explained how he was taken to and from the hotel lying on the back seat floor of a car.

"Did you see anything of the hotel itself?"

"Only the underground parking garage, the lift, and the corridor to our room."

"Did you see anything of the outside from the window of your room? Any landmark that you might recognise if you saw it again?"

"No. The curtains were always closed."

"So it could any one of about one hundred hotels near Reading. Did any of the staff see you?"

"We did have room service," answered Justin hopefully.

"Since we do not know where this hotel is, I don't suppose that will help us at all. Can you think of any witnesses, even one, who might be able to substantiate your story?"

"I did spend some time on the campus of a university in Reading with a guy called Piet, but I doubt if anyone really took any notice of us."

"And who is this Piet?"

"I suspect now that he is also a member of the Special Branch. He is probably back in South Africa by now."

"Well we can forget getting any member of your Special Branch as a witness. So in essence we have no one."

Justin nodded in agreement.

"I am always loath to put the accused in the witness box, but unless you agree to testify we have no defence at all."

"But I would like to stand in the witness box. The world needs to hear how the Special Branch operates."

"It may not be what you expect. Don't think that you can get up there and talk about torture and injustice. It would be ruled as irrelevant. Your testimony would have to be confined to the facts of the case. In other words to the times that you spent with Themba and your trip to South Africa."

"Nevertheless, I would like to have my side of the story told in public."

"You do realise that the prosecution will make mince meat out of you. There is not one iota of your story that we can substantiate. My advice to you still is to plead guilty and take the lighter sentence."

"No way. I am determined to have my day in court."

"Very well. I will do my best to defend you. But be prepared to be disappointed."

The trial went every bit as badly as McDonald had anticipated. The prosecution presented its case methodically and with a nauseating amount of overkill. The strategy was clearly to bludgeon the jury with the indisputable aspects of the case. The immigration official who had processed Justin's arrival confirmed that the passport now in evidence had been presented to him by one claiming to be James Roscoe. An official from the Home Office testified that the passport in question had not been issued by his Department. Three different experts were called in to explain in detail how the passport had been forged. McDonald declined to cross-examine any of them. There was no point in helping the prosecution to hammer home a point that he had already conceded.

Each of the three men who were present when Justin opened his suitcase testified to the effect that Justin had acknowledged that the suitcase was his and that it had contained a number of bags of a substance which might have been heroin. An additional two expert chemists testified that the bags did indeed contain heroin. Again McDonald chose not to cross-examine.

Next Justin's supposed credit card statement was admitted into evidence and an expert called to explain its contents to the jury. The statement showed payments to a coffee shop in Heathrow, the Carlton Hotel, the Independent Car Hire, and to four unknown entities. McDonald objected on the grounds that the statement could in no way be tied to the purchase of drugs and was therefore irrelevant. The prosecution replied that there were sworn affidavits in his possession that would make the connection. McDonald replied that he would oppose the introduction of the affidavits. The judge ruled that testimony on the credit card could continue, and that the question of the admissibility of the affidavits would be dealt with later. The witness then testified that in his view the statements were a valid indication that each of the payments listed had been made. During cross-examination McDonald was able to squeeze a couple of concessions.

"Can you be sure that the final four payments were made to drug dealers?"

"Not at all. Only that a payment was made."

"Please look at the final four payments. They are all between R1 000 and R2 000. Would you say that this amount is enough to buy say one kilogram of heroin?"

"I am not in a position to comment on the appropriateness of any of the amounts, including the last four. For example, the cost of the room in the hotel might seem exorbitant to some, but who am I to say."

The prosecution interrupted, "M'lud all of this will be explained by the affidavits to which I have referred previously."

"Then it is time to decide on their admissibility. Both of you meet me in my chambers. The court is in recess for half an hour."

"Right, tell me more about these affidavits."

"The police in South Africa have arrested the dealers who supplied the accused with ..."

"I presume you meant to say 'allegedly supplied'."

"All right, who allegedly supplied the accused with heroin. Each of the accused has signed a sworn affidavit to the effect that they sold heroin to a person they believed to be James Roscoe."

"For around R1 000. That is ridiculous. The stuff is worth far more than that."

"All of that is explained in the affidavits. Apparently the R1 000 was simply a down payment, a good will gesture, and that they would be given the balance once Roscoe had offloaded the stuff in London."

"So what is your objection Mr. McDonald?"

"I will not be given the opportunity to question the writers of these affidavits, which to my way of thinking seems very fishy, to put it mildly. Hence I request that they be barred from admission."

"I am inclined to agree with you." Looking at the prosecutor he added, "Do you have anything more to say?"

"Yes m'lud. The police in South Africa are keen to cooperate with this case and are prepared to send one, or even all, of the dealers—the writers of the affidavits—to the UK to appear in this court. However it would have to be up to the defence to pay for their airfare. My budget is already in the red."

"Very well. Since the writers of the affidavits are willing to appear in this court, there can be no objection to the admissibility of the affidavits themselves. Thank you gentlemen. I will see you in court in ..." he looked at his watch "... fifteen minutes."

McDonald was disappointed at the ruling, which he now had to break to Justin. "Your defence is being paid for by legal aid. I don't suppose you could raise the money for the airfares."

"No. I am flat broke. In any case it would be futile. The Special Branch would simply send a couple of their own to play the role of my drug suppliers. They will swear up and down that every word in the affidavits is true."

"Even under oath?"

"When you think nothing of torturing people to death, it is no big deal to lie under oath."

It is a different world down there, he thought. This poor fellow. I wish there was more that I could do for him.

When the court reconvened, the affidavits were admitted and read to the jury.

"Do you have anything to say in response?"

"Only that it is the belief of the defence team that they are a pack of lies."

"Your comment is noted. The prosecution may proceed."

"M'lud the prosecution rests its case."

"In that case its is now the turn for the defence to call its witnesses."

"M'lud, I request an adjournment until tomorrow. I need to consult with my client about whether or not to call certain witnesses. I am sure your honour will understand."

"Your request is granted. The court is adjourned until nine o'clock tomorrow morning."

Once in the interview room Justin said, "I thought that we had already decided not to call those phony witnesses from South Africa."

"We had. I am just buying some time. We do need to think of possible character witnesses."

The implication was not lost on Justin. "So you already believe that I will be found guilty."

"To be honest it is a distinct possibility. But I would be remiss if I did not explore every avenue. Can you give me some possible names."

"The only people that I can think of are at my university and then there are also some members of the Anti-apartheid Movement who helped me when I first arrived."

"Let me have some names, and I will contact them this afternoon."

As it turned out McDonald had no luck in securing any character witnesses. With only minor variations, the excuse that each of them gave was that they would love to be of assistance, but that they did not really know Justin well enough.

The next morning the judge began proceedings by asking the defence, "How many witnesses do you intend to call?"

"Just one, M'lud. The accused."

It is generally believed in courts of law that to call the accused as a witness is an act of sheer desperation. McDonald could already envisage the prosecution team licking their collective chops.

Justin was called to the witness box, and McDonald carefully led him through the details of his story. Justin proved to be a credible witness and McDonald hoped that he had at least made enough of a favourable impression on the jury to meet the standard of 'beyond reasonable doubt'.

When he had finished, the lead prosecutor rose to his feet with a look of savage glee on his face. McDonald already could see that Justin was in for a rough time. Indeed, the prosecutor seemed determined to use every dirty trick in the world to humiliate and discredit Justin.

His opening salvo was, "Now tell us Mr. Roscoe, how was it ..."

"Objection M'lud. My client's name is Mr. Roberts."

"I do apologise. My mistake, but he is called Mr. Roscoe on his passport. I find it so very confusing when people call themselves by different names. Seems kind of dishonest to me, but I will earnestly try to remember the name that he is using here."

McDonald seethed with anger, but there was not much more that he could do.

"Tell me once more Mr. Roberts—I do have your name right now do I not—how you first met this elusive Themba Dlamini."

"The man that I meet was Themba Sebe, who turned out to be a sergeant in the South African police. Dlamini is the name of the person I was hoping to save."

"Dear me. Once again I have managed to mix up the names of these two mythical characters. My apologies, but you must admit that your story was rather difficult to follow. Perhaps you should have considered a less complicated tale, which the jury and I might have found easier to follow. I am still not quite clear. Are these two different fictional characters, or does the same man have two different names?"

"Objection. Sebe and Dlamini are not fictional characters."

"Well that is a surprise. In that case I certainly look forward to crossing swords with them in the witness box. But wait a minute. Did you not tell the judge that this is your only witness. Too bad. I would have loved to have a couple of imaginary witnesses to cross-examine. Imagine how that would look in my memoirs."

McDonald could tell that the jury were hugely enjoying this biting wit. To interfere at this point would not help his client. He could only hope that the prosecutor might eventually overdo his jibes and create sympathy for his client. But as it turned out, the prosecutor was too wily a bird to make this mistake. He deftly kept picking holes in Justin's story one thread at a time. He managed to get under Justin's skin and trick him into contradicting himself. It came as a relief when he declared that he was finally done with his cross-examination. All that was now left before the jury retired to consider its verdict was the summing up by both sides. McDonald did he best, but the prosecutor's summation was as brutal as his cross-examination.

The jury took less than and hour to reach its verdict—guilty. In passing sentence the judge was not inclined to show mercy.

"Had you shown remorse for what you have done and indicated that you had learned your lesson, I might have been inclined to let you off with a slap on the wrist. Instead you have wasted the time of this court with a ludicrous tale in which you are the hero and the justice system, those who are sworn to defend society and the law, the criminals.

"As it is, I cannot ignore the thousands of young lives that might have been ruined had the heroin that you brought into this country reached the streets of London. I cannot be confident that once you have served your sentence that you will not immediately revert to your vile trade. Hence I am sentencing you to the maximum penalty allowed by the law—twenty years."

Justin was led from the dock to begin the next phase of his existence as a guest in Her Majesty's prison. He seemed resigned and curiously at peace.

As a young lawyer, McDonald had been taught never to become involved emotionally with his clients. You win some and you lose some, but life goes on. But somehow this case was different. He was now convinced that every word that Justin has spoken was the truth. He had unsuccessfully tried to defend an idealistic, if naive, young man who had chosen to put himself at risk to save the life of a friend. Both he and Justin had failed. Justice had not been done today.

A week later he met with Justin. "I would like to file for an appeal."

"What is the point? There is no new evidence, and the evidence that is there is damning."

McDonald nodded sadly. What Justin had said was true.

"There is however one favour that I would like to ask of you."

"I will do anything if it is within my power."

"Back in my student digs is a photo of a girl and me. I would dearly like to have that photo with me as I serve out my sentence. Could you please get it for me."

McDonald made the request to the university authorities. However once it had become clear that Justin would not be returning, his belongings were either sold off or discarded. The photo had been thrown away.

TWENTY

IT WAS DURING THEIR SECOND YEAR OF STAYING WITH WILMA THAT Julie got married to one of the local ranchers and Colleen was left to fend for herself. Wilma was kind and considerate, but she could not replace Julie as Colleen's soul mate. In the end, Colleen was able to persuade her father to provide the funding that she would need to attend an Australian university. When the time came, Colleen thanked Wilma for the kindness that she had shown and proceeded to make her way to Melbourne to begin the next phase of her life.

Colleen was unsure about what to do with herself, but as she remembered the times she had spent in Soweto with Justin tutoring students, the more she leaned towards a teaching career. Consequently she majored in English literature and then added a teaching diploma to her degree. During her time with Wilma, Colleen's mother had studiously avoided her requests for any news about Justin. It was only once she arrived in Melbourne that her mother finally let on that Justin had been convicted as a drug dealer and that he was now in jail somewhere in the UK. Colleen was devastated by the news and was determined to find out more. Fortunately the university library had an excellent reference section, which included copies of newspapers from around the world dating back for many years. She finally found a copy of a newspaper that carried the text of Justin's defence verbatim. She poured over his words trying her best to believe them, but she had to admit that the case against him was overwhelming. Perhaps the Justin that she knew and loved no longer existed, and that he had come off the rails. But somewhere in the recess of her heart she knew that this was not the case. Had Justin really abandoned her? They only had Snyman's word for that. Had Justin been in detention in South Africa all along before being set up by the Special Branch? How would she ever be able to find out the truth? Would she ever find out? There was nothing to do at this point but to concentrate on her studies. She still had the photo of Justin which she kept on the desk of her dormitory room. It was all that kept her going during those trying years.

It was during the year in which she studied for her teaching diploma that Colleen met John, one of her fellow students. He fell in love with her immediately despite Colleen's attempts to discourage him. After a few months, he actually proposed to her, but she turned him down. It was his third proposal that she finally accepted. He was a solid decent person and someone whom she could perhaps come to love. Besides, Justin would be in prison for years to come and most likely would never want to see her again anyway. She thought of her mother, who had been denied the opportunity to marry the love of her life, but had made the best of her marriage to her father anyway. If her mother had been able to come to terms, as she obviously had, perhaps she could do so as well. She did not want to spend the rest of her life as a lonely spinster. Their wedding was a quiet affair, attended by John's parents, a few friends from university, plus Julie and her husband. Colleen's parents did not feel that they could make the trip. Her father was not in good health.

John and Colleen were lucky enough, not only to find teaching positions near Melbourne, but at the same school. With the help of John's father, they were able to put down a deposit for a small but attractive cottage in a pleasant suburb. Everything was in place for them to settle down into a conventional middle-class existence. They made new friends amongst their neighbours and school colleagues. Weekends were often spent with friends on the beach, or at the local tennis club where Colleen was a much sought after partner, or feared opponent. It should have been an idyllic existence, but somehow Colleen could not shake a nagging feeling of disquiet. People were both friendly and accepting, but she could make herself become one of them. She was an outsider. She did not share a common history with any of their new friends. She doubted that any of their friends could even begin to understand her history and how it had shaped her identity. Their own backgrounds were simply too far removed from hers. Caught up as most of them were with sports—were all Australians so sports mad—there was no way she could make them understand the suffering that she had experienced back in South Africa. When surrounded by friends, she tried to cloak herself in an assumed identity which was not her own but rather an imitation of what she saw around her. But it was the only one that they could relate to. It was a mantle that she assumed to make her appear to be part of the community. She did try to explain herself to John, and he in turn tried to understand. But he usually ended up asking her whether she was not better off here than in a South African jail. Or taking part in endless but futile protests. "Here we are able to enjoy life to the fullest." He was right of course, but also so wrong.

And then there was the memory of Justin. Colleen had chosen not tell John about Justin. It was all so complicated. Even she was not sure whether she loved or hated him—or perhaps did both at the same time. She did not think that John would be able to understand the circumstances under which they had lived and loved. He might ask her if she still loved Justin and she herself had no answer to that question. Or was she deceiving herself on that score?

As time went on, it was becoming obvious that their marriage might not last, but through no one's fault. As Colleen realised later, they simply should not have married in the first place. It was after about a year of marriage that John broached the invisible barrier between them. "You know, whenever we make love it seems to me that you are some place else."

"Perhaps I am just a little tired." She despised herself for lying to John.

But the pretence could not be sustained. A few weeks later John again broached the subject. "When we make love it seems to me that in your mind you are with someone else. Are you having an affair?"

Colleen was taken aback, but decided that it was time to level with him. "You may be right John, and I am so sorry. But I am not cheating on you. However there was someone in my past. I guess that he is still my real love. I do love you but at the same time I cannot put him out of my mind."

"What is his name?"

"Justin. But wait, I have a photo of him that I can show to you." She went to fetch the photo and he studied it carefully.

"What happened?"

"He abandoned me."

"Why? What happened?"

"He fled from the country to avoid the police."

"Why did you not go with him?"

"I was being detained by the police myself at the time."

"So you had both done something wrong?"

"No, we had both done something right."

"I am not sure that I understand. Why would the police want to detain you if you had done something right?"

"It was a difficult and confusing time in my country. It still is. You would have to have been there to understand all that was going on. I don't think that I can explain it to you."

Silence followed. Perhaps if they had spoken more at this juncture, their different histories and her painful past would not have developed into an unbridgeable gulf between them. But as it was, her final sentence was one that shut him out of her life for good.

"I did think when I married you I would be able to put him out of my mind, but it did not turn out that way. I am so sorry. I deceived you by keeping this photo all this time and not levelling with you."

"So what should we do?"

"I would like to ask you to help me bury my past. Please get a candle."

While they both looked on, Colleen took the photo and held it in the burning candle. It caught fire and eventually shrivelled up into nothing but ashes.

"Perhaps by holding on to this photo I have kept his memory alive. Maybe we can start over again. I will always try to be the best wife that I can to you, and I just hope that I can set the memory of Justin aside. Burning the photo might be the first step."

"I can probably settle for that."

Their marriage did limp on for another year. It was one thing, Colleen realised, to burn the photo but another to erase the memory of Justin. In the end she decided that the nettle needed to be grasped. "John, you deserve someone better—someone for whom you are the centre of her universe. You still have your whole life ahead of you. Please do try to find someone who can give you the undivided love that you deserve. I am just not that person. I am too damaged and conflicted. I am so sorry. I really am."

After their amicable divorce, Colleen moved to a small New South Wales town, where she taught English in the local high school and served on the governing board of the town's library. She did not make the mistake of trying to marry again. It was wiser, she realised now, to deal with the old hurts alone rather than to allow them to flow between two people. She did, however, get herself a new dog, a spaniel, which she named Bambi after her childhood pet. She also developed a small circle of women friends, whom she went out with occasionally. But for the most part she preferred to keep to herself. During her free time, she and Bambi would often go and sit in the town park on a bench by the river. It was a placid river, in no hurry to reach its final destination, but it was somehow comforting. It was neither a river of joy or sorrow. The bench became her new rock. A place to which she could come and be alone with her thoughts. A place where she could shed her assumed identity and simply be her self. She now bitterly regretted the impulse which had led her to the burning of Justin's photo—the only one of him she had. It would have been some small comfort if he could be here with her, together dreaming of a different river.

Her main joy in life was to listen to music, of which the library had an ample supply. It was through music that she was able to slip the surly bonds of her discontent to be transported to an alternative world where she was not an outsider, where it might be possible to love once more, and a place where her spirit belonged. Most evenings she would listen to or watch an opera. The one she came back to time and time again was Die Walkure, and especially the final scene that she and Justin had listened to together on their last night together. The poignantly beautiful music that accompanies Wotan's abandonment of Brunnhilde never failed to bring tears to her eyes—or to evoke the memory of how Justin declared that he would never abandon her. Then one day she discovered the opera Thais, as had Justin at an earlier stage, which was to become one of her new favourites. The way it dealt with the theme of yearning for a lover who was forever beyond reach never failed to bring tears to her eyes. It reminded her so much of her own situation.

She would often spend Christmas with Julie and her husband. She was now an aunt to Julie's four children. Events of the past were never part of their conversations.

And so the years slipped by for both Colleen and Justin. The River of Sorrow had ensnared them both in their respective prisons. And then, suddenly, it was 1994.

It was the events of 1994 in South Africa that brought about an abrupt change in Colleen's life. She watched television avidly as the first democratic elections were held in that country and Mandela become its first black president. To her the notion of a peaceful change to majority rule had seemed both unlikely and miraculous. At the same time memories, some pleasant, some painful, of her former life flooded back. She recorded the inauguration of Mandela, and played it over and over again, but the amazement at the event never diminished. The deciding event was the death of her father early the following year. She made immediate plans to return for his funeral.

Even before she set foot back in the country, change was unmistakable. The South African Airways plane that she boarded in Sydney was now adorned in the colours of the 'New South Africa'. The flying springbok had been replaced with a rising sun. The cabin crew, formerly all white, now included one black man and an Indian girl. Passengers were no longer segregated by race. At the immigration kiosk at Johannesburg International (it was no longer called Jan Smuts) the black official scanned her entry application, smiled, and said, "Welcome home, Miss Jansen", two simple words from a total stranger who likely had no cause to welcome back a white person. But these words struck home, releasing long-suppressed emotions of longing and loss. The fact that he was black and she white was rendered irrelevant by a shared common humanity. Was this really a manifestation of the new South Africa? She could have hugged him and very nearly did so.

While waiting for her commuter flight to Nelspruit, Colleen killed time by browsing the CNA book store at the airport, where she experienced more evidence of change. It was stocked with books that previously would have been banned—authors with names like First, Slovo, Mbeki, and so on. She bought a number of them, simply because she could.

Colleen decided to stay on with her mother for a couple of weeks after the funeral. That some earth-shattering changes had come to South Africa was not immediately visible in Sabie, where life seemed more attuned to the older rhythms. However even in Sabie, the new ways could not be shut out. In the evenings Colleen would watch TV with the mother, whose favourite show was Isidingo. One episode, in which an inter-racial couple kissed, caused Colleen's jaw to drop.

"Pinch me mom. Is this really the SABC that we are watching?"

"Yes skattie. This is the new South Africa."

"Papa must be turning in his grave."

"Don't be too sure of that. He did a lot of soul searching after you had left. For instance, he had to acknowledge that the Special Branch were torturing and assassinating people—that these allegations were not just liberal lies. He kept coming back to the phrase 'do unto others' saying we preach it all the time, but do we practice it? You know, although he would not admit it to me, I am almost sure he voted ANC in the election."

Colleen was stunned. "So how did you vote, Ma?"

"By secret ballot."

"Come on Ma, you can do better than that. I am your daughter, remember."

"Okay, yes I did vote ANC. You know before the election your father and I travelled down to Nelspruit to attend an ANC rally. Nelson Mandela himself was the featured speaker. Can you guess where it was held?"

"I have no idea."

"It was in the hall of the Dutch Reformed Church. Can you imagine the irony of that! It is the biggest venue in Nelspruit. We had seats on the aisle. When Mandela entered the hall, he walked down the aisle and shook hands with all those sitting along the aisle, including your father. I tried to push your father out of the way so that I too could shake his hand, but I was too late. By then he had moved on.

"After Mandela had spoken, I knew that I had witnessed something special. Here was a man whom we had jailed for twenty five years, and yet he reached out to us with love and forgiveness. He spoke of a new South Africa where the past would be forgiven and we would stand together to build something special—that what we built would be a lighthouse to the rest of the world. How could I not vote for him!"

Colleen nodded. It finally made sense.

It was a few days before Colleen's scheduled return to Australia when Mrs. Jansen broached the topic that had been on her mind ever since the funeral.

"Skattie, have you ever thought of returning home? The new South Africa could really use a person with your skills."

"I am not sure. What could I do here?"

"Changes are coming, even to Sabie. Next year our high school will become dual language—subjects will be taught in both English and Afrikaans for the first time. There are already a number of black kids in the school, and when English is introduced as a medium of instruction there will be many more. As it is we cannot find enough English speaking teachers, so you would be snapped up if you decided to come home."

"Yes, I will think about it."

"Plus, I am not getting any younger," her mother added. So soon after her father's funeral, the implication was obvious. She had been tempted to add, 'Perhaps you will find yourself some nice man' but wisely had kept silent on the subject.

The next day Colleen drove up to the Blyde River Canyon, and made her way to her special rock—the one where she went to seek consolation or to make important decisions. However, long before she got there, in her heart she knew that the decision had already been made. The river below added its voice to her welcome home.

Two months later she and her dog Bambi were back in Sabie, this time to stay. It was a heady time for her. She would not be appointed as a teacher until the beginning of the new school year. Nevertheless, with the help of her mother, she in effect became an unofficial teacher's aide. Most of her time was spent helping the handful of black students with their English. She was welcomed in the teachers' lounge despite her unofficial status. Here she was able to develop a new set of friends despite the fact that most of the teachers were older than her and Afrikaans speaking. There was one question with which she was constantly bombarded, "Why on earth did you come back?" Many whites still seemed fearful of the future, although not as anxious as before the elections. She heard stories of how people had hoarded food in the expectation that the election would bring with it untold violence. But she was also told stories of how people had stood peacefully in line for hours to vote—and how as they stood there the realisation dawned that it was for the first time as equals. She tried to formulate an adequate answer to the question of her return. Sometimes she simply said, "It is because this is where I belong." If she felt the questioner would understand, she might reply, "There is nothing so exiting as to be part of a country which is the throes of re-inventing itself."

One day a conservation officer from the Blyde River Nature Conservation Area came to the school to speak to the students. Colleen could have been knocked over with a feather when she realised that it was Ian McCall. After his talk she made a bee-line for him. "It's me, Colleen. Do you remember me? Do you have time to stay for a cup of tea?" Ian was equally amazed. "I really do need to get back to the Centre, but there is no way I can pass up a quick reunion tea."

Ian had just enough time to fill Colleen in on the past few years. It had taken two years after her release from detention for Jenny to regain most of her confidence. Ian had patiently helped her to cope with the outside world, one small step at a time. Coaxing her simply to stand in the open front door of their flat took a number of weeks. From there they progressed to short walks to the end of the block and back. After a year of so she could go most places as long as she was not exposed to a large crowd. Inviting friends for social occasions also became possible, starting with just one person and gradually increasing the number. Ian was astute enough to realise that Jenny's recovery required her having a cause on which she could focus her energy. It was obvious that attending lectures would not be possible, so they decided to complete their studies by correspondence, and so enrolled in the University of South Africa. At the same time, they changed the focus of their studies, opting for the biological sciences with a focus on conservation issues. Ten years after their release, and each with a masters degree to their names, they were given the opportunity begin a new career. They were appointed as conservation officers in the Blyde River Nature Conservation Area. Thus they packed up their flat and moved to their new home in Sabie, which was where Colleen had now found him.

As he left he said, "Do come and have dinner with us. Jenny will be delighted to know that you are back, and to see you again."

It was only a few days later that Colleen, armed with a bottle of wine, made her way to Ian and Jenny's bungalow. It was a little way beyond Pilgrims Rest and in the Nature Conservancy itself, not far from the Blyde River Canyon. Colleen could not imagine a more beautiful place to stay. She felt quite envious of them. Ian met her as soon as she pulled into the driveway and showed her inside. She was not quite sure how to treat Jenny, but need not have worried. Jenny immediately gave her a warm welcome hug and led them all to the patio, where they opened the wine and toasted one another, and then the New South Africa. The view from the patio was stunning.

At first the conversation steered clear of anything controversial. Ian and Jenny were keen to hear of her life in Australia, and what she was now doing in Sabie. Having satisfied their curiosity, she felt it was now her turn, but that she had to proceed cautiously. "I would never like to open any old wounds, but there are some things I really need to know. May I ask you questions of my own?"

"Sure. Go ahead. We have both come to terms with the past."

"What I most want to know is what happened to Justin. Did he really abandon me as Snyman claimed, or was he himself detained and had no choice in the matter?"

It was Ian who eventually answered. "It was David and I who convinced him to leave and helped him to escape." He went on to explain the logic of how they had convinced Justin that he had no real choice but to leave. "We told him that if he really loved you, he had to get out to the country as quickly as possible. He only eventually agreed to do so once we promised to put you on a plane to join him as soon as you were released. But then before we could fulfil that promise we were all detained—David, Tony, Jenny and myself. We did not even know at the time whether he had reached safety or not."

"Thank you for sharing this. At last I know the truth. I never wanted to believe that he would just up and abandon me. But what about the others?"

"Who do you have in mind? Just not us. We would rather not talk about ourselves."

"What happened to all the house mates?"

"David, you may have read about, died in detention."

"Yes, I did see that."

"As soon as Tony was released he got an exit permit and now lives in Canada. We have not kept in touch. After our release, we more or less cut ourselves off from anyone we used to know. Adam moved to Australia, Sydney I believe, and is active in the theatre there. You may have seen his name."

"No. I did not know that. I wish I could have seen him again. He was a real character in an arty kind of way."

"So the only one who is still around is Neville."

"So what is he up to?"

"I guess what you would expect. Neville is Neville, cheerful and predictable. He played cricket for Transvaal B for a couple of seasons, but never got further than that. His career as a pilot is more successful. He progressed through the ranks until by the time the new government came into being, he was a captain for South African Airways on the international routes. As far as I know he has settled down with his third wife on a small holding outside Kempton Park—a convenient location for any pilot. We do see from time to when he visits this area."

"And always with a girl other than his wife," added Jenny tartly.

"Do you know what happened to Sipho?"

"Yes. Now there is a happy story. He somehow survived his interrogation at the hands of the Special Branch, although for the rest of his life he will always walk with a limp. He was never broken, but he shrewdly gave his tormentors just enough information to keep them interested, and therefore with motivation enough to keep him alive. When the information he gave was followed up on it was always too late to be of any use. With the new government in charge, Sipho's fortunes changed dramatically. He was rewarded for his role in bringing about the end of apartheid with the post of a deputy minister in the new government of national unity. He lives quite well somewhere in Waterkloof, has a BMW and big house with a pool."

With Colleen's questions answered, the topic of conversation moved to the present again. Ian and Jenny talked about their work—what they were doing and what they hoped to achieve. It was late by the time Colleen left with a promise to keep in touch.

The following weeks past by quickly. Colleen delighted in finding ways in which the changes in the country manifested themselves in Sabie. All the 'Whites only' and 'Non-whites' signs had been removed from all establishments. Sabie did not have that many restaurants, but those that did exist now catered to people of all races. There was no more censorship of newspapers, and books previously banned were now freely available. But some of the changes were more subtle and intangible. It seemed to Colleen that the atmosphere was different—that people walking in the streets no longer had that downtrodden look of trespassers in their own land. Or was she simply imagining what she wished to see? She thought back to the time when Justin had stopped a young white bully from attacking a small black girl. Could that kind of incident still happen today? Yes, but not that likely. There were still racists around, but they tended to keep a low profile these days. In any case, black kids now proudly wore the uniform of Sabie High School along with their white counterparts.

But there was still a pain in her heart. Justin was still languishing in jail. Not only that but she was sure that he was innocent. She had no evidence to back up this belief other than her knowledge of and love for Justin.

TWENTY ONE

THE SENTENCE OF TIME IN PRISON DID HAVE ITS BRIGHT SIDE AS FAR as Justin was concerned. Had he been acquitted, he had nowhere to stay in the UK, no money, and no friends. Plus there would always be questions about his innocence. These worries were taken care of by time in prison. On the other hand, he had always loved the outdoors, and being confined within the walls of a prison would be hard to bear. However, the most bitter pill of all was that fact that he had now been branded falsely as a drug dealer—one of the lowest forms of life. It ate away at him during his first weeks of incarceration, so much so that he became seriously depressed and was considered a suicide risk.

It was the prison chaplain who came to Justin's rescue. Over a series of sessions, he imparted to Justin the tools that would help him to survive in his new environment. At first all Justin wanted was for the chaplain to believe in his innocence. In response the chaplain gently tried to lay out his position. "There are many here who maintain that they are innocent, and perhaps even a few who genuinely are. But at all costs I cannot allow myself to be seen as a judge or as a 'get out of jail' card. I always refuse to discuss their case with those who agree to talk with me. As a matter of principle I know nothing about your case or why you are here. It is this distance that enables me to do my job."

"So there is nothing that you can do to help me?"

"If by help you mean secure your freedom or establish your innocence, then no. That is the job of your lawyer. But there are other ways in which I can help you."

"Such as?"

"I can try to help you find peace of mind, and perhaps even a purpose in your life here. I will not push religion onto you unless that it your wish. There are many paths to finding peace and acceptance, and I am willing to help you in any way you want. Do not fret about those things that you cannot change. Look around and make the most of the opportunities that are on offer. Find ways in which you can help others, and in so doing help yourself."

It was in this spirit that Justin was able to fashion a new life for himself. He volunteered for the various jobs on offer in the prison, starting off by washing dishes, progressing to more pleasant tasks, and after a few years he attained one of the most sought after positions of all—that of assistant librarian.

He did not mix to any great extent with the other prisoners, concentrating rather on his studies. He completed his undergraduate degree through the Open University and went on to acquire a PhD in English literature. Seeking fresh fields of study, he then completed an LLB, thus realising one of his earliest academic ambitions.

As his qualifications increased, so did the demand for him as a teacher of his fellow inmates. His classes on English literature were especially popular. However, what Justice considered the most productive use of his time in prison was the writing of a semi-autobiographical novel.

He did receive the occasional letter from South Africa, mostly from his mother, but also the occasional missive from Ian or Neville. He followed closely the events taking place in South Africa, mainly from newspapers, but also from television.

His trial lawyer, Mr. McDonald did keep in touch, although he was under no obligation to do so. His failure to defend an innocent man—and he was still convinced that Justin was innocent—still rankled. It troubled him thinking about what more he might have done, but there were no easy answers. When consulting with new clients, he made time to see Justin as well whenever he could. When the time came that Justin might apply for parole, McDonald urged him to do so, but Justin declined.

"I do not want to rejoin the outside world as a convicted drug dealer. I would not be able to look other people in the face. No, I would rather stay inside unless there is some way that you are able to establish my innocence."

Justin watched the events of 1994 as shown on TV avidly. The sight of thousands of people queuing up to vote, blacks and whites standing shoulder to shoulder as equals for the first time, brought tears to his eyes. Weeks later he was glued to the TV as Mandela was inaugurated on the steps of the Union Buildings, flanked by generals of the South African Defence Force. He wept openly as Mandela completed his speech. "Never, never and never again shall it be that this beautiful land will again experience the oppression of one by another and suffer the indignity of being the skunk of the world.

"Let freedom reign. The sun shall never set on so glorious a human achievement! God bless Africa!"

And then jets of the South African Air Force, followed by helicopters sporting the new flag, flew over the vast crowd assembled on the grounds below the Union Building. A mighty cheer arose when they suddenly realised that these instruments of their oppression now belonged to them, the people.

However the moment of joy was also infused with sadness for Justin. Much as he may wish it, he would never be able to return after what he had done to Sipho. He would always be a permanent exile from the 'new South Africa' for which he had sacrificed so much.

McDonald was busy at work when interrupted by his secretary.

"Excuse me sir, but you have a visitor."

"Does he or she have an appointment?"

"No sir."

"Who is it, and what do they want?"

"It is a lady from the South African High Commission. She claims to have some important information for you."

"Very well. Show her in."

After introductions had been made, McDonald asked, "How can I help you?"

"Am I correct in assuming that you are the person who defended a certain Mr. Justin Roberts? It would have been some time ago."

"Yes, you are correct. I am that person."

"Then I have some information that may interest you."

"Please proceed. I am interested."

"I assume that you have heard of the Truth and Reconciliation Commission."

"Indeed I have."

"Our government lawyers have been combing through the files of the old police system looking for evidence to bring to the Commission. In the course of their searches, they came across some very interesting details about your former client. Luckily for us the police at the time were required to keep very detailed records of all their spending. We have pages of information about how a certain Sergeant Sebe was instrumental setting up your client to undertake a supposed rescue mission in South Africa."

"Yes, I do remember the details of the case clearly."

"There is also documentation about how drugs were placed by the police in his suitcase, and the British authorities subsequently tipped off."

"And you say you have written documentation of all the you have told me?"

"Yes, I have it right here for you. The person who was captured in that operation, one Sipho Dlamini, is now in the cabinet, and he instructed us to make these documents available to you."

"I cannot tell you how grateful I am to you. I was always convinced that Justin was innocent. With these documents, I should at last be able to clear his name and give him his freedom."

"There is one last thing. Sipho has arranged for Justin to visit South Africa as a guest of the government. You will find an air ticket in this package as well."

McDonald's first instinct was to break the good news immediately to Justin. However, in the end, caution prevailed. He did not want to get Justin's hopes up, only to have them dashed. Nor did he want Justin himself to veto taking action on this new information. Consequently he made an urgent application to the Appeals Board, requesting a review of Justin's case. The appeal was quickly decided in Justin's favour. It had taken no more than a single phone call to South Africa to verify the authenticity of the documents that had been provided to McDonald. The information in these police records coincided exactly with the testimony Justin had given in his trial.

McDonald was the first to break the good news to Justin.

"It is not just a pardon, you have been completely exonerated. Not only that, the compensation for wrongful incarceration means that you are now relatively well off."

Justin thanked McDonald for all the efforts on his behalf, and for believing in him when all others had refused to do so.

"One more item was included with the documents that I was able to use to clear your name." McDonald paused for dramatic effect. "It is an official invitation from the government to visit South Africa. An air ticket is included with the invitation."

It was the last thing that Justin had expected. "The last time I was given a free ticket to South Africa, it did not turn out that well for me—or for others. Would it be different this time, or is it just a trick to get me back where I would be prosecuted?"

"I am sure it would be different. In fact the invitation comes directly from Sipho Dlamini, who is now in the cabinet. If I were in your shoes I would certainly accept the invitation."

Why would Sipho want to see him again? There was only one way to find out.

Two days after his release Justin found himself once again at a now much expanded Heathrow Airport. He would be flying South African Airways for the first time in his life. The cabin crew was now representative of all the races in South Africa. He had a further surprise waiting for him. The welcome on board announcement gave the name of the captain as one Neville Perkins, his old flying buddy. Soon after take off Justin asked one of the cabin crew to take a message to the captain, that a Justin Roberts was a passenger on the plane. He was immediately invited to go up to the cockpit. Neville greeted him like an old friend, which of course he was. He enthusiastically showed Justin all the various controls in the cockpit. He was in his element. However there is only so much fun one can have in a cockpit, even of an Airbus. He next suggested that they retire to the first class cabin, where there were a number of empty seats, and where they would be able to talk more easily. Neville ordered a drink for Justin, who was glad to see that Neville abstained.

"So who is flying this plane while you sit here watching me drink?"

"My first officer will take care of things while I am gone, so no need to worry. At this point in the flight there is basically nothing to do anyway. She is a young girl by the way. Part of the new equity policy at South African Airways."

"Is she any good?"

"I don't know. She locked her hotel room last night so I couldn't get in."

"I meant as a pilot you lecherous old reprobate."

"Well why didn't you say so in the first place? She has the qualifications and experience, but this is the first time we have flown together. I handled the approach and landing to Heathrow, but she will be landing the plane once we get to Johannesburg. So we will both be able to judge her skills for ourselves then."

"She seems to be smart enough to know to lock her door while you are around. So my money is on her when it comes to nailing the landing in Jo'burg."

For a while they chatted about old times and mutual friends.

"You made front page news on your release. I am sure many of your old buddies are anxious to see you again. Talking of which, did I mention before that Ian and Jenny now live down in Sabie. I am sure they would love to see you. I have an idea. Why don't I fly you down to Sabie. You could take the left hand seat and see if you still remember any of your old skills."

"I would love that, but I will first have to see what all Sipho has in mind."

After several hours of catching up, Neville announced that he had better get back to the cockpit. "Passengers tend to get nervous when they see their captain sitting in the cabin, even if he is not drinking. I tell you what. Stay here in first class as my guest. I will square it with the cabin attendant."

Justin was astounded, but apprehensive, to see a banner strung across the arrivals hall with the sign, 'Welcome home Justin'. He knew at some point that he and Sipho would have to meet and deal with the past, but he had hoped to slip back into the country quietly without being noticed. But apparently it was not to be. Standing under the sign was Sipho, who strode forward to meet him, shook his hand, and then gave him a bear hug. It was all so unexpected and confusing. Instead of heading for immigration, Sipho led him through a side door, down a passage and into a VIP lounge. Here he was greeted by a welcoming committee comprising a few cabinet members and other colleagues of Sipho. After handshakes all around, and a few short words of welcome home, Justin was given the opportunity to express his thanks and gratitude to those who had made his homecoming possible.

As they were exiting the building Justin muttered, "I need to explain what happened."

"Not now. We can talk freely later. Anyway I already know exactly how the whole episode played out."

Justin took a deep breath of the Highveld air. "It smells so different, so unique. I would recognise it anywhere."

"Yes. Welcome home. I will take you to my place where you can freshen up and then we will go out to lunch."

Justin noted that there was now a double- lane highway between the airport and Pretoria.

"This is all very different."

"You are going to see lots of changes in the next few days."

"I suppose so. This car is one of them." Sipho was driving a brand new BMW series seven.

"Just one of the perks of the job." In the old days, Justin remembered, cabinet ministers had favoured Mercedes Benz's.

Sipho's house was in the Pretoria suburb of Waterkloof. Having showered and put on fresh clothes, Justin sat down with Sipho on his outdoor patio for a late morning tea.

"You seem to have done well for yourself, living here in Waterkloof."

"Yes, at last I am able to enjoy the fruits of our struggle."

Justin hoped that that would be true for all South Africans, and not just the elite in power, and that the former selfless freedom fighters would not be seduced by luxury and power. From where he sat he could gaze out over the suburbs of the city to the distant Union Buildings, the seat of power for both the old and new governments. Sipho must have divined his thoughts.

"Yes. It belongs to us now, to the people."

"But it came at a cost."

"Yes, a tremendous cost."

"I cannot tell you how sorry I am that I caused your capture."

"There is no need to apologise at all. I know now exactly how you were deceived, and that you put yourself at risk to do what you thought was saving me. It was I who collected the police records on that event and had them sent to London so as to exonerate you. It was the least that I could do, since I was the cause of your troubles. In a sense I too deceived you when I asked you to drive me to Komatipoort. I am sorry for what I did. It is not as if you had volunteered to be part of the armed struggle. I simply used you. I am sorry."

"Thank you. Well, the past is behind us and we can look forward to a new and better future. What is it that Tutu has dubbed us? The Rainbow Nation?"

"Yes. You can also look forward to lunch. I have heard that there is a new Indian restaurant in Brooklyn that I am keen to try out. I have reservations for lunch."

As they walked towards the restaurant, Justin noticed how badly Sipho limped. Up until this point, they had only walked short distances during which time Sipho was able to mostly conceal his limp. "Aren't you getting too old to play soccer?"

"You are referring to my limp? It is nothing to do with soccer. It is a souvenir from my time with the Special Branch."

"I am sorry. Clumsy of me. I was just trying to be funny. Forgive me."

"Not at all. I regard my limp as a badge of honour."

Once in the restaurant they were immediately shown to their table. Their waiter was a young white girl, Afrikaans speaking to judge by her accent. She took Justin's order and then turned to Sipho, "What can I get you, sir?"

After she had left, Justin said, "Did you hear that? She called you 'sir'. Unbelievable."

Sipho laughed. "At first I was taken aback by that sort of thing, but one gets used to it. The young whites in particular seem to have had little trouble in adjusting."

"Does she know that you are a cabinet minister?"

"I doubt it. I have not been here before. To her I am just an ordinary, middle aged client who should be treated with respect."

"No. An ordinary, middle aged, *black* client."

"Black does not seem to matter so much any more—in many situations anyway. But not all."

Justin looked around. Up to half the diners were black and it appeared that they were all being treated with the same respect as

Sipho. Amazing. He thought back to the incident at the café in Beaufort West, and reminded Sipho of it. How different it was now. They both had a good laugh about how Justin had identified himself in Klaserie as 'the idiot from the café in Beaufort West'. They spent the rest of lunch reminiscing about the past, mostly Sipho's exploits as part of the resistance. Justin did not have that many interesting prison stories to tell.

The following day Sipho drove Justin out to Soweto, where he had organised what he termed the official welcome home ceremony. "It will not be like that stuffy reception that they gave you at the airport. This will be a proper African affair." Justin was keen to see the streets of Soweto again. To his surprise, not much had changed. A visitor from the past—from twenty years earlier—would still feel at home. The dusty side streets and matchbox houses evoked past memories when he and his colleagues had come out here on Saturdays for tutoring sessions. After a while Sipho turned off the main road and made his way down a series of side streets. Eventually he pulled up outside what appeared to be a church hall. Justin wondered if it was one of the halls that they had used during the tutoring project, but he could not be sure. In any event the sounds of singing and festivity assailed Justin's ears. "This is our destination. Come with me."

As Justin entered the building, the singing reached a crescendo, interspersed with cheering, ululating, and clapping. "Who are all these people. Why are they here?"

"Mostly they are students who used to attend your tutoring sessions. Some are also umkhonto isibashu veterans—colleagues of mine from my time in the Lowveld. As to what they are doing here, they will tell you themselves."

As Justin was led onto the platform at the end of the hall, the cheering, shouting, and stamping of feet grew even louder. After a while, Sipho called for silence. "We are here today to welcome home one of Africa's greatest sons. He is a man amongst men. He is a true hero with the heart of a lion." And so it went on. Justin had heard about the tradition of a praise singer, but he had never expected to be on the receiving end. It was all rather embarrassing. Apparently the more outlandish the compliments, the higher the esteem in which a praise singer was held. Perhaps Sipho was still an amateur, or perhaps trying to be something that he was not meant to be. After he had wound down his speech, others came forward to offer their tributes and thanks. Students from the tutoring project mostly spoke about how the programme had helped them become what they were today. Veterans from umkhonto isibashu expanded on the theme that had Justin not sacrificed his future, their organisation might well have been crushed while in its infancy.

As the speeches came to an end, Sipho invited Justin to make his reply. However when he rose to his feet he knew that he could not express even a fraction of the feelings that were overwhelming him. He did not even try. Instead he simply said, "My friends, thank you from the bottom of my heart for this welcome. There is no way that I am deserving of any of the praises that you have so generously lavished upon me. No way at all. But it is so good to be home again. I do have one request. My homecoming will be complete if you would sing Nkosi Sikelel'. I would love to hear it again after all these years."

For a moment there was dead silence, and then from somewhere near the back of the crowd came a solo female voice singing, the first line of Nkosi Sikelel' iAfrika. She was immediately joined by the rest of the crowd singing the remainder of the anthem in a haunting harmony. It was all too much for Justin. For the first time since his return he could not hold back his tears. He was home again at last.

As they were driving back, Justin realised to what extent this event had reminded him of Lucky's funeral. He and Colleen had been there together. How he wished she could have been with him today. But then he remembered his resolve not to dwell on the past—not to keep the memories of her alive. It would be harder now that he was surrounded by places that they had been together. She was lost to him forever—something he had to accept. Some years ago he had learned that she was married and living in Australia.

Justin spent the rest to the week being shown around by Sipho and being introduced to various members of the cabinet. He also gave a series of interviews for some of the newspapers and magazines. He contacted his mother, who was now living in a retirement village in Howick, his father having died some years previously, and was able to hear her voice again for the first time in so many years. She told him that she had prayed for this day and that she had never ceased to believed in his innocence. He promised to visit her as soon as feasible. Perhaps he could get Neville to fly him down to Howick as well. Towards the end of the week he told Sipho, "An old friend, Neville, has offered to fly me down to Sabie. Two of my oldest friends live there now. You may have come across them, Ian and Jenny McCall. I would like to take him up on the offer before I go back to London. I also need to go down to Howick and see my mother."

"But why are you going back?"

"I assumed that was the plan. After all you sent me a return ticket."

"That was just in case you wanted to return. But I wish you would stay. The country needs people like you now more than ever."

"Let me think about it. The truth is that I have no reason to go back. There is nothing for me to go back to in the UK. But then I am not really qualified to do anything here either."

"That would not be a problem. I am sure that I could fix you up with a good position in the government. And with all the perks. We have always found ways to reward and look after those that helped us during the struggle years."

"Thanks for the offer. You are a true friend and I appreciate it. Let me sleep on it."

Justin thought it over, and decided if it was possible he would like to stay. Being part of a new country trying to reinvent itself was an exciting prospect. But he would first like to see what Ian and Jenny thought about the idea. They might have a more realistic view on what it would be like to be part of the government of the new South Africa.

Neville picked him up at Sipho's house. They would be flying from Wonderboom airport down to Sabie. The plane was a familiar one, a Cessna 172. Justin took over the controls once they were in the air. He was delighted to find that most of the old skills were still intact. Neville even allowed him to land the plane at the Sabie airport. Ian and Jenny were there to meet him.

The four of them spent a quiet evening together. Ian was much like his old self again. Jenny, too, seemed to have recovered somewhat. She was not her old enthusiastic and bubbly self, but at least she was no longer the emotional cripple that Ian had described to him all those years ago. Their new jobs meant dealing mostly with animals and plants, rather than people, and that suited them both just fine. Mostly they reminisced about the old days, especially the first year in the house that they had shared. There were many hilarious memories, but they could not conceal the fact that of the original six house mates, one was dead and two had fled the country. Their memories expanded to take in other activities—arguments at Student Council meetings, protests in which they had participated, time spent tutoring in Soweto, and picnic outings in the Magaliesberg. But there were holes in these recalled memories large enough to drive a truck through. Never once was there any mention of the two girls who had been packed off to Australia.

That night in bed, Justin tried to focus on the memories of his old house mates rather than on the times he had spent with Colleen, many of them in this very area. The loss of Colleen was still very painful. While in Pretoria he had visited the web page of Sabie High School, and had discovered that there was a new principal. The Jansens must have left town some time ago. He did not even want to ask Ian if he had any knowledge of their whereabouts.

The following morning Neville had to fly back to Pretoria. Ian suggested that the three of them visit some of Justin's old haunts in the area—the waterfalls and the views over the escarpment. And so they spent much of the day going from one tourist spot to the next. The whole area was much more developed tourist-wise than in Justin's time.

"Anything else you would like to see before we go home?"

"There is one special place overlooking the Blyde Canyon that I would like to visit. Perhaps you could take me there." He was deliberately breaking his resolve not to think about Colleen, but this would be the last time he succumbed to this indulgence before burying her memory once and for all. He really did want to visit Colleen's rock just one more time.

The road along the canyon rim was now paved with a number of viewpoint pull outs. Justin was worried that he might not be able to find Colleen's rock again. But the way to the rock had been impressed indelibly on his mind, and he recognised the area when they reached it. To his annoyance there was one other car in the pull out, but since it serviced a large area he would hopefully have the rock to himself.

As he approached the rock, to his annoyance he saw a person sitting on it. He was about to turn around, but curiosity made him continue. As he got closer, his mind played tricks on him. The person looked like Colleen, but that was impossible. The mind is capable of great deception—it sees what it wants to see.

As he got closer still, the figure on the rock arose. It was Colleen, or was it? She opened her arms to receive him as he ran to greet her.

"Colleen. Is it really you?"

"It is indeed."

"I don't know what to say. There is so much I need to explain to you."

"Hush my dearest love. 'Ruhe. Ruhe. Alles, alles weiss ich, alles ward mir nun frei.' I know and understand all. But words will never be adequate in this situation. That is why I have brought some music for this special occasion." She reached down to turn on a cassette player. Music swelled out over the canyon, drifting down to its very depths and rising to its very peaks. It was the final moments of Gotterdammerung, The Twilight of the Gods, where Wagner too had decided that words would only impede that which only his music could adequately express. The music unfolded theme by theme, building up to the soaring, magnificent, and ultimately hopeful motif of redemption. At this point when staged, the River Rhine would be overflowing its banks, obliterating the old world, and making way for the new. Justin and Colleen clung to each other on their rock, as below them the eternal River of Joy flowed on unheedingly through the basement of time as it always had for aeons past.

EDITOR'S NOTE

After the death of her beloved husband of nearly forty years, Colleen Roberts found the manuscript of the novel he had written while in prison. She decided to have it published in his memory, but it was she who added the some of the new material.

Sabie 2038

ACKNOWLEDGEMENTS

I WOULD LIKE TO EXPRESS GRATITUDE TO THE ENTIRE TEAM AT Archway Publishing. Each member of the team was invariably prompt, courteous, and professional.

Then my sincere thanks to friends and colleagues who willingly shared their personal memoirs, many of which found their way into the book in one form or another.

Finally to my wife, without whose encouragement and support, this book would never have come about.

Printed in the United States
by Baker & Taylor Publisher Services